A KINGDOM SCARRED

FAE OF TÍRIA, BOOK ONE

K. A. RILEY

Cover by thebookbrander.com

For Jaime, for giving Lyrinn her name,
and for Lynne, for giving Leta hers.

FOREWORD

A brief caution for my readers—more particularly, my readers' ***parents:***

I have written quite a few books by now, most of which are suitable for younger readers. I try to keep my language light, though there are occasional acts of violence on the pages—and occasionally, a beloved character meets their untimely end.

I've had messages asking if certain books are "spicy," and in this case, the answer is yes. *A Kingdom Scarred* is a novel that is not suitable for younger readers.

So I leave it to you, the parents, to determine what level of "viewer discretion" you wish to exercise when it comes to this book and series.

And to ***my*** parents: I'll send you a nice, clean, redacted version of the book. Promise.

The next books in the series are:

A Crown Broken (Pre-order available until release day)

Of Flame and Fury

And yes, they too will include a fair serving of spice.

For those of you delving into the world ahead, thank you for coming on this journey, and I hope you enjoy!

K. A.

DESCRIPTION

"I was a prisoner in these ruins, captive of a Fae who was as perilously alluring as the lands where I now stood."

A thousand years ago, the mortal realms of Kalemnar were separated from the land of the Fae by a dark, vicious mist that takes lives with all the cruelty of the sharpest blade.

Lyrinn Martel has been told all her life the Fae deserted their lands long ago, leaving them to decay and ruin. Rumors still swirl to this day that the Immortals were malevolent creatures, bent on destroying the realms of humans...and that their departure was a welcome blessing.

But one fateful night, as Lyrinn flees for her life, she discovers a hidden path up the cliff that guides her to the Fae realm of Tíria. There, she encounters a Fae so extraordinary and captivating that she finds herself inextricably drawn to him, despite her fear that he plans to send her to her death.

When Lyrinn escapes the Fae lands, she finds herself summoned to the palace of the mortal king. Even as her journey begins, she discovers that the alluring Fae is not done with her—and he has no intention of ever letting her go.

For fans of Fantasy Romance such as A Court of Thorns and Roses, A Kingdom Scarred is the first book in an exciting new Fantasy Series by the author of Recruitment and The Cure.

The Mortal Realms of Kalemnar

To Tíria
The Rise
Dúnbar
Castelle
River Dún
Belleau
The Lake of Blood
Domignon
Marqueyssal

CHAPTER ONE

Mortals called it the Breath of the Fae.

The poisonous, encroaching mist fell upon the town of Dúnbar from the north, cascading like a torrential waterfall down the sheer, daunting mass of stone known as the Onyx Rise. It lapped at the town's edge, threatening then retreating, its deadly tendrils never venturing far from the cliff.

According to dark legend, one touch of the vapor to a man's skin was enough to melt his flesh away until nothing was left but pristine bone.

Hand-painted signs littered the dead-end streets and alleys that came to an abrupt halt just before the cliff's base:

Stay clear of the Breath, or die.

The message was simple, yet several of Dúnbar's drunken fools had died wretched, painful late-night deaths over the years, arrogantly convinced they could make their way to the cliff's summit without succumbing to the vicious power of the Breath.

Though the mist faded to near invisibility under the glare of sunlight, those who had attempted the climb under the light of day had been no more successful.

Some said it wasn't the Breath that killed you, but wicked creatures known as *Grimpers*—malevolent beings of shadow and bone who swiped razor-sharp claws at any mortal foolish enough to attempt the ascent.

I had never seen such a beast. Nor was I entirely certain that I believed in their existence. Like many in Dúnbar, I had told myself from a young age that they were nothing more than legendary monsters invented to keep curious children from approaching the Onyx Rise.

Still, the tales had proven effective, and Dúnbar's youth had grown up over the centuries to fear the Rise and those who had inflicted it upon us—the Fae who had once ruled our kind from the realm known as Tíria.

Once counted among the Five Realms of Kalemnar, Tíria had, for many centuries, been accessible to the Low Lands' mortals—though even in those days, few dared venture up the Onyx Rise for fear of being stricken with some magical curse or other.

The Fae were said to have been hostile and judgmental, looking down on us for our perceived inferiority. Still, they had tolerated us well enough in those days, and for the most part, they allowed mortals to roam their lands...so long as our kind didn't hunt their wildlife or fell their trees.

But one day a thousand years ago, the balance of Kalemnar's power had shifted.

It was just after the competition known as the Blood Trials, held only once a millennium, that the Breath of the Fae had first begun to cascade over the Onyx Rise, separating human from Fae and altering our lands forever.

My father told me when I was very young about the Breath and the monsters known as *Grimpers*. Both blights, he said, had been sent by an enraged Fae Lord, a punishment inflicted on our kind when the mortal realm of Domignon had bested Tíria's two Champions in the Blood Trials.

"The Fae," my father told me when I was a small girl, his voice low as if he were fearful that an Immortal would overhear him, "despise us now, for the insult mortals inflicted on them. It is unheard of for one of their kind to be vanquished by a human. So, the lord of their highest court accused Domignon's winners of treachery. He closed Tíria off to our kind. Ever since that day no Tírian Fae has shown his—or *her*—face among mortal-kind. The Elders say the Fae fled Kalemnar for Aetherion, the land across the sea, never to return. Some say they would sooner perish than look one of us in the eye. Others say they would strike us down on sight were we arrogant enough to pursue them to those lands."

The tale had at once saddened me and filled me with a wistful longing for a world I'd never known. I had always been curious about the Immortal race. After all, rumors about their exquisite beauty and grace still circulated to this day, whispered among those who lived in Castelle, the realm north of the river where we lived.

Then again, some said the Fae were not beautiful, but frightening to behold, and deceitful; that it was impossible to look one of their kind in the eye without succumbing to a terror that could kill a grown man more quickly than the sharpest blade.

Still, as I strode along Dúnbar's High Street one particular autumn evening, I couldn't help but turn my eyes toward the Onyx Rise's summit and to the mist that flowed over its edge, an eternal, iridescent torrent.

A question flitted its way through my mind, tormenting me just as it had done for years:

If no Immortals dwell in Tíria now, then why does the Breath still threaten us?

A sudden movement on the street ahead pulled my mind away from such thoughts, my eyes drawn to two young men making their way toward me under the dim light of the oil-fueled street lamps.

Each of the men was cloaked in an elegant crimson tunic and equipped with an impressive blade. Their tunics were decorated with a single, silver sword, a design I had recently seen stamped on notices plastered to Dúnbar's walls.

My heart quickened to a violent drumbeat as I realized who they must be.

Scouts, come north to seek Castelle's two Champions for the upcoming Blood Trials.

Suddenly self-conscious, I pulled my gray hood around my face to conceal the angry red scars that had decorated my ears, neck, and shoulders ever since a fire had engulfed our home many years ago, nearly claiming my sister's life and my own even as it took our mother from us.

But the Scouts, it seemed, were not there to scrutinize my imperfect flesh.

They stopped some distance away and turned to face a storefront. One of them unrolled a length of parchment, pressing it to the shop's wall, while the other opened a glass jar filled with some sort of liquid and proceeded to brush it over the parchment's surface.

When they'd finished hanging the notice, the men proceeded toward me. The taller of them looked me in the eye, elbowing his companion and nodding in my direction.

A sudden need assaulted me to ensure my dagger was firmly tucked into the sheath strapped to my right thigh. My hand slipped into the false pocket sliced into my skirt's side, my fingers reaching for the comfort of cold metal.

When I felt the ornate hilt, I allowed myself a quick exhalation as I nodded *Good evening* to the two men.

The taller of them stopped and blocked my way with his body.

"How old are you, Miss?" he asked, holding out a hand expectantly.

I swallowed before replying, "Eighteen years, Sir." With trembling fingers, I pulled at the silver chain I always wore around my neck to reveal a small metal tube that normally hung against my chest. The Scout waited patiently as I twisted it open and pulled out a small, rolled-up piece of parchment, then handed it to him.

"And when will you be nineteen?" he asked, unrolling the delicate paper that revealed a record of my birth.

"On the twentieth day of the eleventh moon."

"I see," he said, squinting at the parchment before rolling it up and handing it back to me. "Too young by two moons. Pity. Carry on, then."

The men, seeming to satisfy themselves that I was of no use to them, kept trudging down the cobbled street toward the town's gates.

Huffing out a relieved breath, I reinserted the paper into the metal tube, screwed its two halves together, then walked on.

When I was confident they wouldn't turn back, I stopped to read the notice they'd just hung.

To the Gifted Mortals
of the Realm of Castelle:
The time has come to select
one young man and one young woman
to compete in the Blood Trials.
Speak to our scouts today
and earn your chance to represent one of
Kalemnar's four realms
in the event of the millennium!

At the bottom of the announcement was the same sword I'd seen emblazoned on the Scouts' tunics.

But it wasn't the sword that drew my eye or tormented my mind.

Instead, it was one simple word:

Four.

Four realms.

Domignon, the king's realm. Belleau, home to the ship merchants and fishermen. Castelle, land of the stone masons. Marqueyssal, known as the Garden Realm, for its beautiful landscape.

But there was no mention of Tíria. Not even a whisper of the disappeared Fae who for thousands of years had proven their indomitable strength in the Trials.

It was as though their kind had never even existed.

Perhaps they never did, I thought sadly. *Perhaps they are a mere legend, invented by the tale-weavers of old. No living human has ever laid eyes upon one of them, after all. There is no proof that they ever lived.*

And yet, I felt in my blood and bones that they were real. I had thought of them every day since childhood, envisioning exquisite faces with all the vivid conjurings of a young mind. I used to see Fae in my dreams, even, though it was an experience I had never shared with anyone, not even my sister Leta.

During my youth I had often found myself consumed by thoughts of what had become of their kind.

But as I grew into maturity, I began to question why they hated humans with such a violence that they had sent mist and monsters to kill our people. Were they really so vengeful that one loss in the Blood Trials had sent them all spiraling into a sort of common madness?

Grimacing, I told myself I didn't wish to know. If they were indeed real, an angry Fae was a terrifying prospect. Best to stop daydreaming about their kind, to cease imagining what it might be like to come face to face with someone of their legendary beauty and their alleged skills with magic and weapons.

Best to forget the word "Fae" entirely.

Keeping my head down, I made my way along the street until I reached the front door of the Raven, the local tavern where a motley assortment of Dúnbar's more repellent men went nightly to avoid interacting with their wives and children.

As I stepped over the threshold, the combined scent of ale and pipe smoke met my nose, melding into something not entirely unpleasant. My eyes were instantly drawn to two men slouched at a nearby table, their voices echoing through the space in the sort of booming timbre normally inspired by copious amounts of alcohol.

"It's far too late to hope for Castelle's victory in the Trials," one of them was saying, his speech slurring. "We have only two moons to find and train two Champions. It can't be done, not without a miracle. Besides, everyone knows Prince Corym of Domignon will win—him and Olivia Brimley. They say she's the most Gifted young woman in all the realms."

"Which is probably why Castelle's lord hasn't bothered searching for our own competitors. There's no point, is there?"

I recognized the man nearest to me. Raleigh was his name, and he was a disrespectful ass. He'd hired my blacksmith father once or twice to craft him weapons, though he was seldom sober enough to wield one without endangering everyone in his vicinity.

I did my best to avoid him each time I spotted his soulless gray eyes coming at me in Dúnbar's shadowed streets.

"All I can tell you is the Scouts ain't likely to find their Champions in this shit-hole of a town," Raleigh added with a derisive snort. "A more useless assortment of flesh there never was."

As if to prove his point, he pulled his eyes up to look at me.

I attempted to ignore him and to stride by their table, my gray linen hood still drawn around my face. But as I moved, Raleigh reached out and grabbed me by the wrist, yanking me roughly into his lap.

"Caught you, *kitten,*" he said, his rancid breath enough to draw an instant swell of nausea from my belly.

The prick never called me by my name, though he knew it perfectly well. Better, I supposed, to dehumanize me just enough to justify his harassment.

"You'd make a fine Champion, wouldn't you, darlin'?" he asked, huffing his vile stench onto my skin. "I hear you're skilled with a blade. And I'll bet that's not all you're good at."

Chuckling, he slipped a hand under my skirt, his fingers creeping up my leg like a slow-moving insect that was begging to be punished for the infiltration.

In retaliation, I shoved my free hand into my pocket, drew my still-hidden dagger from its sheath under my skirt, and jabbed its tip into the back of his hand.

"Move another inch and I'll remove each of your testicles in turn, bastard," I breathed into his ear. "I'll make it quick, I promise. You won't even feel it until you find yourself bleeding to death."

Raleigh froze, his eyes widening in shock, before he finally dragged his hand back down my leg and out from its hiding spot, a trickle of deep red decorating his skin.

I tucked my knife back into its sheath and rose to my feet, scowling.

Emboldened by the meager distance between us, my would-be assailant opened his mouth to speak. But before he could say a word, a deep voice—one I knew better than my own—erupted from somewhere behind me.

CHAPTER TWO

"My daughter has gutted larger game than you, Raleigh. So I advise that you keep that gaping fish-mouth of yours shut."

I turned to see my father towering over me, a tall, broad-shouldered behemoth with a dark beard, waves of ebony hair, and the blackest of eyes.

"Bull balls," Raleigh snorted. "I'll touch her if I want to."

My father advanced toward the table, shielding me with his large frame as he leapt at the man and yanked him to his feet. "I don't care how many pints you've taken in. Utter those words again and I'll take your head." He snarled the words, his voice hoarse with rage. "Do you hear me?"

Raleigh raised his hands, let out a weak nod, then, when my father released him, fell back into his chair as if his legs had no strength in them. "My apologies, Martel," the drunken miscreant said with a half-scowl, wincing when my father took yet another step toward him. "*Sincerest* apologies, truly. It won't happen again."

"Good. Because if it does, I promise you will not see another sunrise."

With that, my father turned and nodded toward a table at the far end of the tavern where a lone occupant was seated.

"You didn't need to do that," I said under my breath as I slipped toward the table. "I was perfectly capable of dealing with him myself."

"I know," my father chuckled. "But I so enjoy it."

I let out a shallow laugh as I stepped over and seated myself opposite my sister, Leta.

She was dressed in a cloak similar to mine though her hood was down, her red hair pulled back into a twisting braid. Her skin glowed in the candlelight, her eyes flickering shades of gold, green, and dark brown.

Leta had always been the beautiful one, the girl the entire town noticed and worshiped. Even her scars, similar as they were to mine, managed to appear delicate and lovely on her otherwise perfect skin. Symmetrically distributed around her ears, her neck, her shoulders, they looked more like exquisite jewelry than cruel reminders of a vicious conflagration.

My father told us years ago that Leta and I were together in our small cradle when the fire had broken out behind us, which was why our burns were so alike. At the time, I was two years old, and Leta a mere one. My father had snatched us from the cradle before the flames could take us, but the scars had remained.

My sister wore them with pride, and it was no wonder. She was beautiful in the secretive, unobtainable way that drove the town's young men mad. She wielded her loveliness like a weapon, looking disdainfully down upon almost anyone who dared meet her eyes.

I, on the other hand, hid among the shadows of my cloak, scrutinizing those around me even as I willed them to ignore my existence.

Better, I had always told myself, *to be a shadow than a blooming rose. A rose has thorns, but it can still be snatched up.*

A shadow, on the other hand, is utterly unobtainable.

"I passed the Scouts on my way here," I announced as I leaned forward, my elbows pressed to the table. "They were headed toward the Iron Gates."

"No doubt they're camping outside the town's walls," my father said. "They'll be back in the morning, sniffing around for their Champions."

"*Human sacrifices* is a more apt term," Leta said with a sneer. "I've never understood why anyone would want to participate in the Blood Trials. At best, you win and are forced to marry some violent psychopath. At worst, you're beheaded in front of hundreds of onlookers. It's a dubious honor, if you ask me."

"If only I'd been born a few moons earlier," I lamented half-sarcastically, "I, too, could have been beheaded in a public square."

My father looked at me with an unexpected sympathy in his eyes. "I, for one, am grateful you came along in the eleventh moon of your birth-year, and not the eighth. It is a blessing that you're still but eighteen and will be until the Trials begin."

"Not that it matters, Lyrinn," Leta told me with a laugh. "Even if you were old enough to compete, it's not as though you have any Blood-Gifts. I'll admit you're decent when it comes to hunting rodents, but you'd be killed by one of those sword-wielding sadists before you could unsheathe your blade, and let's be honest—you have nothing to offer but a keen ability to stab a squirrel in the eye with a hot poker."

"Says the girl who once hurled a throwing knife at a target outside Father's smithy and hit a pig hanging in the butcher's window *next door,*" I scoffed with a chuckle.

"Hush, now." Unamused, our father huffed out a hard breath. "I don't want *either* of my daughters sacrificed for the sake of the High Lord of Castelle's pride," he said, taking a swig of ale before sending the mug clattering down on the table. "We all know Domignon will win, just as they did one thousand years ago." He pulled his eyes toward the window, where we could just see the uneven, thatched silhouettes of Dúnbar's rooftops and the Onyx Rise beyond. "The king's bloodline is strong. His son is more powerful now, even, than the Champions who defeated the Fae."

As he spoke the last words, he looked genuinely puzzled, as though the defeat of the Fae a thousand years ago was a riddle he'd been trying to solve for decades.

I didn't know a great deal about the history of the Blood Trials, but I was aware of their basic rules:

From each region of Kalemnar, a young man and a young woman were chosen as Champions and sent to compete against those selected by the other realms.

The competition lasted several days and consisted of a series of challenges, some of which were violent and often deadly.

There was a reason the Fae had dominated in the Blood Trials for thousands of years. Their magical Gifts were far greater than any mortal possessed, and they were skilled fighters. Some Fae Champions had been capable of summoning flame; others, they said, could see the future, or even control the minds of their foes. Legend held that one competitor many thousands of years ago had been born with the ability to call upon Dragons for aid, though most people agreed that was nothing more than an old wives' tale.

The two most important rules of the Blood Trials were the following:

One: Only two Champions were allowed to live past the Trials' final day. One male, one female.

Two: Before—or after—the vanquished died, their magical

traits known as "Blood-Gifts" were siphoned from their minds and bodies by a creature known only as the Taker. An entity neither human nor animal, the Taker's sole purpose was to leech power from the fallen and grant their Gifts to the new couple, who passed them down to future generations.

The Elders said the Taker dwelt near the Eternity Tree, which rose up near the Lake of Blood at the center of Kalemnar. The tree flowered only once every thousand years during the ninth moon, and it was then that the Taker emerged to perform its sacred duties.

Once the creature had completed its task, the Trials' vanquished were beheaded to ensure the end of their bloodlines.

Kalemnar's Elders had always insisted that such an end was an honor, a sacrifice made to the old gods to acknowledge the weaker realms' submission to the strongest.

To me, it had always seemed like a cruelty beyond measure.

"Raleigh is right about one thing, much as I hate to admit it," I said quietly, leaning forward.

"What's that?" Leta asked.

"Castelle has known the Trials were coming for a thousand years. They should have been grooming Champions for at least the last decade."

Our father shook his head. "Blood-Gifts don't show themselves until a person comes of age—and unless that candidate is of a bloodline like that of the prince of Domignon, there is no telling who will make a good Champion until they reach their nineteenth year. It puts most of the young folk at a great disadvantage. There are few in Castelle who could compete with the likes of the prince, given that his ancestors long ago inherited Gifts of two powerful Fae. Truth be told, I feel for anyone who has to go up against him."

"I have more faith than you, Father," Leta replied with a

shrug. "Marqueyssal and Belleau have been preparing their Champions for some time. At least, according to Gem."

"Gem?" I asked, smiling. "The butcher's son? Have you two gotten close, then?"

Leta sneered at me. "We were simply having a polite chat the other day when I went to sell him one of the mangy rabbits you keep trapping down by the river." She looked to my father and said, her voice animated, "He told me Belleau and Marqueyssal have Champions in training the likes of which no one has seen in a hundred years. I mean, aside from Prince Corym."

"What's so special about the prince, anyhow?" I asked, slightly put off by the admiration in my sister's voice when she spoke of him.

"They say he can decapitate a man just by looking at him."

"That's idiotic," I said. "It's ridiculous. How would he even *test* that? Does the king just give him guard after guard and say, 'Here, my boy, slice this one's head off with your mind like you did to all the others'?"

"Ha. Ha." Leta slow-laughed, sarcasm dripping down her throat. "Anyhow, I couldn't care less whether it's true. The prince is beautiful. Perhaps he should win for that alone. Have you *seen* his portrait?"

I resisted the temptation to roll my eyes. Yes, I'd seen the prince's portrait. Of course I had. It was everywhere these days —in every shop, hanging on the walls like he was the most sacred being ever to grace our lands. Kalemnar's population had an unhealthy obsession with the young man, considering that he sounded vaguely psychotic.

For all I knew, he hunted kittens for sport.

"Enough talk about the prince. I want you two to make yourselves scarce tomorrow morning," my father told us softly, glancing around to ensure no one in the Raven could hear him.

He seemed suddenly agitated, concerned about an invisible threat. "Do not let the Scouts speak to either of you. Don't engage with them. Do you hear me?"

Seeing the look in his eye, I pressed back in my chair, pulling my hands off the table and bowing my chin to conceal my face within the shadows of my hood.

"You don't want them to see us," I said. "It's the scars, isn't it?"

"Scars?" My father leaned forward, slipping strong fingers under my chin to lift my face. In his eyes was a sorrow that felt like a knife in my side. "I take no issue with your scars," he said softly, "and neither should you or anyone else. It is not your fault the two of you were burned, Lyrinn. Always remember that."

"We know that, Father," Leta said cheerfully, glancing sideways at me. She looked exquisite as always in the candlelight, her flame-red hair dancing with color, her large eyes sparkling.

In stark contrast to my younger sister's, my hair was black and unruly, my eyes dark to match. Traits inherited from my father, though the resemblance ended there. My eyes were far larger than my father's, my lips fuller. He had always had the air of someone who was set on scrutinizing those around him, his eyes permanently narrowed into an appraising expression, lips pulled into an almost perpetual frown. That was, until someone cracked a joke that he couldn't resist. It was in those moments that his defenses broke down, and I could see the carefree young man that he had once been before my mother's death.

Leta resembled our mother—at least, judging by the only remaining portrait of her, which was stored in a dresser in our father's bedroom. Hand-painted, the image was small enough to fit into the palm of my hand, but it still showed her blue eyes and flaming red hair in exquisite detail.

"You are beautiful and strong, both of you," my father said, reading my mind as it wandered to thoughts of the woman who had died when we were too young to know her. "Scars or none. Do you hear me?"

"Spoken like a true father," I replied with a smirk.

"You may not see it now, Lyrinn. But you will, one day soon. I promise you that. You will see how lovely you really are."

I went silent and nodded, though I scarcely believed him. The angry red marks slipped down my shoulders like a grim cowl, marring my flesh in strange, asymmetrical patterns that swirled along my skin like a mockery of what could have been.

Perhaps if the fire had never assaulted us, I would have grown up confident, my head held high. Perhaps if the scars weren't a constant reminder of the night our mother died—the night a permanent sadness had taken up residence in our father's eyes—I would have found the capacity to see beauty in my appearance rather than live with a perpetual desire to remain unseen.

Leta didn't feel the same embarrassment that assailed me when others stared, and I had always wished I could understand how she wore her scars with such pride. On her, they seemed beautiful and unique, a baroque decoration along perfect skin.

But my own markings had always felt like a sign of brokenness, a weakness carved into my flesh for all to see.

I was a person forged from pain, a marred shadow of my perfect sister.

"None of it matters," I said. "Whether we're pleasing to the eye or hideous, the Scouts won't test us. As Leta so accurately pointed out, we have no magical Gifts. Even if we were of age, we would be of no interest to those men."

My father took in a breath before replying, "Still, I want you two both far from their minds tomorrow. Castelle is desperate for its Champions. The Scouts may bend the rules and test every resident under twenty years of age, and I would not put either of you through such an ordeal. If others want their sons and daughters suffering the sadistic tests, that's their choice. My daughters will not be subject to abuse by any man."

I looked him in the eye and smiled, almost against my will. Our father had always been so protective of us both. He had warned us early in life about the perils of the nightly Fae's Breath that came from Tíria—its toxic qualities, the danger of nearing the cliffside. But he had warned us, too, about the cruelty of mortal men. Of their greed, their selfishness, their violence.

Not that he'd ever had to say a word about that particular matter—I had seen and felt the threat myself. I'd watched men force themselves on girls far younger than me. Men like Raleigh, who used inebriation as an excuse for vile behavior.

Not that *every* man in Dúnbar was terrible. I'd met one or two in my time who were quite pleasant to be around.

Chancel, the apothecary's son, was the first boy I'd ever kissed, at the age of fifteen. And though I had little interest in him now, I could not deny that he had grown into a kind young man with a warm smile.

There were others, of course—others with whom I'd shared fleeting, intimate moments here or there, in the darkness of an abandoned barn or in a cave by the river.

But I had never been willing to give myself wholly to any of them. That privilege remained on reserve for some mysterious future entity—perhaps a man from the South, from the Realms of Domignon, Belleau or Marqueyssal. It would have to be a good man, one who respected me and saw me as an equal—an attitude that apparently eluded nearly every male who resided north of the river.

"I'll keep myself hidden tomorrow," I promised my father.

"Far from the Scouts. Maybe I'll head down to the river and do some fishing."

"I'll do the same," Leta agreed with a shrug. "I have no desire to be scrutinized like a cow at auction while the Scouts tell me I'm too young to be useful to anyone."

My father pressed a hand to Leta's cheek and mine, and said, "Good girls." With a sigh, he added, "Your mother is looking down upon you both from the Farlands each moment of every day. She would have been so very proud of the young women you've become."

"We know," I replied with a faint smile.

Clearing his throat, he pressed his hands to the solid oak table and pushed himself to his feet. "I think I'll head home," he said. "And you two?"

"I'll come," Leta replied, rising to join him. "I'm about ready to pass out from fatigue. You coming, Lyr?"

"No." I shook my head. "I think I'll have a pint first and do a little reading." I extracted a small, leather-bound tome from the pocket of my cloak and held it up. "I'll be home soon. And as promised, I'll disappear before dawn."

"See that you do," my father half-whispered. He gave me a last affectionate look before putting an arm around Leta, turning away, then shooting a final, angry glare at Raleigh on his way to the door.

I loved my father for not asking if I was all right on my own. After all, he had taught me long ago how to fend off attackers and how to gut a predator with a few flicks of my wrist and a quick manipulation of my razor-sharp blade.

Still, I hoped not to be put to the test that night.

The last thing I wanted was to attract the wagging tongues of the town gossips on the eve of the Scouts' official visit.

CHAPTER THREE

For over an hour, I nursed a pint of local ale in my dark corner, ignoring the pub's population as they grew increasingly drunk, their voices rising to an irritating cacophony.

Finally, accepting that the noise was preventing me from absorbing any more words on my book's pages, I closed it and rose to my feet with a quiet sigh. I told myself I would head home and get some sleep before disappearing through the town's back gates in the morning. I would spend the next day wandering the woods, grateful not to be nineteen yet...

But ever so slightly envious of those who were.

Our father had never explained what the Scouts did to those they "tested." Did they force physical labors upon them? Make them hunt and dismember animals? Wrestle one another in the town square?

The more I speculated, the more grateful I was not to have to find out.

Striding toward the Raven's front door, I was all too aware that Raleigh and his friend were still seated at their table. They locked eyes on me as I moved toward them, stiffening defiantly.

Raleigh's face wore an expression of pure rage.

For all his consumption of alcohol, it seemed he had not forgotten the humiliation inflicted upon him by my father and me two hours ago.

Tempted as I was to sneer back at him, I kept my chin down and pulled my hood over my head as I slipped out the door onto the street and turned to head home.

I walked briskly past several shops before ducking into Barden Close, the narrow, sloping laneway that I frequently used as a shortcut. I told myself the detour would prevent any unwanted company from following me.

I climbed quietly, my eyes locked straight ahead on the massive wall of stone that was the Onyx Rise. The Breath of the Fae was flowing down its surface in a torrent of dark mist, and I had to admit that in its way, it was a beautiful sight—a breathtaking cascade reflecting every hint of the moon's brightness. At this distance, I was unbothered by its inherent danger; after all, I would be turning left long before I was close to the Rise.

As I advanced, though, I began to feel uneasy. The creeping sound of footfalls began to echo behind me, unsteady and arrhythmic. They grew louder and faster with each step.

I didn't need to turn in order to guess who was pursuing me.

"Come back here, girl!" a gruff, slurring voice called out. "I want to talk to you!"

Bloody Raleigh.

I twisted around to look at him, though I wasn't entirely sure what compelled me to do so. Politeness, perhaps, or habit.

"I have nothing to say to you," I called out, my tone curt. "Good night, sir."

Spinning back around, I lengthened my stride and hastened, confident in my ability to leave him in the dust. He was well behind me still, and besides, he looked ready to keel over at any moment. He probably couldn't do me much harm.

Then again, I had no desire to find out.

"I said come here, you little bitch!" he shouted, breaking into a run, the soles of his leather boots slapping against the cobblestones.

This time, I didn't look back. Instead, I simply burst into a sprint, ready to veer left and run all the way home.

But my confidence began to wane as I realized with a jolt of horror that I was running directly toward the Onyx Rise and its wall of deadly mist, and that the familiar alley was nowhere to be seen.

But...how could I possibly have missed it?

My intention had been to turn left between the Butcher's house and the Apothecary, to take the twisting laneway that wove between a series of shops and row houses. It was a route I knew like the back of my hand—one I had taken nearly every day of my life.

In my distracted state, I must have charged past the lane's entrance somehow. And now, I was a mere twenty feet from the Onyx Rise, with Raleigh coming up quickly behind me.

Straight ahead, the Breath poured down the cliff face, landing in waves on the cobblestones and creeping toward my toes, a rising tide of malevolent threat.

On either side of me, the façades of unfamiliar, abandoned houses rose like morbid specters, their windows dark and threatening.

My eyes shot from side to side as I tried to get my bearings, to determine where the hell I was. Dúnbar was a small town, after all.

I should recognize these houses. I should know each of them intimately.

And yet...

"This isn't possible," I breathed, stopping in my tracks and twisting around to try to decipher where I'd gone wrong.

Raleigh was still coming at me, but now, seeing that I was cornered, he slowed his pace, his chapped lips curling into a malicious grin.

I stared past him, searching for the opening of the alley I should have turned down.

Only I couldn't see it.

The only thing that met my eyes was a thick, encroaching darkness, as though my route home was trying—and *succeeding* —to conceal itself from my eyes and mind.

"I've got you, Missy," Raleigh hissed, stepping slowly toward me and slipping a hand into his cloak. He extracted a weapon—a small folding knife, which he pulled open as he licked his lips. "First, I'll have you. Then I'll gut you." He nodded past me toward the Rise. "I'll make it look like them Grimpers did it. You'll be their first lady victim in centuries. How do you like that?"

"You'll do no such thing," I growled, shoving my hand deep into my false pocket to reach for my own blade. *Enough. If I have to slice you open to get home, I'll do it.*

But my blade wasn't there.

Nausea roiled inside me as I felt around, only to come to the awful realization that its sheath, still fastened by a few hanging threads, was split in two.

No. It's impossible.

I had hand-stitched the leather sheath myself. Just tonight, I had inspected it to ensure its integrity. Every stitch had been intact and reinforced. Every single one...

And yet, the blade most likely lay on the Raven's hard-packed dirt floor.

How had I managed to lose the weapon that would be my only chance to see morning?

I can take Raleigh, I told myself, drawing my mind away

from my panic. *He's rocking on his feet like he's about to topple over. I could kick him, knock him down, steal his blade.*

But even as he stared me down, another figure emerged from the shadows behind him—one who was all too steady on his feet.

It only took me a moment to recognize Raleigh's friend from the tavern, who was wielding a weapon of his own—a glinting short sword. He looked far less inebriated than Raleigh, and his grin was even more malevolent.

Desperate, I spun around, hunting for a possible way out. The houses' walls lining the alley were too high and smooth to climb, or I might have contemplated a rooftop escape.

As if to remind me of my limited options, the mist came faster now, rolling waves forming a carpet of pure darkness only a few feet away from where I stood.

Without knowing why, I pivoted around to take in the sight of the Onyx Rise.

Climb, a voice called out inside my mind.

I shook my head, my eyes wide. Had I only imagined it? Was this some enticement of the mist itself?

As if in response, when I fixed my gaze on the swirling Breath, it parted to reveal a narrow row of cobblestones leading toward the cliff's base, beckoning me forward.

I tried to convince myself I was imagining the sight. But when I pulled my eyes up to the vast cliff, the mist continued to spread itself apart.

And in the darkness before me, a grim black staircase emerged, zigzagging up the cliffside.

No. Such a thing does not exist. I'm imagining it because I'm terrified.

A rough hand grabbed me by the shoulder, the tip of a blade threatening to pierce my back.

"Take off the cloak," a coarse voice growled into my ear. "And the rest."

I thought to protest, to tell him I would never do such a thing. But instead, shaking, I nodded my assent. "All right," I said, and pulled slowly away. I drew the cloak from my shoulders, letting it drop, and when I turned to face them the men backed off, looks of pure, smug satisfaction in their eyes.

I stepped back, then back some more until the mist curled around my feet, seeming by some miracle of fate not to want to touch me.

I have a choice. The men, or the mist.

Whatever happens, I die tonight. Perhaps it would be better that the Breath should finish me quickly than these bastards kill me slowly.

There was no way out except back the way I'd come. No way to escape except to sprint between the two men...and the likelihood of that plan succeeding was slim to none.

As I lamented my fate, my name came to me, a mere whisper on the wind.

Lyrinn...

I twisted around again to see the black stairs gleaming in the starlight, calling to me as the mist swirled around them.

Lyrinn...

I shook my head, trying to dislodge the madness from within. I told myself it was nothing more than some creeping old magic, a spell cast by the Grimpers to lure me into a death trap.

Fight it, I told myself. *Do not go toward the voice.*

"What the hell are you doing, Girl?" Raleigh called out. "Take off your damned clothes!"

Lyrinn...

I couldn't resist any longer. I reached down and grabbed my

cloak, pulling it back up around my shoulders even as my feet took over, striding toward the stairs and up, one step at a time.

I turned once to see Raleigh's friend running at me as if to grab me, to claim me before it was too late.

"What are you doing? Are you mad?"

He was right to ask the question.

Only madness could have compelled a person to do what I was about to do.

Yet here I was, my mind overtaken by the dark spell, my body following obediently. I was climbing to my death.

And all I could think was, "At least I won't have to hide from the Scouts in the morning. At least Father won't worry."

There was no fear in my heart. No pain. No sorrow.

There was only a profound knowledge that climbing toward an unknown, dangerous realm was the right thing to do.

As I ascended, a cry sounded below me. I turned to see the mist closing up behind my heels to urge me forward. Horrific wails filled the air, the two men's voices echoing against solid stone as they screamed in life-ending agony.

And I knew without question that the Breath of the Fae was claiming them both.

Someone from the town would find them in the morning, unrecognizable but for their clothing.

They were dying, and it was all my fault.

No, the voice assured me, *it is their own.*

A strange, distant comfort worked its way slowly into my mind and pulled me away from the horrors I had just witnessed.

It was true. They had chosen to pursue me, to threaten me, to try and possess me. They had failed to claim me, and the Breath had punished them for it.

Resigned to my fate, I continued my winding climb. There was no going back now, no going home. The black swirls of vapor were controlling my trajectory, forcing me to continue up the cliff to a fate I could not guess. Would my death be as painful as Raleigh's? I could still hear him scream, though I wasn't sure if the cries were figments of my imagination, or echoes of the Grimpers' triumphant howls.

With a strained grimace, I pushed the thoughts away and told myself I was about to experience something few before me had been through. It was a privilege, in a twisted way. A thing both unique and horrifying.

I didn't know how long it was before I reached the cliff's top. I was simply there, standing above the curtain of mist, looking down upon the town far below, lights glowing in the windows of the houses that lined the curving streets of cobblestone.

I turned away, snapping out of my fog as a surge of fear assaulted me. Turning to face the darkness ahead, I tried to make out shapes I could only vaguely see in the distance. Were the Grimpers awaiting my arrival?

But the shadows were nothing more than trees, twisted and lifeless, lining the clifftop. Beyond them lay more silhouettes, terrifying forms that brooded in the distance like a waiting army.

The Breath had trapped me at the top of the Rise. There was no way to return to Dúnbar tonight. I would have to conceal myself, to huddle in the darkness in hopes that the Grimpers wouldn't find me. In the morning when the sun rose, I could find the stairs and hope the Breath would once again part to let me through.

They said no one in a millennium had ascended the cliff and survived.

My chances of descending seemed even less promising.

CHAPTER FOUR

I STUMBLED forward until I was safely clear of the mist's tendrils.

My breath was heavy, my chest burning as my eyes locked on what looked like a vast graveyard of dead and dying trees, their limbs as gnarled as skeletal fingers. Beyond, the occasional standing stone rose up, darkly silhouetted against the moonlit clouds.

Remnants of a time when the Immortals occupied these lands.

It seemed my father had been right. The Fae had deserted this place a thousand years ago, leaving the land forsaken. No doubt they really had sailed across the sea to join those of their kind who dwelt in Aetherion. The *Lightblood,* those Fae were sometimes called, for their hair the color of snow and their piercing eyes. Their reputation was even more dire than that of the cruel Fae of Tíria; humans said they were vicious, brutal, and entirely bent on the destruction of the mortal world.

As far as I knew, no mortal had ever seen a Lightblood in Kalemnar. And with any luck, no mortal ever would.

I pushed on until I came to a tall, sturdy standing stone, gray and lichen-coated. Pressing my back to its cold surface, I let myself slip to the ground, pulling my legs up close to me, my arms wrapping around them. It was a pose I had assumed a thousand times as a frightened child on stormy nights in Dúnbar, shielding myself from this or that imagined threat.

In the distance, eerie howls echoed through the night. Strange and blood-curdling, they sounded at first like tormented wolves. But there was something grimly human in the timbre of the cries. The echoes of lost lives reverberated through every wail.

Grimpers? I wondered with a shudder.

I tensed, waiting for the pending attack. But the cries faded into the distance until they disappeared entirely, leaving me alone with my thoughts, my fear, my confusion.

I pushed my head back against the hard stone, inhaling the night air. It was fresh, clean, not at all the toxic thickness that I would have expected from the land beyond the mist. But as I breathed in, I could taste a faint odor of something unsettling—something that set a juddering disquiet deep in my bones.

Closing my eyes, I called out silently to Leta, to my father, attempting to reassure them from afar. *I'm all right. I'll be home soon. Don't worry.*

I only need to figure out how to get back to you.

My arms tightened around me as I repeated the words, whispering in hopes that I could convince myself they were true.

I could not say whether it was sheer exhaustion or some other force at work, but after a few minutes, my head drooped down. All thoughts of Grimpers, curses, and malevolence left me...and by some miracle, I fell into a deep sleep.

A voice came to me as I slumbered.

Deep, low, and smooth as the finest velvet, I was certain at first that I was dreaming a sound conjured from the depths of my imagination.

"Rise," it said, "and show me your face."

My eyes popped open to land on a leather-clad boot tapping the sole of my foot.

With a start, I leapt up, only to see that I was surrounded by a series of tall, cloaked figures, each of whom had a dark hood pulled over his—or her—eyes.

Two of the shadowed forms held bows in hand at the ready, their dagger-sharp arrows directed at my head. Despite the fact that I could not see their faces, I knew instinctively that they were perfectly able to see mine, and that their aim would be true.

The tallest of the group stood back from the rest, arms crossed over a broad chest, and when he spoke, I knew without question that he was the one I'd heard in my slumber.

"Take her to the ruins," he commanded, and instantly, two figures reached for me, grabbing my arms.

"What in Kalemnar's realms do you think you're doing?" I cried, throwing my entire body weight backwards as I tried to yank myself away. But they were impossibly strong, their grip unfaltering.

"You are an intruder on the clifftop," the leader said, his tone icy cold. He was walking already, his servants following, dragging me with them. "You will be questioned and assessed. You will likely be tried as a spy. And then, we will figure out what to do with you."

"A spy?" I spat, suddenly too angry to be frightened. "That's ridiculous! I never even intended to come here. I'm heading home at dawn. I'll leave this place and—"

"You will not leave until I allow you to do so," the leader

retorted. "And I will not allow such a thing until I learn how and why you came to be here."

I wanted to tell him I had climbed the stairs. It was a simple explanation, after all. But he would have told me I was mad. I knew as well as anyone how ridiculous such a story would sound. I had heard Raleigh's and his friend's screams as the Breath had taken them.

There was no earthly reason why I should be alive right now.

"I only wanted—" I began, but the leader growled a menacing, "Silence!"

It was enough to convince me to keep my mouth shut for the time being.

The party led me for several minutes, until I saw that we were headed toward what looked like the dilapidated remnants of an old castle—what must once have been Fairholme, the castle on the clifftop that had been inhabited by Immortals.

If so, then it was true. I really had stumbled upon the long-abandoned Realm of Tíria. For thousands of years, its highest lord and lady had ruled Kalemnar and its mortal realms, their power indisputable. But if the Breath had separated our lands a thousand years ago, then how had these cloaked strangers come to be here? Were they bandits? Interlopers who had breached the mist as I had, and taken over the Fae's former lands? Had they, like me, found a gap in the Breath and climbed the Onyx Stair?

My mind, addled as it was with question after question, was quickly overtaken with thoughts of the ruins ahead of us, which may once have been a beautiful castle, but now looked like nothing more than a series of tall, half-broken stone walls that appeared barely sturdy enough to support the meager bits of roof covering the castle's various wings.

"Who *are* you?" I asked the leader as we approached what

was left of Fairholme, trying and failing to muster the strength to sound fearless.

He replied, his voice smoothly ominous. "We are guardians. Caretakers of these lands."

My courage grew a little with his arrogant words. "Since when?" I asked with a sneer. "These are Fae lands—at least, they were at one time. They are not yours, or any mortal's, to claim."

The leader threw me a quick glance, and I got a momentary look at his mouth, which was ticking into a strange smile. "At least you admit that much."

"Let me go," I commanded, unsettled by his tone. "You cannot take me prisoner. If the Lord of Castelle learns of it, he'll—"

"The Lord of Castelle," he scoffed. "The Lord of Castelle cares little for these lands. And I would surmise he cares even less what happens to a young woman who is foolish enough to climb the Onyx Stair."

I glared at him then, unable to come up with an adequate retort. He was right, after all—Castelle's highest lord was a drunken fool, just like so many of the men of our region. He had little interest in our people or in the Onyx Rise, and I suspected, in fact, that he would be perfectly content to lose the Blood Trials if it meant another thousand years of sloth and decadence for his descendants.

After a moment, the leader finally stopped walking and stared up at the ruins before us. "My kind has watched over Fairholme for many thousands of years, and will no doubt watch over it for a thousand more. It is my hope that one day, it will be restored to its former beauty."

"Your...kind..." I repeated, looking around at the shadowy figures surrounding me, their features still concealed from view. "You're trying to tell me you are...?"

I couldn't quite bring myself to utter the word.

Fae.

I wanted to laugh. No, of course they weren't. Why would Immortals remain here, in this wasteland? Every mortal knew Fae were creatures of nature. They loved all things green and blooming.

The lands beyond the Rise were a bleak realm of ash and decay.

Pushing out an impatient breath, the leader turned my way.

"You know what we are," he replied, and an invisible charge shot through the air, the space between us exploding with a powerful, daunting energy. "Though it surprises you, for some reason."

He pulled his chin up briefly, only enough so that I caught a glimpse of his eyes glowing brightly in the darkness.

"No," I said, shaking my head. "It can't be. You left after the..."

I forced myself to stop before mentioning the Blood Trials, for fear that the topic would arouse the leader's wrath.

"My kind still reside in Tíria," he replied, turning to the ruins with a note of irritation in his voice. "Just as we did for thousands of years before mortal-kind betrayed us at the last Blood Trials."

"Betrayed?" I replied with a derisive chuckle, forgetting momentarily that I was speaking to a creature far more powerful than myself. "Every mortal in Kalemnar knows your Champions lost, and then your kind disappeared out of humiliation. Then you sent the mist and the Grimpers to make sure any mortal who tried to get into your land died violently. It's a curse that has plagued Dúnbar and all of Castelle for a thousand years."

"Plagued *Dúnbar?*" The leader spun around to glare at me, his cloak a whirlwind of light twisting through the air so fast that when I tried to focus on it, the flickering illusion of luminescence vanished into the ether.

He strode toward me and for the first time, I saw his face clearly. His eyes, bright amber, glinted in the moonlight like those of a cat. Above them arched a pair of deep black brows that met as he halted before me. His lips, full and defined at once, curved down into an angry sneer.

Something in his stare made me want to melt into my cloak and disappear, never to be seen by such eyes again.

Yet I couldn't look away.

"Is that really what you think?" he snarled. "That *we* created the mist that devours your people? That my kind wreaked this havoc?" With that, he gestured violently toward the ruins and the land beyond.

"Everyone knows it to be the truth," I replied, but my voice had turned meek, my courage dissipating. "It's not a question of whether I think it or not."

"You have been fed so many lies," he hissed, taking my chin between his fingers, his extraordinary eyes piercing my flesh even as his touch sent a shock of heat through my body. "You've been convinced that we are cruel and dangerous, malicious beings bent on harming your kind. And yet you willingly crept into our lands, infiltrator. Tell me, why is that?"

"I..."

No words could explain why I'd come. Why I'd ventured into the mist, knowing it would likely end me, rather than taking my chances in Dúnbar against two drunken fools.

"I don't know," I finally confessed.

"Well, you'd best figure it out. Because I intend to learn the truth about you, with or without your consent."

The two figures who were holding my arms maintained their grip as I hastily replied, "My name is Lyrinn Martel. I live in Dúnbar. I am a blacksmith's daughter. That's all I have to tell you. I am of no interest to one such as yourself."

"Oh—you are very interesting to me indeed." Nodding to his companions, he eased closer and inhaled a deep breath as if taking in my scent.

The two Fae freed my arms at last. But instead of running, I froze in place, unable to move. Against my skin, I felt the leader's breath caress every inch of me as though the air itself was examining my flesh for weaknesses.

"There is something about you," he said, his face so close to mine that his breath teased the strands of hair around my cheekbones. "Something that makes little sense. And I intend to figure out what it is. You should never have come to this place, Lyrinn Martel. No good will come of this—neither for your kind nor my own."

I swallowed deeply as the Fae let out a snarl and turned again, silently leading the way into the ruins.

CHAPTER FIVE

THE CLOAKED figures took my arms again and guided me along until we came to a broad gap in one of the tall, broken walls that made up the outer shell of the ruins.

There was little doubt in my mind that the Fae planned to kill me under the sky's darkness, to do away with my body as though I'd never been here. Why else, I wondered, would they want to bring me to a place so destroyed, so long dead?

As we advanced, I began to wonder where my captors spent their days and nights. Were they encamped somewhere nearby, sleeping under the stars by the flickering glow of firelight? Perhaps they sought shelter nightly among the ruins themselves. Maybe the decayed walls and damaged slate roof were enough to offer protection from the elements.

I wondered if they would protect me from the Grimpers, should those entities choose to seek me out.

As we navigated our way over uneven ground, the stars and the moon disappeared, and an encompassing darkness crept around us so deep and intense that I lost all ability to see even a few inches before me. I had no choice but to entrust myself to those who held my arms, allowing them to guide me to our dubious destination. And they seemed confident enough to guide me over the stone-coated terrain as though they'd made their way over its surface a million times before this night.

Still, I wondered what had happened to the clouds, the stars. Why could I no longer see the outlines of the half-shattered walls against the night sky?

Why could I no longer see the mysterious leader walking before us?

Under my feet, I began to feel the familiar texture of hard, uneven paving stones. The breeze that had caressed my skin when I had first arrived in Tíria had ceased, and now all I felt was a sort of cold clamminess that sent goosebumps trailing along my flesh. We were enclosed now, trapped between walls that I could not see.

Instinct told me to ask my silent captors where they were taking me and what they intended to do with me once we reached our destination. But their determined stride told me there was little point in such enquiries.

I already knew the answers, besides. *You are taking me wherever your leader wishes for you to take me.*

And we will arrive soon enough.

After a few minutes of frustrating, unrelenting darkness, the sound of an iron key scraping its way into a lock met my ears, then I heard a door creak open on worn hinges. My two guides shoved me into a place so devoid of light that it seemed a thick velvet mask had been drawn over my eyes, adding layer upon layer to the already oppressive darkness.

When I heard the door creak shut, I let out a breath and told myself I must be in a cell of some sort.

But I'm still alive.

Which means there's hope, at least.

I stood still for a time, waiting and hoping for my eyes to

adjust to the blackness surrounding me. *I need to ascertain where I am. How I got here.*

How I can escape.

Sure enough, after several minutes, faint shapes began to manifest around me. I could just make out the outline of a set of bars forming a sort of window in the cell's door. The random shapes of the large stones making up the walls. A straw mattress on the floor. A wash basin sitting atop a small dresser that didn't entirely look as if it belonged to such a place.

I turned slowly, assessing each wall, each corner, even as a set of torches lining one wall flickered slowly to life, conjured by some devilry I could not begin to comprehend.

I had been frightened since the moment when the leader had awoken me—not to mention confused. But watching the flames flare to life in front of my eyes without the aid of human implements sent a chill through me like none I had ever known.

This was magic. Some trickery of the Fae.

Either that, or I was losing my mind.

"I want to go home," I said miserably. The words sounded more pathetic than I intended, like those uttered by a terrified child rather than a grown young woman who knows how to wield a blade with some skill.

But I don't have a blade, I reminded myself. *I have nothing but my mind, and it is growing weaker and more vulnerable by the second.*

"I never wanted to come to this place," I said, pleading with the walls to release me. "Please...just let me go. I will never speak of this, I promise you."

With that, the door at the opposite end of the cell flew open, a burst of flame-light from the corridor beyond blinding me until my eyes managed to settle on the silhouette framed in the doorway.

The Fae I had spoken to earlier—the leader—was standing

staring at me. But this time, his cloak was gone. Without his hood, I could now see waves of dark hair falling to his broad shoulders. I could make out the outline of his torso, a narrow waist, powerful legs under fitted leather trousers.

Wordlessly, he stepped inside the cell and strode over to stand before me. I inhaled a sharp, desperate breath as he reached out and pressed a powerful hand to my chest, holding it there, sizing me up with his very touch.

Terrified, I averted my eyes, telling myself I needed to be strong and brave. He had not harmed me yet, after all. Perhaps he only wanted to feel my heart beating—to gauge my honesty. To understand how I'd managed to penetrate the Breath of the Fae.

It was a question I'd asked myself a thousand times last night even as I had ascended the Rise.

Finally, I summoned the courage to look up at his face. But it wasn't his eyes that drew me in now.

Pointed into elegant tips, his ears were unlike any I'd ever seen, other than in the illustrated faerie tales I had read as a child—stories from books that were now banned in Castelle.

It has been a millennium, I thought, *since one of my people has met the gaze of those who dwell in the highest kingdom.*

Tales of beings such as him had circulated since I was a child—of their cruelty, their feral malice. I had been taught to hate and fear them.

But when I pulled my eyes to his, it wasn't fear that scalded me to my core.

It was deep, unrelenting desire.

I had heard rumors all my life that the Fae were monstrous. Yet this being was so beautiful that it almost pained me to look at him.

His eyes shone like gems, his hair a multitude of twisting, dark shades so brilliant that I could scarcely name just one.

"We are alone, and I need you to tell me the truth," my captor said, the quiet hostility in his tone instantly turning the heat inside me to ice. His hand was still pressed to my chest, no doubt assessing the throb of my heart against my ribcage. "None but the Grimpers have climbed the Onyx Stair in centuries—neither up nor down. How did you do it? What manner of mortal are you, exactly?"

I stared into his eyes, taking a deep breath to try and calm my pulse.

"I am Lyrinn Martel, as I told you," I said. "A blacksmith's daughter. I live in Dúnbar."

"So you have said," he replied, his eyes scanning my face for signs that I was hiding some dark truth. He pulled his hand away and added, "I need more than a name. I need to know your nature. You are a curiosity. A puzzle I would very much like to solve."

CHAPTER SIX

I GLARED AT MY CAPTOR, irritated beyond measure that my pain was a source of amusement for him. But I managed to suppress my anger enough to reply, "You will have all the time in the world to figure me out after I've left. There's no reason to keep me here. No one will ever have to know I ever ventured up the Onyx Rise. I could—"

"But you *did* venture up the Rise, which means you endangered the inhabitants of these ruins." He eased toward me again and whispered, "Were it up to me, I might be tempted to have your body flung off the Rise for Dúnbar's townsfolk to find. Your presence here has already drawn the eyes of Grimpers, and worse, no doubt, than them. It was a reckless thing that you did, Lyrinn Martel." He backed away and cleared his throat before adding, "If I am to decide your fate, I suppose I must pay a visit to the Dragon Court."

Dragon Court.

I had heard those two words uttered only a few times in my life, when I was very young. A visitor to Castelle—a southerner from Marqueyssal—had made the mistake of asking a shopkeeper a question about the court. Within seconds, a member of

Castelle's Lord's Guard had advanced on her, taken her by the hair and dragged her, screaming, from the shop.

When Leta and I asked my father why she had been punished so aggressively for what seemed like an innocent question, he told us the Dragon Court was the stuff of dark legends—the ancient domain of the highest of the Tírian Fae lords. It was situated in the far North, inaccessible by mortals even in the days when the border between our lands was open.

"I suspect the court has crumbled to dust by now and is perfectly harmless," my father had insisted. "Still, it was once a place of power. A land where Fae-silver was mined to forge exquisite weapons, and where the Fae grew strong, their magic extraordinary."

With those words, his voice was filled with an admiration I had never heard before or since. "To this day," he continued, "the lords of the mortal realms refuse to acknowledge the court's inhabitants or its former power. The High King was a cruel being, at least according to the old tales. One who could summon fire and flame with little more than a look in his enemy's direction."

Recalling my father's words, I clenched my jaw. "Your kind despises my people," I told the Fae. "Those in the Dragon Court will tell you to kill me. Let me leave this place. I promise you I won't return. You never have to look upon me again—I'll become a fleeting memory, nothing more."

He laughed, his smile lighting up the small cell. "Forgive me for seeming unsympathetic. Need I remind you that you entered our lands willingly?"

"So let me leave willingly."

The Fae smirked, his eyes unreadable. "You misunderstand me. A mortal who enters our lands freely becomes the responsibility of the Fae who presides over that land. It is a law far older than you, than me, than your little town in the Low Lands."

"You deem me your responsibility?" I scoffed. "It seems to me you mean *prisoner*—or, at the very least, property. But you can't lay claim to me. I only came up the cliff to escape two men who were trying to harm me. I had no intention of making my way into these lands, and if you and your...*minions* hadn't found me..."

"But you did make your way here," the Fae said with a grimace. "You sought protection, did you not?"

"Protection, yes," I snapped. "But only because I lost my blade and was defenseless. I had every intention of descending when day broke. Instead of allowing it, you took me captive. That is not what I call protection."

"Had we not taken you, you may have been killed by creatures far fouler than us," he said. "Fortunately for you, I *will* protect you. At least, as long as you are in my lands. No harm will come to you here. If you should try to leave, however, the Grimpers may well pursue you."

"They didn't hurt me when I climbed the Onyx Rise," I said triumphantly, my chin raised. "Maybe I'm immune to their particular form of violence."

"I wouldn't be so arrogant about it, if I were you. Grimpers are more dangerous than you can begin to imagine."

There was pain in the Fae's features. And something else, as well. A sort of frustration, as though he didn't entirely know how to defeat the creatures.

"Can't your fighters stop them?" I asked. "I thought you Fae were powerful—why can't you just kill them?"

He let out a deep, throaty laugh, and his eyes flashed with quiet bitterness. "There is a great deal you don't know about this world of ours, isn't there?"

I lifted my chin higher and challenged him, my eyes boring into his own.

"Yes, there is," I said sharply. "For instance, I don't know your name."

With the last few words, I softened my voice. Maybe I could charm him as Leta would have done. Convince him that I was more curious than afraid. If he thought I was relaxed—if he let his guard down—then maybe I could convince him to set me free.

"I am Mithraan, caretaker and protector of the castle Fairholme," he said, gesturing around us. "At least, what remains of it. And at this moment, I am still trying to determine whether you are a pleasing gift or a walking curse. You have achieved what no being from your lands has in a millennium. Which means it is my bound duty to find out why the mist chose to allow you safe passage to our lands."

"*Chose?*" I echoed. "You speak as though the mist has a mind of its own."

"The mist is more than mere poison," he replied, his tone sharp. "It is the product of a dark, foul magic that has eaten away at Tíria for far too many years. But last night, for the first time in memory, it parted to welcome a young woman from Dúnbar into our lands. I would like to understand why that is—though I am beginning to have my suspicions."

I ground my teeth for a moment before replying, "I would love to tell you. But since I don't know the answer any more than you do, I would appreciate if you would drop the matter. You've been up here alone for a millennium. Perhaps another thousand years will pass before you're forced to look a mortal in the eye again. Let me go, and think of my departure as my gift to you, given that you seem to despise humans thoroughly."

With that, I offered him a smile and a shallow curtsy.

"You are, in fact, the first human whose gaze I have had the displeasure of meeting," Mithraan said. "I am not as old as you might think."

I stared at him, wanting to accuse him of lying, but I realized he had never said he was thousands of years old—only that his *kind* had lived in these lands for millennia.

"Yet you seem to be in charge of this place, which fell when the Breath first cascaded down the Rise," I finally said. "How is that?"

Mithraan narrowed his eyes, and for a moment, a frisson of terror shuddered its way through my body. I only hoped he couldn't read the fear in my eyes.

"My father was High Lord of Fairholme when it fell all those years ago," he said. "He was alive when the last Blood Trials took place. He lived to see our lands destroyed, and he watched over the ruins for hundreds of years after that. When he died not so long ago, I was granted title of lord—though *Lord of the Ruins* seems a dubious honor."

"How old are you, then?" I asked, fully aware of the impertinence of such a question.

At that, the Fae simply issued me a look of warning. "Age is of no consequence to one such as me. What matters is knowledge—and of that, I have plenty."

Without explaining his meaning, Mithraan turned and moved toward the door, stopping only when he reached it. "I will consider letting you leave eventually, if only for the sake of those who dwell here with me. On one condition."

"Which is?"

"You will remain here for a few days. I would like a chance to observe you."

I contemplated his proposal for a moment before asking, "Do I have a choice?"

He chuckled before replying, "I'm afraid not."

"Fine, then," I said, attempting in vain to force a pleasant note into my voice. *Best for him to think me compliant, because I intend to escape at the first possible chance.*

"You must be craving the caress of clean clothing, so I offer you the opportunity to bathe and change. And then, I would like for you to dine with me."

I gawked at him, frozen in place. "Bathe?" I asked, as if I'd never heard the word before.

He turned to look at me, puzzled by my question.

Gesturing to the cell's walls, I said, "Where, exactly?"

"My men will escort you to the bathing chamber," he replied. "I may not know exactly how you came to be here, but I am not without manners. Whoever you really are, Lyrinn Martel, I am keenly aware that you do not belong in a cold cell. It's time you saw a little of this once beautiful castle."

Castle, I thought. *More like dark, dead, shadowy remnants.*

Not exactly a place I care to explore.

Mithraan lifted a hand, gesturing mildly with his fingers, and immediately, two hooded figures in light armor strode into the cell. Instead of grabbing me as the Fae had done on the clifftop, one of them simply said, "This way, Miss."

I followed, too baffled to refuse—and too excited by the possibility of a bath.

Our home in Dúnbar never had a bathtub. When Leta or I wished to cleanse ourselves, we headed to a secluded place along the river and bathed. It was a refreshing, if occasionally frigid, form of ablution, particularly during the colder months.

The Fae led me down the long, dark stone corridor until we reached a door of wood and iron. After unlocking it, they guided me through, and as I glanced back over my shoulder, I spied Mithraan watching me from a distance, his eyes narrowed in scrutiny as if he was still trying to figure out what demon had conjured me.

I still couldn't tell if he abhorred or admired me for infiltrating his lands. I told myself I didn't care—that all that mattered was finding my way out of this place and back to my family. By now, someone had likely found Raleigh's and his repugnant friend's remains in the alleyway, and my father was probably worried that I might have suffered the same fate.

But I almost forgot about all of it when we turned a corner and stepped into a wide corridor.

The space around us, which had appeared dark and stained from years of moisture, turned bright and airy. The ceiling was suddenly intact and beautifully vaulted, the plaster walls topped with delicately carved moulding. The floor extended before us in elegant slabs of polished marble. Along the walls, rows of torches sparked to vivid life, their flames dancing in synchronicity with our footfalls.

Beneath the torches hung various tapestries depicting forest scenes replete with birds singing, foxes scampering about, and other wildlife mingling with exquisite, flowering trees. There was a depth to the images so vivid, so realistic, that a part of me wished to walk straight into them and lose myself among the scents and sights of the wilds.

The scene around us was the absolute opposite of the world outside. The ruins had, by some miracle, solidified into some semblance of what must have been the castle Fairholme's original beauty.

I had to bite my tongue to restrain myself from asking what had just happened. How had our surroundings altered so dramatically? Were we still in the ruins, or had we somehow moved through time?

Worse still, had I gone mad?

Even as I grew more tempted to inquire, a strange, soothing sensation flitted through my mind. All of a sudden, my questions vanished, trivial and forgotten, as did every worry that had infiltrated my soul since I'd entered this realm.

All I wanted was to remain in this place forever, to inhale the sweetness of its air, to behold its beautiful denizens and extraordinary architecture. I never cared to look upon another of Dúnbar's questionable residents again—men like Raleigh whose lives consisted of imbibing and assaulting women while moaning about their unfulfilling existence.

Or even men like...like...

My father.

His face came to me in graphic detail, and I tried in vain to hold it in my mind, to remember why it was that I needed to get home. The importance of him, of Leta.

They'll think I've died. I cannot let them suffer that sorrow.

But even as I focused my mind on them both, the thoughts vanished in a mental puff of smoke, and all I could think about was the bath awaiting me and the Fae who had brought me to this strange, mercurial paradise.

Fairholme had cast a spell over me—one that I knew to be incredibly dangerous.

I was a prisoner in these ruins, captive of a Fae who was as perilously alluring as the lands where I now stood.

CHAPTER SEVEN

WHEN WE REACHED a set of double doors at the farthest end of the long corridor, they opened inward in greeting, seemingly of their own volition.

Inside the room, two female Fae awaited me. Each was dressed in white, hair flowing in spiraling curls past their shoulders. They were both beautiful, their eyes large and expressive. One had skin of alabaster, the other of deep onyx. The former's hair was golden, the latter's was silvery white, as fine as silken thread. Their ears, like Mithraan's, were pointed into delicate tips.

The chamber was large, with a window at the far end covered in light, billowing curtains. I could just make out the bleak, blackened landscape beyond—it seemed that we were on the second level, though that seemed impossible. I had no recollection of ascending a staircase. Then again, my mind had played tricks on me since my arrival at the top of the Onyx Rise.

The sun had risen, casting a warm glow over the chamber. At the center of the stone floor sat an ornate tub filled with steaming hot water. Covered in filigree of gleaming faerie silver, its ends were curved like the necks of elegant swans.

"Come," one of the women said, gesturing me to advance. Hesitating for a moment, I stepped toward her. She smiled reassuringly, seeming to understand my trepidation.

"I am Isibeth," she said, her voice sweet as a lilting melody. "And this is Asta. We're here to serve you as—" She exchanged a look with her companion before proceeding. "As our guest."

"My name is Lyrinn," I replied, unsure what else to say. "I... was told I would be able to take a bath."

"Yes. We are here to assist you," Asta replied.

"I can bathe myself," I retorted more sharply than I intended, my brows meeting in involuntary defensiveness.

The two Fae exchanged a look, then Isibeth said, "Yes, of course you can. We will assist you into the tub and provide you with clean clothing. If you wish for privacy while you bathe, naturally, you will have it."

I forced my face to settle into a more pleasant expression as I said, "Thank you."

Asta slipped over to me and gently pulled my cloak from my shoulders. The euphoric feeling that had overtaken me a minute earlier was gone now, and I found myself struggling to relax under the Fae's touch. I wasn't accustomed to being handled—let alone disrobed—by strangers.

But I told myself she meant me no harm, and that soon I would be soaking in the tub with my eyes closed, my fears washing away.

It wasn't long before my clothing was lying in a pile on the marble floor. Isibeth gathered it in her arms before laying out a long, flowing dress of light blue on a nearby chair.

"Please," Asta said, holding out a hand. I took it, thankful for her help as I stepped over the tub's high rim.

The water was hot, but not scalding, and I sank every inch of myself into it until my head, too, was submerged, before coming up and inhaling a breath of cool, fresh air. Brushing my wet hair away from my face, I turned toward the window only to see rolling green hills in the distance like those in the tapestries that lined the corridor.

But...I had to be imagining it, surely. The land of Tíria was dead. Blackened, decayed, and crawling with menacing creatures of shadow. I had seen it with my own eyes only a few seconds ago.

"What's happened?" I asked aloud before I could stop myself. "How is this possible? Why does the landscape look so...alive?"

Asta glanced briefly toward the window, then issued me a sympathetic smile.

"Mithraan has a few spells up his sleeve," she said. "He wanted make you feel at home."

The Fae exchanged a knowing glance, then both lowered their chins, hands clasped before them.

"Let us know if you need anything more," Isibeth said as they turned and headed for the doors, which opened just long enough for them to move through before closing tight.

I was alone with my thoughts, steam swirling about my face as I sank into an unfamiliar sensation of pure, luxurious bliss.

So, the caretaker of the ruins was a spell caster. And clearly, he was impressively gifted. So why had he and his companions not managed to fight off the mist and the Grimpers?

Unless the stories were true, and the Fae *were* responsible for those blights upon these lands...

Idly washing myself, I turned once again to stare out the window at the distant hills, at their impossible greenness, the blue sky above as clear as any I'd ever seen.

After a time, an irresistible curiosity began to eat away at me. I wanted—no, *needed*—to study the lands more closely. To witness the spell that Mithraan was casting on my behalf. I wished to understand what would compel such a cruel being to change the entire landscape for my benefit.

Pushing myself up, I slipped out of the tub and walked over to press my hands to the thick stone windowsill, staring out at a scene that beckoned to me as nothing ever had. I was only vaguely aware of the chilly breeze caressing my damp skin, of the water I was leaving on the floor around me. I was aware, too, of my nudity.

But for once, I didn't feel a hint of self-consciousness.

My mind and my eyes were fixed on the distant, wooded hills and on what lay beyond. Somewhere in the far distance, I knew, was the Dragon Court, where the Highest Lord of Tíria resided.

How vast *was* this land? How much of it had the Immortals once occupied, and how much of it was now overrun with vicious Grimpers?

After staring toward the horizon for a time, my gaze roamed to a tall stone wall surrounding a courtyard below me. A single tree stood at its center, its trunk white, its leaves silver and shining.

I sensed a quiet strength inside the tree itself. I felt its heart struggling to survive, even as its life was sucked slowly away by the toxicity of the land.

It was beautiful and devastating, all at once.

Several seconds passed before I realized a lone figure had stepped up to stand a few feet from the tree's trunk, his face pulled up, eyes locked on mine.

Mithraan.

He could see me from the waist up, naked, vulnerable. But for some reason I couldn't explain, I did not recoil from his gaze. Was he casting a spell right now? Forcing me against my will to expose my body to him? Was this some cruel joke on his part?

As I fixed my eyes on his, the truth flowed through my veins, prompting my cheeks to flush with shame.

Because I knew in my heart that he was not forcing me into this position—though telling myself so would have been a convenient excuse for my folly.

The truth was, I *wanted* him to see me. And as I studied his face, so exquisitely defined in the daylight, I longed to feel him close behind me, his arms wrapping around my body, his lips on my neck.

In that moment, I desired him as I had never desired any human male, and the ache that set into my core was enough to make me want to cry out in a feral, frustrated agony.

A violent gust of wind slammed against my skin and I inhaled sharply, backing away, my arms crossing to cover my chest. I strode back to the tub and climbed in, hiding myself.

I closed my eyes and told myself I'd only imagined Mithraan down below—that everything I'd seen since entering this chamber was an illusion conjured by his devious, twisted mind. He was simply part of a pretty picture of Tíria—one he had painted to lure me deeper into his clutches, to convince me to stay in this place.

Some of the old tales told that the Fae enjoyed teasing and taunting humans to the point of madness, forcing our kind to fall for them, then leaving us lust-filled and desperate.

I told myself to be wary. If Mithraan was pulling those tricks with me—trying to force me into a state of rampant desire—it would be difficult to convince myself to return home.

I soaked in the tub for countless minutes. The water never grew cold, and my flesh never shriveled. Over time, my embarrassment faded, and I began to feel embraced, even at peace with the notion that Mithraan's eyes had caressed my flesh so aggressively.

When I found myself stripped of all anxiety, I finally

climbed out of the tub and slipped into the long blue dress Isibeth had left for me, which was soft as the finest silk, embroidered with vines that twisted and curled around one another like lovers locked in an intimate embrace.

Though the garment didn't look like much as it lay over the chair, when I pulled it on it conformed to my every curve, neither too tight nor too loose, accentuating my waist, my hips, my shoulders. Enveloped as I was in such a beautiful creation, I almost felt as though I belonged in this place alongside its population of Immortals.

I peered at myself in a tarnished mirror that sat against the wall, and an unfamiliar thought reached my mind.

I look almost beautiful.

Though my sister and I didn't look very much alike, for the briefest moment, I saw a flash of Leta in my face. But I wondered if this was more of Mithraan's magic. Another spell cast to comfort me and set my mind at ease.

I had never once in my life thought myself pretty, let alone beautiful.

But I supposed if it was the worst thing that was to happen to me here in the Immortal lands, perhaps this place wasn't so bad, after all.

CHAPTER EIGHT

After a few minutes, a knock sounded at the bathing chamber's doors.

"Come," I called.

The doors opened and a male Fae in a golden tunic walked in.

"Mithraan requests your company in the dining hall," he announced in a formal tone. "For dinner."

"Dinner?" I asked, stunned. "Already? Isn't it morning? Shouldn't we be having breakfast?"

"It is evening, my Lady," he said, looking a little confused.

I was about to protest when I scolded myself. I was certain I had been in the bath only for an hour or so, but for all I knew, I had soaked in the delicious heat for an entire day.

Whatever reality-twisting spell engulfed this place and rendered it whole and beautiful had skewed my mind.

"I see," I replied. "Very well, then."

I followed him wordlessly, my heart throbbing in my chest as we moved along corridor after corridor until at last we reached a magnificent room of sage, white and golden accents. Its ceilings were high and ornate, its walls decorated in yet another mural depicting woodlands filled with beautiful wildlife. My mind was soothed once again as my gaze slid over every surface, filling me with a renewed sense of calm to counter any feelings of quiet terror I had about seeing a certain dark-haired Fae again.

A long wooden table stood at the room's center, flanked by twelve chairs, with one positioned at each end.

I waited until a door at the room's far end opened and Mithraan strode in, followed by two male Fae in similar garb to his. Each was wearing a tunic of rich silk with layered leather belts at their waists.

On Mithraan's tunic was embroidered a silver eagle, but the other two were unadorned.

His companions were exquisitely handsome, one with hair of fiery red and deep blue eyes. The other, like Mithraan, had dark hair, though his was shorter and cut into angular spikes that fell sculpturally about his face. He wore a mischievous expression as he appraised me, his eyes moving from my face to my body, then back again.

"Sit, Lyrinn," Mithraan commanded, his eyes locking on mine for only a moment.

My cheeks heated with the sudden recollection of our exchanged look through the bathing chamber's window. I saw no sign of it in his eyes, no sly sideways glances.

Was it real? Had I merely imagined it through some trickery?

I pulled up a chair and took a seat, and Mithraan's two companions seated themselves opposite me. Mithraan claimed the chair at the head of the table, appraising all three of us at once.

"Lyrinn," he said, pointing first to the black-haired man, then to the one with red hair. "Meet Khiral and Alaric. They are my most trusted friends."

I nodded, but remained silent, unaccustomed as I was to strangers' eyes peering so intently into mine.

"You have questions," Mithraan added when I said nothing.

"I do," I replied, finally finding my voice.

"Well?" Khiral asked. "What does a mere mortal who has no business in our lands wish to know?"

Mithraan shot him a look of warning, but Khiral simply sat back, his arms crossed, a smug grin on his lips.

I raised my chin and looked into his eyes.

"All right, then," I said. "Tell me why your friend here sent the mist and the Grimpers down to our village to kill our people."

"Mithraan?" Khiral laughed, exchanging a look with Alaric, who offered up a cryptic smile. "You really think..."

Mithraan held up a hand to silence him. "The Grimpers are not under my command, nor have they ever been," he said, ice coating his voice. "They are malevolent beings, controlled by one far crueler than I."

"Who?" I asked.

"No Fae of Tíria," Mithraan replied, offering up a frustrating non-answer.

"But I thought..." I stammered, failing to conclude my question. I wasn't even sure what I wanted to ask at this point.

"You thought they were the result of a spell cast centuries ago to keep our kind and yours separate," Mithraan said. "Because we are bitter at having been defeated in the last Trials. Yes, I know. Many believe the same as you—including some of our own kind. But the Grimpers were not conjured by the magic of Tíria. They are the cruelest curse on our lands. They attack our kind, just as they attack yours—ironic though that may seem to those who know their true nature."

I was almost afraid to ask, but I mustered the courage to utter the words, "What do you mean by true nature?"

Mithraan and Khiral both went silent, their mouths drawn into a clench as anger seemed to surge through them both.

"The Grimpers were once Fae," Alaric said quietly. "Each and every one of them was one of our kind. Their bodies, minds, and souls were stolen from them. They are nothing now but cruel shadows of their former selves."

A sense of horror permeated my flesh, my veins, my bones. To do such a thing to beautiful Immortals—to steal their lives from them and condemn them to an existence filled with torment? It seemed a crueler fate than any I could imagine.

"Who did this to them?" I asked, my voice tight.

He let out a slow breath. "There are some who say the Taker did, when our lands were cut off from the mortal realms. Some claim the creature has been corrupted by men, its mind taken over."

"But I thought the Taker was beyond corruption," I replied. "I thought it extracted the Gifts from the vanquished at the Blood Trials. They say it's incapable of cheating, of being manipulated."

"Every living thing can be manipulated, provided it has something to lose," Mithraan said. "Though I have my doubts about the Taker. It is a mindless creature, and devoid of much of the greed that destroys men and Fae." He went silent for a moment before asking, "Tell me, Lyrinn, have you ever been to the Lake of Blood?"

I shook my head. "I've never so much as crossed the River Dún," I replied. "But I know of the lake—I know it's near the grounds at Kalemnar's center, where the Trials take place."

"The Eternity Tree towers over a nearby wood," Mithraan replied with a nod. "It is larger than any other, its bark twisted and laced like intertwining tendons."

I nodded. "I've heard of it."

Mithraan continued. "They say that there is a cavern

beneath the tree's roots. It is there that the Taker dwells. The creature only leaves it once every thousand years, to serve those who win the Blood Trials. It used to be that the Taker was the Faes' to control, because we never lost. The creature granted the winners the Blood-Gifts of the vanquished, our Champions were wed, and our kind grew stronger over many, many generations. But contrary to your skewed tales, we ruled over mortals with kindness and patience. We were not oppressors. Still, a thousand years ago, Kalemnar's mortals decided they needed to put an end to our long reign through subterfuge and murder."

"The Trials were rigged against us by our enemies," Khiral said with a snarl. "No human was ever meant to win them. You know it as well as we do."

"I'm not sure she does know," Mithraan replied. "She was not alive then, remember. She didn't witness the fall."

"Fall?"

Mithraan let out a sigh. "As Khiral said—as every mortal knows—our Fae Champions had won every Trial with ease. The Blood Trials themselves were a mere formality—a means for the Fae to prove their dominance. As you said, no mortal could have beaten one of our Champions in competition—and every human in Kalemnar knew it."

"Yet mortals did beat Fae," I said impatiently. "Which means our Champions must have been more powerful than your kind gave them credit for. I realize that's difficult to accept, but—"

"It was not the mortal Champions' power that won them the competition," Mithraan interrupted with a shake of his head. "On the final day of the Blood Trials, when they should have been declared winners, our two Champions both collapsed at once. They fell to the ground, their bodies suddenly lifeless. A young man from Domignon went on to win, alongside a young woman from Belleau. When the Taker had siphoned the Blood-Gifts and the other vanquished had been slaughtered, the two winners wed. The king who now rules Domignon is their descendant."

"To this day, we don't know how our two Champions died," Alaric said. "We are Immortal. We do not succumb easily."

"Had they been killed in combat, we might have forgiven the travesty," Khiral added bitterly. "But our Champions' lives were taken through foul play, and we all know it. No one was ever able to prove it, however. The Blood Trials are a game of death, with few rules of conduct. There was little sympathy for our kind."

"We were cut off from the rest of Kalemnar after the Trials ended and the remaining Fae returned to Tíria," Alaric said. "The mist began to pour down the Rise, and despite our strength, it proved toxic to our kind. The Grimpers began to herd the Fae away from the cliff's edge, forcing us back. During those confusing days, we lost some of our own. Our High King's own daughter Kaela, who had attended the Blood Trials, went missing soon after our Champions fell. Some say she was turned into a Grimper, and that she still roams the Rise, looking for victims."

"That's horrible," I replied, but I forced myself to swallow and harden against his words. I had no idea if these Fae were telling me the truth. I had heard the tales all my life—of Fae deception, of their cruelty. But I had also heard that they were incapable of uttering falsehoods. And at the moment, I wasn't sure whether I could take anything they said at face value. "You don't believe it, surely? I mean, why would she have been turned?"

"I cannot say," Mithraan said. "I know only that her father, our High King, loved his daughter, and that her disappearance left him an empty shell as devoid of light and beauty as this land is now."

"It doesn't matter," Khiral snarled. "It is done now, and there is no way back for us. There is only one way to break the curse that has destroyed this land, and it is an impossibility."

"Why is that?" I asked.

The Fae exchanged looks, then Mithraan finally replied, "One of us would have to compete in the Blood Trials and win, so that we might regain our former strength."

I stopped myself from replying too quickly, unsure if I should dare venture an answer. But finally, I said, "So why don't you compete?"

"Is that a serious question?" Khiral sneered.

"It is," I replied, swallowing hard in an attempt to keep my voice in check.

"The Fae of Tíria cannot compete," he replied. "Domignon's king has decreed it. And even if we could, descending the Rise is impossible. The mist and the Grimpers would take us before we could get halfway down."

"What if the mist parted for you, like it did for me?" I asked. It was probably a foolish question, and from the look on the Fae's features, it was disrespectful, too.

"The mist is not ours to control," Mithraan said before Khiral could interject. "We cannot simply command it."

"Our lord is being modest," Alaric said with a half-smile.

"Oh?" I replied.

"Mithraan is powerful. He could part the mist long enough for a few of us to descend, I'd wager."

"It would take a great deal out of me," Mithraan said. "I would have no chance of victory in the Trials if I were to die simply trying to descend the Rise."

I sat back in my chair, silent.

Why did I even care if the Fae competed? It wasn't my problem. Besides, I cared little for the Trials. All I wanted was to return home, to escape this place and be with my father and

Leta. I longed for my own bed, for a bowl of rabbit stew in our tiny house.

The Fae had lived up here for a thousand years, and they were doing just fine. Not thriving in a lush green wilderness, perhaps.

But fine.

No. It definitely isn't my problem. I was never meant to be in this place.

As a plate of delicious-looking food appeared on the table before me, a door at the room's far end opened and a Fae female walked in wearing a long, white gown.

When my eyes landed on her, I gasped.

She was the most beautiful creature I'd ever seen. Her hair was dark brown and fell in ringlets around her shoulders. Her eyes were large and black, her brows shapely. Her cheekbones looked as though they could cut through diamonds.

Smiling, she strode directly toward Mithraan.

She slipped her arms around his neck and kissed his cheek, and I found myself overcome with a fierce, cruel envy that I struggled to shake from my own mind.

Mithraan smiled and laid a hand on her arm, slipping it to her hand and rising to his feet.

"Nihara," he said. "Please, sit with us."

She seated herself next to Khiral on the opposite side of the table from me, and her eyes locked on mine. As I looked at her, her irises seemed to lighten for an instant to a sort of golden hue before darkening again.

"Lyrinn," she said.

"That's right," I replied icily, wondering if she'd invaded my mind to extract my name.

She let out a quiet laugh, not quite mocking, but not entirely kind, either.

"You did what no mortal man has done in a thousand years. How does it feel?"

"The climb, you mean?"

She nodded. "The climb."

"I'm beginning to wonder if I should have let the men in Dúnbar kill me, to be honest," I told her. "Your...leader here is holding me hostage."

"Not hostage," Mithraan corrected. "You are a guest. For now."

"Guests are allowed to leave when they wish to."

Mithraan fixed his eyes on mine and pulled his chin down. I wanted to look away—I demanded it of myself—but I could not. As I stared into his eyes, he asked, "Tell me, Lyrinn, do you wish to leave at this moment?"

I opened my mouth to say yes, but nothing came out.

Mithraan rose to his feet and slipped over to stand behind my chair. With both hands, he grabbed its back and pulled me away from the table, twisting me around so that I was facing him.

He took my hands and pulled me to my feet. I turned to look at the woman called Nihara, who was smiling mischievously like this was all a great joke to her. But Mithraan cupped a hand under my chin and pulled my eyes back to his.

His scent wrapped itself around me like a tantalizing breeze, infiltrating my every pore and making my mouth water as though I were suddenly starving for the merest taste of him.

Around us, darkness began to swirl, and the table, the chairs, the other Fae all disappeared. We were alone, standing in a void together, isolated from everyone and everything. I could have kissed him then. I could have satisfied my craving, if only a little, and no one would have been the wiser but the two of us.

Except I knew in my mind and my heart that we had not left

the dining chamber. I knew Khiral, Alaric, and Nihara were still close at hand.

Was this glamour? Part of his trickery? Was Mithraan making himself captivating on purpose?

"Do you really wish to leave me, never to set eyes on me again?" he asked, gently this time, his voice like a soft breeze on my mind. "Do you really think your life will ever be the same, after what you have seen and felt in this place?"

"The...same?" I retorted, trying to snap myself out of the spell. "What makes you think you've changed me?"

"Maybe you're right." Mithraan pushed closer and pressed his mouth to my ear. I felt his lips caress my lobe as he said, "Perhaps it's you who have changed *me*, Lyrinn. Perhaps it is you who are tormenting me. You have filled me with a need unlike any that has ever consumed me. I am desperate for you."

I pulled back and looked into his eyes, which were swirling with light and flame. I stared at him for a long moment, absorbed in his gaze, telling myself not to succumb to the desire that was so close to overtaking me.

"I..." I stammered. "I need..."

He pulled away abruptly, let out a laugh, then, as the chamber flared back to life around us, returned to his seat.

My heart pounding, mortification seared my cheeks as I pushed my chair back to the table and sat down.

"Come now, Lyrinn," Nihara said, watching me with a satisfied smirk on her lips. "Mithraan was simply playing with you. He enjoys doing that to his prey before devouring it whole. Don't you, my Lord?"

But Mithraan didn't reply. Instead, he watched me, his expression impossible to decipher.

"Hysterical," I muttered, glancing over as he laid his hand over Nihara's.

So, they were a couple, were they? They both had an air of

cruelty about them. I was quite certain they couldn't have cared less for the feelings of anyone but themselves.

"A plain little thing, isn't she?" Nihara asked, leaning close to Mithraan. "She could be pretty, if not for..."

"Don't," Mithraan shot, stopping her from completing her thought. He pulled his hand back, curling it into a tight fist on the tabletop.

It sounded like a warning, and Nihara bowed her head.

"As much as I appreciate your kind hospitality," I said with a snide clearing of my throat, "I would like to get some sleep. Could someone please show me to my quarters?"

"Of course," Alaric said, shooting a sideways glance at Mithraan, who waved him away. "Come with me, Lyrinn."

CHAPTER NINE

ALARIC LED the way down a long, gray-walled corridor until we reached a spiral staircase of dark, worn stone. Taking hold of my dress to avoid falling on my face, I climbed after him until we reached a small landing with a wooden door to one side.

"You've been given the Tower Room," he said, pushing the door open. "It has the best views."

I slipped inside to see that he was right—there was only one arched window, but it looked out toward the edge of the Onyx Rise and the realm of Castelle far below, stretching all the way to the River Dún, south of my home. So strange to see the world I had always inhabited from this vantage—from the viewpoint of the Immortals who had watched over us for so long in the days before I was born.

I turned to survey the Tower Room, which contained a single bed covered in white linen. On the wall next to a mirror hung a white robe of raw silk.

"There is a bell here if you should need anything," Alaric told me. "You will not be locked in, but trust me when I tell you that you don't want to think about escape. In the evenings, the land by the Onyx Rise crawls with malevolent beings. Should you try to get home, you will no doubt encounter them."

I wanted to point out that they hadn't troubled me on my way up here, but instead, I nodded. "Don't worry. I'm too tired to go anywhere."

He was about to leave when I stopped him.

"Alaric—may I ask you a question?"

"Of course," he replied, his expression kind.

"How old is Mithraan?"

He smirked and shook his head. "He doesn't like to speak of his age. Suffice it to say that he is quite young—far younger than Khiral or myself."

"If that's the case, how does he know so much about the past? He speaks of it as though he has seen it. Felt it, even."

Alaric let out a slow breath. "His blood is knowledge," he said simply, but I grimaced in response.

"I have no idea what that could possibly mean."

"It means he has lived the lives of ten mortals, thanks to the Gifts bestowed by his ancestors. Those with the blood of Immortals have the ability to pass knowledge wordlessly down through the generations, from one to the next. Mithraan is in possession of his father's memories—at least, some of them. He recalls sights and sounds from the last Blood Trials. He recalls the faces of those who attended, even if he never met them. He can tell you precisely what each competitor was wearing on the first day, because his father saw and greeted each of them in turn."

"That's...astounding," I said. "It must be a little overwhelming, too."

"It can be," Alaric replied. "But the knowledge comes in waves—it does not flood one's mind all at once. Mithraan has studied the memories. For years, he has tried to piece together what happened back then—why it is that our kind failed, and why we were cut off from mortal lands, ostracized like carriers of contagious disease. And to this day, he has not managed to solve the mystery—and neither have the rest of us." He paused for a moment before adding, "And now, a new mystery has wandered into our lands. You are a puzzle, Lyrinn. I fear you may drive Mithraan to distraction."

When he had left, I lay down on the bed, my mind reeling. I told myself to be calm—to rest easy in the knowledge that no harm had come to me. I had experienced something no human in many generations had. I tried to convince myself, even, that I was *fortunate* for having ventured to this place.

But even as I attempted reassurance, everything that had occurred since my arrival began to cascade through my mind—my imprisonment in a dark cell; Mithraan's cruel teasing; Nihara's comment about my looks.

This place was cold and hostile, and the Fae saw me as nothing more than a toy to use for their amusement. The Lord of Fairholme had found my weaknesses, and he prodded at them with needle-like precision, taking pleasure in the small wounds he inflicted.

Against my will, a single tear rolled down my cheek. I hated this place and its inhabitants. Tomorrow, I would figure out how to get home. I would find a way out of this forsaken place, away from these awful creatures. They were beautiful, yes. But they had the capacity to make me feel like nothing more than a sewer rat, and for that, I despised them.

I lay on the bed for some time before a knock sounded at the door. I rose and strode over, running a nervous hand through my hair.

"Who is it?" I called out.

"Mithraan."

Setting my jaw, I pulled the door open to see him standing

in the twisting stairwell. His eyes flashed bright in the shadows, mischievous as always.

I expected him to waltz into the room, but he stayed still.

"I came to see if you needed anything," he said.

"I'm surprised that you would care enough to bother, my Lord."

"I am your host," he retorted sharply. "I am the overseer of this castle, or what remains of it. I have a duty."

"You didn't seem to care for duty at dinner, when you acted like an ass." I slammed my mouth shut and resolved to say nothing more.

I had revealed too much, shown my vulnerability when I should have tried to appear strong.

Fool.

"I teased you," he said. "I suppose I was putting on a show for Nihara's amusement. I should not have used you like that."

He sounded genuinely contrite, and for a moment I softened.

"Nihara—is she..."

"My lover?" he asked, and once again, that amused, mischievous grin took up residence on his lips. "No. She is not. Though perhaps one day soon, she will be."

With that, he eased forward into the room. I took a step back, but he moved closer, his chin low. His eyes shone with an intensity that penetrated some place deep inside my chest—a heat so enticing that I wanted nothing more than to push myself toward him and drape myself in the sensation of it.

"Did you feel envy toward her when you saw her touch me?" he whispered. "Did it bother you when I touched *her*?"

"Of course not," I snapped, avoiding his eyes. But my voice was a weak rasp, my resolve crumbling with each word I uttered. *How dare you do this to me, Fae? How dare you weave your spells to take hold of my mind?* "Why would I envy her? All I know of you is that you've imprisoned me, that you claim my people have been cruel to you, and that the only cruelty I've seen is on your part."

"How have I been cruel?" He slipped a hand onto my cheek, his thumb stroking my skin, but I refused to look at him. "How have I been anything other than kind to you?"

I couldn't reply, because if I did, I would have had to confess my attraction to him. That I *was* envious of Nihara. That even now, as he stood so close to me, all I wanted was to tear his clothing off and press my hands to his chest, to taste him on my tongue. I would fall to my knees before him and consume every inch of him.

But I would never, ever have confessed such a weakness.

"No. You have been kind, mostly," I finally said. "But...I'm very tired. Please, let me have some rest."

"Very well." He pulled his hand away, combing it briefly through his dark hair. "Good night, Lyrinn."

I watched as he turned away and left me standing, breathless, in the doorway. Wondering if I should loathe him for making me feel this way, if I was weak for wanting him despite what he was to me—a prison warden in a ghastly ruin.

As I turned away and closed the door, I commanded myself to be wary. My father had always taught me not to trust men, and a Fae, after all, was not so different. I was rapidly learning that Fae males played all the same games as human men—the only difference was their impressive prowess.

I lay down on the bed once again, exhausted and relieved to be free of the torment that was Mithraan's presence.

Within a few minutes, I had fallen asleep, dreams coming to me in vivid waves of color.

I dreamed of a female Fae, and it took me only a little while to realize she was the High King of Tíria's daughter—the one who had disappeared at the last Blood Trials. I tried to conjure her in my mind's eye but failed. I could make out nothing more than a nebulous form with a featureless face.

Through a veil of fog, I saw the Fae princess dancing, celebrating the coming of the Trials. I heard her voice ringing through the air.

And then, she was gone, her voice faded to silence.

A bitter frost settled into my mind, a void where she had been.

Alaric's words came to me then about how some believed the High King's daughter had been changed into a Grimper, her soul torn from her body.

As if in reaction, a series of cries stormed through my mind. Screams of rage, terror, and pain tore through me like blades.

I shot awake, my chest pounding, my back coated in sweat as a terrible realization invaded my mind:

The screams were not part of my dream, but of the reality I was about to face.

CHAPTER TEN

A cacophony of shouts assaulted my ears, a discombobulated chorus of male voices intermingled with something awful, animalistic. A screeching cut through the night like the cry of a wild creature doing battle. It reminded me with a shudder of the lupine howls that had met my ears when I'd first climbed the Rise.

I leapt out of bed and raced to the window, pressing my hands to its sill. Far below, I could just barely make out dark shadows of Fae and beasts fighting.

For some reason I would never fully understand, I wanted more than anything to run toward them.

I dressed quickly in a pair of trousers and a tunic I found in the room's wardrobe, then raced out the door and down the stairs, seeking a way out. I sprang toward the cries, searching as I went for any object I could use as a weapon.

Some part of me was fearful, terrified of what I would find, yet I kept running toward the fray.

A siren's song, luring me toward my death.

When I got to the large clearing that spanned the lands between the ruins and the Rise, I spotted a group of male Fae standing back-to-back, their weapons drawn and glowing in the pale starlight. It was a moment before I noticed a familiar figure—Nihara, standing among them, her hands in the air before her, glowing with dancing flame.

I watched as she thrust her palms out, darts of fire shooting into the darkness.

Around them, creatures advanced—forms devoid of color, made of swirling mist and exuding an aura of danger and death. Their heads were large, with glistening teeth that resembled threatening silver spikes.

They swiped unnaturally long arms at their foes, accented with fierce talons at the ends of their terrifying fingers.

Without ever having seen one, I knew exactly what they were.

Grimpers.

The Fae were fighting the creatures with silver blades and gleaming, metallic arrows, but each time they thrust or shot their weapons at one of the creatures, the Grimper would fall back, recover, then advance again.

I watched as one of the beasts lunged at a Fae dressed in gray. He waved his arm in vain, trying to slice at the creature, but it evaded him easily, swiping an outstretched limb at his chest and letting out a harrowing cry.

The Fae fell to the ground, clutching at his torso, and I watched with terror as his exquisite face turned ashen, his eyes sinking and darkening into his flesh.

Within moments, his body had disappeared, and he became nothing more than a swirl of dark mist, rising from the ground to form another Grimper.

I raced toward the group of male Fae. As I moved, another shape emerged from the darkness and lunged in my direction. It stopped mid-stride, its twisting face contorting this way and that as it studied me.

I froze, my fingers splayed at my sides, too terrified to move. The creature was soulless, a being of shadow and void.

I could feel its malice twisting in the air between us.

Before I could blink or breathe, a shape came darting out from behind me, leaping at the Grimper and slicing its head off. The monster tumbled to the ground as I let out a cry—not of fear, but of torment for a Fae's soul that had been denied the chance at the life they should have lived.

I turned to see that it was Mithraan who had saved me. As the Grimper's body lay on the ground, its headless corpse oozing black bile, the Fae lord took me by the arm, twisting me angrily around to face him.

"What are you doing here?" he shouted. "Go back inside. Bar your door!"

I wanted to reply, to protest. As he spoke, I looked down at his hands, searching for the weapon he had used to kill the creature.

But there was no weapon.

Instead, his hands had altered to something not human—something animalistic. His fingers were thickened and curled unnaturally, accented by long, shining talons like those of a bird of prey.

"You..." I stammered. "How..."

"Leave this place," he growled, and his voice sent a shudder through me. "Go! You must not distract us, Lyrinn!"

He looked so enraged that I did as he commanded without another second's hesitation. Behind me, I heard Khiral say, "They're here because of her. We should give her to them!"

"We will *not*," Mithraan retorted. His tone was final. "We will not give her up to them or anyone else. She is too important."

"Mith..."

"Silence!"

I turned once to watch the Fae lord as he let out a wail and took down another Grimper with nothing more than his bare hands.

I had heard tales in my youth of the Fae's ability to shapeshift. And though Mithraan had not entirely altered from his human form, I had sensed a feral power coursing through his body and mind—a strength I had never sensed in any other creature.

As I made my way back up to my chamber in the tower, I wondered what he looked like when he changed completely. Did he morph into a beautiful, dark eagle? A hawk?

Or something dire and frightening?

I *should* have been afraid. Of him, of the Grimpers, of the darkness that ate away at Fairholme's ruins like a plague.

But instead, I found myself strangely calm as I stepped back into my room, closed and barred the door. I changed into the white robe and lay down on the bed, staring at the ceiling.

My mind swirled with wonder at how the caretaker of this destroyed castle managed to make me feel so safe and in such danger, all at once.

An hour or so later, the cries had finally died down when a knock sounded at the door. I was sitting on the bed, my arms wrapped around my legs, my chin resting on my knees.

Apprehensive, I rose from the bed and stepped toward the door, calling out, "Who is there?"

"Mithraan," a deep voice called softly.

I pulled up the bar and opened the door, only to see that he was bleeding from a wound in his cheek. On instinct, I reached up, but he flinched away, shaking his head. "Don't," he said, his tone chilly. It softened when he added, "It's all right. I will heal. It was not a Grimper that did this to me, but a stray arrow."

I backed away, and he stepped into the room.

"What if a Grimper *had* done it?" I asked, my voice tremulous in anticipation of his response.

"You know the answer," Mithraan said, "You saw what happened to Eron tonight."

"Eron," I echoed. "That was his name..."

The memory of the Fae's transformation sickened me. His beauty, his strength, being torn from him as though his skeleton had been ripped through his very flesh.

"Is it true?" I asked. "Did they attack your men because of me?"

"I cannot say. I do know, however, that you were never meant to come to this place. And yet, despite your wishes and mine, here you are." Mithraan grimaced. "Which means you were lured here by a force greater than either of us. What I'd like to know is what is it that willed you to our lands?"

I shook my head. "I don't know. I told you—I was escaping from two men who wanted to—"

"I know what you told me," he said. "But those men did not part the mist for you. They did not keep the Grimpers at bay while you climbed. Why allow you to come to this place, only to attack when you're here? It makes no sense."

"I can't begin to imagine," I said miserably. "I'm putting you and the other Fae in danger, though. I wish..."

"You wish you could close your eyes and bring yourself back to a time before any of this had come to pass."

He stepped closer, and for a moment, it looked like his hand was going to reach for my face once again. He stilled it, though, and brought it back down to his side.

In the candlelight I studied every inch of him—his hair, his exquisite eyes, his lips. He was my enemy. My captor.

But he was now my savior, too, and I wasn't entirely sure how to absorb all of him at once.

"It was going to kill me," I said. "You stopped it."

"No." He shook his head. "The Grimper was not moving to attack you. It was merely observing you. Why, I cannot say." Pulling his eyes from mine, he moved toward the window and peered out.

"*Observe* me? Why would it do that?"

"Because someone is seeking knowledge, just as I am. They are searching for the truth about you, and in luring you here, they were hoping to learn it."

"And what have *you* learned?"

He turned and looked into my eyes with such an intensity that I nearly lost my balance, my legs going numb beneath me.

"That I don't believe you are who you say you are. Yet I cannot say *who* you are—and I'm not certain you know yourself."

I sat down on the bed, my strength sapped. "The Scouts are in my town, seeking Champions. If I don't return, my father will worry about me. He'll think they took me, or worse."

The Fae took a step toward me and, his voice tinged with frost, said, "The eyes of a powerful enemy are on you, Lyrinn. If you do return, I fear you will be in danger—as will anyone else you care about."

"Why?" I asked, pulling my chin up, my eyes damp with tears. "Why would anyone want to hurt any of us?"

Mithraan's jaw tightened, his eyes narrowing. "I have only theories at the moment, and theories are not enough. I cannot speak of them, not yet. If I'm correct, the truth would endanger you, me, and everyone who guards these ruins, as well as all the Immortals of Tíria."

I stared at him for a few seconds, then shook my head as if loosing a nagging thought. "No. There is no truth other than the one I've told you. I'm not whoever or whatever you think I am. I have a home. My life is quiet and dull. Please—let me go."

Mithraan looked genuinely tempted for a moment, but he crossed his arms over his chest and replied, "I cannot risk more harm coming to the Fae of these ruins. I will travel north to see Rynfael, High King of the Dragon Court. I will seek his counsel in this matter, and then return here to tell you his decision."

"How...how long will it take you to get to the Court?" I asked.

"If I leave now, I should be there by tomorrow nightfall. I will return in the next day."

Two days. Two days in this place without Mithraan.

For some reason, the thought of it filled me with dread, as well as another emotion—one I didn't wish to acknowledge or admit, even to myself.

"Can't you send someone else?" I asked. "One of your Fae? You—"

I realized as I was speaking how desperate I sounded, how needful. Since when did I want this Fae lord anywhere near me? He had been nothing but a thorn in my side since I'd first set eyes on him. I should have been delighted to be rid of him.

Heat swirled through the air between us, a fraught whirlwind of confusion.

"You dread my departure," he said, and I thought I detected a note of malevolent bliss in his words.

You enjoy my suffering, do you?

"I don't know if I trust your kind enough to want to be left alone with Fae such as Khiral," I replied. "That is all."

"Are you telling me you trust *me*?"

"No. But I think you understand honor. I think you will do as you promised and protect me. I can't say the same for Khiral."

"He will not harm you, Lyrinn. At most, he and Alaric will

get drunk on Faerie Ale and ignore you entirely. They have far less interest in you than you imagine they do, trust me."

Good, I thought. *The less they notice me, the better.*

"Fine," I replied, rising to my feet and averting my eyes. "I will see you in two days, then."

The Fae stared at me. His eyes heated my flesh, caressing me as intently as the tips of hungry fingers. They slipped over every inch of me, taking in the curves of my shoulders, my waist, my hips, and I felt every single curious stroke.

He reached for me then, the back of one hand slipping so gently over my breast that I wasn't sure whether I'd imagined it or manifested the sensation through a profound, insatiable desire.

My breath caught in my chest, my core aching for another touch—more aggressive this time. I wanted him to grab me, to pull me close. I wanted to feel every inch of him against me.

Yet I hated him...for so many reasons.

For imprisoning me.

For looking at me as he did.

For leaving me.

"That robe is far too thin," he said softly, taking its fabric between his fingers and studying it, his head cocked to the side. "I'll have Asta bring you one that's a little warmer—and less transparent. You are beautiful, Lyrinn. The others see it, too, and I wouldn't want any of the weaker Fae to be tempted to try and get close to you."

He slipped a hand to my waist and pulled me closer, his other hand gliding down my neck, then down some more, until it reached the valley between my breasts. I held my breath, willing my heartbeat to slow itself in case he could feel it pounding against his fingertips.

"I saw you through that window," he told me in a whisper, his eyes roving greedily over my body. "In the bathing chamber.

You are a work of art, and if I had an ounce less self-control than I do, I would tear this garment from your shoulders and wrap my lips first around one nipple, then the other. I would show you what it is to be consumed by desire, to burn with it. I would have you beg for my length, Lyrinn—and for you...I would grow as hard as the Onyx Rise itself."

I was no longer holding my breath.

I simply...couldn't breathe.

All I could do was pull my eyes to his, to try and determine whether he was teasing me again.

In his golden eyes, I saw a flash of flame—red-orange and hot—burning bright as the sun.

There was no answer in those eyes. No reassurance. Nothing but mystery.

"But I fear you are meant for another," he said, pulling away, his irises fading. "Not for me."

"What do you mean?" I managed to ask, my voice shaking.

I should have kept my thoughts to myself and pushed away the cruel desire that was churning inside me like the most brutal of storms.

Slipping still closer, he pushed my hair back, freezing as his gaze found its way to my left ear and my neck. On instinct, I raised a hand to cover my ear, but he grabbed my wrist, pulling my arm down to my side.

Taking me by the shoulders, he twisted me around to face the cold stone wall, and I found myself crying out as I pressed my hands to its surface. "Please!" I yelped. "Please, don't! I..."

But his touch didn't soften for a moment. Instead, he pulled at the robe, yanking it away from my right shoulder and drawing a terrified whimper from my lips.

A deep exhale met my ears as his eyes landed on the scars embedded in the flesh that ran from my neck down to my shoulder blade. His breath stroked my skin, sending a trail of heat in its wake. My body was tense with a sensation so foreign to me that I could not tell if I was feeling pleasure or agony, fear or delight.

I remained frozen, my hands against the stone wall as his fingers glided their way along the tokens of grim remembrance from the fire that tried to take my life so long ago.

"Face me," he finally said quietly, pulling away. "Look me in the eye."

I turned, and in the shadow of my captor's beauty, I cowered, certain that he would slaughter me for my imperfection, for my weakness.

I was as ruined as the very castle where we now stood. Broken, useless, and filled with dire shadow.

"Those scars," he breathed, his gaze skimming every detail of my face. "How did you come by them?"

Somehow, I summoned the courage to yank my nightgown back up and gather it around my neck. "An accident," I told him, lowering my chin. "A fire, years ago. I was very young at the time. I don't remember the incident."

"A fire," he repeated, his mouth pulled into a fierce snarl.

He shook his head, and in his irises flames began to dance again. Intense and destructive, the fire mocked me as if to remind me what it had once done to my flesh.

"It was no fire that caused those scars," he whispered.

"Of course it was," I said, my courage returning. "Our house burned. Our mother *died*."

At that, Mithraan went silent for a moment.

He brushed his hair back from his face, inhaling deep. With each second that passed, he seemed to grow more angry, more agitated. I only wished I could determine whether his hostility was directed at me or at some other invisible entity. There was something in the air between us—some incident in the past that was eating away at him, though I could not understand what, or why.

"You are being truthful," he finally said. "You have no memory of what caused the scars, which means that if I am to find out who inflicted them, I will have to do so another way."

Heading for the door, he stopped, turned, and said, "Goodbye for now, Lyrinn. I fear that our next meeting will not take place in the happiest of circumstances."

Without another word, he left, closing the door behind him.

I collapsed onto the bed, my fingers gripping the edge of the mattress.

Though I could not understand why, tears had begun to stream down my cheeks.

My courage had deserted me, and I felt as alone as I ever had in my life.

CHAPTER ELEVEN

There was no chance of sleep after Mithraan's visit.

Instead, I lay in bed for the rest of the night, listening, half-awake, for the terrifying sound of the Grimpers doing battle with Fae. But nothing met my ears except for eerie silence.

When morning finally dawned, I half expected another knock on my door and to find Mithraan standing in the twisting stairwell outside, asking how I'd fared for the rest of the night.

But when no knock came, I rose from my bed and dressed in an olive-colored linen tunic and gray leather trousers that the servants had left for me, before heading down to the dining room. They seemed more like the clothing of a hunter than a female houseguest, but I was grateful that someone in the ruins seemed to understand my particular aesthetic. I had little need of flouncy dresses or ladies in waiting to style my hair for me; more than anything, I wanted to blend in with my surroundings—particularly after the previous night's madness.

I still didn't entirely understand the spell Mithraan had cast to seemingly rebuild the castle Fairholme around us. Illusion or none, I could not fathom how the walls rose up around me despite the fact that, from the outside, the ruins looked like nothing more than broken down walls and stony detritus.

Though my rational mind knew it to be nothing more than a pleasant illusion, I felt safe, protected from the vile creatures lurking on the outside.

In the dining hall, I found Khiral seated at the table, a book in hand. He rose to his feet as I entered, a grudging look on his face as he nodded in my direction.

"Is Mithraan...?" I asked, standing awkwardly by the door. I was hungry, but the last thing I wanted was to be alone with a Fae who seemed to loathe every fiber of my being.

"Gone," he said. "Thanks to you. He has left for the North."

"He really left?" I asked under my breath. "I didn't think—"

"No. Of course you didn't think," Khiral snapped, refusing to let me complete my thought. "You have endangered us all once again. Mith is the primary defender of this fortress, or what's left of it. He keeps the Grimpers at bay. He keeps the walls solid around us. Without him, we are vulnerable."

"But why does he need to go to the Dragon Court at all? It seems like a great risk. What could possibly be so important that he's willing to leave Fairholme behind?"

Khiral clenched his jaw for a moment, then shook his head quickly and sat back down. "Who the devil knows?" he asked. "He said something about a question of blood, whatever that means. I suspect he's still trying to work out how the hell a mortal made her way up the Rise to us. You should have stayed in Dúnbar. Our lands may be forsaken, but we have grown accustomed to our isolation. You have made Mithraan question the life we have all come to know. You're a troublemaker, and nothing more."

"Well," I retorted, irritated that Khiral was so quick to blame me for all the Fae's ills. "Mithraan needn't have left. If he had questions, why could you not have gone in his stead to find the answers, if you're so keen to protect Fairholme?"

After all, I didn't force Mithraan to leave.

I didn't even *want* him to leave.

The question I found myself asking was why. Why did I want my captor to stay? After all, my best chance at escape was in his absence. With his eyes and mind focused elsewhere, I had little to worry about. Khiral clearly had no interest in me, and Alaric seemed too soft-spoken to wish to hold me against my will.

Still, I found myself wishing for Mithraan's presence in a way that set a quiet discomfort streaming through my veins.

Khiral chewed on the inside of his cheek for a moment before replying, "I do not have Mith's gift for quick travel," he said. "He is the swiftest of us."

He said nothing more, and instead of looking me in the eye, he simply returned to his book.

I was contemplating leaving without eating when a female Fae entered the dining chamber and smiled at me, bowing her head gracefully. She was dressed entirely in white, and like every Fae I'd set eyes on, she was exquisitely beautiful.

"May I get you some breakfast?" she asked.

"Thank you, yes."

She left the room, and I took a seat some distance from Khiral, who set his book down and stared daggers at me once again.

"Stay close today," he said. "I don't want to lose any more of our own to the Grimpers."

"I don't understand why all of you don't head north," I retorted without thinking. "If this part of your land is overrun with shadows bent on killing you, why don't you leave? Mithraan said the North is still beautiful."

Khiral let out a snort, leaning back in his chair as he ran a hand through his black hair. "Look around, mortal. Do you actually think we *choose* to live like this?"

My eyes caressed the walls—the murals, the high ceilings, the beauty of it all. But as I stared, our surroundings faded, revealing nothing but crumbling stone, cobwebs, and a foul odor of rot. A gust of ill-smelling wind caught my breath.

I gasped as I began to comprehend the power of Mithraan's spell.

"Why, then?" I asked, my heart pounding, my voice near its breaking point. "Truly, I want to understand, but I don't. Why would you stay here? You could sail across the sea to Aetherion, could you not?"

"Aetherion!" Khiral looked as though he was about to rise to his feet and throw himself across the table to throttle the life out of me. But instead, he took a deep breath, stiffened, and said, "There is an old tale. A prophecy, I suppose you might say, that dictates that one day, the mist will fail. We are here as wardens of this land, waiting for that day to come. Because only when it does can the Fae of Tíria regain the power we once had. Our power does not lie in Aetherion. The Fae of that land are not allies to us, and never have been. If they had their way, we would be wiped off the face of this world, alongside every mortal in the land."

The walls rose up around us once again, beautiful and comforting, and I could feel Khiral settle into the state of quiet annoyance I'd come to expect of him.

"For now," he said, "we will remain in Fairholme. Mithraan will do everything in his power to keep us safe—though if anything should happen to him, most of us would most likely perish. He is the thread that binds us all together and keeps us whole. He is the one who makes the castle walls appear solid, and keeps the Grimpers from killing us in our sleep."

"I'm sure nothing will happen to him," I said hastily. "He

seems..." I was about to say *strong. Powerful. Indomitable.* But I didn't want to be seen to praise the Fae lord who tormented me more than any other living thing.

"He is a good leader," Khiral said, filling in the conclusion of my statement. "And believe it or not, he is kind. His hatred of mortals is founded only in his love of his people. He would kill for us. He *has* killed for us. And make no mistake—he would burn your town to the ground, if it meant freeing our people from this curse."

I shuddered at the thought. But it was true; Mithraan was passionate and protective.

Still, I couldn't quite envision him as a murderer of innocents.

The door opened and the Fae servant in white came in with a large plate covered in eggs, toast, and other assorted food. She laid it down in front of me and wordlessly left again.

"I would advise you to keep to your quarters today," Khiral told me. "Do not venture beyond the courtyard, and stay out of our way."

With that, he rose to his feet and left the room.

I spent the next several hours in my room as Khiral advised, peering out the window occasionally at the landscape beyond the ruins. The distant hills were gray and lifeless, inhospitable to the point of seeming like a vast graveyard.

I found myself wondering how the Fae cultivated their fruit, vegetables, and meat—where they could possibly have acquired such delicacies in such a barren land.

The only answer that came to mind was Mithraan.

From the moment I had first laid my eyes on him and heard his voice, I had felt a power simmering quietly inside him. Like a wild animal stealthily stalking its prey, he was more than he appeared—though his appearance was already impressive enough. He exuded a commanding presence, that of a daunting lord who could intimidate even Fae like Khiral.

Mithraan was a puzzle, and I wanted more than anything to solve him, just as he wished to solve me.

As I stared out at the trees that had lost their healthy appearance in his absence, I envisioned his conversation with the High King of the Dragon Court. I imagined my name being uttered in such company, though I could not imagine that the king would have anything good to say in response. I was the enemy, and I had wandered into the Fae realm uninvited and unwanted. I had probably broken some sacred, ancient law, and I could see no conclusion to this venture other than my own death at Mithraan's hand.

He had asked me not to leave.

Khiral had warned me.

And I knew perfectly well that the Breath of the Fae may never part for me again, even if I should walk straight to the edge of the Onyx Rise.

But if I stayed here, there was a good chance I would never see my father or Leta again...and the thought was too much to bear.

Sometime in the late afternoon, I left my room, padded down the stone staircase to the bottom of the tower, and wound my way down corridor after corridor until I finally came to a door leading out to the courtyard where I had seen Mithraan standing a day earlier.

The ground was now blackened with decay, the walls crawling with dead vines and lichen.

Looking over my shoulder to ensure that no one was watching, I walked the length of the courtyard's wall. I focused my eyes and mind on the fragile, uneven stone, wondering how much of what I was seeing was real and how much had been created by Mithraan's spell to convince the Grimpers and his allies that the wall was solid and strong enough to prevent their infiltration.

I examined each stone, slipping my palm along the wall's surface, until suddenly, my hand pushed through what felt like a large opening. Though the wall still looked entirely solid, I was able to shove my entire arm through until I felt a cool breeze sweep over my fingertips.

I stared at the surface until much of it faded away before my eyes, revealing a gap large enough for me to walk through.

"Please, let me go," I said under my breath. "Please don't close in on me and crush me to death."

Glancing around to make sure I was still alone, I stepped through the gap, holding my breath until both of my feet had settled onto the soil just beyond the castle walls. I was free, and there was nothing between me and the Onyx Rise except for dead trees and wasteland.

Only one small problem remained.

The Grimpers are out there.

I shook my head, raising my chin, determined to force confidence into my mind and body.

Mithraan told me himself that the Grimpers don't want to hurt me. He said they were merely studying me.

The question was, would they ever allow me to leave this place?

CHAPTER TWELVE

I HAD ALWAYS BEEN quick on my feet and adept at ducking stealthily between Dúnbar's houses in games of hunter-and-prey with Leta.

I could easily have outrun Raleigh the other night, too, if not for the fact that the town itself had ensnared me in a sort of cruel magic, forcing me toward the Onyx Rise.

Now, as I fled the ruins of Fairholme, I was running as fast as I ever had in my life. I could only hope the eyes of my Fae guardians were not on me.

With every ounce of my being, I willed them not to discover my disappearance until I was long gone.

I heard no threatening sound from behind me as I sprang toward the Rise's edge. Nothing but gusting wind met my ears. No Grimpers howled their ominous, blood-curdling threats. No Fae called out for me to stop, or threatened to shoot arrows into my back.

Only a few minutes of fearful sprinting passed before I began to make out the jagged outline of the Rise before me. Stunned to have made it this far, I slowed my pace to a quick walk, breathlessly turning to see if anyone was in pursuit.

At first, all I saw were the twisted trees I had seen upon my arrival in Tíria. Ghostly figures outlined against the horizon. I was convinced I was alone—that, in some miraculous twist of fate, I truly had evaded my captors.

But my heart ceased to beat when next to one of the dying trees, I spotted a solitary a tall, slim Fae in a silver dress. Her hair was dark, her chin held high.

Nihara.

I stared at her, waiting for her to hurl one of her fiery bolts at me, to kill me where I stood.

But she did no such thing.

Instead, she smiled, turned, and walked back toward the ruins, utterly indifferent to my departure.

Against my will, I let out a quick, triumphant laugh.

I pictured Mithraan scolding her and Khiral harshly for failing to watch over their captive human. "Fools!" his imagined voice rang inside my mind. "How dare you allow the weak, useless girl from Dúnbar leave before I had a chance to tear her head from her shoulders?"

Reminding myself that my good fortune might prove limited, I turned and slipped toward the Rise's edge, my eyes searching for any sign of the elusive Onyx Stair.

But as I drew near, I froze, my eyes widening with terror.

Silent, dark shapes had begun to materialize around me. Swirling shadows flickered and waned in the daylight—the vile outlines of Grimpers.

Just beyond them, I could just make out the Breath of the Fae rolling, barely visible, over the cliff's edge.

The grim creatures faded in and out of focus before me as though sunlight alone could not quite bring itself to reveal their true forms. I spotted a large head here, a set of glistening fangs there. Hands like contorted tree branches tipped with brutal claws.

Twenty or more of the creatures lined the clifftop, facing me in a militaristic row.

It was no wonder Nihara had dismissed me so easily. I had little doubt the Grimpers were intending to tear into me in a wild frenzy, rendering her task of watching over me utterly obsolete.

I cursed my chest's rise and fall with each fearful breath. My eyes locked on the cliff's edge as I contemplated leaping over it and ending this cruel nightmare.

As I stared straight ahead, the two Grimpers nearest me pulled apart, creating a gap two or so feet wide. Perhaps they could read my mind, and wanted to encourage my quick demise. Maybe they were as cruel as they were vicious.

A strangely familiar voice—the same one I had heard in the alley the night I had fled Raleigh and his companion—called to my mind. I knew now that it was not Mithraan himself, but someone else—someone more frightening, even, than the Lord of Fairholme.

Lyrinn...you are free.

Drawn to the gap between the two Grimpers, I advanced, my legs shaking. It was madness, I knew. I should have fled back to the ruins and begged for mercy. Instead, I was walking toward my death.

But I soon found myself standing at the top of the long, winding descent known as the Onyx Stair. The Breath of the Fae swirled around its edges, threatening to lap over the steps but never quite touching them.

Pausing on the cliff's edge and all too aware of my vulnerability, I turned to my right to see one of the Grimpers staring at me, its dark, glistening eyes barely visible on its translucent, near-featureless face.

Lyrinn, the voice called again. *I look forward to our next meeting.*

"I do not want to see you," I hissed at the entity. "Not ever again. Do you hear me?"

The Grimper simply stared. Mindless, lifeless, like a dark boulder perched atop of the Rise. If not for its coarse breaths and the vague outline of threatening claws, I might have convinced myself it was nothing more than harmless shadow.

Terror filled me as my foot landed on the first stone stair. I took a deep breath and told myself I would make it home—that for a reason I did not begin to understand, I was safe on these stairs.

I would head to Dúnbar and find my way to our house. I would embrace my father and Leta and return to my former life. I would forget I had ever come to these lands.

I told myself, too, that I would forget Mithraan.

I would cast the memory of his amber eyes, his voice, his touch, far from my mind.

But of all the threats that surrounded me now—of all the danger swelling around me—it was the thought of forgetting him that frightened me the most.

I reached the bottom step after what felt like hours of careful maneuvering on the treacherously uneven steps, and found myself once again in the narrow, twisting alleyway where Raleigh and his friend had cornered me not so long ago. The Breath of the Fae swirled close around my feet, its threatening tendrils ebbing and receding but never touching me as I stumbled forward along the cobblestones.

In the stark light of day, Barden Close looked entirely different. The uninviting houses that had confronted me two nights earlier looked welcoming and pretty, green vines crawling down their façades, laced with pretty pink and white flowers.

The sensation of disorientation was gone, and the narrow passageway felt as familiar once again as my own room at home.

As I strode forward, distancing myself quickly from the Onyx Rise, I realized with profound relief that the laneway I had meant to turn down a few nights earlier had returned.

All was once again right with my small world.

Issuing one final glance over my shoulder to assure myself that I really had escaped Tíria, I hastened my pace, turning right when it came time to head toward home.

That was far too easy, I thought in the comfort of familiar surroundings. *Too simple. But why did Nihara let me go? Why didn't Khiral hunt me down and kill me?*

I reprimanded myself. *Just be grateful that you're alive, you idiot.*

There was no word in any language to describe the emotion that overtook me when I threw open our front door and leapt inside, slamming it shut behind me. I pressed my back to the coarse wood, my breath heavy as tears streamed down my face.

I should have felt happy to be so close to those I loved. Euphoric, even.

But somewhere inside me lingered a terrible, profound sadness. A feeling of loss like none I had ever encountered was stirring away at my insides.

I would never see the Fae again.

I would never see *him* again.

"Lyr? Is that you?"

The voice came at me from the next room. A moment later, I saw Leta's face peering through the doorway. Her brows met when she laid her eyes on me.

I drew a sleeve over my cheeks and looked at her. "I..."

"Where have you been? We've been worried sick!"

But there was no way to explain what had happened to me

over the last day and a half. No way to recount all that had occurred since the moment I had left the Raven, expecting to sleep in my own bed that night.

Leta strode angrily toward me, her expression softening only a little when she noted my red eyes. "Are you..." she began. "What's wrong?"

Shaking my head, I simply said, "Nothing. Long night, that's all."

Our father walked in after a moment and threw me an indecipherable look. He showed no emotion, but there was a wisdom in his eyes. A strange, deep understanding that unsettled me.

Does he know, somehow? Can he sense where I've been, and what I've seen?

No. My father couldn't possibly know. No one would believe the tale, even if every word I spoke was the exact truth. My father, of all people, had warned us for almost two decades that the Onyx Rise was unscalable. That the Fae were long gone. That the Grimpers would tear us to pieces at first glance.

Whatever he's thinking, it's as far from the truth as Domignon from Dúnbar.

"I was...hiding," I finally stammered, pulling nervously at my sleeve. "Just as Father asked."

"The Scouts have picked three potential Champions to represent Castelle," my father said in reply, his tone casual, as though my disappearance was perfectly normal. "So you have no need to worry anymore, Lyrinn. They've selected two young men from Castelle proper, one young woman from Dúnbar. The innkeeper's daughter, Sharilh. They say she has a Mind-Gift of some sort—an ability to summon weapons of stone, or some such nonsense. The young men, they say, are skilled in other ways, though if you ask me, there is no way in hell they'll be able to compete against whatever Domignon's prince throws at them."

He was rambling, which was unlike my father. He was normally a man of few words, careful not to reveal too much of himself or anyone else.

"Yes," I said, smiling with gratitude that he had chosen not to interrogate me. "I'm sure you're right. It sounds like Prince Corym has the Trials well in hand. Now it's only a question of a female Champion worthy of him."

"Where were you hiding?" Leta asked sharply, crossing her arms. Apparently my sister wasn't willing to let me off the hook quite so easily as our father.

"I...I'll tell you later," I said, turning to head to my room. "I need to wash up, and I'm tired."

"Those clothes," Leta shot before I could leave, indifferent to my desire for solitude. "I haven't seen them before. They're not exactly Dúnbar's style. In fact, that tunic is gorgeous. It looks like it's worth a fortune. Where did you get it?"

I had no reply to offer, but it seemed she was already formulating an answer of her own. Her eyes went wide as a possible explanation made its way into her mind. "Gods! You were with a *man*!" she finally said, letting out a chuckle. "You borrowed the clothing because yours was probably stained from rolling about in a hay loft. Or the mud, knowing you." She pressed her hands to her hips and did a little dance that was enough to make my cheeks heat. "My big sister was enjoying the pleasures of the masculine touch," she half-sang.

"Leta!" my father's voice warned. "Where she has been and who she has been with is no business of yours. Lyrinn is an adult, and free to make her own choices." His voice shifted as he spoke the last few words, and again, he threw me a look that communicated knowledge that should not have been his to convey. "I'm sure that whatever she's been doing since we saw her last, it was for her own good—and for ours."

I stared at him for a moment. *If only you knew how I have wanted to come back home. How much I wanted to free myself of the shackles of the Fae.*

And how much I'm aching to be back with them now.

The last thought came to me against my will, and I cursed myself for it. I chastised myself, commanding my mind to expel the Fae once and for all.

One, in particular.

"Ugh," Leta replied, but she finally dropped the subject. "Oh, gods, Lyr—did you hear about that awful Raleigh? The mist got him that night, after we saw him in the pub. He and his friend Dahrin—the one who was sitting with him."

"I...yes," I said. "I heard something about it."

I heard them screaming for their lives.

"Such an end was well-deserved," my father said under his breath. "Lyrinn, go. Get washed up and changed. We'll eat together this evening. I...want my family close right now."

"Why?" I asked, troubled by his tone. "What's happened?"

"Nothing has happened, dear girl." With that, he issued me a quick look with his dark eyes, shook his head slightly, then left the room.

"What's going on with Father?" I asked, turning to Leta. "Did something happen while I was gone?"

My sister shrugged. "Nothing except for the Raleigh business. But you know, you could have told us where you were off to. I'm quite certain Father nearly lost his mind when he heard someone had been killed by the mist. But you know how he is—he hides his feelings. For all I know, he was in his room weeping the entire time you were gone."

"I doubt that," I replied. "Father is not a weeper."

"Perhaps not, but he cares about you. About both of us. If

you ask me, he's incredibly relieved the Scouts didn't come for either of us rejects. But—gods, I almost forgot to tell you!"

"Tell me what?" I asked impatiently, desperate to get to my room and collapse onto my bed.

"It was the strangest thing—some men *did* come looking for you—the morning after we left you at the Raven. I was meant to be out of the house, so I hid myself away in my room the entire time. But I heard what they said to Father. And I saw them, too."

A strange tightness set itself into my chest at the news. No one ever came to see me. Not men, not women. Not even local dogs, seeking a piece of meat.

"Men? What men?" I asked.

"That was the odd bit. I'm not entirely sure who they were. They only said they were seeking Lyrinn Martel. At first, I thought maybe it had to do with Raleigh and his disgusting friend—that maybe they had some questions about what had happened after we'd left the Raven, since you stayed there. But then I saw their silk tunics. They were very elegant. Swords, baldrics, the whole bit. But Lyrinn—they were wearing the silver mountain—the sigil of Domignon's Royal Court."

"Domignon?" I repeated. "Why on earth would the king's men be looking for me?"

"A very good question," Leta laughed. "Honestly, I think they had the wrong person. Father told them you were away for a day or two, and asked what they wanted. They told him they were here to make an inquiry about your birth records. He showed them your papers, and they left."

The tension in my chest finally dissipated and I was able to breathe normally once again. "You're right, they must have had the wrong person," I replied, assuring myself that it had to be the truth. "I am of no interest to anyone in the king's circle. Maybe they were just doing the Scouts' job for them—though I had already shown my birth papers to the Scouts the night we met at the Raven."

"Who knows?" Leta shrugged. "Maybe they were looking for a new scullery maid in the servants' quarters of the palace." With that, she wrinkled her nose at me and laughed.

"A real wit, my sister," I replied, turning to head for my room at last. "Well, *this* scullery maid is going to rest for a little. Wake me when the world has begun to make sense."

CHAPTER THIRTEEN

Once in my room, I splashed water on my face and stared at myself for a moment in the silver mirror over my dresser.

I couldn't say how or why, but I was certain I looked different than I had before my journey up the Onyx Rise. My skin seemed brighter, softer, as though I'd been enjoying a quiet holiday in the mountains rather than the trauma of emotional abuse set upon me by a Fae captor.

I attributed my healthy glow to simple joy at having found my way home safely. All was once again right with the world.

The Scouts had found their Champions.

Whatever strange men had come for me would be long gone by now...and I was back to being Lyrinn Martel. Simple, dull, plain Lyrinn. The young woman who dwells in shadow.

A young woman scarred.

I finished washing up, then, after tidily folding the clothing I had taken from Fairholme, changed into a belted linen dress. Light blue with a wide sash, it was one of my favorites. And in this moment, it felt like a reassurance that I had found safety and normality once again.

As a final touch, I extracted a dagger from the top drawer of my narrow dresser, pulled my skirt up, and strapped the weapon, along with another hand-stitched sheath, to my right thigh.

This time, I promised myself, *I will not lose the blade. I will never again find myself face to face with a predator without a weapon at the ready.*

I will sleep with it by my side every single night.

As if to prove I would hold to the vow, I lay down on my bed, threw an arm over my eyes, and allowed myself to drift into a deep sleep. Before long, my mind spun with an amalgam of interwoven dreams. In my mind, I saw the ruins, the decaying trees lining the clifftop. A party of Fae searching for me. Grimpers crying out, attacking their enemies with fierce, destructive claws.

Finally, I saw Mithraan moving as swiftly as the wind as his eyes hunted for me. His voice, deep and rich, came to me.

I will find you, Lyrinn.

I shot awake to see Leta standing in my doorway, a smile on her lips.

"Nightmare?" she asked.

I opened my mouth to say yes, but the truth was not so simple. Seeing Mithraan's face, if only for a few seconds in my own imagination, had filled me with quiet longing that made me want to fall immediately back asleep in hopes of finding him again.

But I shook the thought free, telling myself I had conjured an ideal, unrealistic version of him. He was a danger to me, to my family. He was a menace, and I never wished to see him again.

"Nightmare," I replied with a nod, rubbing the sleep out of my eyes.

"Well, dinner is ready, your Highness," Leta said, taking a low bow.

"Highness?" I asked sharply. "Why would you call me that?"

"No reason," she replied, pivoting and heading toward the kitchen, calling out, "except that you looked like a princess, all sprawled out luxuriously on that bed of yours!"

I chuckled. I was the last person on earth who could ever be accused of looking like royalty. *Leta* was the princess. She was the one who would look natural in a crown or draped in gold, rubies, and diamonds.

I was a thing of shadow, a Grimper without the malice. A stalking, observant entity who wanted nothing more than to remain far from any sort of drama for the rest of my days.

I rose, stretched my arms over my head, and strode toward the kitchen, lured by the scent of rabbit stew.

My father was seated at the table already, and Leta served us each a bowl as he sat back in his chair and assessed me.

"Get some rest?" he asked.

"I did, yes, thanks."

"You probably needed it, after your time with the Mystery Man," Leta began, but our father shot her another look of warning. "Oh, come now, can't I tease her just a little?"

"No. Not after what she's been through these last few days."

I looked sideways at him, hardly daring to meet his eye. What did he mean? What did he know of what I had endured?

"Been through?" Leta asked. "If you mean she's been snogging some young man in an abandoned shed somewhere, then—"

"Leta," Father cautioned. "Stop."

A heavy silence fell over the room, but it was Leta who finally broke it, jumping into conversation about Castelle's selected Champion candidates, the coming Blood Trials, and our realm's likely dismal failure. We ended up laughing as we pictured the region's most useless citizens fighting the other realms' young men and women, who would inevitably be impeccably trained in combat.

"Denyss, the baker's son, would be the funniest to watch," Leta said. "The only weapon I've ever seen him wield is a sausage one time when he got into a fight at the Raven with young Colin. Do you remember?"

"I remember," our father said with a grin. "The sausage didn't last long. As I recall, a dog ate it."

"Yet Denyss survived the ordeal," I pointed out with a chuckle. "It's too bad the Trials aren't well-suited to those who are adept with weapons made of meat. I seem to recall that his opponent got some grease in his eye and called for pity."

"Pity is as powerful a weapon as any, and can go a long way in a fight," Father said. "Those with a shred of empathy seldom have the heart to strike down one who begs for his—or her —life."

"Something tells me the Champions fighting for their own lives won't be blessed with a great deal of empathy."

"I wonder who the prince will marry when he wins," Leta said with a sigh. "Probably the beauty from Belleau, given that he can have his pick. Much as I hate the Trials, I do envy that young woman. She'll have all the riches she can handle when they're wed."

"She'll also suffer from massive trauma," I retorted. "You seem to conveniently forget that in order to position herself to marry him, she'll probably have to murder several people."

Leta shrugged. "There are worse things in this world than murder."

"Absolutely," I concurred. "*Being* murdered, for one."

"What do you think, Father?" Leta asked, turning his way. He looked deep in thought, his eyes fixed on the window that looked out to the street. "Have you heard anything about the female Champions, other than our own from Dúnbar?"

He shook his head, his jaw clenched tight. "I know only that Prince Corym is the most powerful mortal man in all the Kingdoms," he said. "That his father is hoping to find him a worthy wife—and I can almost guarantee that she will not be a native of Castelle."

"No, I suspect not," Leta said with a laugh. "Both our Champions will end up vulture meal before the Trials are through."

"Leta!" I chastised. "Don't speak of it so lightly. You're talking about people dying. It's morbid."

"We all die," she replied with a dismissive frown. "Just at different times. At least our Champions will die with some kind of honor, as opposed to that disgusting Raleigh and his friend."

Our father remained strangely silent, and when I looked at him again, his eyes were still locked on the window.

"What is it?" I asked, leaning toward him. "What do you see out there?"

He went very still for a moment, then shook his head and turned my way. "Nothing. It's only...a feeling." He put his hand over mine and squeezed, adding, "Take care of your sister, will you, Lyrinn? Always?"

"Of course," I laughed. "Why are you behaving so strangely?"

He looked deep into my eyes, his irises dark as coal, and said, "A moment is coming that I have been awaiting for many years. One I had hoped would never find its way to us—but I suppose I've always known it was inevitable." He glanced at Leta and added, "I hope you both know I love you dearly, and that I have done everything I could to give you each a good life."

"Of course, Father," Leta said, rising to her feet and embracing him from behind. She looked at me, raising her eyebrows questioningly. No doubt she was as confused and concerned as I was. "We both know it."

"Good," he said, patting her arm gently.

He looked sad, distant, as if basking in a bittersweet memory from long ago. “I am going to sit by the fire and read,” he told us at last, issuing a deep exhalation. “Be wary tonight. Keep to your rooms, would you?”

“I have no intention of going anywhere,” I told him.

“Nor I,” said Leta.

“Good. That’s good.”

With that, our father rose to his feet and headed to the small sitting room to seat himself in his worn leather chair by the flickering hearth.

Silently, I helped Leta clean up then went to my room, closing the door behind me.

Exhaustion overtook me once again, and I soon found myself lying back on the bed, my eyes drooping closed.

For the second night in a row, I bolted awake when a blood-curdling scream pierced the night’s darkness.

CHAPTER FOURTEEN

I SHOT UP WITHOUT THINKING, twisting myself so that my bare feet hit the floor, and darted toward the door. Reaching into my dress' open side seam, I felt for my blade, creeping forward as another scream met my ears.

What was screaming, I couldn't say. All I knew was that it was close—far too close—and horrific.

"Father?" I called out. "Leta!"

But no answer came. Only a crash, another shriek, then...silence.

I yanked my door open and raced to the sitting room, where my father was lying on the floor, a large, shadowy form hunched over him.

A wave of nausea surged through me, and I froze, staring.

A Grimper.

My father was breathing heavily. In the dull orange light cast by the embers still glowing in the hearth, I could see dark red staining his tunic. I held my knife up, though I knew my blade would likely do nothing to stop the creature who had infiltrated our home.

"Leave," I hissed, my hand trembling with rage and fear.

"Leave, and never return to this place. You are not welcome here."

The creature stared at me with lifeless, dark eyes, looked down at my father once, then fled through the open front door.

"Gods!" I cried, leaping to my father's side and crouching next to him, my hand hovering in the air above his bloodied chest. I couldn't bring myself to touch him, to feel for the severity of his wounds. The injuries, I knew without even looking, were too deep. There was nothing I could do to stop the bleeding.

Nothing anyone could do.

"Why did this happen?" I asked, almost certain there would be no answer.

Mithraan had warned me. *I fear you will be in danger—as will anyone else you care about.* I had assumed his words were a threat, meant to keep me trapped in Tíria—a warning issued to instill fear in me, and nothing more.

It had not occurred to me for a moment that he could possibly be telling the truth.

"Lyrinn," my father whispered faintly, his voice little more than a weak rasp. I leaned closer, tears falling now, mingling with the blood staining his face, his neck, his chest.

"I knew this night was coming," he said. "It's all right, my girl. I have known for many years. I know you have seen them—the Fae. It was only a matter of time before you found your way to them."

"But..." I murmured. "The Grimper—did it come because I escaped? Was it the Fae who sent it?"

My father winced against the pain, shaking his head ever so slightly. "You know by now that the Fae of Tíria are not to blame for the Grimpers," he said. "You understand that they are not so cruel as mortals claim. Some Fae are quite wonderful, in fact."

He managed a strange, distant smile as he spoke the words.

"But you always said—"

Another weak shake of his head. "I only told you those lies to shield you from the truth. It was for your safety...yours and Leta's."

Leta.

I twisted this way and that, looking for my sister, but she was nowhere to be seen. Surely she must have heard the cries. Surely...

"Where is she?" I asked, desperate. "Why hasn't she come?"

"She was here with me, checking on me, as she always does when they came for her."

"They?" My heart hammered in my chest. "The Grimpers?"

"No...not Grimpers...Men." Reaching a hand out, he took my own and squeezed, but the strength of the powerful man I'd always known was gone. "The days ahead will be difficult for you, but your sister will be safe. They won't harm her. But...you must follow your heart, Lyrinn...You must trust yourself."

"Follow my heart?" I asked. "No! I need to find Leta! Who took her? I need to..."

My father's hand slipped from mine, his arm falling to his side. He lay still, his eyes glassy as he stared up at the ceiling's dark wooden beams.

The sound of footsteps on the cobblestone street outside drew my eyes from him to the doorway, where two men in dark blue tunics stood now, staring in at us. On each tunic was a silver mountain peak.

The sigil of Domignon.

"Lyrinn Martel," one of them said. "We have been sent to find you. You must come with us."

Through my tears, their faces were little more than a blur. I shook my head, my hand going to my father's arm.

"I can't leave him!" I cried. "I can't..."

I leaned over my father, grasping his hands in mine. They were so cold now, and clammy. Not at all like the hands that had held mine so often over the years.

"I won't leave him," I said.

But even as I wept, the hands I clasped so tightly in my own disintegrated. My father's body, so large and strong, faded to ash before my eyes, crumbling into a dark pile on the floor, his blood-stained clothing sagging loosely onto stone.

The Grimper's poison had taken my father's body from me. I could not even grant him a proper burial.

"You must come with us, Miss," the man said again, more insistent this time. "Your life is in danger. When you return to this place, you can hold a service for your father. But if you do not accept our protection, the Grimper will return and he will take you next. We are the King's Guard—you can trust us."

"My sister," I stammered, turning to look at the men through tear-filled eyes. "Someone has taken her!"

The two of them exchanged a look. "We will have our men search for her," the one who seemed to be in charge told me. "But we need to take you to Domignon, on the king's orders."

"*Domignon*?" I found the strength to rise to my feet, wiping the tears from my eyes to clear my vision. "Why would Domignon or the king want me? What is happening?"

"If you come with us, all will be explained. Look—we will do all we can to reunite you with your sister. But as I said, if you stay here, you will die."

Somewhere in the distance, a piercing cry ripped through the night, a cross between a wild animal and a human. The sound chilled my blood and enraged me at once, and in that moment, all I wanted was to stalk into the night with my dagger in hand and slash the first Grimper I saw into ribbons.

"Please," the guard said. "We don't have much time."

"Promise me," I said. "Promise your men will find Leta, my sister, and I will come."

"I promise. Every King's Guardsman available will search Kalemnar until she is found."

"Fine." Forcing a sob away from my chest, I rose to my feet. "I want someone to burn my father's clothing. I don't want it there if—when—my sister returns."

"Of course," one of the guards said, signaling a man outside. "It will be done immediately."

I accompanied the men out of the house and toward the town gates, the cries of desperate malice still echoing behind us in the night as Dúnbar's residents sealed themselves behind locked shutters and barred doors.

"The carriage awaits us at the town's gates," the leader said. "It will take three nights to get to Domignon. We must leave now. The king is most eager to see you."

"But why?" I asked, my jaw set as I tried to push away thoughts of what had just happened. "How does the king even know who I am?"

"I cannot say," the young man replied. "I am only a messenger. I only know that we were meant to collect you tonight. Four of the king's guards will accompany you on your journey, as well as one other."

I wanted to ask more questions. *Why tonight? Why did you not come before the Grimper killed my father? Why didn't you protect him or my sister, if you're so intent on protecting me?*

But I kept my mouth shut, my thoughts numbed by shock as I stumbled through the gates toward a waiting carriage of intricately carved wood, with Domignon's mountain sigil emblazoned on its doors. It looked more suited for a princess than for an insignificant young woman from Dúnbar, and I had yet to understand how or why it had made its way so many miles to me, of all people.

One of the men helped me into the carriage. The second went over to speak to two other men. I could only hope he was instructing them to hunt for Leta and to bring her to me.

The inside of the carriage was spacious, its long seats broad. Velvet and silk pillows lay on every conceivable surface, as well as blankets of soft fur and wool.

For those small comforts, at least, I was grateful.

When I'd sat down, I pressed my head back and thought of my father's strange, nonsensical words as he lay dying. Of the lies he had told me for so many years—lies about the Fae, about Tíria.

Why had he kept the truth from me for so long? And how had he foreseen his death on this night?

Most baffling of all, why was I about to be transported the length of the King's Road to the southern realms and King Caedmon himself?

I was contemplating a multitude of new questions when a man I hadn't yet seen climbed into the carriage to take a seat across from me. He slapped a palm against the roof to signal the driver, and we began to lurch forward.

The man was dressed in a green tunic adorned with an embroidered golden arrow, a golden belt at his waist. His hair was graying, his face finely lined, and he was handsome—at least, by human standards.

"I am Nallach," he said. "One of the king's most trusted advisors. I will be riding with the party for some time, as I have a little business in Kortland, a small town on the way to Domignon. But for now, I am here to answer any questions you might have. I understand that this must all be somewhat confusing for you, Lyrinn."

"Questions," I repeated, my voice dry and weak. "Yes, I have many...My sister..."

The man held up a hand, interrupting immediately. "We have several parties searching for her, including the Scouts who were in Dúnbar. They will bring her to you as soon as they find her. And before you ask me who has her—I can't say, as I do not know."

I nodded miserably, wondering if I would come to regret leaving with these men so readily, so quickly after my father's death. I had not allowed myself a second to grieve, to mourn. I was still in shock, incapable of rational thought.

Still, I managed to speak. "Why were your men—the king's men, I mean—looking for me? Who am I to them?"

Nallach cleared his throat and pulled his eyes to the darkness of the passing countryside as the horses picked up their pace. "That, I do not know," he replied. "The king sent us several days ago to make our way to Dúnbar. He told us only to find you and bring you to him...and to look into your birth records."

"Why my birth records? How could they possibly be of interest to the king?"

"Ah," Nallach replied. "That I can tell you. It seems King Caedmon knew your mother."

"My mother," I repeated, my mind overflowing with more questions. "He couldn't have known her. She was from Dúnbar."

Nallach shrugged. "Whatever the case, they were friends long ago, it seems. I suppose he has an interest in you because of it."

"My mother, friends with the king?" I asked. "Are you quite certain?"

"King Caedmon will explain everything, Lyrinn. I have every

faith in it. He is excited about meeting you. The prince, too, is looking forward to it."

"Prince Corym?"

Nallach's lips curled up as he nodded, leaning forward and speaking quietly. "I probably shouldn't say anything about it. It's all meant to be very hush-hush, you see."

"I fail to understand any of this," I replied in a tremulous voice. "There are plenty of young women in Kalemnar. The prince has no reason whatsoever to take an interest in me. Besides which, he is preparing for the Blood Trials, is he not?"

"He is."

"In that case, I would appreciate if a messenger would ride ahead and inform both the king and his son that they have taken the wrong woman from Dúnbar. There is no way the king knew my mother, and there's certainly no way Prince Corym is anticipating my arrival."

"It's possible that they are indeed mistaken," Nallach said. "But, given what has just occurred, perhaps you would not lose anything by hearing what the king and prince have to say to you. It seems to me you have just endured a harrowing experience, and you ought to allow yourself to embrace whatever small pleasures life may throw your way in the near future."

It was an oddly unsympathetic manner of acknowledging the loss of both my father and my sister in one night.

I barely knew Nallach, but I already disliked him intensely. He made my skin crawl, though I couldn't put my finger on what it was about him that I found so utterly repugnant. I supposed it was his lack of humanity, of empathy.

Still, some part of me was desperate to follow his advice and seek out whatever pleasure I could find. Grief was threatening me like an ebbing tide, and I wanted nothing more than to suppress the feeling of torment that would soon tear at my insides.

I had a chance to meet the king, the prince. To see the realm of Domignon and the city that bore its name, legendary for its splendor and beauty. For the first time, I would get to inhale the scent of orange trees and fresh southern pastries, to walk down a broad street filled with happy people and bathed in sunshine.

I may even see the inside of the palace, I thought. *After all, I am to meet the man who rules over all of Kalemnar.*

I turned to look out the window, pressing my forehead to the delicate leaded glass window and reveling in its coolness.

"You are tired," Nallach said gently. "I can see that you need rest. I will head up to the front and ride with the driver." He knocked on the carriage's ceiling, and the horses promptly slowed to a halt. He climbed out, leaving me to my solitude.

I realized as I found myself alone that he had answered hardly any of my questions, and in fact, had left me with more.

He'd said the king had known my mother. A woman I knew only from a small portrait in my father's room. She had been a mystery to Leta and me all our lives, only ever revealed in tiny morsels that our father had doled out as he saw fit.

But on that strange night, she had become far more than a mere mystery. My mother allegedly had royal ties. And as devastated as I was, another emotion had started to mingle with the sorrow inside me: a deep, unrelenting need to understand who my mother was and why, after all these years, the king had seen fit to send his men to locate her eldest daughter.

I curled up on the long, broad seat, grateful for its lavish abundance of velvet cushions, and closed my eyes, only to feel the carriage surging forward along the uneven King's Road that led from Dúnbar south across the river.

An hour or more passed before the horses let out a harrowing whinny that made my blood run cold.

CHAPTER FIFTEEN

The carriage pulled to an abrupt halt, and I had to grab hold of the edge of the seat to keep from tumbling off.

Voices rang through the air outside, punctuated by the clatter of clashing weapons, and for a moment, I was convinced we were under attack by some rebel army.

"You have a young woman in your custody," a deep, masculine voice bellowed. "Let me see her, or this night will not end well for you."

My chest tightened.

That voice...How is this possible?

"Go back to the North." I could hear the derisive sneer in Nallach's tone. "You are not meant to be here. Leave the King's Guard in peace, and we will not harm you."

"Peace," the other voice said with a toxic chuckle. "Like the 'peace' you mortals have inflicted on my kind and my home for a thousand years?"

If there had been any doubt in my mind as to the speaker's identity, it was gone now. I pushed open the carriage door and leapt out, showing myself.

Mithraan stood over Nallach, a threatening, dominant presence. The Fae was far larger than the silver-haired man, his shoulders like boulders, his arms thick with muscle.

And to add insult to injury, he held a fine silver blade at his adversary's throat.

Two members of the King's Guard, who had been riding along beside the carriage, were standing by with their swords drawn. Both looked terrified, and I knew without asking that neither imagined a day when they would come face to face with an Immortal.

As I stepped toward Mithraan, he turned my way and issued me a less than friendly smile.

"How did you come to be here?" I asked, my heart threatening an explosion in my chest. "The Breath...the Grimpers... You said no one could climb the Onyx Stair."

"Yet you did," he retorted. "Both up *and* down, it seems."

It was then that I saw the glint of perspiration on his brow —not to mention the deathlike pallor in his cheeks. His dark hair was streaked and wet from whatever exertion had brought him here.

"You know this creature?" Nallach asked, turning his face my way, the blade still at his throat.

"I do," I replied. "Though I never thought I would see him in these lands."

"I never thought I would see the likes of you in our lands either, Lyrinn, yet here we are," Mithraan replied. "An eye for an eye—isn't that how the saying goes?"

I ignored his words and, nodding toward Nallach, asked, "Are you going to kill this man?"

"That depends," the Fae lord replied. "Would you like me to?"

I thought about it for a moment. Nallach was not remotely likeable, nor did I trust him. He had failed to soothe me when I needed it, and done nothing to answer my questions.

But his irritating presence wasn't enough to warrant a death sentence. "No. I don't think I do."

"Very well," Mithraan replied, backing away and sheathing his weapon, then locking his eyes on mine. "But you will come with me back to the North, will you not?"

"Why would I do that?" I asked, venom on my tongue. "There is nothing for me in the North. My father is dead, my sister disappeared."

Mithraan looked pained, but the expression quickly turned to anger. "I warned you," he said. "I told you what would happen if you left Tíria before I let you go."

"You would never have let me go," I said, almost under my breath. "You would have killed me."

"Is that really what you think?"

"I hate to interrupt," Nallach said, flattening out his tunic and sweeping his silver hair back from his face, "but we need to keep moving. The king is waiting."

I nodded and addressed Mithraan once again. "These men have given me no reason to fear them. I will accompany them to Domignon. I wish to hear what the king has to say."

Mithraan looked like he wanted to argue, but, seeing my clenched jaw and narrowed eyes, he relented. "Then I will come with you," he said with some finality. "The carriage is large enough for us both, is it not?"

"You certainly will not come," Nallach retorted. "You cannot simply invite yourself along, Fae."

"I certainly *can,* according to the Pact," Mithraan replied. "Or have you conveniently forgotten the laws that still exist between Fae and human?"

Nallach went quiet, searching for a reply but failing to come up with one.

"Pact?" I asked, an eyebrow raised. I had never heard of such a thing.

Then again, I had been misinformed all my life about the Fae, about the origin of the Grimpers, about Tíria. I could only imagine how much there was for me yet to learn about those who dwelt beyond the Rise.

"Between Fae and mortal-kind," Mithraan said. "If a Fae lord announces an offer of protection, it must be accepted—even if that means allowing him into a fancy carriage with an irritable young woman. I offered you my protection, and I intend to keep my promise."

I tightened, shooting him a look. "We are in the mortal realms now. I don't need your protection in this place."

"It is not for you to decide. My offer stands, and as such, you are obliged to accept it."

I glared at him, angry that he was imposing himself upon me in my time of grief. Angry, too, that some irritating part of me was sending a pulse of excitement throbbing through my bloodstream. I had expected never to set eyes on Mithraan again, and I had felt the loss acutely when he had left me in Fairholme with his companions. But now, he felt like a relief—a joy, almost—despite the fact that I wanted to despise him.

At the very least, he was a distraction.

I glanced around. "Where is your horse?" I asked. "If you insist on coming, you should ride alongside the carriage."

"I have no horse. I came here on my own."

My brow furrowed, but Nallach interrupted my thoughts with, "For the gods' sake, let's go."

"Fine," I replied, turning to climb back into the carriage. Mithraan followed me in, seating himself next to me.

"What are you doing?" I asked, turning to scowl at him. He was too close now—so close that I was convinced he could hear my heart racing.

"Watching over you. Ensuring those mortal bastards don't

get their hooks into your mind. I don't want them corrupting you with their tales of the beautiful land of Domignon."

"Corrupt me? They're looking *after* me. I told you—it's not as though I have anything keeping me in the North. My father is—"

I stopped, bit my lip, and turned to look away.

My father is not just dead. He is gone.

He no longer exists in any form.

"These men are transporting you to a fate you're not ready for," Mithraan said more gently than I expected. "To a world and a life that you will despise. In the king's domain, you will find nothing but pain, Lyrinn."

My sadness was quickly replaced with a feeling of annoyance, and I tried to level him with a glare. But once again, my mind was overwhelmed by his dark intensity.

His beauty, his power.

Much as I wanted to feel like a lioness in his presence, I felt like nothing more than a mouse.

But I told myself not to soften under his gaze. Since I had first laid eyes on him, my entire life had been turned upside down, and I had no desire to discover how he could further destroy me.

"What do you know of my pain?" I asked. "I am alone in this world, and unless I find Leta, I will remain alone. If the king wants to offer me a life better than any I could have had in Dúnbar, I will accept it without question."

Mithraan lowered his chin, and I watched as his irises danced with an abundance of impossible colors. Green, gold, blue, mixing like watercolor paints before settling on deep amber once again. "Beware the lure of pretty things," he said. "Prince Corym, they say, is a handsome man with many talents. You will find him hard to resist."

Is that it? I wondered with a laugh. *Is this Fae lord jealous of the prince?*

"And why should I resist him? If he's all that you say, why shouldn't I want to spend every waking moment with him?"

I knew full well that the prince was not bringing me to Domignon for himself. The prince had the Blood Trials to prepare for. A female Champion would be his bride. All of Kalemnar knew it.

But there was part of me that wanted nothing more than to stir up jealousy inside Mithraan...just as he had done to me.

"Perhaps you should," the Fae replied. "It's possible that I have misread you all this time."

"*All this time*," I scoffed. "You and I have barely spent any time together. You don't know me."

He went quiet then, leaning back in the seat, and the grim silence between us felt like a growing weight around my neck.

"What do you intend to do when we get to Domignon?" I finally asked, unable to stand the tension in the air any longer.

"I will decide that when I have learned the king's reasons for bringing you to his realm," he told me. "I wish to protect you until I know his intentions. You are..." He paused, clenching his jaw for a moment before finishing. "You are of some importance to me."

Importance.

His flattery always felt as if its roots lay in something nefarious, even cruel. As if whatever part of me he deemed extraordinary was one he wanted to steal for himself, for his own ill purposes.

"You don't seem angry that I left Tíria," I said, ignoring his odd choice of words. "I must admit, I'm surprised."

"I'm not angry. I expected it, in fact. And Nihara facilitated it. It seems she wanted to be rid of you."

"Facilitated it?"

"She is powerful," he said. "She cast a sleeping spell over every Fae in Fairholme. It was her fault you escaped with such ease. I suppose you should write her a thank-you missive."

I shuddered to think of what punishment Mithraan had inflicted on Nihara for her disobedience, but I chose not to ask.

"I am sorry about your father," the Fae said. "I am sorry you found your way home, only to be greeted by such grief."

"I..." His kindness took me aback, but I tightened and forced out a "Thank you."

"I should have foreseen his fate more clearly. I should have seen all of what's happening to you now. But there is a veil over my mind—something preventing me from seeing clearly. I fear that you and I are going to need each other in the days to come, Lyrinn. We will need to help one another to seek the truth."

"Truth?"

"Do you not wonder why the king has taken such a keen interest in you?" He chuckled softly. "Though I suppose I should point out that I don't blame him."

"The king has his reasons," I snapped.

"We'll see about that," he said, and when I turned to him, he had pressed his head back, dark hair flowing about his shoulders, and closed his eyes, a smile on his lips.

CHAPTER SIXTEEN

We traveled for countless hours, the carriage rocking and jostling its way over the uneven King's Road.

I awoke at one point, realizing with horror that I had fallen asleep with my head on Mithraan's shoulder. I pulled away, daring a glance at him that revealed another amused grin on his lips. But he said nothing.

Now and then, the carriage stopped to allow us to stretch our legs. The guards gave me bread, cheese, and water, which I shared with Mithraan as we traveled, though we said little to each other. It seemed he sensed my dark mood, and he was gracious enough not to attempt light conversation.

He kept vigilant watch out the window, though I wasn't sure what, exactly, he expected to see.

When the second night fell, the carriage slowed once again before coming to a full stop. I heard a voice calling out in the distance and peered out the window to see that we'd come to a large wooden building—an inn, from the looks of it.

"My Lady," one of the guards said when he had descended and made his way to the door. "The horses need to rest, so we will remain here tonight. I will show you to your room."

"Where is Nallach?" I asked.

"We dropped him off some time ago," the young man said. "In Kortland."

"Ah, right. He mentioned that," I replied. I gave Mithraan a quick glance before taking the guard's offered hand, grateful for the opportunity to stretch my legs once again.

We headed into the inn, followed by another guard who carried a large pack with him.

"What's that?" I asked, gesturing to the bag.

"Fresh clothing for you, and other necessities," the man said.

The guard guided me through a pub on the first floor that smelled pleasantly of roast chicken and ale, and up a set of stairs to a room on the second level. "You know this place well?" I asked.

"The Feathery?" he replied. "Yes. I stop here frequently on long travels. My brother-in-law owns the place."

"I would like to have a drink downstairs," I said. "I'm thirsty after the long voyage."

"I would advise against it. Not every man who makes his way into this place is reputable. Travelers show up at the inn from all over the land, and—"

"I can look after myself," I interrupted, patting my leg surreptitiously to ensure my blade was still firmly sheathed.

"My Lady..."

"I'm not your *lady*," I snapped, but immediately regretted my tone.

"I simply meant..."

"I know," I said, attempting to steer my voice into a more charming timbre. I thought of Leta then, of how she had a way of rendering herself sugary-sweet when she wished to get her way. "I only meant that I am a blacksmith's daughter, a girl born in Dúnbar. I am very accustomed to men like those who frequent places like this."

The man still hesitated, but finally, the second guard, who was carrying the pack, said, "We'll be nearby. We'll hear if anything goes awry."

The other man relented, and the two of them guided me into my room, laying the pack on the bed.

"Thank you. I'll be down in a few minutes," I told them. "I'll call for you should I need anything."

When I'd closed the door, I rifled through the pack and found an unadorned linen dress. I changed into it and splashed some cold water on my face from the pitcher on the nightstand. I stared in the mirror, wondering where Mithraan had ended up.

I scolded myself, insisting that I didn't care, that he was nothing to me. Just as I had infiltrated his lands, he had done so to mine. As far as I knew, he was the first Fae to enter the lower kingdoms in a millennium—but that didn't mean I had to waste a moment thinking about him.

"Anyhow," I muttered. "The instant the king sees him, he'll order him back to the North."

When I opened the door a moment later, Mithraan was standing in the hallway, a hand pressed to the wall as though he was casually awaiting me.

I started when I saw him, but tried my best to conceal my surprise.

"Do you know," he said, staring me up and down, "the old saying that Fae cannot lie?"

"I've heard it," I told him. "Is it true?"

Mithraan laughed at the irony of my question.

If he was a liar, he would say yes. If he was not, he would *also* say yes.

Neither was a useful answer—and we both knew it.

"The truth is," he said, "we Fae are notorious liars. What is glamour, after all, but a lie? We manipulate mortals' perceptions of the world at large, of our appearances. We make ourselves more pleasing to your eyes and conceal our true selves. We find ways to blend into human society when we feel that mortals find us threatening. We are devious creatures who prey on weak minds, and so I have always found it ironic that humans think us truthful."

"Are you saying my mind is weak?" I asked, my body tightening under his unreadable gaze.

He moved toward me, gliding like a stalking cat.

"No," he replied. "But then again, maybe you should not believe me. I have just confessed to being a liar, but it is in my interest to make you feel safe, secure, and most of all, to gain your trust."

"Oh?" I asked as I felt the caress of his breath on my skin, my cheeks heating to what was no doubt a deep shade of crimson. "Why do you want my trust?"

"Because I'm quite certain you are not the sort of woman who allows just *any* man to sleep in her bed...yet that is precisely where I intend to find myself tonight."

I let out a laugh, pulling back to assess him. "You can't be serious."

"Can't I? I've told you, Lyrinn—I am here to protect you. I can hardly do so if I'm relegated to the hallway, can I?"

"You will *not* sleep in my bed." My voice bit at the air as I said the words.

He leaned in close again, whispering into my ear.

"*Sleep?* Chances are there will be no such thing. I would not waste a night by your side with such a banal activity as snoring."

With that, he turned and headed down the stairs to the pub.

I stood back, leaning against the wall, and breathed deep, commanding my heart to slow its relentless pace.

Damn you, Fae, for doing this to me.

Damn your eyes, your lips, your body.

Damn you for the cruel ache at my core.

"I will defeat this," I said under my breath. "He will leave me when we reach Domignon, and fade into the memory he was always meant to be."

I headed down the stairs after what felt like hours spent trying to regain control over my mind and traitorous body.

Mithraan was seated alone at a small table in the pub's far corner. Despite the darkness, I could see his eyes flickering, reflecting every ounce of firelight in the room as he studied me. A predator, assessing his prey for the hundredth time.

I proceeded toward the bar and asked for a pint of local ale. Almost instantly, I felt eyes on my back, then my ears met the sound of chair legs scraping against the stone floor.

I refused to turn and look. The Fae lord could wait until I'd had at least one sip before expecting me to speak to him.

But when the barkeep had handed me my ale, I turned to see that it wasn't Mithraan standing beside me, but a large, lumbering man with a beard of reddish brown. He was tall and broad, built like a stone wall.

"We don't often see the likes of you in these parts, darlin'," he said with a repugnant attempt at a friendly smile.

"The likes of me aren't often in these parts," I said, trying to push past him. "Now, if you'll excuse me..."

"Excuse you indeed," the man said, blocking my way each time I tried to navigate around him. "Pretty thing, ain't ya?

But..." he said, gesturing to my right ear. "Where did you get the scars?"

I reached up and self-consciously pulled a lock of hair forward to cover the red marks. *Damn it. I should have brought my cloak.*

"I don't see how that's any of your business," I scowled.

"Don't be sensitive, love. I'm just wondering what other bits of you are pink and pretty," he said with a lick of his lips, reaching a hand out to pull at the front of my dress.

I was about to warn him about my blade when a powerful hand grabbed his shoulder and yanked him backwards, throwing him across the room and knocking several chairs to the floor in the process.

The large man scrambled to his feet, snarling a threat as he spun around to face his assailant.

Mithraan had already maneuvered to stand between us, his shoulders heaving with protective rage. I pulled away to look at him, my eyes pleading.

Don't do anything foolish.

Do not risk both our lives.

"Touch her again," he snarled at the man, ignoring me, "and I will end your life in the most miserable of ways."

His foe yanked an arm back, his hand curled into a boulder-like fist, preparing to ram it into Mithraan's perfect face. But even as he thrust it forward, his body froze in mid-movement, his face straining with effort.

Mithraan crossed his arms and stared, his lips slowly ticking upward. "You are paralyzed," he said. "It's all right. Many men suffer this ailment on occasion. Perhaps if you learn not to be such an ass, you'll eventually recover." He pulled his eyes to mine and asked, "Did he hurt you?"

I shook my head. "No. I told you—I don't need your protection."

"No, I don't suppose you do. But you are, unfortunately, stuck with it for a little while. Come, sit."

I wanted to ask what would become of the still-frozen man, but instead I simply walked around the jackass and joined Mithraan at his table.

By now, every face in the pub was turned toward us, whispers slinking their way through the air.

"Do they know what you are?" I asked in a whisper of my own, taking a seat and leaning forward.

"Yes," Mithraan said. "And if they don't, they will in a second."

He flicked a hand into the air, and behind me a loud thud sounded as the bearded man hit the floor like a sack of potatoes.

"Let them gossip," he said. "Let them be afraid, even. They should be. The likes of them thought they were done with my kind. They thought we had lost our power. But instead, they've made us angry—and nothing strengthens a Fae like rage."

"How did you get down the Onyx Rise?" I asked, changing the subject. "I mean, really? If you weren't able to descend for a thousand years, how did you manage it now?"

Mithraan looked for a moment as though he was contemplating his answer, then he lowered his chin and said, "The Breath of the Fae allowed me through."

My brow furrowed. "Did it, then?"

He nodded enthusiastically. "It was the strangest thing. When I returned from my journey to the Dragon Court and discovered you were gone, I headed to the Rise. The mist, it just...disappeared for a time. The Grimpers, too. It was as if they'd taken the Breath with them. I simply climbed down the Rise. It was the easiest thing in the world."

"Strange indeed." I narrowed my eyes, not believing him for a single second. "And your journey to the Dragon Court?" I asked. "What did the High King have to say?"

I could have asked the question during the long carriage ride, but I had been too irritated, too sad. Now, sitting with a pint as I was, my courage had begun to find its way back to me.

"Ah," Mithraan replied. "I was wondering when we would come to it. Our High King had plenty to say, in fact, though none of it was useful. You see, I went to him believing that perhaps you were someone special. Someone with secrets untold and a history to unearth. I thought the mist had parted for you because you were some sort of blessing on our lands. You see, there is an old legend that says 'One will come who can restore Tíria to its former beauty, and the days of old will come again.' I told the High King I believed you could be the One."

I studied him, trying to detect a smile on his lips. He looked entirely serious, but I was certain I could feel the lie in his words.

Again.

"And?" I asked, my tone cold. "What were his thoughts?"

The Fae shrugged. "He believes there was a temporary weakening in the mist. That you were fortunate enough to ascend, but that you are simply a mortal who found herself in the wrong place at the wrong time. Or perhaps it was the right place. Who's to say?"

He pulled my ale toward him and took a long sip.

"But you disagree with him," I said slowly, reading his thoughts. "Tell me, why is that?"

"Because the king of Domignon has coincidentally called you south. The prince, his son, will be a Champion in the Trials. Which means he will be forced to marry the chosen female co-winner. Strange, don't you think, that he should send for a young woman such as yourself at this, of all times?"

"I cannot be a Champion, if that's what you're implying," I said. "So it is not a topic that merits discussion."

"Not exactly. It means he could marry you *if* you competed and won alongside him."

At that, I laughed. "I can't compete. I have no Blood-Gifts, and I'm under the required age, besides."

"Ah." Mithraan issued me a strange smile. "I suppose you're right about that. Still, the big man with the beard thought you were something special," he added, nodding toward the creature who had collided so violently with the pub's floor. "Perhaps he knows something we don't."

I turned to see the man sitting with his back to the wall, his eyes looking unfocused as he stared warily in our direction.

"All drunken men think eighteen-year-old girls are something special," I retorted, pivoting back to the Fae. "I don't exactly take his keen interest as a compliment."

I leaned back in my chair, debating whether or not to give up on this conversation, head to my room, and bar the door behind me.

"You are irritated with me," Mithraan said.

"Is it that obvious?"

"I can smell it on you, even if your face didn't already betray you," he said with a soft laugh. He leaned forward and added, "And your irritation is not all that I can smell on you."

I narrowed my eyes at him, annoyed by his heightened senses. "I don't know what you mean," I said, fighting to keep my tone innocent.

"Ah, but I think you do," he told me. "You desire me. It's all right Lyrinn; you wouldn't be the first mortal woman ever to ache for a Fae lord."

"I don't *ache for* you, you arrogant bastard," I snarled. "I literally fled south to get myself as far from you as I—"

I stopped, my voice catching with the realization that I had just offered up a horrible confession: that I had not, in fact, agreed to accompany the king's men because my father was dead, or because Leta was missing. It wasn't even because I feared for my life.

I had done it to get myself far away from the Rise. To escape the constant reminder that Mithraan was close yet utterly inaccessible.

For the first time, I realized the whole, pathetic truth: I did not want to live the rest of my days being tortured by the shadow of the Fae lord.

"You are angry that I followed you on the King's Road," Mithraan said. "I suppose I can't exactly blame you. Would it help if I told you I did it only to help my kind?"

"I don't see how," I replied. "Your kind needs you in Tíria. Following me to Domignon will do nothing for them."

"The Tírians need their lands back," he said, crossing his arms over the broad chest I was trying—and failing—to ignore. "Do you know how beautiful our land once was?"

I shook my head slightly, recalling the murals and tapestries inside the ruins of Fairholme. The images that felt so strangely real that I had wanted nothing more than to climb inside them, to dwell in the lands they depicted for the rest of my days. I recalled, too, what the landscape looked like out the window of the bathing chamber, thanks to Mithraan's cast illusion. "No. But I can imagine it."

"The powerful force that took our world from us did so maliciously," he said. "It has been a thousand-year-long siege. An attempt to starve us out, to force us from our lands. But we cannot and will not leave. Our roots run too deep."

"You speak of a force," I replied. "What force? No mortal is capable of destroying Tíria—and I don't believe it was the Taker who did it. So who is responsible?"

Mithraan sat back. "I have told you that I have theories," he said. "I need to be certain before I level accusations, however. These are serious matters—and I intend to get to the truth."

"Still, your Fae would be better off elsewhere than in Tíria," I told him, and my voice had softened a little. "Let the past go. Move on with your lives. I don't understand why you followed me, rather than take your kind to a place of beauty and peace."

"Don't you?" he asked, pressing close to me, his eyes dancing with light. "Does it really surprise you that I would want to be close to you, Lyrinn?"

I could feel the power of those words, the seductive music in his voice. Lilting, lyrical, almost a song. But I told myself he was attempting to charm me for his own amusement again, and I would not fall for it.

"If you want to be close to me, it's for your own reasons," I said. "If you don't wish to divulge them, fine. But don't pretend it has anything to do with my allure."

With that, I rose to my feet and headed for the stairs.

CHAPTER SEVENTEEN

Once in my room, I washed up and changed into a white nightgown the King's servants had packed for me, then climbed into bed.

The entire time, I found myself wondering where the Fae lord would spend the night.

Mithraan has his own room, I told myself. *He was teasing me when he said he would spend the night in my bed.*

He enjoyed getting a rise out of the naive mortal, derived a perverse sort of pleasure from watching my cheeks flush crimson.

I wasn't about to play into his hands by spending another moment thinking about him.

I had just rolled onto my side, my eyes sealing shut, when the door to my room opened slowly, quietly, and I heard the creak of nearby floorboards.

I reached for my blade, which I had lain on the nightstand before climbing into bed.

"You're awake," a deep, silken voice said.

Pulling my hand back from the dagger's hilt, I twisted

around to glare at Mithraan, who was bathed in moonlight pouring in through the window.

"Barely," I replied. "You shouldn't be here. It's not proper for us to be..."

"To be what?" he asked with conspicuous amusement.

"In a bedroom together like this," I said. "Not that it should need to be said."

"You're not betrothed to the prince quite yet," the Fae said, stepping over to a chair by the window. He sat down and removed his boots, then proceeded to unfasten his leather belt and pull off his tunic.

I gasped against my will when his bare torso revealed itself, sculpted muscles defined to perfection in the shadowy light of the moon.

I had stroked my gaze along young men's torsos before. I had kissed necks, chests, run my hand down taut stomachs.

But none of them had come close to Mithraan's unearthly beauty. No man I had ever seen had looked so masculine, so powerful.

Nor had I ever desired one as much as I desired him in that moment.

Teasing me, he rose to his feet and stepped toward the bed.

"Your King's Guardsmen do not know I'm here, in case you really are concerned," Mithraan said. "I saw to it that they imagined me heading out to the woods. They're convinced I'm off hunting for the night. I suspect they think me some kind of vampire who feasts on deer and wolves."

I swallowed, unable to come up with a suitable retort as Mithraan pulled the covers back and slipped into bed.

"I will shield you from enemies," he said softly as he climbed over me, his arms, roped with muscle, forming rigid prison bars to either side of my head. His hair fell in a frame about his face as he eased himself slowly down, his lips trailing along my neck. "I offer you my body as protection against all ills."

I inhaled sharply, my hands reaching for his chest, fingers clawing gently at his flesh. I was trying to push him away from me—only I *wasn't* trying at all. If anything, I ached violently with the temptation to pull him closer. To feel those lips on my own, to taste his tongue against mine.

The blood in my veins was flowing too fast, too hard, as though my body would tear itself apart if he didn't claim me.

I needed him. Every. Single. Inch.

I reached for his neck, pulled his face close, asking him —*begging* him wordlessly to kiss me. My back arched under me as I pressed myself to him, my legs parting, inviting him to do with me everything he could want, and more.

I am yours. Claim me. Devour me.

Feed me.

His lips were so near now that I could almost taste them. He kissed my chin, my jawbone, then moved to kiss my own lips...

But he pulled away and rolled onto his side, his face resting on his hand, a smile spreading across his features as my chest heaved up and down in frustrated torment.

I wanted to curse him for his cruelty.

How dare he?

He knew the king had summoned me. He knew where I was headed. He had basically said he believed I was intended for the prince, as absurd a theory as it was.

"You're a devil," I said, turning my back toward him.

"Devils don't exist," he replied, easing closer—so close that I could feel the deep, glorious agony of his heat penetrating my flesh as he pressed his body to mine. "And if they did, they would hurt their victims. Torture them, even."

A hand crept around and pushed my nightgown up to my waist, slipping its way up some more until his fingers trailed up my stomach, then slowly traced the curve of my breast.

"Am I torturing you, Lyrinn?" he breathed. "Because the thing is, I rather think you're enjoying this."

When I didn't reply, he found my nipple and rolled it gently between his fingers, driving me to cruel distraction.

"Don't..." I began, but there was no conviction in my voice. "I can't..."

I didn't mean it.

I can. I would. I want to.

His mouth was on my neck again, his body pressed to mine. I felt his stone-hard length against my backside, my breath catching in my throat as I ground into him. The anticipation of a moment that could not come soon enough was brutal, like a hand around my lungs squeezing the air out of me.

Surrendering at last, I twisted around to face him, to kiss him, to savor him. To give in to every wicked desire that had assaulted my body and mind since the first moment I had felt his presence atop the Onyx Rise.

But when I turned to look him in the eye...there was no one there.

I shot up, looking over to see that he was seated once again in the chair by the window, that cruel, playful smile on his lips. His tunic was still on, and still belted. He was wearing his leather boots.

Just as he had been when he'd first entered the room.

Had I only imagined the feeling of his fingers on my breast, his mouth on my neck? Had I dreamt it all?

Or was this another of his devious tricks—some sort of sensual glamour?

"Damn you," I said under my breath.

"What's wrong?" he asked, his tone infuriatingly innocent.

I scowled at him, pulled the covers up to my chin, and closed my eyes. "I'm going to sleep," I replied.

"Good night, Lyrinn. And...thank you. That was...quite pleasant."

CHAPTER EIGHTEEN

When I awoke in the morning, Mithraan was gone.

I wasn't entirely convinced he had ever been in my room in the first place. The previous night's delicious, infuriating moments of torment now seemed like a dangerous dream, pleasant and cruel at once.

Pushing thoughts of the Fae lord away, I washed up in the basin on the dresser, then clothed myself in a dress made of a series of fine silver scales before heading downstairs, where the king's men awaited me.

"Where is Lord Mithraan?" I asked, looking around.

"He went hunting last night, and he hasn't returned," one of the guards told me. *Right. I wasn't the only one taken in by Fae deceit.* "Good riddance, I say. We must be on our way, my Lady. There is some breakfast awaiting you in the carriage."

"We can't leave without him," I replied abruptly. Probably *too* abruptly, given that I kept insisting I didn't want Mithraan anywhere near me. "I mean—the Pact," I stammered. "We wouldn't want to cause difficulties for the king."

"He'll catch up," the guard said. "The Fae found us on the road once; there is no doubt he will do it again. His kind is clever, and the road is long. But we should depart now, if we wish to reach Domignon by nightfall."

"Nightfall? I thought we had another day of travel yet," I replied, my eyebrows raised.

"Our horses have been fed and watered. They will move quickly for several hours, and we will exchange them at an inn at our midway point."

I nodded, unable to think of any excuse to put off the voyage any longer.

A guard fetched the bag from my room and proceeded to escort me to the carriage. Before climbing in, I glanced up and down the road, half-expecting Mithraan to appear.

But he was nowhere to be seen.

As I seated myself for the ride, an irritating blend of relief and disappointment gestated inside me.

Mithraan was a complication, a distraction. He was mischievous, even malicious, and he toyed too often with my mind.

I was best rid of him.

Yet I felt what had become an all-too-familiar hole forming in my chest at the thought of being separated from him.

I chastised myself, insisting the void had nothing to do with Mithraan, but was a symptom of the sorrow I felt for my father, for Leta. That they were the only two beings in my life who had ever truly mattered.

Before I could convince myself of it, the horses had begun to charge down the road, the lush green of Kalemnar's landscape flying by outside.

I forced myself to swallow a few bites of the bread and cheese the guards had provided for me, washing them down with a bottle of water. But my appetite was minimal, my mind reeling with too many thoughts and too much conflicting emotion.

It wasn't until late afternoon, the horses having already been changed at an inn on the King's Road, that I heard a commotion outside and the carriage ground to a halt, the driver growling with displeasure.

I looked out through the window to my left to see Mithraan pulled up atop a sleek black horse, blocking the road ahead.

Without thinking, I threw the door open and climbed out of the carriage, my heart racing once again as I strode toward him.

"My Lady," Mithraan said with a nod.

"Where did you get the horse?" I asked, my tone accusatory.

"From a farmer a few towns away—one who was very obliging. Don't worry—I will send him back when we're done with him."

"He will be exhausted by the time we arrive in Domignon."

"He'll be fine," Mithraan said with a confidence so profound that I could not bring myself to doubt him. "Now," he added, turning to the driver and guards, "I assume we can proceed on our way, yes?"

"Fine," the leader of the guards said. "But try anything, Fae, and we will bring you to the king in silver wrist cuffs."

"I wouldn't *dream* of it," Mithraan said, shooting me a quick, knowing glance.

It was real, I thought. *Last night. Every touch. Every caress.*

Damn you, Fae.

I spun around and climbed back into the carriage, impatient to begin the journey once again.

"Four more hours, Lyrinn Martel," Mithraan's voice said from outside as he guided his steed to the window. "Then you will meet your charming prince at last."

I was certain I detected a hint of venom in his tone, as if he had nothing but disdain for the noble young man he had never so much as met. But I ignored him and pressed my head back into the seat, delving deep into my thoughts as Mithraan rode silently along beside the carriage.

With the beginnings of a smile, I pondered what Leta would think if she could see me now, on route to Domignon to meet King Caedmon and Prince Corym. She would have accused me of a lie, then told me how much more deserving she was than I of the prince's attentions. And she would have been right.

My mind quickly shifted to other thoughts, bleak memories flashing through my consciousness. My father's bloodless face as the last vestiges of life left him.

My sister, taken to some place I could not begin to imagine.

Was she a prisoner? A guest? Was she being well looked after?

I couldn't quite imagine anyone abusing Leta. When she wanted to, she had all the charm of a summer cottage bedecked in roses, her cheeks dewy and glowing pink, her eyes clever and enticing at once. As much as she and I liked to prod and tease one another, I had no difficulty in recognizing her goodness.

And I had no doubt that even the cruelest jailer would eventually succumb to her charms.

The hours passed quietly. Every now and then, I would peer out the window to see Mithraan talking to the Guardsmen, or riding silently next to the carriage, a stoic guardian.

His presence was reassuring and daunting at once. I wondered if I would ever be free of the hold he had over me, of his strange, awful magic and those glimmering eyes that called to me like beacons in a storm.

Part of me wished he would speak, if only to tease me. But something in his posture told me he was on high alert, looking out for threats.

I had to wonder what sorts of threats could possibly come upon us on the road so close to the capital.

As time passed, I closed my eyes and envisioned life in the palace among the members of the Royal Family. A secret part of me longed to be dressed in elegant clothing, to be pampered by ladies in waiting, to enjoy the life of luxury girls like Leta always dreamt of.

Another part wished I could be outside, riding alongside the Fae and inhaling the fresh country air. The carriage felt too much like a cage, and the silver dress was just a little too constricting and revealing at once. I wanted my cloak back. I wanted the comforting shadows and corners of Dúnbar to conceal me.

Instead, I was on my way to be examined by a king.

Sometime shortly after dusk, the carriage came to an abrupt halt, jarring me out of my thoughts. Distant shouts met my ears. Violent and piercing, they sounded like the shrieks of desperate men.

Closer to the carriage, a voice sliced through the air, and then the distinct *whish* of an arrow, mere inches from the carriage itself.

A horrifying thud met my ears, and I peered outside, gasping to see one of the Guardsmen lying on the ground.

"Archers!" Another guard's voice sounded. "In the woods!"

"What's happening?" I cried, pulling my skirt up and reaching for my blade.

"Bandits," Mithraan replied, his voice low. By now, he had dismounted and was wielding his own blade, his eyes narrowed into the darkness as he stood just outside the carriage door, blocking my exit. "Or worse."

"Worse? What's worse than people shooting at us?"

With a *thwack*, an arrow slammed into the carriage's side.

"Stay where you are. Do not leave the carriage," Mithraan said, and without another word, he darted toward the woods.

Another arrow hit the door, then another, the collision so violent that I felt the entire carriage vibrate with the impact.

I knew I should follow the Fae's advice and stay put. Every rational part of my mind told me so.

Yet for some reason, I could not.

I *would* not.

I pushed the door open and stepped into the night, only to see signs of utter mayhem all around me.

Men in dark gray linen tatters were creeping out of the woods toward the carriage, their weapons drawn. Two Guardsmen were fighting hand to hand with several others. The carriage's driver lay on the ground, an arrow in his heart, eyes staring blankly at the stars.

Mithraan was nowhere to be seen.

Without understanding what compelled me to do it, I began to walk slowly toward the woods, my eyes fixed on the trees ahead of me. I couldn't think, couldn't control my movements as my feet slipped silently along the grass, the silver dress sliding along the ground like trailing water.

"My Lady!" a guard's voice cried. "Get back in the carriage!"

I didn't reply, didn't so much as shake my head. I simply kept walking until a man emerged from the woods just before me, a short sword in hand. His round face was dirty, his eyes bright. When he smiled at the sight of me, I was confronted by a mouth largely devoid of teeth.

To my horror, he brought his blade to his lips, jutted out his tongue, and licked it as he stared into my eyes.

Flashes of Raleigh came to mind then—of what that man had wished to do to me on the night I had fled to Tíria.

"Coming right to me, pretty thing?" the man asked. "I didn't think it would be this easy to snag me a young lady."

I looked down at my hand, searching for the blade I had been clutching since before I'd left the carriage.

Only it was gone. My hand, clenched into a tight fist, was empty.

I was defenseless.

The man continued to move toward me, and I stopped, freezing in place even as he grabbed me and pressed the sword to my throat.

"Come with me into the woods," he hissed. "We're going to have a time of it before the others get to you, eh?"

I expected whimpers from my lips. Sobs, even. But instead, a voice—*my* voice—simply said, "No. I won't be going anywhere with the likes of you."

The man pulled back, cocked his head to the side, and let out a laugh. His breath smelled like rot.

I winced, refusing to inhale the foulness.

"A feisty lass!" he chuckled. "I like that."

Clearly, he thought I was toying with him, playing hard to get.

"You misunderstand me," I said quietly. "I'm not going anywhere with you, because I aim to kill you."

At that, the man let me go, stepped back, and let out a full belly laugh. "A court jester, at that!" he exclaimed, offering up a low bow. "Incredible. I'm going to enjoy taking you, my Lady. Now c'mere, before I gut you."

A sudden movement drew my eyes momentarily to the edge of the wood where Mithraan was emerging, his blade in hand. He stared at me, at the man making threats against my life, and took a step toward us.

I raised a hand to stop him, and the Fae lord did as I commanded...

But not for the reasons I was expecting.

My hand, suspended in the air between us, tingled and

glowed, its veins brightly lit against the darkness. I stared at it —at my own flesh, taken over by some wild magic.

I looked at Mithraan, my eyes wide. "Is this your doing?" I asked.

He shook his head. "I assure you that it is not," he said. In his eyes was a look of horror, and for a moment I wondered whether I was about to die.

I took a long step back, which seemed to send my would-be assailant into a spiraling rage. He leapt toward me, trying to close the gap between us. But Mithraan was between us in the blink of an eye, his body forming a protective shield.

The bandit held his sword up, twisting it to reveal its sharp edge.

"Mine's bigger than yours," the toothless wretch said.

Mithraan moved then, leaping at the bandit faster than I could register. His free hand shot out from his side, grabbing the man's arm. The man shrieked in pain and dropped the sword to the ground, and all of a sudden, he was facing the road, his forearm firmly in Mithraan's grip.

"Call off the others," Mithraan said.

"Or what?"

Mith shoved his blade into the man's back and said, "or you lose a vital organ, and then another and another, until they're all on the ground around you."

The man sneered and let out something like a growl, but he shouted, "Let 'em go!" to his companions.

The others, who were still fighting the King's Guardsmen, stopped, backing away. Two Guardsmen lay on the ground; another was bleeding and clutching his side.

And just like that, the team of miscreants went running back into the woods.

Mithraan whispered something into his captive's ear, then

shoved him hard toward the forest so the man stumbled, almost fell, then regained his balance and fled.

"Are you all right?" the Fae lord asked, sheathing his blade, turning to me, and reaching for my shoulders.

I looked up at him, my mind twisting this way and that. Whatever force had compelled me to leave the carriage was gone now, and all I wanted was to seek shelter and comfort. Part of me wished to throw myself into his chest, to feel the warmth of his body. To feel his strength like a cloak of strong mail wrapped around every inch of me.

But instead, I pulled away and turned to head back to the carriage.

"Lyrinn," Mithraan said, but I ignored him and climbed in through the open door, my eyes scanning the interior.

There was my blade, lying on the seat as if I had simply dropped it.

"How can this be?" I asked under my breath.

I grabbed the dagger and pulled my skirt up, sheathing it quickly.

"What *was* that?" I asked. "What happened to me out there?"

Mithraan was standing in the carriage's doorway, elbows bent, his hands holding onto the top of the door frame. "I don't know," he said softly, but I could tell from his evasive eyes that he had a theory. "Look—we need to leave this place. There may be others out here, and there are not enough guards left to protect you. I, too, am weakened after..."

After coming down the Onyx Rise, I thought.

"Weak?" I said, nodding toward the woods. "You didn't look weak out there. You moved faster than anyone I've ever seen."

"Your mind was playing tricks on you."

I shook my head. "I know what I saw." With that, I looked down at my hands. "What happened to me out there?"

"Lyrinn."

I looked at him. "What?"

"You have been through an ordeal these last few days, and you are imagining things. You lost your father. Your sister is missing. I told you, your mind is playing tricks on you, probably to shield you from your grief. It is a natural reaction to shock."

"But you saw it," I replied. "I know you did."

"I saw you holding out your hand," he said. "I saw that you were in danger. I placed myself between you and that...*man*. I would have killed him for the threats he made against you—but the king would gladly imprison me if I murdered a human so close to Domignon, bandit or no. It's a risk I cannot afford to take just now."

I was about to protest again, but instead, I gave in. He was probably right. The blade, my hands—all of it—was just my mind twisting inside me. My sadness, my rage, my confusion, all melding inside me to create a mess of emotions.

"Come," he said. "There is no driver left. I will take you the rest of the way on horseback."

He reached a hand out, and I hesitated only briefly before taking it and allowing him to guide me out of the carriage.

Mithraan led me to his horse and lifted me as if I weighed nothing, helping me onto its back. I was stunned to realize he had not been using a saddle.

The Fae approached the one remaining Guard and spoke a few words to him. The young man nodded, and I thought I heard him say something about seeing to the horses and the bodies.

A few seconds later, Mithraan leapt up behind me, his body pressed to mine.

"We will be in Domignon soon," he whispered, his lips close to my ear. "You will be given a warm, comfortable bed for the night. You will be safe for now, Lyrinn."

"And you?" I asked. "Where will you be?"

"Close," he said. "But not quite as close as I am now. Which, I suppose, is for the best. Taking in your scent is almost more than I can bear, my Lady."

For once, I didn't mind him bestowing the title on me. I allowed myself to sink back into his body, telling myself I was exhausted, cold. *Anything* to give myself an excuse to be closer to him.

The truth was, I was frightened of what I had seen. Either my mind really *was* playing tricks on me, or worse—my blood was tainted with some strange, terrifying magic.

Right now, I was a rudderless ship thrashing wildly at sea, and Mithraan's breath against my neck felt like a much-needed anchor.

CHAPTER NINETEEN

DOMIGNON, the city at the center of the realm bearing the same name, was a white-walled wonder of marble inlaid with exquisite, swirling designs of silver and mother of pearl.

My heart had calmed since our altercation with the bandits, and a quiet excitement flourished inside me as Mithraan and I neared the largest city in all of Kalemnar—and the wealthiest—at least, among mortal-kind.

Even in the moonlight, I could make out ornate walls rising up majestically. The silhouettes of tall, delicate towers stood out against the cloud-laced night sky like delicate saplings, and as we rode, I grew more and more eager to see them up close.

Having lived in Dúnbar all my life, I was accustomed to men and women in sweat-stained linen garb trudging up dusty cobblestone streets. But something told me the residents of Domignon would be more discerning about their appearances. I looked forward to wandering the streets and seeing for myself what sorts of denizens tread the cobblestones daily.

Two guards in braided silver chest-pieces and elegant helms topped with white feathers stood guard at the gates, pikes in hand.

With his eyes fixed on Mithraan, one of the guards bellowed, "Who comes this night to Domignon's sacred gates?"

"Mithraan of House Irion, Lord of Fairholme and Guard of the Onyx Rise," Mithraan replied, his tone oddly soft, almost soothing. "I am delivering Lyrinn Martel to King Caedmon. Her driver was killed on the road by bandits, and I chose to accompany her the rest of the way, to ensure her safety."

"Let her dismount, then," the guard said. "We will see to it that she is brought to the king. You may take your leave, stranger."

"I will not leave her," Mithraan said, a possessiveness in his voice that pleased me too much for my own good. "I, too, wish for an audience."

His body tensing, the guard took a step toward us, weapon held tightly in his fist. It almost looked comical, the ceremonial, tall spear too unwieldy to use effectively against a foe so close at hand.

He eyed Mithraan irritably at first, but as he approached, his expression quickly altered to one of confused apprehension.

"You're...a Fae," he said after a few moments. "Aren't you?"

At that, the other guard stepped forward, moving like a timid dog afraid that it might be hit for some sin or other.

"I am." Mithraan let out a low laugh. "Despite what you may have heard, we still exist—as does the Pact between human and Immortal realms. And that very Pact states that if I ask for an audience with a mortal lord, it will be granted."

The pike-bearer turned to look at his companion, who nodded gravely. Neither seemed particularly pleased about the truth of the matter, but both called out simultaneously to the guards inside the courtyard to open the gates.

A few seconds later, we rode into the city, my breath catching in my chest.

The broad street, paved with smooth marble of white and

gray, was elegant, so clean that the ground glistened like ice in the light of the street lamps. Lined with pleasant shops with gold-lettered signs, the place felt immediately welcoming, even seductive, in a way no street in the entire realm of Castelle ever had.

I fell in love instantly with Domignon, my eyes wandering from one marvelous sight to the next. The visual feast reminded me of the sensation of slipping a square of pure, exquisite chocolate onto my tongue after days of eating nothing but flavorless porridge.

Flickering lamps of silver and glass illuminated the shop windows as we proceeded up the street. Large windows revealed baked delicacies, toys, elegant clothing fit for kings and queens. Banners hung over the street, one announcing the weekend market, others advertising the upcoming Blood Trials and singing the praises of Prince Corym.

I wondered silently why there was no mention of Domignon's female Champion, Olivia Brimley. She had been named weeks ago, so why did she receive no credit while the prince was lauded for his skill?

But I quickly forgot the question as my eyes were lured this way and that, my mind flowing in a constant stream of pleasure at the sights and scents of the marble city.

I thought of Leta, of how much she would have adored this place. How well it would have suited her to be in a city as lovely as she was.

I thought of my father, too. Of how much happier we three could have been down here in this wonderland than in the constant, looming shadow of the Onyx Rise.

And then, as I looked around, my mother made her way into my mind. My mother, whom I'd never really known.

My mother, whose lovely face seemed reflected on every surface around us.

She was here, I thought. *She walked these streets. What possessed her to leave this place?*

The white-towered palace was situated at the city's far end, visible at the end of a winding road that led steeply uphill. As we rode in silence toward the vast complex of stone and slate, I found myself pulling away from Mithraan, stiffening in the saddle as if suddenly remembering that I should not lean into his body so casually.

He was still my enemy, after all. And with any luck, within a matter of days he would be sent away from this place, and I would be free of him at last.

As we neared the castle, a small group of mounted men wearing gleaming silver-white mail came trotting out of the gates toward us.

"I am Tobin, Captain of the King's Guard," the first of them said to us. He was middle-aged, with white hair and dark brows. His face was sternly lined, but kind. "I have been instructed to greet you, my Lady."

He appraised Mithraan, his eyes roaming up and down his form. "I never thought I would see the likes of you here," he said, and I couldn't figure out if his tone was hostile or impressed.

"Neither did I," Mithraan replied with a gleaming smile. "Yet here I am."

Tobin said nothing more at first, but turned his horse, and we followed him through the palace gates.

"The king will greet you upon your arrival," he told us after a few minutes, turning in his saddle to address us. "He will dictate where you stay."

"Thank you," I said softly, suddenly wracked with disquietude. For the first time, it struck me that I had no idea how to behave around royalty. No idea what I was supposed to do when I met the king.

Curtsy? Avert my eyes? Unfortunately, at the moment, it felt like my most likely reaction would be to double over with terror-induced nausea.

I was grateful when we soon found ourselves in a pretty courtyard whose walls crawled with green vines and delicate white flowers. To one side was an elegant stable containing a multitude of horses.

"You may leave your mount here," Tobin told us. "He will be well looked after."

"He should be set free at the city gates," Mithraan told him when we had dismounted. "He needs to return to his home."

"You have my word," Tobin replied, gesturing to one of his men before leading us through a broad door in the castle's wall.

"The king awaits you in the throne room," Tobin said nonchalantly.

"Before we see him, I was wondering," I replied. "That is, it's been some time since we last had a chance to change our clothing. Do you think—"

"I'm afraid there is no time for that. The king asked that you be brought to him immediately."

For the briefest moment, I felt Mithraan's hand on my back as though warning me to keep my thoughts to myself.

I wasn't sure why he was being so quiet, so compliant. He was a born leader, not one to go along for the ride while a human led him around.

Then again, it wouldn't help his cause to be rude to the king's men. As far as I understood, this was to be the first time King Caedmon had ever lain his eyes on a Fae—which meant Mithraan would have to tread lightly.

Tobin brought us to a large room with round, stained glass windows decorating its walls. What looked like two gilt thrones, one of which was occupied, sat perched on a dais at the far end. Several guards stood against each wall, armed and ready to fight as they narrowed their eyes at the Fae in their midst.

Mithraan, meanwhile, seemed entirely unperturbed as he locked his eyes on the man dressed in red and gold seated in one of the two thrones.

As we approached, the king nodded to us, then rose to his feet. With a surprisingly spirited gait, he leapt down three stairs to find himself on the same level with us.

He looked forty or so years old, with graying hair and broad shoulders. His stomach was a little round, his cheeks red, and his eyes were bright blue as the sky on a cloudless day.

He eyed me cautiously, his gaze moving from the top of my head to my feet, then back up again. As he stepped closer—too close—I tried not to tighten or flinch. He reached out, tucked my hair behind my ear, and studied my seared flesh, seemingly unbothered by the scars.

"So," he said with a smile, "you're real after all, Lyrinn."

I nodded. "I am...your Grace," I said, my chin low. *Why wouldn't I be?*

"And the Fae who came with you apparently is, as well."

I pulled my eyes up to look at Mithraan, whose chin was also pulled down. But his eyes were locked on the king's.

"How did you come to be here?" King Caedmon asked Mithraan. "How did you leave Tíria?"

"I suspect you know the answer, your Grace," Mithraan replied. His tone was sweet, even charming, but I could almost taste a bitter hint of poison in the last two words.

The king glared at him, and for a moment, I thought he was going to eject Mithraan on the spot. But instead, he chuckled.

"If I knew, I would not have asked," he said. "They say the Breath of the Fae still cascades down the Onyx Rise. Only this morning, a Sight-Hawk confirmed it for us, in fact."

I shot Mithraan a sideways glance. He had told me the

Breath had parted for him just as it had for me, and I had known it was a lie the second he'd said the words, if only from the playful glint in his eye.

But now, I found myself wondering if he was about to reveal the whole truth.

"There is magic deep in my blood," he told the king, "despite what was done to my kind so long ago. And though it weakens me to call upon my ancient Gifts, I find myself able to do so in times of need. I was able to part the mist just long enough to descend, your Grace."

"Times of need?" the king repeated. "What, may I ask, was it that made you feel this was such a time? Why have you come all this way, when your friends are trapped in Tíria?"

Mithraan raised his chin now and leveled the king with a look that would have brought most men to their knees. But King Caedmon didn't so much as flinch.

"The Blood Trials approach. My Ancestral Sight means that I have an understanding of the Trials that no living mortal possesses. I would like to offer my services to help train your Champions."

The king bowed his head slightly and said, "I thank you, Lord Mithraan, for the offer. But you needn't have come. My son the prince is in good hands, and training with the best fighters and minds that Domignon has to offer. You are free to return to your homeland."

I felt Mithraan tighten beside me. Saw his fingers curl into tight fists, then release.

The king didn't mention Olivia Brimley, and who would train her, and once again, I wondered what had become of her.

"I have also offered Lyrinn Martel my protection," Mithraan said. "And I intend to maintain that offer until the Trials have passed."

"That is curious," the king said, a note of quiet anger in his voice. "May I ask why you would do such a thing?"

Mithraan's jaw tightened. "She ventured into my lands a few days ago. You are, of course, aware that such an ascent has not been accomplished by a mortal in many centuries."

"I am. But I fail to see why you insisted on following her here. It was I who summoned her, and I do not recall asking for a Fae escort."

"Had I not chosen to escort Lyrinn," Mithraan said, "she may well have been killed when bandits attacked the carriage and your men. With respect, your Grace, your guards did little to protect her."

At that, the king went silent for a moment, then flicked a finger, summoning Tobin to his side.

The two exchanged a few whispered sentences, then the king turned back to us. "Since you are here, Fae," he said to Mithraan, his voice chilly, "I cannot turn you away. It may be an age since last I saw one of your kind in these lands, but I am well-versed in the ancient laws."

Mithraan bowed his head in polite acknowledgment, and I found myself wondering when the king had ever met a Fae before, given that Tíria had been cut off for so many centuries.

But something else was nagging at my mind, too—something far more pressing.

"Your Grace," I said before the king had a chance to end the conversation. "I need to ask you about my sister."

"Ah, yes," King Caedmon replied. "I heard that she has gone missing."

I nodded. "Before he was...killed," I said, swallowing in hopes of stabilizing my quaking voice, "my father told me some men had taken her. He seemed to think she would be safe, but... if I may...I was wondering if your guards or the Scouts had heard anything."

"Not yet, unfortunately," he said. His voice was kind and swollen with sympathy. "But they will continue the search until she is found, my dear. And—I am very sorry to have heard about your father."

"Thank you, your Grace."

"Now, it is late, and you must be exhausted after your ordeal. My servants will take you both to your chambers. Lyrinn, you will sleep in the East Wing."

I glanced at Mithraan, wondering what would become of him.

"Don't worry about your companion," the king said, reading my thoughts. "I owe him a great deal, if only for looking after you so well. He will be given an exquisite room—one fit for royalty."

"I thank you, your Grace," Mithraan said with a bow of his head. I wasn't sure if I was imagining the vague sarcasm in his tone. The Fae and I exchanged a look, and in his eyes, I was certain I detected a hint of warning.

As the guards moved toward me, I wasn't sure if I only imagined the deep, velvety voice that spoke to my mind.

We will go our separate ways for now—but I intend to keep my eyes on you, Lyrinn Martel.

CHAPTER TWENTY

As promised, two of the king's men guided me toward a distant wing of the palace.

Mithraan, meanwhile, was led in the opposite direction, and it took all my strength not to turn and watch him go.

No doubt I'll see him soon enough, I thought. *He never fails to show up when I least expect him.*

When we reached a set of elegant, carved wooden double doors and the guards pushed them open, I was greeted by an enormous bed chamber. Tall windows at the room's far end opened to reveal a courtyard below, a cool breeze billowing in through diaphanous white curtains. A massive bed was draped in white linens, and to one side of the room, a door led into a bathing room of white marble streaked with gray veins, a large silver tub sitting at its center.

A wardrobe stood open to one side of the bedroom, filled with dresses of every possible color—all in what appeared to be my exact size. As I approached to examine the garments, I even noted a few pairs of trousers and matching velvet or silk tunics.

Someone had not only anticipated my arrival, but had

managed to inform the king's servants of my measurements and even my tastes.

I was beginning to think the Fae were not the only ones capable of magic.

"My Lady," one of my escorts said. "Will you be needing anything more this evening?"

I glanced toward a table by the window, laid with bread, cheese, water, and wine.

"Nothing at all," I said with a smile and a nod. "Thank you very much."

With that, the men left, closing the doors gently.

"How on earth did this happen to me?" I asked under my breath as I spun around, my arms outstretched to the enormous room. For the briefest of moments, I allowed myself a frisson of amusement at the absurdity of my situation. "Why on earth do they want me—*me*—here so badly?"

The only answer I could think of—the one link to the king—was my mother. He had not mentioned her during our brief conversation, but in his eyes I had seen a look of familiarity and fondness, though we had never met before this night.

Well, my mother may have known the king, but that did not mean *I* was anything special. Regardless of her brief time spent in the company of royalty, I was still just a girl from Dúnbar. A young woman who drank ale in a tavern and read for pleasure, who scoffed at men and their usual pursuits, and who had no patience for most girls and their obsession with pretty dresses.

What could I possibly have to offer this realm?

With no answer to give, I ventured to the open window only to see a lamp flare to life in a room across the large courtyard from where I stood.

A figure made its way to the window, pushing it open and peering out into the night.

I gasped when I realized I was looking at Mithraan, who perused the courtyard below before his eyes landed on me.

He pressed his palms to the window frame, his muscles taut as his eyes flared bright. As we watched one another, he relaxed his arms and pulled off his tunic to reveal his sculpted, exquisite body. I flushed when I saw him shirtless, reminded that this was not the first time.

And yet, I still couldn't say if what I had seen last night at the inn was real or imagined.

Mithraan lifted his chin, pulling his eyes up to look at the sky.

I, too, glanced up, as much to avoid ogling him as to see what he was looking at. But all I saw were clouds moving slowly across the moon, and the occasional star twinkling in the far distance.

When I pulled my eyes back to the Fae, his silhouette had altered. Above his shoulders were strange, silvery shapes that looked at first like two broadswords jutting out from his shoulders.

But as they began to spread, I realized what I was seeing. Gleaming in the firelight of his room, translucent, beautiful, magical...was a set of perfect feathered wings, each so large that I couldn't see them in their entirety when they were fully extended.

I had heard in my youth that some Fae could fly, but I had always assumed it to be a made-up detail from the folk tales. It had seemed too improbable. Besides, having met a few Fae by now, I had seen no evidence of wings. No concealed lumps on their shoulder blades, nothing to indicate such a gift.

Yet I had seen talons jutting out from Mithraan's hands when he fought the Grimpers. The sharp claws of a bird of prey, sharp as daggers and twice as deadly.

I had no doubt that his wings, delicate and powerful at

once, were real—and I longed to see him transform further, to leave his Fae body behind and reveal his other form to me.

I was still staring when a gentle knock sounded at my door. Mithraan, seeming to hear it, moved away from the window, disappearing into the depths of his bed chamber.

Reluctantly, I pulled the windows closed and headed over to answer the door, thinking it must be a guard come to deliver a message for the king.

As it turned out, I couldn't have been more wrong.

CHAPTER TWENTY-ONE

A YOUNG MAN of nineteen or twenty stood in the doorway. He was tall—several inches taller than me, at least—with light brown hair and intense blue-green eyes the color of the sea. He wore a white tunic, gray leather trousers, and tall riding boots.

Something about him was deeply familiar, though I was certain we had never met.

"Hello," I said, the word sounding more like a question than a greeting. "May I help you?"

The young man looked me up and down, then, pressing a hand against the door frame, said, "I was wondering if I could help *you*, actually. Is there anything you need, my Lady?"

I quickly assessed him. He didn't look like a servant, and he wasn't dressed in the armor of a guard. Was he some sort of squire, maybe?

"I...nothing at all," I replied with a forced smile, trying to imagine how Leta would behave in this moment, confronted by a young man so handsome he looked like he'd been custom-designed. "I have everything I could possibly need, thank you."

The young man straightened up and gave me a quick bow. "Good. I suppose I'll see you in the morning, then."

"In the morning?"

"At breakfast in the dining hall," he replied, spinning away and striding down the corridor, waving a hand in the air. Just as he made it to the stone staircase, he turned and called out, "Wait—I just realized I didn't tell you my name."

"No," I replied with a puzzled smile. "You didn't."

"Corym," he said. "Good night, Lyrinn."

With a quickly flashed grin, he disappeared down the stairs.

My heart instantly began hammering in my chest, a coat of perspiration beading on my brow as I backed into the room and closed the door.

Corym.

The Prince and Champion of Domignon.

Of course.

I had often seen his painted portrait in Dúnbar. But a painting and an actual face were two very different matters, and it seemed the artists had not done him justice.

He was far better-looking in person—and far more approachable—than I would ever have suspected from those stuffy portraits.

I pressed my back to the door, breathing hard.

Corym was handsome, to be sure. And from the looks of it, he had a playful sense of humor. But if I'd known he was coming, I would have changed my clothing. I would have bathed. *I must look awful. I...*

I shook my head, letting out a brief laugh.

The prince had done it deliberately. He had known of my arrival and ambushed me in my natural state so he could assess me honestly. And I couldn't blame him for it—I would have done the same.

I moved toward the window again, thinking about what I might say to Corym in the morning. How I could possibly bring myself to have a casual conversation with such a man—

a man the entirety of Kalemnar worshiped as some sort of demigod.

In spite of the sadness that washed over me in waves when I thought of my father or Leta, I couldn't help but smile again. My father would have been so proud to know his daughter had made it to Domignon—not only to the capital, but to the palace itself to dine with the prince and king of all of Kalemnar.

If only Father could have been here with me, I murmured under my breath, wandering over to pull the windows open once again. *Maybe he could have answered some of the questions excavating their way through my mind.*

I looked across the courtyard toward Mithraan's room. The fire still glowed within, but I saw no shadows, no flicker of movement to indicate whether the Fae was inside. Perhaps he'd flown off into the night on his glorious wings.

I told myself it was no matter to me, that my focus lay elsewhere.

This beautiful place was my future.

My home.

I slept deeply that night, my mind invaded by vivid dreams. I saw my father trapped in a swirling, dark mist, his hand reaching fruitlessly for my own. Leta, somewhere in the distance, calling out to me.

The dreams weren't unpleasant or nightmarish, though perhaps they should have been. Instead, they fed some part of my soul I had never entirely realized was starving. Despite his ensnarement, I could hear my father speaking soft words of reassurance. Leta, too, comforted me, telling me she had come to no harm.

After a time, I dreamt of a figure flying through the sky on silver wings, his eyes searching the lands below. For what, I couldn't say.

I awoke feeling oddly refreshed, like I knew without a shadow of a doubt that the answers I needed would soon come to me.

I had just slipped on a blue dress from the wardrobe when a knock sounded at the door. Studying myself only briefly in the mirror, I determined I looked decent enough for whatever company had come calling.

I pulled the door open to see a young woman dressed in a gray linen uniform. Her cheeks were rosy pink, her hair twisted around her head in a series of impressive braids.

"My name is Anira," she said, gesturing toward the inside of the chamber. "I've come to assist you, my Lady."

"Assist me with what?" I asked.

"Your hair and...anything else you should need before breakfast."

Relieved not to have to rely on my own poor hair styling skills, I told her to come in. I walked over to grab hold of a chair that sat by the window. Pulling it closer to the bed, I seated myself, unsure whether I was supposed to issue Anira orders or simply wait for her to make a move.

"I thought perhaps a crown of braids like my own," she said, taking my hair in hand. "For the newest Noble-lady of Domignon."

I pulled away, twisting to look up at her. I must have appeared a little fierce, because she recoiled, an expression of fear in her eyes.

"I didn't mean to offend," she said.

"You didn't offend me," I told her. "It's only that I'm not noble—and I'm certainly not from Domignon. I'm only in this place because the king summoned me here."

"I'm sorry," she replied, bowing her head. "I had heard that

—" She stopped speaking and bit her lip, then smiled. "Well, you know how servants can be, my Lady. Gossip circulates, stories expand to legend, and before you know it, entire fictions have been crafted that have no basis in reality."

"I do know all about that," I said with an attempt at a friendly smile.

I sat back and allowed her to take hold of my hair once again.

"All the staff are talking about you," Anira said. "They—we —were so excited about your arrival. When we learned who you were..."

I tightened at those words. "Wait—who am I, exactly?" I asked, struggling to keep my tone sweet and friendly.

"The daughter of Alessia," she said. "Who was here many years ago, when the king was young. He was smitten with your mother, they say. But I suppose that never came to anything, since she ran off to marry that vile..."

Anira stopped, seemingly realizing she was about to say something disparaging about my father.

"My father was a good man," I said, my tone icy.

"Of course, yes. I'm sorry, my Lady. It's only—I couldn't imagine turning down a future king—especially one so powerful."

"No," I replied. "Neither can I, really." Admiration swept through my mind for the woman I never knew. Leaving a king behind in favor of a blacksmith showed impressive character—and that my parents must have loved one another deeply.

I relaxed a little when I asked, "What else do you know about my mother?"

"I remember hearing about her when I was younger—about how beautiful she was, how perfect and clever. I was just so excited to hear they had found you. It's like a miracle. Your mother must be so excited to know her daughter ended up here."

"My mother died in a fire when I was very young, so no—she isn't excited."

Anira stopped what she was doing and eyed me in the mirror, a sudden, aggressive pity in her eyes that forced me to look away. I did not like being pitied, sincere as the sentiment might be.

"I'm so sorry," she said softly. "I didn't know. Goodness, I've really put my foot in it, haven't I?"

I shrugged, attempting to rid myself of my discomfort. "I barely knew her," I said. "My sister and I were raised by our father."

"Ah," Anira replied, sealing her mouth as though afraid she'd say yet another insensitive thing if she was fool enough to speak.

Her silence didn't last long, though. After a pause, she said, "Your sister...is she..."

"My sister is missing," I said curtly. "She disappeared the night my father was killed. The night the king's men came for me. Tell me, is there anything else about my disastrous existence you'd like to know?"

Anira was on the verge of tears by now. "No, my Lady," she said. "I apologize...again."

She seemed like a nice girl, pleasant and polite, and I knew I was being a little cruel by being so direct.

But there was no sense in sugar-coating or lying. The truth was, I was alone in the world. The king, the prince, this place—they were my greatest hope for any sort of meaningful future.

But in the meantime, I was, without a doubt, a walking disaster.

"What do you know about the prince's Blood-Gifts?" I asked, watching Anira in the mirror.

Her eyes went wide with gratitude and she smiled. Finally, a subject she could discuss without the potential of wretched awkwardness.

"They say he is as Gifted as the ancient Fae lords," she said. "Which I suppose makes sense, given that many of his Gifts *came* from the Fae. Do you know—when humans show extraordinary skills—speed, strength, intellect, an ability to predict the future...they say it all comes from ancient trysts between human and Fae? Rumor has it that our most talented all have Fae blood running through their veins."

"Seems like the sort of rumor a Fae would start," I replied with a smile, thinking of Mithraan and his stubborn insistence that his kind were superior to ours.

Annoyingly, it was a claim I could scarcely dispute. The Fae were clever, their Gifts plentiful and extraordinary. It would be folly to claim humans as their equals.

Not that I would ever have admitted as much to him.

"When the last Blood Trials were won," Anira continued, "the Taker gave the Fae Gifts to the human Champions, as is the rule. For a thousand years and from generation to generation, those Gifts have developed and evolved. The prince is basically an Immortal now."

"An Immortal?" I asked, surprised. "Are you telling me he'll live for thousands of years?"

"Oh," Anira laughed. "I couldn't say." She leaned in close and spoke low, as if confiding a dark secret. "But I've heard he's older than he looks, if that means anything."

I pondered that for a moment, unsure what to do with the information. Was he a year older? Twenty-five years? What?

"Anyhow," Anira said with a sigh, "he's handsome. And he can cast so, so many spells. I've seen him summon flame and ice, but they say he is saving the best for the Trials."

I went silent for a moment, remembering the sight of

Mithraan with his exquisite wings. Gleaming silver appendages that signaled freedom, power, and a strength I had never witnessed in another being.

For all the prince's so-called Gifts, I wondered if Corym was capable of anything so beautiful.

"I wonder how powerful he really is," I said softly, more to myself than to Anira. "I wonder if we will ever see the extent of his strength."

"The prince, you mean?"

I shook my head and smiled. "Sorry. Yes, of course. The prince."

It was a lie, albeit a small one. The unfortunate truth was that I was far more interested in Mithraan's skill than any mortal's.

"I think we will," she replied with a broad grin. "Just you wait."

A few minutes later, Anira told me she was finished. I thanked her, rose to my feet, and watched her leave.

A quick glance in the mirror told me she had done a fine job, taking care to cover the worst of my scars with thick, twisting braids.

She was capable of *some* modicum of discretion, at least.

CHAPTER TWENTY-TWO

I FOUND the dining chamber empty except for two guards stationed at each door. A long table stood at the room's center, draped in a white cloth and covered in an assortment of delicious-looking fruit, bread, chocolate pastries, and other delicacies.

I turned to a guard and, in my most authoritative voice, said, "I thought I was to break my fast with the prince and the king."

The guard looked apologetic when he replied, "They are otherwise occupied this morning, I'm afraid. But I believe one of the king's servants left a note for you, my Lady."

He gestured to the centerpiece, and for the first time, I noticed a small white envelope sitting on the table, my name scrawled tidily on its surface.

I opened it and extracted the elegant note inside that read,

Lyrinn Martel:

You are cordially invited to
a Celebration in your honor
In Domignon's Grand Ballroom

this Evening at Sunset.
A suitable dress will be provided for you.
Please arrive
when the sun meets the horizon.

I stared at the note. *Celebration in my honor?*

Why, exactly, was I being honored?

"My Lady," the guard said quietly. I realized then that I was standing frozen, my eyes locked on the note. "Would you like some food?"

I nodded, pulling out a chair and seating myself. "Yes, please," I said.

The guard reached over and pulled at a delicate golden chain that seemed to emerge from the stone wall. A few seconds later, a young woman in a servant's dress strode into the room, curtseyed at me, then proceeded to load a plate full of various delicacies.

"Do you know what's happening tonight?" I asked her.

"Only that the ballroom is already being decorated," she replied. "They say it's the event of the century."

"What is?"

The servant shrugged. "I'm sorry, m'lady. I don't know."

Against my will, I found myself longing for Mithraan's presence, for him to stalk over to me and whisper an explanation for the invitation into my ear.

I nodded again. "And the...Fae? The one staying in the castle? Do you know where he is?"

"He is enjoying breakfast in his suite, m'lady."

I fought to mask my disappointment when I said, "Oh."

Of course he didn't care to see me. He had come to Domignon for other reasons, after all. And now that his mission was more or less accomplished, I was of no use to him anymore.

"It is my understanding that he is invited to tonight's festivities, however," the servant added.

My heart lightened a little with the revelation. As grateful as I was to be safe here in Domignon, the simple truth was that I didn't know anyone. And though Mithraan drove me mad at times, I couldn't deny that his presence, in its twisted way, was a comfort. I felt safe when he was near...though, if I were to be fully honest with myself, it was something far more enticing than personal safety that drew me to him.

After I'd finished eating, I excused myself and headed outside to wander the castle grounds for a little, exploring a few of the well-groomed gardens filled with perfectly trimmed shrubs and flowering trees.

I seated myself on a long stone bench and watched as two swans swam lazily around a large pond speckled with lily pads. In the distance, I could see men and women strolling about, dressed in elegant clothing that told me they were not servants of the king's, but most likely wealthy guests, here for tonight's mysterious affair.

As I watched them move around, I imagined their lives of luxury and privilege. I couldn't help but wonder if any of them had ever known a day of hardship.

Wrapped up in my vaguely hostile thoughts, I didn't notice the figure approaching from my left to seat himself at the far end of the bench.

"Good morning, my Lady," a deep voice said.

I turned to see Mithraan watching me, his eyes unnaturally bright in the sunlight.

Something inside me ignited when my eyes landed on his. It was as though I had forgotten something of his beauty overnight—forgotten the effect his face had on my body and mind. His cheekbones looked more defined than ever in the dappled sunlight that pierced through the tree limbs dancing overhead. He was a being of splendor, grace, and beauty, and my pulse throbbed just to be near him.

A flash of memory came to me then—the image of the Fae standing in his window, his wings spreading behind him.

But I saw no trace of them now. No hint that they had ever been there.

Perhaps it had been nothing more than one of his tricks.

"Good morning," I replied, forcing an artificial chill into my voice to counteract the heat surging through my veins.

Mithraan smiled, pulling his eyes to the pond to watch the swans. "Beautiful creatures, aren't they?" he asked. "Not the most elegant flyers, but in the water, they're wonders."

I nodded silently before asking, "What birds are the best flyers, would you say?"

He looked at me again, his smile fading. "No need to be coy about it. You may ask me about my wings, Lady Lyrinn."

"Don't call me that," I hissed.

With a chuckle, he replied, "You won't last very long here if you find yourself objecting so vehemently to the title. It is what you are now. You are the daughter of a lady. That makes you one."

"My mother, a lady?" I asked, scoffing. "*Hardly.* No 'lady' would go running off with a blacksmith, for one thing—and more power to her for it."

"I wouldn't be so certain of that. People have done stranger things for love."Mithraan eased closer when he said, "But since you seem curious, I should tell you that I have learned a few things. I know nothing of your mother's ancestry, but I did hear some servants chittering about her. It seems she is of a noble bloodline—which explains why you came to be dragged through Kalemnar and brought to this godforsaken place."

"Servants like to gossip," I said, recalling my conversation with Anira. "They invent stories for their own amusement.

That's all it is. My father would have told Leta and me if we have nobility in our ancestry."

"Fair enough," Mithraan said with a shrug. "Well, perhaps I should leave you to enjoy your day."

"Your wings," I blurted out, reluctant to let him go just yet.

"What of them?" he asked without looking at me.

"Are you..."

"A shape-shifter?" he asked. "Yes, I am. I can turn into many things, but my favorite form is that of a silver eagle."

"Is that how you escaped Tíria? Did you fly over the mist?"

He shook his head. "No. One cannot, or many of us would have left Tíria years ago. The mist—the Breath, as mortal-kind likes to call it—rises as well as falling. I had no choice but to slice it apart temporarily—to cleave a sort of tunnel to walk through. I did, however, fly once I found myself in Castelle. It's how I managed to catch your carriage without a horse of my own."

"I see. And how, exactly, did you cleave your tunnel?"

"A magician never reveals his secrets," he said with an impish grin.

I wanted to ask more questions—so *many* questions—but I refused to give him the satisfaction of knowing I found him fascinating.

"You met the prince last night," he said, slipping closer to me.

"How do you know?"

"I was watching you through the window when he came to your door."

"Oh. Right." I flushed, not having realized Mithraan could see quite so much of my suite from his own. "I did meet him briefly, yes."

"And? What did you think?"

I winced slightly as I looked away and said, "He's very...handsome."

"He gets that from the Fae's Blood-Gifts in his ancestry."

"Of course he does," I said with a snicker.

"Do you trust him?"

I scowled. What sort of question was that? And what business was it of his?

"We only spoke briefly," I replied. "I couldn't tell you if I trust him."

"Hardly a ringing endorsement, is it?"

"I only mean that I don't know him properly. I suspect we will remedy that soon enough." I paused for a moment then asked, "Do you know anything about this celebration tonight?"

Mithraan tensed. "I know the king intends to make an announcement." He moved closer still, eyeing me as he said, "And I know you will look exquisite, just as you do now."

My cheeks heated as I told myself to reject his flattery. *More devious Fae charm.* "The king has been generous."

"You deserve every gift he grants you, Lyrinn."

I twisted around, lowered my chin, and glared at him. "Why are you being kind to me?"

"Kind? Kindness has nothing to do with my observation of simple fact."

"You have teased me for days," I said. "Now you're telling me how exquisite I am, and that I deserve gifts from kings. What are you playing at?"

Mithraan pushed himself to his feet. "I suppose I wanted you to know of my admiration before we part ways for good. Truth be told, I do not know if I will remain at the palace for long...and I would hate to part, knowing I had never told you just how lovely I find you."

With that, he bowed his head slightly.

When he turned to walk away, I found myself gasping for

breath as though he had just delivered a vicious blow to my chest.

I tried and failed all afternoon to rest in my bed, rising after a few hours of tossing and turning only to hear a knock at the door.

I opened it to find that Anira had come by once again to prepare me for the evening's party. She carried with her a white gown of silk and lace, which she laid on the bed as I gawked at the garment.

"What is that?" I asked, my voice tight with a dose of panic.

"Your dress for this evening, my Lady," she said. "Isn't it lovely?"

"It is," I concurred. "But why is it so...That is, it looks like..."

"A wedding gown?" Anira laughed, then shrugged. "Don't worry—this style of dress is worn every thousand years in Domignon, near the time of the Blood Trials. It's a tradition older, even, than wedding garb. Come—let's try it on you."

The dress looked even more splendid on my body than on the bed, much to my surprise. Anira fastened its laces tight, its bodice narrowing my waist and accentuating my chest in a way no garment ever had. From the neck down, I felt as though I was looking at someone entirely different from myself—a woman, rather than the girl I had always been.

As I stepped toward the mirror, I noticed for the first time that delicate lines of red stitching wove their way along the dress's seams and elsewhere, running over the entire garment like a series of hair-thin veins.

"You're wondering about the red?" Anira said. "It represents bloodlines."

"My bloodline," I repeated. My mysterious mother. "I don't

know anything about my ancestry, as it turns out. But I don't suppose that matters." With a forced smile, I changed the topic. "What are they saying in the servants' quarters about tonight?"

"Nothing, really," Anira replied with a small shrug. "They say it's a celebration to mark the official naming of the Champions."

"I thought the prince and Olivia Brimley were the chosen two," I said. "As far away as Castelle, we heard about it weeks ago."

"Yes," Anira said, seeming to mull her words carefully. "But..."

"But what?" I asked, a hint of impatience taking over my voice as a feeling of dread seized at my chest.

"Olivia Brimley was selected, but never in an official capacity. I suppose that's the point of tonight—to give her the proper title."

"Well then, I'm sure we'll hear the official word tonight," I said, breathing a long sigh of relief. *Good. Mithraan's unhinged theory is clearly far from reality—Domignon has its female Champion.* "And I'm sure Olivia and the prince will win, and go on to wed."

"Oh, they'll win, no question about it." Anira leaned in and spoke under her breath. "They say the Champions from the other realms are appalling. No real Blood-Gifts to be found among the lot of them. It will be a slaughter."

She seemed to delight in the notion of a massacre of innocents, and I found myself shuddering with horror at her words.

Anira seemed to sense my disgust, because she hastened to add, "Now, let's get your hair done. We'll add some lip stain and line your lovely eyes, as well. I promise, my Lady—you will be remarkable when you walk into that ballroom tonight."

I hesitated before saying, "There's one thing—about my

hair..." I didn't want to confess my insecurities, so instead I bit the inside of my cheek and searched for my next words.

"Your hair will be tied up loosely," she assured me. "It will flow down your neck and shoulders—and cover your ears, if you'd like."

With a nod, I said, "Yes. I'd like that very much."

CHAPTER TWENTY-THREE

At seven o'clock precisely, the doors to the ballroom opened and I strode in, chin raised, legs trembling beneath me.

The room teemed with strangers dressed in elegant gowns or silk tunics. But to my surprise, no one else was clothed in what Anira had said was the traditional garb of the Blood Trials.

I felt uneasy and out of place in my flowing white gown, its red veins slipping along its surface as though pulsing in synchronicity with my pounding heart. Eyes flicked to mine as I walked by, and guests leaned in to whisper to one another, no doubt assessing Domignon's newest acquisition.

For too long, my natural habitat had consisted of concealment in my long cloak. I had been a shadow on Dúnbar's streets, like the mist that had slipped down the Onyx Rise for so many years. But now, I was floating off to sea with no tether, nothing to hang onto, no one to guide me.

As I stared nervously out at the crowd, a hand reached for my arm and a deep voice said, "You look beautiful, my Lady."

I turned to see Prince Corym, his eyes moving down my body in a way that wasn't entirely unpleasant—but nor was it particularly appropriate for a man who was intended for another woman.

Still, I smiled and thanked him—not only for the compliment, but for standing between myself and the abundance of watchful eyes that rendered me self-conscious to the point of nausea.

"Thank you," I said with an awkward smile, his compliment taking me by surprise.

Be like Leta, I told myself. *Be charming. Make him grateful to be in your presence.*

The prince was wearing a waistcoat and trousers of white silk. Like my dress, its stitching was deep red.

"You look...handsome," I added, using every ounce of my strength to try and appear relaxed. "Your clothing is very well-tailored."

"I see that we have been outfitted to match," he said with a grin. "White is so pristine, so...*clean.* Not at all an indicator of the horrors to come. I suppose that's the whole point, isn't it? To forget how vicious the Trials can be while we drink ourselves silly."

I smiled, glancing around the room. "Olivia Brimley," I said. "Is she here?"

"Oh, probably," the prince replied with a quick shrug. "She was invited, of course."

Relief assaulted me again. *His co-Champion will be here. Good.*

Olivia Brimley, too, would likely be dressed in white. She would no doubt be lovely and impressive, the jewel of the realm.

"They say the Trials are a great honor," I replied. "But sometimes I do wonder..."

"Wonder what?" the prince asked, one eyebrow raised.

I wanted to tell him I thought something about the Trials

seemed barbaric and cruel, not to mention unnecessary. But if I said the words out loud, I could offend the prince, or worse, the king.

"Nothing," I finally said with an uncomfortable smirk.

It seemed the prince sensed my discomfort, because he quickly shifted the subject. "You resemble your father, you know."

My heart leapt in my chest. I had tried not to think too much about my father since my arrival—and, more than that, to push away memories of my last moments with him as his powerful body disintegrated to ash.

The thought of it was enough to make me want to collapse in a heap and weep until my eyes were parched of tears.

"You knew my father?" I asked.

He nodded. "Not personally, but I've seen an old portrait of him. I was told he was an apprentice smith here in Domignon when he met your mother." Something in his tone was tense, as if he was trying to hold back an emotion, to imprison it inside his mind.

"Do you know anything about their courtship?"

He shook his head. "I'm afraid not," he said. "But perhaps one day you can corner my father and ask him. I believe he knows a little more."

I nodded nervously. The thought of asking the king anything was slightly terrifying. After all, I had already imposed upon him by inquiring about Leta.

"I—I don't suppose you've heard anything about my sister?" I asked the prince. "Have you discovered where she was taken?"

Corym opened his mouth to reply, but just then, a bell began to chime somewhere in the distance. He took my arm gently and whispered, "My parents have arrived. We must greet them."

As the crowd parted, the king walked in through a door at the ballroom's far end. A slight woman with blond hair and blue eyes—the queen, I assumed—had her arm interlocked in his own, her chin held high. Both were dressed in silk of deep crimson. The queen wore a flowing gown, the king a fitted tunic and trousers tucked into tall, black leather boots. He smiled through his thick beard when his gaze landed on Corym.

The king's eyes darted to and fro, taking in every guest as he passed them. Picking up their pace, he and his wife made their way directly toward us.

"Lyrinn," the king bellowed when he was near, "may I introduce you to her Royal Highness, Queen Malleen of Domignon?"

I curtseyed awkwardly, lowering myself in a weak attempt to display reverence.

"Your Grace," I said.

"Ah," she replied. Her eyes assessed me when I stood up straight, judgmental but not harsh. "So, this is Alessia's daughter. Yes. You do look strong." She reached a hand out and stroked it over my left ear and my neck before pulling back and smiling.

I struggled to keep my brow from creasing as I stared at her, trying to figure out why she was appraising me like a prize steer.

Normally, had someone reached out and stroked a finger along my scars, I would have snapped at them like a wild animal. But the rules were different for kings and queens.

Had she stripped me naked in that moment, I would have had little recourse but to accept it.

"Have you come into your Blood-Gifts yet?" the queen asked.

I wondered why she would assume I would *ever* come into any Gifts. But instead of daring to ask, I simply shook my head. "No, your Grace," I said.

"You will." She pressed in close and laid a delicate hand on my arm. "After tonight, your Gifts will come."

I looked at her questioningly. *After tonight? What's so special about this evening?*

"Thank you, your Grace," I said, stumbling over the words as I curtseyed once again.

The king and queen finally made their way across the room to seat themselves at a long table and watch the guests mingling, and I turned to the prince, hoping to gain some insight into what had just happened.

"I need to go say hello to a few people," he said apologetically, his eyes roving over the crowd. "Will you be all right on your own?"

I nodded. "Just one thing—have you spotted your other Champion yet?"

The prince smiled and nodded across the ballroom to a young woman dressed in a silver gown who was watching us intently, a scowl on her lips. "Olivia Brimley," he said. "The most Gifted young woman in this realm. But here's hoping that will all change tonight."

He touched my back briefly before making his way across the large room through a sea of jostling figures, and once again I was left with more questions than answers.

I wandered the room for a time, reaching for a glass of sparkling wine whenever one was within my reach, if only to have something to occupy my hand.

It was when I'd already consumed three full glasses that I spotted Mithraan across the ballroom, dressed entirely in black. His amber eyes stood out like beacons against the backdrop of colorful gowns, and my breath caught in my chest when he began to move toward me.

I squirmed in place, hunting for an escape route. But all

doorways were blocked with guests, so I froze and awaited my fate.

When the Fae lord was ten or so feet away, the same bell I had heard earlier began to clang loudly. The chatter ground to a halt, and an echoing voice called out, "King Caedmon wishes to make an announcement!"

I turned my attention to a dais at the front of the chamber where the king and queen now stood, Corym at their side. I looked around, curious as to why Olivia Brimley wasn't with them.

I spotted her on the far side of the room. Her eyes were locked on the king, a look of pure hatred on her face.

When I pulled my gaze back away, I noticed Mithraan staring at Olivia, a wary expression in his eyes.

The king cleared his throat and began to speak.

"Honored guests, a time of great excitement is upon us all! The Blood Trials are coming." He clapped his hands together and added, "But I don't need to tell any of you that."

The crowd chuckled and guffawed as though he'd just uttered the most hilarious joke of all time.

"As many of you know, my son was long ago named Champion of Domignon. His ascension to a position of such power came as no surprise to him or to any of us—our lineage is directly descended from those who were victorious one thousand years ago."

Cheers erupted. Cries of "Domignon!" and "Prince Corym will be victorious!" echoed through the large space.

Why are you not cheering for Olivia Brimley? I asked the crowd silently.

"As some of you may know, we have struggled," the king continued, "to find a co-Champion for Prince Corym. Someone worthy both of competing by his side and of bearing his children. Given the importance of both preserving and enhancing our bloodline, his mother and I have had many frank discussions on the matter."

Mithraan turned to me, raising a dark eyebrow, and I thought I detected a faint, knowing smile on his lips.

Why aren't they naming Olivia? I thought. *Why not just say her name and be done with it?*

"Long ago, we discovered the whereabouts of a young woman with a bloodline that was...quite impressive," the king said.

Okay. Here we go—the big reveal.

He's about to name Olivia the official second Champion.

But instead of looking over at the young woman in the silver dress at the far end of the ballroom, the king fixed his eyes on me.

And, to my horror, so did every other person in the room.

"Lyrinn Martel," the king called out, "I believe it's time you learned why I summoned you here."

CHAPTER TWENTY-FOUR

My cheeks went instantly fever-hot, my pulse throbbing like war drums in my ears.

In my mind, I cried out:

Why are you all looking at me?

Instinctively, my hands reached up to pull my hood around my face. But I wasn't wearing a cloak. There was nowhere to hide; no shadows to conceal me. I was on full display for every wealthy resident of the great city of Domignon.

"Lyrinn Martel, you must wonder why you're here," the king said with a deep chuckle. "It's only fair that we should tell you once and for all."

I looked around, stepping toward him. Somewhere to my right, I could feel Mithraan tensing like a cat ready to pounce.

"I'll admit I'm very curious, Majesty," I said. "I...I still don't fully understand how you even know who I am."

"Did you know that your mother lived here in Domignon?" he called out. The spectators' eyes were bouncing back and forth between us as though our words were a ball in a sporting match.

I inhaled a sharp breath and held it. "Yes," I finally exhaled.

"That is, I only learned it recently. My mother died when I was young. I never knew her. I knew nothing of her past. You say she lived here, in the city?"

"Here on the castle grounds, in fact."

"You did know her, then?" I asked, curious beyond words.

The king nodded, a look in his eye that seemed suddenly distant, as if he was recalling a far-away dream. "I did, for a time. She was a lovely thing, and so intelligent. She was..." He stopped himself as if he was on the verge of saying something he might come to regret. "Come closer, Lyrinn. You should be in front of the guests when I tell you this."

I threw Mithraan a quick sideways glance. He nodded once, his face solemn, and I strode toward the king, the crowd parting to allow me through.

"Your mother's bloodline," the king said, "was...well, let's just say it was impressive. And because of that, I have long wished I could find her firstborn daughter. You see, because of your ancestry—because she lived here—you are eligible to represent Domignon in the Blood Trials. I would like for you to be Prince Corym's co-Champion."

I shook my head. "But that's insane!" I stammered, forgetting momentarily who was in front of me. Thankfully, the king and Corym looked amused, though the queen appeared shocked. "I'm sorry, your Grace. That is, I mean—" I stopped myself. I was arguing with a king, for the gods' sake. Wasn't that grounds for beheading or something? "What I mean is, I'm only eighteen, your Grace. I am too young to compete. Not to mention that I am not a Blood-Gifted."

The king smiled again, and, gesturing with his left hand, summoned a man in a long robe who was carrying a piece of rolled up parchment.

"Your birthdate has been a matter of some confusion for a long time. Dúnbar's records say you were born in the eleventh moon, but that's not entirely accurate. Funnily enough I recall your birth, as it occurred here in this very palace."

My legs nearly gave out under me as his words sank into my mind.

"Your Grace?" I half-whispered.

"Your mother gave birth here," he said again. "And as it turns out, you were born in the eighth moon. Which means you are very soon to be nineteen years of age—and eligible to compete."

"Are you certain?" I asked, my voice trembling with the weight of what his words might mean.

"I am," he laughed, gesturing once again, and this time, the man with the parchment stepped forward to unfurl it.

I grasped at the metal tube around my neck and considered opening it to show them. But that would have been ridiculous. The paper I was looking at was a royal document.

It was law.

"Born at Domignon," the man called out. "Lyrinn, daughter of Alessia."

"Just Alessia?" I asked. "There's no surname? No Martel? No mention of my father?"

"These are the palace's records. No surname was necessary."

"But—" I began to protest. I wanted to tell them there must be another Alessia—it would explain the mix-up.

I am not meant to be here. And I certainly am not meant to be a chosen Champion.

"You aren't pleased," King Caedmon said, the expression in his eyes one of confusion combined with disapproval. "I feel that I should remind you, Lyrinn, that being named Champion is the greatest honor one can bestow on any mortal in all of Kalemnar."

I felt the eyes of a hundred onlookers judging me, questioning me. *Despising me.*

I swallowed and said, "It is an honor, your Grace, and I am humbled. Forgive me—I am simply surprised. I didn't see this coming."

Mithraan did, though. He knew, the second he learned I was headed to Domignon.

The king's expression softened a little when he said, "Of course, my dear. Sometimes life throws surprises at us—but we rise to the occasion, and we prevail, don't we? Just as I know you will, with my son by your side."

"Yes, your Grace," I said, pasting a smile onto my lips.

King Caedmon rubbed his hands together and said, "Very good. You will train here for the Trials. And when you and my son are victorious, you will be free to bear children with him."

I tensed when he paused and looked me in the eye. For the first time, the depth of my fate hit me.

When the prince and I were victorious—*if* we were victorious...

We would marry.

Our children would carry inside them the strength of our bloodlines, and every Gift that came with our victory in the Trials.

"My son, the prince, is more Gifted than any other mortal in the realms," the king said proudly. "He will watch over and protect you in competition. And in the end, you will both win."

With that, he raised a glass of red wine to toast the blissful future he had crafted so carefully in his mind.

An uproar thundered through the room, and I started at the sound. Strangers, delighted by the announcement of a fate that had been thrust upon me without my desire or consent.

Me, married to a Prince.

I pulled my eyes to Corym's, only to see him smiling down

at me. He looked genuinely happy. Delighted, even.

I should have been happy, as well. I should have been proud, excited, euphoric.

But instead, I was more lost than I'd ever been. I had walked into a wild dream, and I couldn't entirely decide if I should be pleased or horrified at my inability to extricate myself.

Leta would have lost her mind if she had been present to witness this madness. She would probably have offered to take my place—not that I would have allowed it, even if she were of age. Leta's fighting skills left a great deal to be desired, and the last thing I wanted was to see her hurt, or worse.

Leta...

"My sister," I blurted out.

"Sister?" the king asked.

"You mentioned that your men were looking for her, your Grace. I would...love to share the happy news with her. Have you heard anything?"

"I'm afraid not. But you have my word that my men are combing the realms for her as we speak."

"Thank you so much," I said, holding back tears.

I needed Leta by my side—I needed to know she was safe. I couldn't imagine facing my future without her to cheer me on, to ground me. I was desperate to hang onto some vestige of my former life, and my sister was all I had left.

"Now," the king said, raising his glass to the gathered crowd once again, "let's get on with the festivities, shall we? It's time to celebrate the coming union of two great families!"

Once again, the crowd erupted. I spun around, looking for Mithraan, for Olivia Brimley, for any face that could assure me none of this was really happening.

But instead, I felt a hand on my arm and heard the prince's voice.

"Lyrinn."

I turned to look up at him.

"You look terrified," he said with a chuckle. "It's all right. Trust me—it's understandable on every conceivable level. You believed I was to marry Olivia. This is a shock to your system—and for that, I am deeply sorry."

"A shock," I repeated. "Yes." I still didn't understand. How had my father assigned me the wrong birthdate all my life? Why did the king want me as Champion when Olivia Brimley, who by all accounts had proven herself worthy and powerful, was readily available?

"I will protect you, of course," the prince promised. "Just as my father said. Though something tells me you won't need my protection. You are a strong woman—I can feel it in you. And after tonight, I believe with every fiber of my being that your strength will only grow. You will prove more Gifted than anyone ever imagined. Trust me."

Thinking he was joking, I let out a nervous laugh.

"There will be competitors from Belleau, Marqueyssal, and Domignon," I said. "Six people trying to beat me in competition, or even kill me. My odds aren't wonderful, Highness. I have no experience as a Champion. The truth is, I still think your father has the wrong person. There must have been more than one Alessia—"

The prince looked at me with a quizzical expression, tilting his head to the right as if trying to understand my meaning. "My father has searched for you for a long time. Do you really think the King of Domignon would commit such an error?"

I took a deep breath and held it in my chest. "No, of course not," I said. "I apologize."

"At any rate," he added, "You needn't worry about six Champions trying to harm you. The three women from Belleau, Castelle, and Marqueyssal will be the only ones looking to take you down, remember. Only the women will have a vested interest in your demise. Any man worth his salt will want you as a potential mate—including me."

His eyes were focused intently on mine, and now his hand came up and brushed a stray lock of dark hair behind my right ear.

"You are exquisite, Lyrinn," he said softly, his fingers trailing down the scar tissue lining my neck. I struggled not to flinch under his touch. What was it with his family members, that they were so eager to fondle my scars? "When you arrived here —when I first set eyes on you—I was relieved beyond compare. I am beyond excited to know you are to be my wife."

Wife.

I wasn't sure what I'd expected when I'd climbed into the carriage in Dúnbar. But whatever distant theory had worked its way through my mind was a million miles from this scenario.

Had I known the king would be naming me Champion, I would probably have run back to the Onyx Rise and taken my chances with the mist and the Grimpers.

And now, my eyes were fixed on those of a handsome, powerful prince who seemed to genuinely *want* me. A prince who had offered me his protection, who wished for me to be mother to his children.

Corym was kind, not to mention beautiful to behold. His voice was rich, his eyes expressive and striking. He was polite and good-natured, with the exception of the occasional sneer in Mithraan's direction.

The prince was everything Leta used to imagine he was, and more.

If only I had my sister by my side right now, I told myself, *I might even find a way to be happy.*

"I need to survive," I told Corym. "I want to live—for my sister's sake. Whatever it takes. Now, if you'll excuse me, Highness...I'd like to get some air."

CHAPTER TWENTY-FIVE

SUFFOCATING under the weight of all the king had announced in front of a hundred people or more, I made my way to a set of doors that sat wide open to a vast marble terrace outside.

Desperate, I inhaled a deep breath of fresh air as I raced across the smooth surface and down a set of stairs.

I didn't stop until I reached a well-groomed garden filled with tall, trimmed hedges. A place where I could conceal myself at long last. I'd spent far too much time this evening with the eyes of strangers grazing on my flesh. Too much time being scrutinized.

Slipping through an arched opening in the first hedge, I strolled along a quiet, gravel-strewn path, my pulse slowing as I took in the perfectly coiffed shrubs.

It was only when I rounded a bend in the path that I spotted another figure. Tall, dark, and broad-shouldered, his amber eyes were locked on the first bright star shining in the evening sky.

He did not turn my way as I approached.

"They say the Southern Star contains the soul of the first Fae Lord," he said almost absently, as if it didn't particularly matter that I was there. "Burning eternally as it watches over many, many worlds. The other stars are our ancestors, killed in battle, departed for the Farlands."

"What about humans?" I asked. "Are we not important enough to merit our own stars?"

"Some are," Mithraan said softly, turning my way, his irises shining bright as always. "Something tells me your star would shine brightly indeed, Lyrinn."

"I would have to die first," I said, pulling my eyes to the sky. "Which is beginning to seem more likely with each passing moment."

"No," he said with a shake of his head. "You will not die."

I let out a bitter chuckle and replied, "You heard what the king said in there. It seems your theory was correct. He was bringing me here to compete alongside his son. But I'm no Champion. I'm capable of gutting a squirrel or a fox, but I have never really fought, let alone cast a magical spell. This is a case of mistaken identity, nothing more. They have the wrong Lyrinn."

I turned back to glance over the hedges at the silhouetted figures visible through the castle's windows—dancing, singing, making merry. But Mithraan turned to stare at me with a hard look on his features.

"That dress," he said, his eyes moving down my body. "It fits you very well, though I despise all that it represents."

"I suppose they wanted to make the prince's future spouse look like she fits into high society."

"Future spouse," Mithraan scoffed. "You are actually considering it, then." He lowered his chin and looked into my eyes more intently, his lips slightly parted. "Tell me, how do you feel about your future husband?"

His eyes flared bright in the darkness as he awaited my reply.

"He's a good man," I said simply. "And kind. He genuinely wishes to protect me."

"I see." Mithraan's jaw tightened. "I am glad to hear it. But perhaps you don't need his protection any more than you need mine. There is magic in you. Never forget it."

"Magic?" I said. "I've never seen evidence of it."

"You're forgetting what happened last night—when the bandits came for the carriage."

I was about to respond that I didn't know what he was talking about when a flash of memory came to me—of my hands, glowing white in the darkness.

But Mithraan himself had insisted my mind was playing tricks on me. That I hadn't really seen such a thing. It was little more than a half-forgotten dream. Something so unreal that I had pushed it from my thoughts entirely.

And now, I didn't know what to believe.

"If there's magic deep inside me," I said, "I have no control over it."

"You will," Mithraan replied. "But I fear the king and the prince are using you as a pawn. You do realize this is your choice, do you not? You were raised in Castelle. You don't have to compete on behalf of Domignon, and you certainly don't have to marry that ivory-skinned dolt."

His disdain for the prince might have made me laugh if I weren't so terrified of the days to come. I would rely on the prince, whether Mithraan liked him or not.

"If I win alongside the prince, I won't have a choice but to marry him. Not that there's any chance of my winning. If I compete, the Blood Trials will be my end."

"Not if I have anything to say about it," Mithraan growled quietly, and something inside of me heated against my will. An ache, a longing deep in my core for this strange, hostile creature who seemed to abhor me...yet had risked his life to protect me more than once.

"The prince seems like a gentleman, besides," I snapped, trying to push away the emotions overtaking my rational mind. "A young lady could do far worse."

"A young woman's sole purpose in this world ought not to be to produce heirs for egotistical monarchs," Mithraan scowled. "You, Lyrinn, should be as free as our people once were. You are not meant to be shackled in a place like this. You are more than..." His irises seemed to catch fire before he pulled his gaze back to the sky. "You are more," he said quietly.

The gentleness in his voice fractured something inside me, my defensiveness fading.

"Perhaps if I win by some miracle, and marry the prince," I said, "I could find a way to free your people once again. Maybe you should be cheering for me, rather than discouraging me."

Mithraan stepped close, his scent enveloping me like an intoxicating cloak that sent my head spinning.

"Do you feel the importance of this night?" he asked softly, his hand reaching for my face, then pulling back as though fearful that my flesh would burn him. "Do you feel it in your blood, in your bones? Do you know why the king held the celebration this evening? Why he and the prince are so confident?"

"No," I said. "I have no idea why they would be confident, given that I'm no one."

Mithraan looked to the sky again when he said, "Nineteen years ago on this night, you were born in this palace."

My heart leapt in my chest. "Tonight?" I breathed. I thought I had more time. Days. Weeks, even, to absorb all that I'd learned this evening.

Mithraan nodded. "In just a couple of hours, you will reach your exact birth-date. And in that moment, if indeed you have Blood-Gifts, they will begin to show themselves with all the clarity of a rose's petals on a sunny day. You, Lyrinn, will be nineteen winters old. And this—" He gestured toward the castle. "This is a party to celebrate your coming of age. By morning, you will have changed. In what way, I don't yet know. The question is, who was this Gifted mother of yours?"

Who indeed.

"How exactly do Gifts reveal themselves?" I asked. "When *you* came of age, how did it happen?"

Mithraan smiled a little. "If you are, say, a flame wielder, you may find yourself accidentally conjuring a fireball. Or you may find your mind addled as you read another's thoughts. But in your case, I suspect something else entirely will happen."

"Why is that?"

"I saw what you did on the edge of the woods. I felt a power in you I have only ever seen in my father's memories. One that frightens me a little."

He reached out, and this time he didn't pull back. Instead, he touched my face, slipping his fingers slowly down my cheek, activating my every nerve ending at once. I resisted the desire to lean into the sensation, to savor it, to show him how enthralled his caress made me feel.

"There are things you don't know," he whispered, moving closer. "You are in danger here, Lyrinn. And if you enter the Blood Trials, you will be in grave danger there, as well. Unless..."

His lips were so close to my cheek that I could feel them brushing against my skin, and the sensation set a craving into my core. More than anything, I wanted to turn my face toward him, to feel his lips on my own. To taste him at long last, and quench the thirst that had tormented me since the first moment I'd seen him.

"Unless?" I repeated, fighting my most base urges.

He pulled away abruptly, taking a long step backward. "We

aren't alone," he whispered, narrowing his eyes at me. "It is torture, being so close to you, knowing you are intended for that bastard."

A second later, I heard the sound of feet treading on gravel a few feet away and looked over to see the prince standing on the path, staring at Mithraan. Rage overtook his features but the expression passed quickly, morphing into a smile as he pulled his eyes to mine.

"There you are!" he said. "I've been searching for you. You are the guest of honor, remember. It's time we returned."

I threw a look toward Mithraan, whose face had gone cold, his expression unreadable as always. He simply nodded silently, watching as I took the prince's offered arm and walked toward the castle.

The prince and I stepped back into the ballroom to be greeted by the sound of rich, lilting music. For the next hour we danced, our feet gliding lightly along the marble floor as others stopped to watch us. Ladies smiled and gentlemen nodded approvingly as the prince guided me expertly through the steps.

I was incredulous when I realized how easily I managed to keep up with him despite my lack of experience.

And pleased to know what an adept teacher he was.

Maybe there was hope for me as a Champion, after all.

"My father told me of your mother's beauty long ago," Corym said as we moved. "But I did not dare hope her daughter was as beautiful as she. Yet here you are, as lovely as a rose."

A rose. The very thing I thought of when I looked at Leta.

"Thank you, Highness," I said shyly.

Just then, my eyes landed on Mithraan, who was standing by a twisting column, his shoulder pressed against it, arms crossed over his chest. The way he stared at me sent a shudder through my body, and I had to force myself to look back into the prince's eyes and smile. What color were they, anyhow? Blue? Green?

Right. Blue-green. Focus on them.

When a bell sounded a moment later, I was relieved for the excuse to stop dancing and found myself looking for Mithraan. But I could not find him before the king stepped onto the dais at the room's far end to make an announcement.

"Prince Corym. Lyrinn Martel. Please—come stand by my side."

I pulled my eyes to the king and smiled politely as the prince guided me forward and then stopped, gently turning me around to face the crowd.

"We are gathered tonight," the king bellowed to the rapt audience, "to celebrate our two Champions. But it is with pleasure that I say *Happy Birth-Night, Lyrinn*. Tomorrow, you will awaken as a young woman who has come of age—a young woman with a legacy unlike any other. The Change—if there is a Change to come, and I suspect there will be, given how Gifted your mother was—will begin in you, and your full potential will begin to emerge. I have faith that you will prove powerful. You will make a fine Champion of Domignon...and eventually, you will make a wonderful, powerful queen."

Queen.

I had not seen that far into the future...

Nausea ebbed in my belly, but I forced it away and said, "I thank you, your Grace, for the kind words."

I only wish I had half your faith in my nonexistent abilities.

"With that said, Lyrinn, you must enjoy yourself tonight. Tomorrow may prove...difficult for you. But once you have recovered, the training will begin. I am pleased to announce that we have a very skilled trainer at our disposal. One who knows the Trials, and the style of combat necessary to emerge victorious, should you make it to the very end."

With that, the king turned to his left, and Mithraan stepped out of the shadows, bowing his head slightly.

Some in the crowd gasped, shocked to see a Fae in their midst. A few looked frightened, even angry at the sight of him.

Why did his presence come as a surprise? Had they not noticed him earlier?

The questions faded from my mind as I recalled how adept Mithraan was at altering others' perceptions. He had no doubt used glamour on the crowd to convince them that he was merely another mortal face among many.

"Your Grace," I said. "I hadn't realized Lord Mithraan would be training me."

"You are under his protection," the king reminded me. "He has offered to train you. I'm afraid I had little choice but to accept." With that, he chuckled uneasily and shot an unfriendly look in the Fae's direction.

The notion of finding myself alone with Mithraan for hours at a time sent a wave of excitement shuddering through my body, but I told myself it was merely my nerves getting to me.

If—**if**—*I survive the Trials,* I told myself, *I have no choice but to marry the prince...which means I must stop craving the touch of a Fae lord.*

CHAPTER TWENTY-SIX

THE REST of the evening passed in a haze. Eleven o'clock came and went, and still, the prince and I danced, to the delight and amusement of all.

All but one.

Mithraan stood to the side of the dance floor, chin low, eyes locked on us. I found myself looking in his direction more than once, trying to read his thoughts. Was he studying me? Trying to work out which weapons would best suit me in our training sessions?

Was he judging my poor dancing?

After a time, the prince wandered off to speak to his mother, and I searched the crowd for the Fae. I wanted to approach him, to reprimand him for the unwanted attention he insisted on bestowing upon me.

But as much as I hunted, I couldn't find him.

Finally, I stepped into the corridor outside the ballroom and wandered along until I came to its end, where another hallway led off to the right. I was about to glance into its depths when I heard Mithraan's voice echoing through the space.

"I know why you brought her here. I know what she is to you," he said.

I peeked around the corner to see the Fae towering over the king, whose shoulders were thrust back, his head held high. An expression of rage had taken over his features.

"She is my son's future wife, if that's what you mean."

Mithraan took a step forward. "She is far more than that, and you know it. Her life has been a lie—her age, her mother's origins. Your plan will fail if you continue to conceal the truth."

I pulled myself away, pressing my back to the wall for fear that they'd see me. Why were they arguing about me? What was this about?

"Conceal?" The king laughed. "On the contrary—I hope her Gifts emerge with flying colors, and soon. She will help Corym to victory. She will give my son Gifted heirs, and our bloodline will be unlike any the world has ever known."

"You underestimate her," Mithraan said. "When she learns the truth, she will rebel. She is not as weak as you might think."

"She will not rebel," the king snarled. "She will be a queen of mortals. It is her fate—it always has been."

"Not if I have anything to say about it," Mithraan snarled.

"Is that a threat, Fae?"

"Perhaps you underestimate me as well as Lyrinn, your Grace."

"Do not try me, Fae. I have powerful allies."

"I would be very interested indeed to hear of those allies," Mithraan retorted. "Though I already have my suspicions, King."

"Speak a word of it, and I will have your tongue cut out." At that, I heard loud footsteps moving quickly in the other direction.

The king was gone.

I poked my head around the corner and watched as

Mithraan leaned back against the wall, his head pressed to cold stone so hard that I got the distinct impression he wanted to push his way through it.

He turned in my direction, his amber eyes flashing with bright flame. He strode over and stopped mere inches from me, looking down into my eyes, unblinking.

"What you do to me," he said, cupping my cheek in his large hand. "You are a scourge on my soul."

"What were you talking about with the king?" I asked, my tone sharp. I was in no mood for his manipulation, his strange, almost violent brand of flattery.

"The king," he scoffed. "King of men. King of fools. Ask yourself why they were desperate for you, a girl from Dúnbar, to come to this place. When you are writhing in bed later—when you feel the Change overtake you—ask yourself that question. Why those scars line your ears and neck. Ask yourself what happened to your mother. Why, for all your life, you have stared longingly at that cliff and pondered how to ascend to the land of the Fae."

My eyes met his, and I could not decide whether to be angry that he had dug through my thoughts and my memories, or impressed by his skill.

"You do not know what I have wanted all my life," I said. "You do not speak for me."

"I know more than you think," he replied, turning away and striding down the hall.

Leaving me with more questions than answers.

CHAPTER TWENTY-SEVEN

After I reentered the ballroom, the rest of the evening passed in a whirlwind of confusion and activity combined. The prince found me once again and, taking my hand, led me out to the dance floor.

He barely let me rest between dances, ensuring that we were front and center in our red-laced white garments, spinning over the shining marble for all to see.

I finally excused myself after a few hours, telling Corym I was exhausted—which was the truth. But exhaustion was hardly my greatest concern.

My head had begun to spin despite the fact that I had not had a sip of alcohol since shortly after my arrival at the ball. I felt disoriented, traumatized, excited, and baffled, all at once. It was as though I were watching myself through someone else's eyes, stunned by the rapid transformation of a life that had always been calm and simple.

I made my way back to my chamber, grateful when I finally threw open the door.

I hadn't seen Mithraan since his tense conversation with

the king, and I had no doubt that it was for the best. He offered me nothing but confusion and a terrible, reluctant intoxication that took over my mind and body each time I laid eyes on him.

My sleep was restless that night. I tossed and turned, my head reeling with ugly thoughts, my stomach churning with sickness. I told myself it was a reaction to learning of my fate, of my birth in Domignon, of my mother's mysterious history.

But when I finally tried to rise from the bed in the morning, my discomfort only increased. My head was pounding, my stomach churning. When I tried to push myself up to a sitting position, I collapsed, sweat soaking through my nightgown.

When Anira wandered into the room and saw my face, she almost dropped the breakfast tray she was carrying. With shaking hands, she set it down, backed out of the room, and shut the door.

Shortly thereafter, a man in a white tunic rushed in, all but sprinting to my bedside.

"Lyrinn, is it?" he asked, pressing an unwelcome hand to my cheek.

I nodded weakly.

"I was told you're not feeling well, and I must say, you look..." He stopped speaking as if afraid to offend me.

"The king warned me," I murmured. "He said the night would be diff...difficult..."

"I'm the king's personal physician," the man added, ignoring my words. "It looks as though you have a fever, likely brought on by your journey down here from Castelle. I will be giving you some medicine and a cold compress, and if we're fortunate, that will be enough to heal you."

"It's the Change," I half-whispered, recalling Mithraan's and the king's words from the previous night. "It's...what happens to those with Blood-Gifts. It will pass."

The doctor lowered his chin and shot me a skeptical look. "I have seen Blood-Gifted when they turn nineteen. I was with Prince Corym when it happened to him."

"So you know," I rasped, my chest heaving. "You know what happens."

"Yes," the doctor said, reaching into the bag he had carried into the room and extracting a dark brown glass vial. "I know very well. Which is why I know you are not showing mere symptoms of your coming of age. I don't mean to alarm you, but..." Instead of continuing, he simply shook his head. "Your eyes are dull. Your fever is high. You will need a good deal of help to get through this illness."

"Illness?" I repeated. "No...I am perfectly well."

The thing was, I didn't feel well. I felt as wretched as I had in my entire life. I felt Death lurking in shadow, waiting to claim me.

The doctor was right—if this was the Change, then most Blood-Gifted probably didn't live to see adulthood.

He offered me a vial of some bitter drink, which I downed quickly. He then pressed a cold cloth to my sweat-soaked forehead, seeking to relieve me of the fire burning its way through my veins.

But his treatment had nothing like the desired effect. The fever didn't break; instead, I began to tremble violently. The world around me went hazy as I began to hallucinate visions of Leta, of my father. I may have cried out for them more than once. I saw myself running toward each of them through a field of tall grass and wildflowers. I felt free and light, as if I'd left my body entirely and entered a dreamworld that was both beautiful and bittersweet.

An image came to me, too, of a vast wood. I could see it from above, as though I were soaring over the treetops. Far below, sprinting through the trees, were a number of men and women seemingly fleeing for their lives.

At some point, I was vaguely aware of the doctor's presence at the far end of the bedroom, speaking to another man—one with a deep, familiar voice that reminded me of chocolate.

No, I murmured. *No...don't let him near me. Please.*

A hand pressed itself to my cheek, and the deep voice spoke directly to me.

I tried to focus on his face, but all I saw was a sort of blinding halo of light that made me cover my eyes with my forearm. I shook my head violently, willing the Fae away.

But he didn't leave.

I couldn't tell how much time passed, only that a point came when I grew certain that I was going to die. I would never see Leta in the flesh again, or Dúnbar, or the river. I would never marry, never have children. I would never find my place in the world—as a fighter, a mother, or a lover. My brief life was at its end, even sooner than I had come to expect.

The hand lingered on my cheek throughout my torment, sometimes stroking my skin, sometimes running its way through my tangles of dark hair. At one point, I felt it pull away, heard the deep voice commanding the doctor and everyone else present to leave us alone.

There were protests and argument, but ultimately, the room emptied. A lone figure stood some distance away as the door to my chamber closed. Slowly, he turned and moved back to my bedside, taking my hand.

"You are fighting, Lyrinn," he said. "That is what the doctor wants. But I don't want you to fight. I want you to give in to the sickness."

I turned my head to stare at him, calling upon all my strength to focus on his face.

Mithraan. You want me to die. It's what you've wanted all along, isn't it?

You told me soon after we met that you wished to throw me off the Onyx Rise.

You despise me.

"No," I rasped, my throat lined with coarse sand. "I won't give in. You—"

I tried to snap at him. I wanted to tell him to get out and never to come near me again, but when I attempted to speak, my chest erupted in a coughing fit that left me winded.

"Lyrinn," he said softly. His hand slipped to my chest, his touch gentle. I tightened under his fingers, too weak to force him away. Too soothed by his hand to want him to stop.

He slid his fingers up to my neck, muttering under his breath in a language I did not know. I could feel his fingertips trail along the scars that had made me self-conscious all my life, tracing their outlines.

I wanted to push him away, to snarl at him. But I was too weak.

"I have seen you in my dreams, Lyrinn," he whispered, leaning in close. "For many years, you have come to me in my mind's eye. I have waited for you all this time, though I did not know what form you would take. I did not know you would be so lovely. Please..." His voice broke a little with the final word, and he cleared his throat. "Please, give in to the force inside you. For your sister. For this world. For all of Kalemnar. For Tíria."

His voice came clearly, the fog in my mind lifting as I turned to see that his eyes were damp. He was fighting back tears, willing them not to fall.

"Why?" I asked, my voice hoarse. "Why would you see me in your dreams?"

"Because you are..." he said, slipping down to kneel next to the bed, stroking a hand through my damp hair. "You are the stars. You are the hills. You are all that was once beautiful and is now lost. And I *need* you to survive this."

"Why?" I asked again. "You..."

You hate me.

He laid a hand on each of my cheeks. Leaning in close, he kissed me gently, his lips soft against my own.

It was an innocent touch, that was all.

Yet the intensity of it made me feel as though the bed had disappeared from beneath me, and I was tumbling endlessly through space into an endless void I would never escape.

"Your destiny," he said, "is tied to my own. I do not yet fully understand how or why. But I do know that I cannot lose you. I will not. I will give my life to protect you, if it comes to it. If I could do so right now and take away your pain, I would."

I winced with confusion. "But...you told the king..."

At that, Mithraan let out a quiet laugh. But he didn't confirm or deny my statement. Instead, he said, "You *are* coming into your Blood-Gifts, despite what the doctor may think. It happens to all who are blessed with the ancient strength of the Ancestors, though some suffer more than others. You must surrender to the Change in order for it to come. You're strong, and you're fighting too hard. Let your mind go for a little. Let your body ache. In the end, you will be greater for it. When the pain leaves you, you will feel stronger than you ever imagined."

"What Gifts could I possibly have?" I breathed. "I have never been like the prince. He's known he was special from the beginning—his parents knew. I've never been special."

"His parents' insistence that he is special does not make it so," Mithraan chastised. "And telling yourself you're nothing, Lyrinn, is a cruel disservice. You are a miracle. You simply haven't seen it yet."

I pulled my eyes to the ceiling and let out a quiet sob. "Why didn't my father ever tell me about my mother?" I asked in a whimper. "Who was she?"

Mithraan caressed my skin gently. "Perhaps he wanted to protect you. He loved you. He never wanted you to compete in the Trials, because with the competition comes a high chance of death. So he hid you away in hopes of keeping the Scouts at bay."

"He loved me, so he hid the truth from me all my life?" I asked, anger roiling up inside me. *He lied to me. To Leta. For years on end.*

"He loved you enough to try for years to protect you from the fate that has now come for you. The fate that caught up to you both, the night the Grimper came for him. He died trying to keep you from harm, Lyrinn, and in the end, his lie came to claim him. Do not allow yourself anger now."

None of it made sense. What had my father known? Was he aware that my mother was Gifted, that there was a good chance Leta and I would inherit her skills? Why had he not told us so that we could prepare ourselves and gain strength over time? Why had he never told us about our mother's life in Domignon?

Mithraan took my hand and kissed it gently, pressing it to his cheek. I was too exhausted to question his behavior, and instead, I simply closed my eyes and savored the sensation of his touch.

As my body writhed, I accepted the pain that would pulse through me in waves for the next several hours.

As the day passed, Mithraan never left my side. I moaned and rolled in agony, the sheets soaked with perspiration. My mind alternated between vivid, terrifying hallucination and reality.

I was aware at some point of the prince entering the chamber, of Mithraan standing by as Corym tried to speak to me, to ask if I was all right. I was aware, too, of a nurse, the doctor, and others.

But never did Mithraan move more than a few feet away from me.

Nor did I want him to.

CHAPTER TWENTY-EIGHT

In the late morning of the second day, I awoke to see that the window was wide open, the curtains billowing gently in the breeze. Far beyond the palace's high walls, I could see the rolling green hills to the east, their color more intense than anything I'd ever beheld.

On one hill in the far distance, I made out the shape of a small sapling, and as I focused on its outline, I began to notice each variation in its bark, each leaf on its branches.

I breathed, "Why does the world look so..."

"Different?" Mithraan's voice replied.

The Fae lord smiled when I turned to look at him. As usual, reading his expression proved almost impossible. But I was certain I detected a note of relief in his eyes.

"Yes," I said. "It's so detailed. It's like...I can see *everything*. What's happened to Domignon?"

"It's not Domignon that has changed. It's you, Lyrinn."

I tried to pull myself up, but my body nearly gave out with the exertion. Mithraan helped me to a sitting position, one hand supporting my back. "It will take you a moment to get used to this," he said. "Your mind and body are adjusting to the novelty of the Change."

I nodded, turning to the window once again.

"Do you want to take a closer look at your new world?" Mithraan asked.

I nodded.

He helped me out of bed and guided me to the window, where I seated myself in a wooden chair and stared out at the landscape. I could see every stone in Domignon's palace walls. Every sheep grazing on the distant hills. Scents of the city's shops and restaurants wafted to me in individual streams. Chocolate. Bread. Roast chicken.

"Is this a Blood-Gift?" I asked. "Seeing everything so brightly? Is that the extent of my abilities?"

"It is only the beginning," Mithraan said with a shake of his head. "You will not know for some days what you're truly capable of. At first, though, you will find your senses heightened, your reflexes quickened, your mind sharper. But if I'm right about you, other changes will occur, as well."

"No one ever taught me about any of this," I said. "My father told me about the Gifted years ago, but he never mentioned the Change."

"Many mortals have traces of the old bloodlines in them, from thousands of years ago. But for some, the Blood-Gifts come as a surprise."

"When you speak of the old bloodlines, I assume you mean the Fae?"

"Fae, Elves, the wild folk of the woods and mountains," Mithraan replied. "There were many in the past who wielded magic as a tool, a means of simple survival. As for you..."

"I what?" I asked when he stopped speaking.

I realized with a start that I could hear footsteps in the

hallway—the soft padding of leather-soled shoes—and he must have heard it, too.

A knock sounded a moment later, then the door creaked open and Prince Corym poked his head in. He looked first at the bed, then over to where I was sitting with Mithraan by my side, his hand on my shoulder.

Mithraan pulled away as the prince strode over to us. My skin went instantly cold where he'd been touching it, and I found myself aching for his lost touch, resentful of the prince for interrupting us.

"Lyrinn," Corym said, crouching before me and taking my hands in his own. "Are you well?"

"Quite well," I said with a nod. "I believe I'm on the mend."

"She did change—didn't she?" he asked, glancing at Mithraan, who nodded. "I went through the same thing when I turned nineteen, though it didn't hit me quite so hard. A restless night, a headache, and then..." He let out a chuckle. "The rest is history. So, my father's instincts were right. You *do* take after your mother."

I smiled, though I had yet to see any evidence that I had a single Blood-Gift other than my enhanced senses.

The prince laid a hand on my cheek, smiling. "I am so glad to see you like this. Your cheeks are flushed, your eyes brighter. You look strong and healthy. I cannot wait to see how your training goes."

I wanted to tell him my cheeks were flushed because of the Fae lord standing behind me. Because of his words, his touch. Because he had watched over me from the beginning.

But all I could do was pretend.

I could smile, nod...and feign pleasure.

I was fated to be with the prince. If I was to survive the Blood Trials, I was to be his.

And no amount of confusion over my feelings for Mithraan would change that destiny.

"Thank you, your Highness," I said. "I am excited to begin training."

"So," Mithraan said. "You have decided to compete, then."

I nodded. It was the best chance I had at providing Leta with the life she had always wanted. If the rumors were true and the other Champions were indeed weak, the prince and I had a real chance of winning.

"If I can make it to the end," I replied with a glance toward the prince, "we will have an opportunity to do great things for Kalemnar."

"You will survive, my Lady," Corym said. "You have my word."

"I'll leave you two alone," Mithraan announced abruptly, his eyes locked on the view of the outdoors. "There are matters I need to attend to in the North."

"The North?" I asked, my voice rising against my will.

The prince shot me a surprised look as if to ask, *Why should you care?*

"That is," I stammered, "I didn't realize you were leaving, Lord Mithraan. I thought you were going to help me train. I have a great deal of work to do before the Trials."

"I will help you when I return," the Fae replied, a cold edge to his voice. "But for now, you need to rest. There is something I must do, and I'm afraid it cannot wait. I will be back in a few days, if all goes well."

He turned to the prince and said, "Her strength will return, but for now, she needs to recover. She should not push herself too hard in the first few days."

Corym's brows met in a look of quiet annoyance. "I know perfectly well what she is going through, Fae. As I said, I've been through it myself."

The prince's tone was sharp and hostile, and reminded me too much of the king's own when I'd heard him snarling at Mithraan a few nights earlier. Their disdain for the Fae lord was all too clear.

"Lyrinn," Mithraan said, ignoring the prince, "allow your strength to come, and whatever accompanies it. Do not fight your body and mind—don't resist what is happening. Do you understand me?"

"She does not need advice from the likes of you, Fae," the prince said even as I nodded assent.

"With respect, your Highness," I replied, forcing a hint of sugary sweetness into my voice, "I *do* need his advice, particularly if he is to train me. I wish to win the Trials alongside you, remember. The stronger I can be—the more I can embrace my Gifts—the more likely our victory."

The prince ground his jaw for a second then said, "That is noble of you, my Lady." He turned back to the Fae lord and said, "My apologies, Lord Mithraan. I simply wish to protect Lyrinn. You understand."

"No apologies necessary from one such as you," Mithraan said with a sly grin, and I could feel the tension building like a steel wall in the air as he turned to leave.

When he'd reached the door, he spun around, gave me a final, deep look, then left without another word.

CHAPTER TWENTY-NINE

For two days, I wandered the castle grounds, exploring hidden gardens, libraries, even kitchens. All in an attempt to distract myself.

I was healed and healthy. But a darkness sat inside me that never seemed to fade. Mithraan hadn't returned, nor had I heard word from him. I couldn't understand why he'd left so abruptly, without explanation, after spending so many hours by my bedside.

The prince came to see me now and then, and even offered to teach me a few fighting techniques. Aching for further distraction, I took advantage.

He showed me various techniques for combat with a short sword, and helped me to refine my skill with my silver dagger. He offered me the use of his small training courtyard, where I spent countless hours hurling blades at various targets.

"I've trained here all my life," he told me when we'd just concluded a session with a bow and arrows—a skill that was not exactly my forte, in spite of my enhanced vision.

"Did you always know?" I asked him, nodding to a target he'd just split apart with a perfect shot from a crossbow.

"Know I'd be a Champion?" He issued an amused smirk. "Of course I did. In Kalemnar's four mortal realms, it is well known that I am the most powerful man."

"Powerfully modest, too," I said with a laugh, curious to see how he would take the slight.

Fortunately, he let out a laugh. "I am simply blessed with good fortune," he said, his voice soft, almost sheepish. "Fortunate beyond measure to be descended from such powerful mortals. As are you, my Lady."

"My mysterious mother, you mean," I said with a sigh. "Tell me—what do you know of her Gifts?"

"I have heard she could summon beasts, for one thing."

"What manner of beasts?"

"Exotic animals. Cats. Bears. Wolves. My father once told me she would do it for the amusement of the Court—that she was the talk of the city when they were younger. The beasts, he said, were made of shadow, glowing with faint blue light. They were as deadly as those who dwell in the woods. But your mother could make them vanish as quickly as they had come."

I inhaled a deep breath and held it there, refusing to give away the feeling of shock that coursed through me. Refusing, too, to reveal the sadness I felt for the extraordinary woman I had never known.

I wondered if my father had known of her Gifts when he wed her—if she had ever conjured those beasts in Dúnbar for the northerners to see.

No—if she had, there would still be talk of it to this day.

"Have you..." the prince began, seeming to contemplate his words carefully.

"Have I shown signs of such Gifts, your Highness?" I asked.

He nodded, grimacing slightly. "I wasn't quite sure how to put the question to you."

"The answer is no," I said. "Nothing so impressive. I am

afraid I may turn out to be something of a disappointment, if people are expecting a recreation of the great Alessia."

His jaw clenched, but only for a second before he smiled and said, "We both need to have patience. I have every faith that your true self will be revealed very soon."

I studied his face, wondering why he would say such a thing. Why be so confident that I would inherit my mother's skills at all?

With a shudder, I wondered, too, what he and his father might do to me if I turned out to prove as useless as I felt.

It was on the evening of the third day, when I was out in the training courtyard alone, that a cry tore its way through my mind.

A summons, called out by a voice so familiar now that it felt like a part of my own flesh.

Lyrinn...

I froze, petrified at the feeling of loss I sensed in those two syllables.

I dropped the bow I was holding and began to run, dashing through the courtyard's arched entrance and down a laneway that led to the dense wood north of the palace.

My chest burned as I sprinted past the forest, branches slashing at my skin like blades. I was like a desperate animal running for its very life.

It was when I finally stumbled into a small clearing that I saw three familiar figures.

The sight sent ice shooting through my veins.

Two were standing.

The other was on the ground, his chest heaving unnaturally.

The first two turned to me, their expressions helpless, panicked.

"Khiral!" I shouted as I leapt toward them. "Alaric! What's happened?"

Mithraan was lying between them, a blanket draped over his chest. His skin was ashen, his face beaded with sweat. His eyes were closed, and he was struggling for breath.

Before the other two could reply, I fell to my knees next to Mithraan.

No. You will not die on me. I need you if I am to survive the Trials. You promised me...

But the words were a mask, a means of concealing my true fear.

I cannot bear to live in a world where you don't exist.

"The mist is gone at last," Alaric said, kneeling down next to me. "But it...it took all of Mithraan's strength to rid our lands of it. And the Grimpers, they..."

I pulled at the woolen blanket that was covering Mithraan's torso to see slash marks in his tunic, dark crimson from the wounds he had suffered.

"Grimpers did this to him in the North, and he made it all this way?" I asked, incredulous.

Khiral shook his head. For once, he looked frightened rather than arrogant. "They came for us in the woods near here, as we approached Domignon," he said. "How they came to be here, we don't know. It felt like an ambush—like they knew we were coming."

"There were too many of them," Alaric interjected. "We took them down one by one, but Mithraan was their target. They attacked with such speed, and he fought valiantly. But one of them..."

I tore at the tunic until I saw his flesh beneath, three claw marks torn deep into his chest. His skin was gray and dark, as if death had already claimed some part of him.

"Water," I said. "Get him water. Quickly, now."

But as I stared at the wound, I knew there was little hope. One of his kind could live for centuries, but a wound like this would drain the life from him quickly. It would destroy him within a matter of hours and turn him into a Grimper—unless some miracle occurred.

While Alaric ran off to fetch water, I pressed a palm to Mithraan's cheek. His eyes opened and he looked up weakly, a strange smile turning the corners of his lips up.

"I knew you would come," he said softly, taking my wrist in his fingers.

"Of course I came," I told him, tears in my eyes. "Alaric is getting water. Khiral is here. We will stay with you."

"I will die," he rasped, his voice inhuman. "I knew it when the attack occurred. But I needed to...to lay my eyes on you one last time. It's why...why I called for you."

I shook my head. "I heard you...but...it can't be the last. I need you, Lord Mithraan. The Trials..."

"The Trials," he replied with a chuckle. "Alaric and Khiral can help you. You will marry that sniveling prince and live happily ever after, as they say."

"I don't see it," I confessed with a shake of my head. "I don't see myself with him. I don't...*desire* the prince."

"What is it that you desire, then?" he asked, the tiniest flicker of life in his dull eyes.

I hesitated, then smiled and said, "Perhaps I'm meant to be alone."

"I will leave you to your solitude, then, Lyrinn Martel. Now, let me rest."

With that, his eyes drooped closed.

"No!"

I said the word over and over again. I said it under my breath, my hands moving to his hair, his neck, searching for a word of reply.

I could not bear to part with him. Not like this.

He was the bane of my existence.

And yet he instilled in me the greatest bliss I'd ever known.

I had lost too much already. I wasn't ready to let him go, too.

Without knowing why, I held my hands over his torso, over the deep gashes in his flesh. I looked to the sky, asking some unknown power to help him.

It is not his time, I said silently. *I refuse to accept a future in which he doesn't exist. Bring him back to me.*

My hand moved slowly over his wounds, and when it hovered for a moment above his chest, my palm burned with a cruel, searing heat. I cried out with the pain of it, but I didn't pull away.

My skin glowed with pulsing veins of white, just as it had when Mithraan and I had confronted the bandits in the woods.

In that moment, I had been terrified. But now, it wasn't terror that assaulted me, but determination. I knew what I must do. For the first time, I understood the power growing inside me.

I pressed my hands down until they covered his deep wounds, and closed my eyes, my lips moving of their own volition. I muttered words in a language I had never spoken, one from another place and time entirely. *Another life.*

I willed my strength to move into Mithraan's body. For his flesh to heal, his eyes to open, his heart to beat once again inside his chest.

He was stiff beneath my touch, his flesh cold. I held out little hope, but still, my lips kept repeating the unknown words.

"*Raith min dir,*" I whispered over and over again. "Raith min dir."

"Lyrinn! What are you—" Alaric's voice called out from behind me. Opening my eyes, I turned his way. He stopped, staring, then leapt over next to me, a sack slung over his shoulder. He knelt down, his eyes wide, and looked at Khiral, who was watching in silence.

"Keep going," he said. "Don't stop."

Alaric seemed to hold his breath next to me as I repeated the same three words over and over again.

Raith min dir.

My hands felt as though the skin was sloughing off from the heat, my every nerve flaming with pain. But I held them steady, focusing every ounce of my strength on Mithraan.

"Open your eyes," Alaric finally whispered, taking me by the arm. "Look what you have done."

I did as he said, daring a glance down at Mithraan's chest.

The wounds had sealed themselves the blood and terrible grayness of his skin faded. His tunic was still in shreds, but his chest heaved up and down in regular breaths, the color returning to his lips, his cheeks.

"He needs to rest," I said softly. "He needs a fire for warmth. We can't move him until morning."

"We'll watch him," Khiral said with a nod.

"I will stay, as well," I replied. I fully expected a protest, but Khiral simply leaned against Alaric and let out a slow breath as his eyes moved to his lord's face.

"I have never liked you, Lyrinn Martel," he said, a tear making its way down his cheek. "I believed Mithraan was wrong—that you were nothing more than an irritating gnat. But now I see that you came to us for a reason." Pulling his eyes to mine, he added, "I will do whatever it takes to help you on your journey. I will help you to train for the Trials, if you'd like."

"As will I," Alaric added. "Gladly."

"Mithraan will help me when he is better," I told them with a smile. "Just as he promised. But thank you both."

The two Fae exchanged a quiet look. I wanted to ask them why they had come all this way. Why, if the mist was gone, they didn't stay and begin to rebuild Fairholme.

But I was exhausted after my strange show of power, and so I simply sat down, my legs crossed, and stared at Mithraan as his breathing slowed and his strength returned to him.

Khiral and Alaric built a fire and hunted down a few small animals to roast while I stayed by Mithraan's side. When night fell and my eyes began to droop with fatigue, I curled up next to him, grateful to feel his warmth.

The other two Fae curled up together on the opposite side of the fire. Alaric's arm was wrapped around Khiral's waist, and I found myself smiling as I looked at them.

During my brief time in the ruins of Fairholme, I hadn't ever observed the intimacy between them. Then again, I'd done everything I could to stay away from the two of them and their ilk.

It was soothing to see them like this. So affectionate. So different from one another, yet so perfectly compatible.

I didn't dare touch Mithraan for fear of waking him, though I wanted more than anything to hold him as Alaric was holding his companion. I wanted the reassurance that came with touch, to feel tethered to something stronger than myself.

But instead, I simply mouthed the words, "I will see you in the morning," closed my eyes, and allowed myself to fall into a deep sleep.

CHAPTER THIRTY

I WAS the first one awake in the morning.

The fire had deteriorated into a pile of ash and glowing embers, but the air was remarkably warm and fresh. For the briefest moment, I forgot where I was...or why.

Turning to Mithraan, I was relieved to see that his healthy glow remained, and his chest still rose and fell in a slow, even pulse.

"Is he awake?" Alaric whispered, pulling himself up to a sitting position.

As he spoke the words, Mithraan's eyes opened. They shone bright amber in the morning light. I looked at him, a surge of pleasure rushing through my chest as though I were watching the first ever sunrise.

He was exquisite.

He was strong.

He was whole.

Wordlessly, he reached for my hand, holding it tightly.

He didn't speak. He didn't need to.

The words passed silently between us.

You have done the impossible, Lyrinn.

You have healed me.

I didn't know how I had done it. The power inside me had taken me by surprise, just as it had done for the others. But somehow, by the grace of fate, I had brought him back to us all.

"She—" Alaric breathed, but Mithraan interrupted him with a raised hand.

"*She* is Lyrinn Martel," he said. "That is all that matters. She is stronger than any of us knew, herself included."

Mithraan pulled his hand away and pushed himself up. "Thank you, Lyrinn," he said softly. "You know what would have happened had you not come along."

"Yes," I said. "I know. And..." I paused, sucking my cheeks in. "I am glad to hear about the mist, both for your kind and for my own."

"Although the mist's disappearance is beneficial for both Tíria and Castelle alike, I destroyed it for other reasons entirely," Mithraan said mysteriously. "Let us hope the gamble pays off."

I nodded, not sure I wanted to know what he meant.

"Well," Mithraan added, leaping to his feet, "I think it's time we headed to Domignon. Now that our protector is with us, I don't suppose we'll be running into more Grimpers today." He nodded to me as he said the words, then turned to Alaric and then Khiral, who was just now beginning to stir. "I will ask the king to give you two rooms as lovely as my own. He may or may not oblige."

"We'll be lucky if he doesn't toss us in the dungeons," Khiral said with a snicker.

We hiked back through the woods toward the palace walls. As we drew close, I stopped in my tracks, convinced that I was losing my mind.

"Do you hear that?" I asked.

Khiral nodded. "Someone called your name."

Thank the gods I wasn't the only one who made it out.

Mithraan stopped and pulled his cloak tight around his chest, concealing the slash marks in his tunic. He stood with all the strength and dignity of a High Lord.

After a few seconds, two men came charging toward us down the wooded path, their swords drawn. They were dressed in mail, their cheeks flushed from what had likely been a long sprint.

"Looking for something?" Mithraan asked.

"The king...and the prince," the guard nearest to us, who was panting hard, said. "They asked us to look for the Lady Lyrinn. They said she would be in danger out in the woods alone."

"She was not alone," Mithraan said. "Not by any stretch."

The guard nodded, breathing heavily. "I can see that," he said. "Still, we have been ordered to accompany her back to the palace."

"Of course. But may I ask what the king and prince thought presented such a dire threat to the Lady Lyrinn?"

I glanced sideways at him, wondering if he was trying to bait them into admitting they were aware there were Grimpers nearby.

"Bandits have been seen in these woods of late," the other guard replied.

"Ah, yes. We've met some of their ilk before." With that, Mithraan threw me a knowing look. "Well, then. After you, my Lady."

I walked silently ahead of the three Fae as the guards escorted us toward the palace walls. Behind me, Khiral spoke in hushed tones to the other two.

"We must meet with them," I heard him say said under his breath. "The prince, the king. Now that the mist is broken, we must make things right."

“We will,” Mithraan replied. “All in good time. For now, I care about one thing only—and that is ensuring that Lyrinn prepares for the Trials.”

“But—”

“Hush,” Mithraan said, his tone ominous. “Speak of nothing else for now—not to the king or anyone. We have a duty to perform—a debt to repay. And I intend to do it. The icy hand of death was at my throat last night, and Lyrinn drove it back. I owe her my life.”

I allowed myself a shallow smile as we proceeded through a narrow iron gate into one of the castle’s courtyards.

What did it mean to a Fae, I wondered—to owe such a debt?

CHAPTER THIRTY-ONE

The prince came to see me after the Fae had been escorted to their quarters and I had retreated to mine.

"Are you all right?" Corym asked quietly as he glided across the room. I was positioned next to the open window, a warm breeze wafting in. "I heard you were lost in the woods last night—it must have been terrifying for you."

"I..." I was about to correct him, but an invisible hand rose up, cautioning me not to tell him about the Grimpers' proximity to Domignon, or about my miraculous healing of Mithraan's wounds. "I am perfectly well," I finally said, shifting my gaze to admire the countryside beyond the castle grounds.

I wondered idly if Mithraan was resting after his ordeal.

Turning back to the prince, I smiled, pushing the thought away. "I'm fine. And you?" I asked, all too eager to change the subject.

"Just fine," he said. "More so for finding you looking so healthy, my Lady. It brings me so much joy to see you looking so strong after your Change."

With those words, his light eyes slipped their way down my body. My cheeks heated when I read the hunger in his expression. Corym had given me looks in past—glances of admiration, or even of lust.

But right now, there was something in his eyes—a possessive sort of greed I had not seen before.

"I look forward to the day when we can be bonded, you and I," he said, moving closer and speaking low. "More precisely, I look forward to bedding you on our wedding night."

I nearly choked.

The words were forward, even brazenly presumptuous.

"*Bedding* me," I repeated.

I understood my perceived duties—that I was expected to emerge victorious at the Trials and to marry the prince.

But my future remained an abstract notion in my mind. I had not thought a great deal about anything but the coming competition, nor had I given any real consideration to a wedding night or the time beyond.

I had yet to successfully envision myself living with this man.

Let alone trying to *love* him.

There was plenty about him to love, of course. He was ideal in many ways—intelligent, handsome and, by all accounts, as Gifted as many Fae. But it struck me as I stared at him that I did not care deeply for him, and I wondered if I could ever bring myself to do so.

Seeing the trepidation in my face, Corym reached for my hand and pulled it to his lips. "I am sorry if I sounded a little too eager. But the truth is, I have desired you since the moment we met, Lyrinn. It is...difficult for me to hold back my excitement when I know the day is coming when we can finally be together. If I'm to be honest, I had been looking forward to meeting you since long before you came south to Domignon."

"But why?" I asked with a self-conscious chuckle. "I've kept to myself my entire life. I have no reputation, so it couldn't possibly have preceded me."

"Perhaps not," he said, an eyebrow raised. "But your mother did."

"Ah, yes. My enigmatic mother," I repeated with a sigh. "And her mysterious Gifts. I only wish I had gotten to know her, and seen what she was capable of. Maybe it would have given me courage."

"I have little doubt that you're just as powerful," the prince said. "In fact, I'm confident that you will prove even more so."

I winced at his words. He couldn't know what happened in the wood last night, could he? Surely he hadn't watched me.

Watched *us*.

I forced a smile when I asked, "Why is that, exactly?"

"I have my reasons," he replied with a grin. "Tell me, what Gifts have come to light since the night you changed?"

It wasn't the first time he'd asked the question, and I was beginning to wonder if he was questioning my honesty as much as my talents.

I hesitated, not wanting to reveal too much.

"My...senses are improved. I can see leaves in trees a mile away. The landscape is more vivid, as is everything else. My sense of hearing, of smell—they're stronger than ever before."

"Ah," Corym said. "Good. That is only the beginning." He backed away a little and said, "What else?"

I stared into his eyes, convinced that he knew something of my healing power.

"Nothing yet," I lied. "Though I am hoping that with your help, I can uncover some hidden talents."

"Of course I will help you, as will the Fae lord. He is intent on it, in fact. It seems he's eager to see us win at the Trials. He must be looking forward to seeing you and me wed."

He eased closer and I stiffened. I still tried to smile, to

behave as if I were excited by him and eager for his touch. This man was to be my husband, after all.

More importantly, if I wanted his protection in the Trials, I would need to convince him that I cared for him—that I was as thrilled about our coming wedding as he was.

"Speaking of the Fae," the prince added, pushing my hair from my neck, "they say your friend, Lord Mithraan, has destroyed the mist at long last. That he has broken the spell cast a thousand years ago, though the Grimpers still wander the land. It seems some of those horrid creatures have broken free and are now roaming the mortal realms."

"Oh?" I replied, desperately hoping to convince him I knew nothing of any of it. "I suppose that's good. The mist has killed many over the centuries. And maybe if the Grimpers are separated from one another, it will be easier to kill them."

A look of rage crossed the prince's face. "For centuries, the mist and the Grimpers protected our lands from those bastard Fae. Not only Castelle's population, but all of Kalemnar. Our people are now at risk, Lyrinn—or do you not care?"

I tightened with his tone, anger heating my blood. "Of course I care, your Highness," I said. "A Grimper killed my own father, or are you forgetting that?"

He looked like he was going to curse at me, but he stopped himself and said, "You're quite right. I apologize. That was inconsiderate of me."

"Perhaps the Fae will remain isolated in Tíria," I offered. "They don't exactly love mortals, remember."

The prince nodded. "Perhaps you're right. But tell me—now that the mist is gone, you don't suppose Lord Mithraan intends to compete in the Trials...do you?"

I froze.

The greatest reason to break down the mist, to destroy it

entirely, is so the Fae can compete against mortals and take back the power they once had. Mithraan and the others had told me it was the only way to restore Tíria to its former glory, after all. With the mist broken, the Fae were once again eligible to compete. The king had said as much—he had all but *promised* it, in fact.

Why had the thought not occurred to me until now?

If Mithraan and a female Fae took part in the Trials, there would be little chance to beat them.

If they compete, I will die.

I had brought Mithraan back from the brink...and now, he would likely take my life.

I had just healed my likely murderer.

"I...couldn't say," I replied, my voice trembling. "But why would he compete, when he knows he would lose to you? We all know you're the most powerful man in the Five Realms."

"Clever girl," Corym replied with a gleaming smile. "The Fae is powerful indeed if he took down the mist. But you and I both know he is nothing compared to me."

I nodded, mirroring his smile despite the nausea that roiled in my belly. "Of course. You're everything they said you were when I was back home in Dúnbar. All the young ladies spoke fondly of you. I'm sure I'm the envy of all of Castelle."

The truth was, I had seen no evidence of the prince's so-called Gifts. No evidence of his power. All I knew was his reputation—and that alone would not be enough to conquer two Gifted Fae.

"I don't care for the other ladies," the prince snickered, slipping closer to whisper, "I only have eyes for you. But I must issue you a warning, my Lady."

"Oh?"

"The Fae lord," he said, scrutinizing me as though awaiting my reaction. "He's not what you think he is."

My smile faded, and all my strength wasn't enough to coax it back to life. "What do you mean, Highness?"

"He is deceitful. Early this morning, just after you had returned with him, he came to my father, to me. Told us he had sapped the power from the Breath of the Fae. He said his realm is once again open to mortals—but it's my belief that he wishes to destroy us and our lands."

The words were like a knife in my side, and I told myself not to believe them. I had seen Mithraan's eyes, felt his touch, his voice, soothing me, grateful to me for saving him.

I owe her my life.

"Don't worry," the prince said. "I will do everything in my power to keep you alive. You are to be the mother of my children, after all. The Queen of Domignon. You will soon be the most powerful woman in this land. Just promise me you'll be wary of the Fae. He is charming—even I can see that. He has eyes that could melt the iciest heart, that one. But his charm is his most potent weapon, and I fear he has used it on you more than once."

I tried to laugh, but my mood was glum.

The prince stepped toward me, slid his fingers down my neck, then farther down, slipping them towards my chest. "You know, there's no reason we need to wait until the Trials are over to enjoy one another's...*company.*" He pressed in close—too close. "No reason we should not bond before we are wedded. The Trials will be difficult and challenging, Lyrinn. Perhaps we can seek some comfort in one another's arms..."

I pulled back abruptly at his words, and his eyes went wide with shock at my apparent revulsion.

"I apologize, Highness," I said, forcing another smile. "It's... it's only that I wish for our bonding to be...*special.* You are such an important man, and I want to prove myself worthy of you before we are united."

He looked skeptical for a moment but finally offered up a white-toothed grin. "I suppose I can wait a little, if I must. Your Gifts, after all, will continue to develop and reveal themselves as the days go by. You and I have a few weeks yet before the Trials begin. Just...do me one favor, would you?"

"Of course," I said, nodding eagerly.

"Train with Lord Mithraan if you must, but do not let him charm you with his deceitful ways. It would only make life more difficult for you and me. Remember—I am your only true ally. It was my father who brought you here to save you from the threat in the North. You can trust us with your life. We will do everything in our substantial power to ensure that your life here is perfect."

But a perfect life would include...

"Have you heard any word of Leta?" I asked, my voice jagged.

He looked surprised at the question, but nodded. "We have found some evidence of her whereabouts, and I believe we are close to locating her. And when we do, as promised, I will have her brought to you. Would you like that?"

"More than anything," I replied. "I...believe it would give me strength."

"Then I will redouble my efforts and insist that my men bring her to you within the week," he said.

I nodded gratefully. "Thank you, Highness," I said. "You don't know what it would mean to me."

Cupping my cheek, the prince inched toward me and pressed a kiss to my lips, seemingly accepting a reward for a feat he had yet to accomplish.

His mouth was soft, gentle and hungry at once. I did my best to return the kiss, trying not to tighten when he pushed his tongue past my lips. I told myself to enjoy the moment, to revel in my first kiss with my future husband.

But I failed miserably.

"Forgive me," he whispered with a low moan, pulling back and pressing his forehead to mine. "I needed to taste you, Lyrinn. I ache for the day when I will be able to stroke my tongue along every inch of you."

I wanted to reciprocate, to tell him I desired the same. That I would be all too pleased to give myself to him, to feel his lips and tongue caressing every nerve, every inch of my bare flesh.

But instead, I simply nodded, straining my lips into another pleasant expression and feigning shyness.

"You have a training session with the Fae today," Corym finally said. "Use your time wisely. I am counting on you, my Lady." The prince stepped toward the door, but turned at the last moment. "Oh—I should tell you, the Champions from Marqueyssal and Belleau will be arriving at the palace soon. I expect those from Castelle will follow before long. You and I will have a chance to assess our competition—though I have little fear of any of them."

With that, he left, and I turned back to the window, filled with a sudden dread.

Champions, here?

The competition was becoming too real, too close. I was nowhere near ready, either physically or mentally, for what was to come.

But more than mortal Champions, I had begun to fear that the prince might be right about Mithraan's intentions.

I had stupidly allowed myself to think he—a Fae lord so powerful that he had broken through a thousand-year-old curse—had developed actual affection for me. I had believed he cared for me when clearly, he was as bent on my destruction as he had ever been.

As much as it pained me to think it, the prince was probably right. A Fae lord such as Mithraan would only ever declare his affection for me or stroke his fingers over my flesh in an attempt to charm me into submission.

And because I was a fool, it had worked. I had fallen for his charms. I had ached for more of him—for his lips, his scent, his...everything.

Worst of all, I had brought him back from the brink of death.

"You will not weaken me with those eyes, those words, that tongue of silver," I hissed under my breath. "I will not cave to you again, *my Lord.*"

CHAPTER THIRTY-TWO

AFTER I'D DRESSED myself in an outfit made up of linen pants, a gray tunic, and a worn leather sheath at my waist, I half-heartedly consumed the breakfast of eggs, bread, and fruit that Anira had brought me.

I cautioned myself not to think too much about Mithraan. Instead, I focused my mind on the training session that was coming—on what it would take to stay alive during the Trials.

The problem was, my survival in the Trials depended largely on whether or not the Fae were likely to compete.

But would Mithraan really do such a thing to me? Competing meant ensuring my death. It meant the potential of slicing my throat open with his silver talons.

With a wave of nausea, the realization came to me that his entire goal in following me on the King's Road—in imposing himself on me as my so-called "protector," had been to find some way to compete in the Blood Trials.

Which meant that my pending death was a guarantee.

After a few minutes, a knock sounded at the door, and I was grateful to be temporarily pulled out of my wretched thoughts.

"Come," I called out. The door opened and Mithraan stepped in, bowing his head slightly.

"Are you ready for our first session?" he asked.

I was wary of him, and cold, and I could see that he sensed it as he studied me. I rose to my feet, nodding.

"Where will we be training?" I asked, my tone curt.

"The small courtyard at the grounds' southeast corner."

"Let's go, then."

In silence, I accompanied him out of my suite and down the corridor, and we wound our way to the courtyard he'd mentioned, where we found Khiral and Alaric shooting at a target with a pair of shortbows.

Their aim was incredible. Arrow after arrow was split down the middle, and I swallowed hard to see what sort of skill I was up against. I could only imagine that Mithraan's prowess was even greater than that of the other two Fae, if he was able to name himself Champion.

Mithraan grabbed hold of a bow and handed it to me. "Do you know how to use one of these?"

"I have some idea," I told him, forcing away the tightness in my voice. "Our father taught us when we were young, though we didn't train as much as we should have."

"Ah. But you didn't know you would end up a Champion one day." Mithraan shot a look toward the other two Fae, who had wandered off to a corner and were now absorbed in some intimate conversation. "Have you told the prince you healed me?"

I looked into his eyes, assessing. "No," I said. "I saw no reason to. It's not exactly the Blood-Gift they were hoping I would display after my Change. It's not like I can murder foes with healing hands, is it?"

"No, I suppose not." Mithraan played idly with an arrow sitting on a nearby table. "Why is it, do you think, that the king and prince were so eager to make you Champion without knowing if you possessed a single Blood-Gift?"

The knowing look in his eye told me he knew the answer far better than I did.

"Other than my mother's supposed talents, I don't have the first clue," I said, nocking an arrow in my bow and aiming it at the target. I shot it, hitting the target's edge and just barely embedding the arrow. "I am clearly not so Gifted as they think."

"Oh, I don't know. I'd say you're extremely talented." Mithraan slipped up behind me and took my arms to re-angle them as I nocked another arrow. I took a shot, and this one hit close to dead center.

"How are you feeling, Lord Mithraan?" I said, pulling away from him. My voice was formal, icy.

"Fine. Very well, in fact. Better than I have in some time."

"That's good." I lay the bow down on the table and turned his way, unable to stand the nagging feeling tearing at my insides. "Tell me—do you intend to compete in the Trials?"

He sucked his cheeks in, his jaw tensing, and for once, he avoided my gaze. "The prince has been speculating, has he?"

"Answer the question," I said.

"Does it matter?"

"I would like to know why I'm training with a Fae who may well intend to end my life."

He looked away then, his eyes landing on Khiral and Alaric. "I need to restore Tíria, for the sake of my kind," he said softly. "Of course I will compete, Lyrinn."

I winced against the pain inflicted by those words. "I see. And who will the female Champion be?"

My breath trapped itself as I awaited the answer, knowing already what it would be.

"Nihara," he said with a shrug. "She is powerful, and loyal to our realm."

"Yes. Of course," I said, stepping to the other end of the table, where an array of throwing knives was laid out.

I picked one up, turned to the target, and focused my eyes on its center before flinging the knife and hitting the bull's eye. I was not yet accustomed to my enhanced eyesight. *If I could just learn to focus all my energy, my rage, on my opponents...*

I held up another knife, playing with its tip with one finger as I glared at Mithraan.

"You are angry," he said. "But of course you are. You saved my life, and now I aim to take yours and the prince's."

"I am angry because you didn't tell me of your plan. You told me in Tíria the Fae weren't allowed to compete, and now, I discover that was a lie."

"Not a lie. The king never expected one of us to find the power to destroy the mist. He has no choice now but to allow us two Champions."

"Of which you will be one, of course," I said bitterly.

"I will. Yes."

"You should have warned me of all of this before I accepted my role as Champion. You had ample opportunity, and you—" I swallowed hard, fighting against a lump in my throat. "And now, I will die. I will leave my sister alone in this world. I could have walked away, Mithraan, and now..."

My voice was breaking.

Yes, I was enraged.

But I was also hurt beyond words. I had come to trust the Fae lord, if only a little. I had healed him. I had heard him tell the others he owed me his life.

And this was the thanks I was to receive?

"I have the Fae to think of, Lyrinn," Mithraan said gently, taking a step toward me.

"So why train me at all? Why waste your time? Is this your way of mocking me some more—pitying the poor mortal girl, the walking joke who will die horribly within a few weeks' time?"

Mithraan shook his head. "I never meant to mock you."

"But you admit that I will die, and that you knew it when you took down the Breath of the Fae? You knew you were driving nail after nail into my coffin, did you not?"

"Your fate is far more complex than you think," he said, his tone smooth and even. "If only you knew—"

"Knew what?" I snarled. "Have you looked into the future and seen my death? Have you foreseen your plan to end me, my Lord?"

"I will not end you," he said, combing his hand through his dark hair. "I could never do such a thing."

I laughed. "Of course you could. You said it yourself—if you don't, your kind will suffer. If you do not end me, Tíria will never return to its former glory. Now, if you'll excuse me, I think I'll train elsewhere. I'm afraid I do not trust you as far as I can fling you, Lord Mithraan. Prince Corym can train me just fine."

He stiffened, his spine as straight as a pike, and backed away, nodding. "Yes. Perhaps it's for the best that you spend your days by the prince's side. If he is the one you desire, then I will not stand in your way."

With those words, he bowed and stepped away, heading for a door next to where Alaric and Khiral were still standing. They looked puzzled as their leader stormed by, but followed him inside the castle.

I grabbed a handful of knives and hurled them one by one at the series of targets, hitting dead center with each throw.

When my hands were empty I finally stopped, my chest heaving with rage.

If he is the one you desire, then I will not stand in your way.

It didn't matter if I desired the prince, or if he desired me. I was going to die—we *both* were, most likely.

I clenched my jaw and told myself the words were nothing but more of Mithraan's cruel manipulation. He was pulling at my heart. Torturing me all over again.

I would not fall for his trickery this time.

For the rest of the week, I avoided Mithraan, the prince, and every other living creature in the palace. I headed out daily to the woods with various weapons I had taken from the castle grounds. Knives, a short sword, a bow and quiver filled with sharpened arrows.

I had decided to train myself. I would hone the skills that my father had taught me when I was younger, and when the time came, I would do my best to take down my foes.

As the days went on, Champions from the other realms began arriving in Domignon, just as the prince had predicted. I watched them from a distance, wary but curious.

From Belleau, a young man called Arvan, with shoulders so broad I wondered how anyone had managed to craft him the armor he was wearing. His female counterpart, on the other hand, was tiny, with large eyes, black hair, and hands that looked too frail to hold a blade, let alone wield it with any conviction. Her name was Elana, and I liked the look of her immediately. She didn't exactly fit the traditional norms of beauty I'd been led to expect of Belleau's Champion, but I found her much more appealing for it. There was something elven about her—delicate, fragile, yet strong.

The Champions from Marqueyssal were both tall and broad, and each looked as if they could down entire forests with their bare hands.

The two from Castelle—Gwyr and Sharilh—both looked terrified. Neither had the air of a fighter, and I could tell just by glancing at them that they had been forced into this endeavor.

"Daunting, aren't they?" the prince said to me at dinner one night as we dined in the hall together. "All but those from your home realm, I mean. I'm sure you've gotten a look at them all by now."

I nodded. "They are a little terrifying," I confessed with a faint smile. "But I've been training with ranged weapons for hours a day. I have faith that I won't have to get too close to any of them in combat. It's a small comfort, at least."

"Ah, good. But you do realize most of the Trials don't involve hand-to-hand combat, don't you?"

"I—," I replied. The truth was, no one had yet filled me in; I had only ever heard vague rumors about mind tricks and riddles. But no one seemed to know what would occur during the Trial period.

I found myself regretting pushing Mithraan away before I could prod his mind for information. He had seen the last Blood Trials in his Ancestral Sight, after all; he had more insight into them than any of us.

"It's all right," the prince said with a chuckle. "I didn't know much until recently, either." He leaned in close and half-whispered, "They change every thousand years, of course. The Trials are designed by an outside party—one who is impartial."

"Outside? What does *that* mean, exactly?"

Corym's eyes lit up as he said, "Lightblood Fae, from Aetherion."

My mouth dropped open, my eyes going wide. "Lightblood?" I said. "Here? I thought they were considered mortal enemies to Kalemnar."

The prince let out a chuckle. "They don't love us, it's true—but they do love a spectacle. Every thousand years, they send a party across the sea to set the magic of the Trials in motion.

They've done it for many millennia. I'm surprised Lord Mithraan never told you."

I shook my head. "Not a word about it." *Then again, Mithraan and I aren't exactly on speaking terms right now.* "So—what sorts of events are we expecting?"

"I'm not sure—it's all kept very secret until the Trials begin. Let's just say that you should sharpen your mind, as well as your sword. There will be challenges you never foresaw. Most of them do not require strength or speed, so much as wits. There are several Trials over seven days—sometimes four, sometimes five, depending."

"Depending on what?"

"On how many of us survive the first few days."

I shuddered. Four would be preferable, of course. But five meant more survivors. More hope. Less violence.

"In all likelihood," the prince continued, "they will begin simply enough—at first, there may be no threats to any of our lives. But as the days pass, we will certainly encounter some danger. That's when the fun begins."

"Fun?" I shot, irritated. "Aren't you concerned that the Fae will kill us?"

The prince let out a derisive laugh. "The Fae failed last time. They'll fail again. I have a few tricks up my sleeve, my Lady."

In spite of myself, a jolt of fear collided with my chest then. Fear for Mithraan, even for Nihara. The prince seemed so sure of himself, so confident, that I couldn't imagine he was wrong.

Still, how could a mortal from Domignon, even a Gifted, best a Fae? Whatever had happened at the last Trials seemed to have been a fluke, at best.

Or subterfuge.

"Come," the prince said, taking me by the hand. "It's late, and you need your rest. I hear that the Fae consortium from Tíria is arriving via ship tomorrow—and if that does not motivate us to train with all our focus, I don't know what will."

As we rose to our feet, I slipped my arm into the prince's and we made our way to the door just as it opened and Mithraan stepped into the dining hall.

His eyes flared as he took in first the prince, then me, and he bowed abruptly.

"My Lady. Your Highness," he said, his voice cold, before making his way toward the table.

"We were just on our way out," the prince told him, guiding me toward the door. "Enjoy your dinner."

I turned to look over my shoulder at the Fae, who was staring at me, his expression a mystery as always.

In the days that had passed since last I'd seen him, I had almost forgotten how beautiful he was.

But I told myself his exquisite face and extraordinary body were nothing more than lures. He was like a pretty, poisonous insect, attracting its naive prey in the hopes of devouring it even as it attempted to devour *him*.

CHAPTER THIRTY-THREE

I DID NOT SEE Mithraan or Nihara over the next few days.

I insisted to myself that I wasn't avoiding them, though it was a silent lie.

I ate every meal in my suite. Occasionally, the prince joined me, and we discussed strategy or theories on what may be expected in the days to come. The prince vowed repeatedly to stay by my side when necessary, that he would grant me protection, though I reminded myself a hundred times at least that I would need to be my own protector.

I spent the hours between meals in the woods, training in the same way I had for days. Occasionally, the prince would send a King's Guard to spar with me, and we would cross swords in a test of my speed and dexterity. Corym watched sometimes, complimenting me or offering me advice on my stance. But he never raised a weapon to me, never attempted to train me himself.

Finally, one afternoon, he came to me in the small clearing I used for target practice, and said, "Are you ready for tomorrow, my Lady?"

"Tomorrow?" I asked, wiping my hair from my brow.

"The Opening Ceremony. Not that we have to do anything other than show our faces. The ceremony is a spectacle—a celebration of past Trials."

My heart thrashed in my chest to realize the day had come so quickly. "I can't believe it," I said breathlessly, panicking. I could have done more to prepare. I should have. Maybe I should even have allowed Mithraan to train me.

I was flying blind, with no idea what was coming.

I had watched the other Champions train from the comfort of the castle's rooms, observing them surreptitiously through windows in order to assess my competition. They were, each of them, impressive.

The large man and the small young woman from Belleau were like dancers, the man flailing a large sword around as if it weighed nothing while his counterpart managed to avoid each swing as if she saw it coming from a mile away. Her tactic seemed primarily to be avoidance, and her speed was extraordinary. I wondered if she could even avoid an arrow flung at her head, if it came down to it.

The two from Marqueyssal were strong, as well. The young woman—Krita—conjured weaponry with her mind, though mostly it consisted of stones, sticks, and other elements one might find in nature. Paneth, on the other hand, was a behemoth, larger and stronger than anyone I'd ever seen.

I watched Mithraan and Nihara, who seemed to embroil themselves deep in conversation during their sessions, rather than actually train. Each wore a stern, serious expression as they spoke, and I noticed they never touched one another as they had done on my first evening in Fairholme. Most likely, they were intent on figuring out how to end us all, and wary of giving away their tricks.

As I watched them, my heart ached with conflicting emotions. Angry as I was, I didn't want Tíria to remain a barren wasteland. I wanted their realm restored, and something in me felt the pain of it acutely. But the only way that could happen was if every mortal Champion failed—and if we failed, we died.

Leta would be left without a sister, after having lost her father.

For that alone, I had no choice but to fight for my life.

I would fight not for Castelle, Domignon, or the other mortal realms, but for my sister's future and my own.

I rose with the sun on the morning of the Opening Ceremony.

The celebration was not to begin until mid-day, but I could not bring myself to sleep any longer. All night, my mind had raced with visions and wild, restless dreams. Swords of flame flying through the air; birds calling out in terrifying, threatening cries. Wounds carved deep into my body, my mind, my soul.

I couldn't help but think my Gifts were beginning to develop into a sort of gruesome prescience, and in my mind's eye, I was seeing the coming of my death

After an hour or two spent lying in my bed, staring at the vaulted stone ceiling, a gentle knock sounded at my door. It was one of the palace's handmaidens.

"My name is Kara," she said. "I've come to help you prepare for the ceremony."

"Thank you," I replied, my voice trembling slightly. "Anira usually helps me. Is she—"

"She is well, my Lady. She is simply occupied elsewhere today."

"I see."

I had spent hours each day in training. I had seen my own improvement, gauged my progress. Yet on this morning, I felt like a small child thrown into a den of wolves with no defense but my fear.

"The king has requested that you wear this, my lady," Kara said, holding up a dress of deep violet that had been draped over her arm.

"Interesting choice," I replied with a nervous half-chuckle. Purple was traditionally a regal shade, reserved for those of noble blood. I felt as unworthy of the garment as I felt of competing in the Trials in the first place.

The handmaiden smiled—was that sympathy in her eyes? —and proceeded deeper into the room.

"I will braid your hair, as well," she said. "Something stylish and eye-catching. Tell me—do you know much about the Opening Ceremony?"

I shook my head. "I thought I knew a great deal about the Blood Trials," I confessed as I took a seat in front of the dresser, staring into my own eyes in the mirror. "But it seems I was dead wrong."

"Few know about the Trials," she said, twisting a thick strand of my unruly hair and revealing my scars. Instinct told me to press a hand to my ear, my neck, to conceal them, but Kara didn't react.

I raised my chin, choosing to embrace the markings as Leta would have done. Perhaps they would give me some unforeseen advantage in the Trials. Maybe my foes would be intimidated, thinking I had already fought valiantly a number of times, that I'd earned my war wounds.

If they knew the truth of the matter, they would laugh.

"The thing is," Kara continued as she brushed away at my hair, braiding it and securing it this way and that, "None of us were alive when the last Trials took place, were we? How could we really know anything about them? The castle has records, of course—a written account of what occurred."

"Oh?" I asked. "Have you ever read it?"

She looked at my reflection, smiled, and shook her head. "Oh, no. I don't read much. It bores me, if I'm to be honest. But others have—those who were preparing the Trial grounds for this day. You know, so they could figure out the order of things and mark out the arena's borders."

"Borders?" I twisted in my seat to look at her.

"You don't know about the arena?" she asked. "I thought all Champions were told ahead of time..."

"I haven't been a Champion for long," I said. "I have trained some, of course, but...I only know the grounds are north of the Lake of Blood."

She smiled again, this time reassuringly. "Yes, of course, you're new to this," she said. "Well, you don't need to worry. The prince will protect you and guide you every step of the way, I'm sure." She leaned in a little and whispered conspiratorially, "Word has it that he is very taken with his bride-to-be."

I smiled back at her reflection, my cheeks heating. *Bride-to-be.* The words were jarring. It was as though our fates were sealed already.

"If only the Trials were so simple as a wedding," I murmured.

"They are simple," Kara said. "You and the prince will win, thanks to his Gifts and yours. You will marry and raise children. For the next thousand years, your descendants will rule Kalemnar. Your legacy will be astounding."

"The only way to win the Blood Trials is to see others die," I said quietly. "It is not a fate I ever desired, truth be told."

Kara straightened up, tightening at my words. On her face, I read a quick expression of horror that dissipated as quickly as it came. "It is the greatest honor known to mortals," she said. "Many would give everything and anything to be in your place."

My eyebrows met and I looked her in the eye once again.

"There is no honor in killing," I said, my voice a tight wire ready to snap.

The handmaiden cowered. "Forgive me, my Lady. You are right, of course," she said as though suddenly recalling that I was soon to be named the future queen.

I sighed and sat back in my seat, irritated with myself. Taking advantage of a social hierarchy was hardly in my nature. But I did not care to be lectured by a young woman on why I should be delighted to be on the verge of a competition where blood would flow like wine.

Where I would be forced to make choices that would cleave my soul in two.

It was then that it hit me: at some point very soon, I would have to face Mithraan. I would likely have to fight him. And he would win, unless a miracle occurred.

Even if he didn't finish me off, Nihara most certainly would. She wanted him, and victory in the Trials would ensure her a future by his side.

I had known from the night we met that my death would likely come at Mithraan's hand, but never had I pictured it all ending this way, as Champions of Domignon and Tíria, pitted against one another for the very survival of our realms.

Kara finished with my hair in silence before applying a little rouge to my cheeks and lips, followed by some sort of cream around my eyes that appeared to brighten my entire face.

By some miracle of design, she had styled my hair so that my scars, trailing down my neck from my ears, looked like ornamental strands of red to accompany my dark hair.

"Thank you," I said softly.

"The prince will fall to his knees when he sees you looking so beautiful," she replied with a bow of her head.

"I can only hope."

It took a few minutes to get me into the dress of violet silk and lace. Its belled sleeves were long and elegant, its bodice tight around my frame. The skirt trailed on the floor, an exquisite silken river flowing behind me as I took a few steps forward.

"Today should be a day of relaxation for you," Kara said. "A day to show you off while you watch others perform. The king's men will be waiting outside in a little while to take you to the city square."

I thanked her again and made my way down to the dining room, where a platter of fruit, cheese, bread, and other food awaited. My appetite was nonexistent, but I forced down a roll and an apple, telling myself I needed strength to get through today, not to mention the days to come.

As I took a seat and contemplated my tenuous future, Mithraan and Nihara strode into the chamber. Mithraan stopped some distance away, nodding curtly in my direction.

"Ah," Nihara said, stalking over to stand before me, her exquisite face almost glowing in the sunlight pouring in through the large windows. "Lyrinn. How nice to see you."

"How nice to be plotting to kill me" is more like it, I thought as I rose to my feet, but I forced myself to utter a pleasant, "And you, Nihara."

With a slight bow of my head, I left them, glancing only briefly at Mithraan, who looked tense and concerned at once.

But I told myself to disregard his feelings and my own. Emotion had no room in what we were about to undertake. My task was clear: survive long enough to see Leta again. Beyond that, I didn't much care. Anything more than simple survival was a fool's hope, after all.

When I was clear of the dining hall, I heard footsteps behind me. Before I could turn around, a hand grabbed my arm and a deep voice said, "Lyrinn."

I turned to look Mithraan in the eye, then yanked my arm violently away.

"What do you want?" I hissed.

"There are things you should know about the Trials. Things I haven't told you."

"You've had weeks to tell me. So whatever it is you have to impart now can't be so important as all that."

"I beg to differ," he said, glancing around. "Look—the Champions will sleep in the Trial grounds. Each will have his or her own tent."

"Why should that matter?"

"Because you must be wary. You have a target on your back. Everyone knows the prince has chosen to take you to the end, and after what happened at the last Trials, I would not trust in the honor of the other Champions. Watch yourself." He stopped speaking, ran a hand through his hair, then said, "I will watch over you when I can. If you ask me to, I will sleep by your side."

I put up a hand and shook my head. "I am not going to seek shelter with you," I hissed, nodding toward the door to the dining room. "Nihara would slit my throat for less, for one thing. For another, I don't trust you to keep me alive."

"She will not harm you. And neither will I."

"She has wanted me dead since the first second she laid eyes on me," I retorted. "Look—you said it yourself. Everyone will be out for my blood. I walked into Domignon with a target on my back, and it only makes matters worse that I am the worst fighter here."

Mithraan's lips twisted, and I could tell immediately what he was thinking. "Fine. Castelle's two are worse. But they hardly count."

"Just...stay in the shadows, as is your nature," Mithraan said, his voice low.

A chill worked its way through me then. He was right—it

had always been my nature to conceal myself, since my youngest days. I knew every alcove, every close, every doorway in Dúnbar where a child could tuck herself and remain unseen. Never had I sought the sort of attention I was about to receive from dozens of nobles—let alone from a number of Champions who wanted to see my head on a pike.

"I will stay alive as long as I can," I told him. "But I do not expect to make it to the Trials' end. And don't worry—I certainly do not expect any help from you."

With that, I turned on my heel and left.

CHAPTER THIRTY-FOUR

I MADE my way outside only to be greeted by a long carpet of crimson and gold, stretching out toward an elegant arena now set up on the castle's grounds. The moment I stepped outside, Nallach approached me with an effusive smile and said, "Hello again, Lady Lyrinn."

"Hello," I replied, feeling wary. I hadn't seen him since his altercation with Mithraan outside of the carriage on our journey to Domignon, and though I had no legitimate reason to dislike him, there was something about him that I still found cold and reptilian.

"The prince is waiting for you, my Lady," he said. "Come—it's almost time for the introductions."

"I thought those took place later in the day," I protested.

"The official Ceremony begins then," Nallach said. "But the prince wishes for you to meet the lords and ladies of the other realms. You may be interested to hear that High King Kazimir of Aetherion has come all the way from the land beyond the sea to witness the Trials."

"Aetherion," I repeated. *The realm of the Lightblood Fae.* "Yes

—I was told their magic is involved in the goings-on at the Trials. I'll admit I'm curious to see how." I forced away thoughts of how much the Lightbloods supposedly despised mortals and Tírians alike.

Let alone the question of why their High King would ever want to set foot on these lands.

"Their magic is rather impressive," Nallach said, and he seemed genuinely awestruck. "Perhaps most spectacular is the Gift of Birdsight bestowed on the leader of each realm."

"Birdsight?"

Nallach looked flustered for a moment as if puzzled by my ignorance, then said, "It's the ability to see through the eyes of a bird sent to witness the Trials. Each leader is assigned one: A hawk for Domignon. A dove for Marqueyssal. A vulture for Belleau, and a heron for Castelle. An eagle for Tíria—though the High Lord of the Dragon Court will not be joining us. Oh—and a white falcon for Aetherion. The Lightblood Fae do love a spectacle."

Yes, I thought. *That's what Corym told me, too.*

"The birds watch the competition, which is too far afield and sometimes moves too fast for an audience to observe through traditional means. Thanks to their assigned bird's special Gift, the leader and all their subjects are able to witness the Trials via a sort of mental conveyance."

"Impressive," I said. But my heart was rapidly sinking. Not only was I to be scrutinized and judged by mortal nobles, but by those from across the sea—Fae I never thought I would have to encounter. The High King I was about to meet would doubtless be hoping for my swift death. He would be expecting it, cheering for it alongside a multitude of others.

My legs trembled as I advanced with Nallach toward a tent where the prince and his father were engaged in deep conversation. When I was close, the prince stepped over with a smile and said, "My lady, you look truly wondrous."

"Thank you," I replied, trying my best not to reveal my apprehension. "As do you."

Unlike me, the prince was dressed in red—the color of Domignon's court.

He offered his arm and told me he wished to introduce me to the lords and ladies of Belleau, Marqueyssal, and Castelle. "Unless you know them already," he said.

With a laugh, I replied, "I have not exactly spent my life in the presence of nobility," I told him.

"Well, then, prepare yourself to start," he said, guiding me along the carpet until we came to his father and mother, who were in the midst of a conversation with a short, bald man with a carefully sculpted, pointed beard, and an even shorter woman in a gold dress. They were friendly-looking and cheerful as they turned our way.

"Ah," the man said. "Prince Corym. And this must be Lyrinn." He bowed his head toward me, and I curtseyed in return.

"Lord and Lady Dubois of Marqueyssal," prince Corym said as I clung to his arm.

"Pleasure," the lord said, and I cleared my throat before replying, "The pleasure is all mine," in the most docile voice I could muster.

Corym took me around the large tent, introducing me to the nobles of Castelle, whom I recognized from my youth when our father had brought Leta and me to see our capital city's royal gardens.

"It is unfortunate that you could not have been chosen to represent our realm," Castelle's lady told me. "But we are proud of you, nonetheless."

Proud, I wanted to say. *You had no idea I existed. You have done nothing for Dúnbar, not when we had droughts or floods or fires. Nothing to protect us from the mist or monsters that killed our people —including my father.*

You would not have cared if I had died on the Onyx Rise that night...

But I smiled and thanked them for their support, turning away to conceal the quiet expression of hostility I knew would be showing itself in my eyes before too many seconds had passed.

Corym guided me next toward a tent adjacent to the one we were in. This one was gold, with intricately crafted lace streamers flowing down from its high ceiling, whispering in the breeze in a strange, quiet melody.

I froze when I saw Mithraan standing at its center with a party of Fae.

It wasn't Mithraan who prompted me to freeze in my tracks, but the male Fae he was speaking to. He was tall, broad-shouldered, with skin of bronze, light hazel eyes, and ivory hair. He was beautiful—more beautiful, almost, than any creature I'd ever seen.

But it wasn't his beauty that stole my breath from me.

Though I was certain I had never met him, there was something about his face that felt as familiar as my own. I was convinced I had seen him in my dreams—in nebulous visions of a faraway place I'd never been.

A place only conjured in the depths of my imagination.

Or so I had thought until this moment.

"Who...is that Fae?" I asked.

"That's King Kazimir," Corym said. "Leader of all of Aetherion. He is the most powerful of the Lightbloods, they say. An extraordinary Fae."

"The High King," I uttered, my eyes moving back to Mithraan.

"What's wrong?" Corym asked, taking hold of my arm. "Lyrinn, you look as though you've seen a ghost."

"I…it's fine," I said. "No ghost. I'm just a little overwhelmed."

"Understandable. But don't worry—in a few days, this will all be over, and you and I will be on our honeymoon. Perhaps we could even travel to Aetherion and solidify the bond between our people."

I looked up at the prince with a smile. As always, he was wholly confident and utterly secure in the notion that together, we would prevail in the Trials.

And once again, I wondered why.

"Come, let's say hello," the prince said, leading me over. I followed, my body taken over by some force not entirely under my control as I stepped toward the figure I'd seen a thousand times in my dreams.

King Kazimir turned my way as we approached, his eyes locking on mine. His face was expressionless, his eyes light and piercing. They reminded me a little of Mithraan's, but there was a coldness in them that sent a bitter chill through my bloodstream.

His lips curved into a smile, the corners of his eyes crinkling, though I wasn't entirely convinced the expression was sincere.

"High King Kazimir," Corym said. "I would like to introduce Lady Lyrinn—"

"Martel," the king said with what sounded like a healthy dose of disdain.

Oh, wonderful. He already despises me, just as all Fae do.

I shot Mithraan a look, but he, like the king, was expressionless.

"Your Majesty," I finally said with an awkward curtsy.

"So, this is the famous daughter of Alessia," the king said, and I jolted to attention.

My brows rose. "You know of my mother?"

"Of course. We met some time ago, when I was here in Kalemnar for a visit."

"I...did not know one of your kind had been to Kalemnar in recent years," I replied. "It was my understanding that the Fae from across the sea had stayed far from this place ever since the last Trials."

For a moment, he looked surprised, but the expression faded quickly, replaced by a tightening of his lips. "Ah," he said, leaning in close. "Let's just say it was a...*secret* visit. Business dealings, if you must know. But it's all very dull."

His words did nothing to allay my own confusion, but I simply smiled and nodded, trying to piece together the timeline. If this Fae High King had met my mother, it must have been before she and my father had married.

Before Leta or I had been born.

And yet, our father had never said anything about it. Then again, perhaps he never knew.

With the thought of my father and sister, my heart sank. The Trials were to begin in one day, and I still had not received news of Leta.

Do not worry, a deep voice said as if in response to my sorrow. *You will see her soon.*

I looked toward the Fae king, certain at first that it was his voice I'd heard. But by now he was embroiled in conversation with Corym.

Mithraan stood some distance away, watching me silently as he sipped from an elegant glass of clear liquid. I glanced at him, wondering if there was any chance it was his voice that had made its way into my mind.

His eyes narrowed briefly, then he looked away, a grim expression on his lips.

The voice came again.

A war is coming, Lyrinn—one far more important than the Blood Trials. I can only hope that when the time comes, the right side is victorious.

CHAPTER THIRTY-FIVE

When he'd concluded his conversation with the High King, Corym introduced me to Lady Isabella, the leader of Belleau.

"The lord of the realm died two years ago," Corym explained to me after our brief meeting. "She is in charge, and by all accounts, an excellent leader."

When I had been introduced to all the important lords, ladies, kings and queens I was to meet that day, Corym told me we were to head to Domignon's largest town square for the Opening Ceremonies.

"Some of the city's residents will be in attendance," he said. "Those who cannot will witness the ceremony through Birdsight."

My mind was addled. The day thus far had been surreal, strange, and filled with fleeting slivers of memories I didn't know I possessed. I reeled with questions about the Lightblood king and my mother—about how a young woman such as her would have come to meet such a Fae.

Corym led me to a golden carriage decorated with Domignon's sigil on its doors, and took my hand as he helped me inside. I was relieved to seat myself, my gown's immense skirt flowing around me in a river of violet. Corym sat opposite me, smiling as he studied my features. He pulled his eyes to the window only when we started moving.

"The High King was impressed with you," he said as we left the palace grounds. "Which isn't exactly surprising. You are, after all, an impressive young woman."

"Thank you," I said, trying to take the compliment at face value. I had never done a thing to impress the prince, and I was still half-convinced that he and his father were delusional. "Though I'm not sure why such a Fae would ever want to meet someone like me."

"He told you—he knew your mother years ago."

"Which in itself is strange, don't you think?" I asked, leaning forward. "I'm still not entirely sure why I never knew that my mother lived here in Domignon. Or how she ended up with my father in Dúnbar, or..."

I stopped speaking, smirked, and shook my head. Surely the prince didn't want to partake in my rambling questions about my ancestry. My mother had secrets, clearly—ones I might never learn. Something in her life had led her to my father. Some event, some moment—but before that moment, she had lived through a series of events that I couldn't begin to imagine.

The prince pulled his eyes to mine, leaned forward, and reached for my hands. I offered them to him, savoring the reassurance of his touch as he squeezed them gently. For the first time, I felt a connection to Corym. I appreciated him. I *needed* him—at least I told myself I did.

"You must focus on the future—not on the past," he told me. "*Our* future. In a few days, Lyrinn, you and I will be married. I understand the temptation to think about other things—to allow your mind to wander to questions about your mother, about the past."

I opened my mouth, but the prince continued before I had a chance to protest.

"And," he said, "I need you to consider the future of the mortal world. You and I must stand together at the end of the Trials, victorious. So that Domignon and the other realms might enjoy another thousand years of peace, far from the oppressive thumb of the Fae."

He was right—at least in part. I had a choice: allow myself to become distracted, then likely die in the Trials—or fight for my life and all the lives of Kalemnar's mortals.

But what I did not tell him—what I would *never* tell him—was that I did not wish for the Fae of Tíria to suffer the same fate they'd been dealt for the last thousand years. As much as Mithraan had hurt me—as much as he had *infuriated* me—I had already silently resolved that, were I to be victorious alongside the prince, I would hold to my promise and find a way to free their lands for good.

The mist may have disappeared thanks to Mithraan's power, but the Grimpers remained. I wouldn't rest until their reign of terror had ended, the lands were restored, and all Fae could be free.

I looked out the window to see a carriage coming around the bend in the road behind us, an elegant silver eagle painted on its door. In its window I could see Mithraan's face, his bright eyes burning into mine, even from this distance.

A surge of searing heat flooded me in that moment—a strange, violent pulse of desire that I tried and failed to push away. I tore my eyes from his, forcing myself to lock them on the prince.

"I will do everything in my power to ensure our victory," I told him.

The prince smiled warmly, and I reminded myself why I needed to focus my energy on him and on my future.

Any past, fleeting moment when you thought Mithraan was an ally—any moment you thought he might care for you—was a deception. Do not fall for his charms, his beauty. Do not succumb to his power.

He will not protect you.

He said himself that he never wished to see you on the throne of Domignon.

We arrived at the city square after a few minutes to a deafening chorus of cheers. Townspeople flooded the area, which had been converted into a sort of makeshift tournament zone, its cobbled terrain covered in thick layers of earth. Seating was set up in risers along each side of a long arena, rows of raised benches crafted for the townsfolk to watch the celebration unfold.

"What exactly are we about to witness?" I asked Corym, terrified that he'd tell me we were expected to perform for the massive crowd. Too many surprises had already thrust themselves upon me since my arrival in Domignon. One more, and I might die of a heart attack.

"We will be introduced," Corym replied proudly. "As will the pairs of Champions from each realm. Once that is done, we will become spectators for the rest of the day. Today is an enjoyable spectacle for our pleasure—a celebration in anticipation of the Blood Trials."

"I see," I said, though his words did little to reassure me. Even the thought of being introduced to the masses was a terror. Who was I to stand before such a crowd? A Champion named for no reason other than her mother's tenuous connection to the king?

Corym reached out once again, took my hand in his, and raised it to his lips. "I will look after you, Lyrinn. I will not leave your side. All my life, I have been in the spotlight...but trust me when I say I have some understanding what it is to be *thrust* into it. You are not alone."

My eyes threatened to well with tears at his words. I was so grateful for his empathy, for his kindness in this, of all moments. I needed it more than I was willing to admit to him or anyone.

"Thank you," I said, then bit my lip to hold back the tears I refused to let fall. "It's a lot to take in, I'll admit...and I'm overwhelmed."

"Of course you are," he said. "Who wouldn't be?" He smiled, sat back, and crossed his arms. "But don't worry. You are skilled, particularly with your knives. I have seldom seen anyone able to throw with such accuracy."

"Thank you," I said. "My father is—was—the one responsible for teaching my sister and me. I've always had a way with knives, though I never seem to have one on hand when I need it."

"Well, you will have all the weaponry you need during the Trials. Don't you worry for a second about that." The carriage pulled to a stop as he spoke, and he laughed and said, "Now, what say you and I make our first public appearance together?"

I nodded and accepted his offered hand as one of the king's men opened the door. The prince stepped out to screams, cries, and whoops from fanatical spectators, then he turned and helped me down from the carriage.

Cries of "We love you, Lady Lyrinn!" met my ears, much to my shock. No doubt there were posters and banners up around the city announcing Domignon's new Champion, but I had not seen them—nor had I so much as given them a second thought.

Never had it occurred to me that I would turn into some sort of celebrity.

I smiled, then issued an awkward wave to the crowd, which only augmented the shouts and screams.

Corym escorted me to a section of velvet-upholstered seating where all the Champions and the lords, ladies, kings and queens of the various realms were to sit and watch.

All but the king and queen of Tíria.

Despite the fact that two Champions now represented the Immortal realm, King Rynfael had not come. Perhaps he had lost faith in the Trials after losing his daughter and both Champions a thousand years ago.

I could hardly blame him if that was the case.

The prince and I sat down next to Domignon's king and queen, who were seated next to High King Kazimir.

A now-familiar voice spoke deep in my mind as I shifted uneasily.

Hello again, Lyrinn Martel.

I looked over to see Kazimir looking out toward the Trial Grounds.

It was you.

I'm sure of it.

The prince touched my hand, jolting me out of my thoughts, and leaned toward me, whispering, "The spectacle is beginning. First is a tribute to our guests from Aetherion. Watch."

I kept my eye on the arena ahead of us as two large gates opened, and two armored figures on white horses came riding into the arena's center. They dismounted, and each drew a long, silver sword. Each wore a long white wig to mimic the silver hair of the Lightblood.

On the tunic of one of the actors was a sword, burning with white flame. On the other was a silver rose.

"Those are two Houses who battled many years ago," Corym told me softly. "The sword represents High King Kazimir's House. The rose belonged to a rival. Kazimir's ancestors won, obviously."

I watched as the knights engaged in an elegantly choreographed battle, swinging their swords and ducking effortlessly, then leaping and dancing around the arena to cheers from the crowd. They moved with all the lightness of ballet dancers, leaping through the air to avoid blows from one another's weapons until finally, the knight wearing the sword sigil swung fiercely at his opponent.

In mid-stroke, his sword disappeared, turning into a flowing white ribbon of silk. It floated through the air, light and beautiful, before striking the other knight in the chest with a terrifying slashing sound that echoed through the entire arena.

Ribbons of deep crimson shot out from the victim's armor, flowing and trickling down to the ground as the man fell.

"The white ribbon represents the Lightbloods' greatest weapon," Corym whispered. "Rumor has it that the most Gifted among them are capable of conjuring projectiles of pure light, capable of cutting through even the thickest steel. They say High King Kazimir possesses the Gift—and that he has used it to cut down entire armies."

As the crowd roared with cheers and shouted pleas for more, I stared out at the arena, at the two men who were now on their feet, bowing to our section. As those around us cheered with excitement, Mithraan turned in his seat and looked me in the eye for only a moment before turning away.

He and Nihara were the only two spectators in the place who weren't applauding.

The next spectacle involved a series of people—men and women, all in battle gear, trudging to the arena's center. All of them looked exhausted, dirty, battle-worn. One of the men and one of the women wore comically large, pointed ears crafted of paper.

Corym laughed when he saw them and once again leaned toward me. "You'll enjoy this one."

I watched as a couple of old men in robes strode out from the arena's opposite end, medals in hand, and one of them exclaimed, "It is time to award the title of Victor to two Champions! After witnessing the Blood Trials these last several days, it is clear that the winners are the two Champions from Tíria!"

A smattering of applause, and a loud chorus of boos sounded from the townspeople.

As the man approached the two actors dressed as Fae Champions, the two tumbled to the ground, making gagging and gurgling noises as they thrashed about, then finally lay still.

The crowd leapt to its feet, screeching its common approval.

I stared, horrified that they would put on an exhibition in such poor taste in front of Tíria's current Champions.

"Cruel," I said softly.

"The truth hurts," Corym replied with a shrug as the fake Elder on the arena floor handed the medals to two mortal winners, then proceeded to feign beheading the other surviving Champions with a paper axe.

I looked down at Mithraan again, only to see Nihara leaning in and whispering something to him. His shoulders were tight, his spine rigid, but both kept their composure while the actors moved off the field.

Over the next couple of hours, we watched jousting, sparring, swordplay, all of which was impressive...but none of which made up for the insult the realm of Domignon had hurled at the Fae.

I couldn't help thinking it was the king's idea—an attempt to diminish Mithraan and Nihara, to remind them of their kind's vulnerability.

But all the cruel gesture had done was remind me that something had gone awry a thousand years ago—that Tíria's two Champions had fallen not in battle, but during the Closing

Ceremonies. Someone had done this to them, and it wasn't a fellow Champion.

I was grateful when we finally climbed into the carriage to head back to the palace, and more grateful still when I found myself alone in my suite, away from the crowds of bloodthirsty mortals eagerly anticipating the death and destruction of the days to come.

CHAPTER THIRTY-SIX

AFTER I'D FINISHED EATING the dinner that one of the king's servants had brought me, a gentle knock sounded at my door.

"Who is there?" I asked, my heart racing as I contemplated the possibility that it could be Mithraan. It was the eve of the Trials, after all. Tomorrow would be the beginning of a fight for our survival.

But no. Why would the Fae come to see me? We had barely spoken in days. We were no longer civil to one another. There was no reason he would waste his time on me—and nor should I waste mine on him.

"Corym," a deep voice said from beyond the door as I approached.

I scolded myself when my heart sank. I should have been happy to see him, tonight of all nights. But I was tired, anxious, and in no mood for company.

"I have brought you a gift," he half-sang from the corridor.

I trudged reluctantly to the door and pulled it open. "A gift?" I asked, plastering a smile to my lips. I had no desire for trinkets or the like, but there was no point in letting my partner in battle know it. *I should at least pretend to be happy,* I told myself.

But when I saw what the prince had brought, there was no need for pretense.

I nearly collapsed to my knees at the sight of his gift, and had to reach for the doorframe to steady myself.

Leta?

No.

I can't believe it.

Yet there she was before me with her beautiful smile, her torrent of red hair, a dress of dark green muslin flowing to the ground around her feet.

I grabbed her wordlessly, pulling her close and wrapping my arms so tightly around her that I felt her gasp.

I didn't care if I hurt her a little. I needed to know she was real and whole, and most of all, unharmed by any cruel enemy.

"Is it really you?" I asked, a sob sticking in my throat.

With a laugh of surprise, she nodded against my shoulder. "It's me, Lyr!" she half-croaked. "Please don't kill me with love!"

I pulled back and shot the prince a look of pure gratitude, then focused once again on my sister. "Where have you been all this time? How did they find you?"

"She'll tell you all," Corym said, laying a gentle hand on my shoulder. "I know you need rest for tomorrow's first Trial, Lyrinn—but I also know you need strength. I have been working to get Leta to you, and the timing of her discovery, as it turned out, was perfect. So enjoy each other, and rest assured that I will watch over you tomorrow. For tonight, though, I want you to remember what you're fighting for."

My eyes went to Leta again and I nodded, then simply said, "Thank you, your Highness. I am more grateful than I can say. Truly."

The prince bowed his head and left us both, me with tears in my eyes, my sister with the amused grin she had worn since our reunion had begun.

"Come, sit," I said, taking her by the hand and dragging her into the room. "Tell me everything."

I perched on the edge of the bed, but Leta stood a few feet away, staring at me. She crossed her arms as she replied, "You first, Sister. I'd love to hear you explain how you came to live in Domignon's palace, Champion to the realm, set to wed Prince Corym, of all people. What the hell has happened since we last saw one another?"

For the first time, it hit me that she had lost both my father and me on the same night I'd lost them both. All this time that I'd been worried about her, Leta had no way of knowing what had happened to me—if I was still alive, or...

I took in a deep breath and gestured for her to sit. "That night," I said when she'd obliged, "the night you went missing... I heard cries from our living room. Father..."

My voice creaked to a halt in my throat. I couldn't bring myself to say the words.

But Leta nodded, her smile finally fading. "I know," she said with a nod. "They told me what happened."

I wanted to ask who told her about his death, but we would come to that in due time. Instead, I exercised patience and told her about the men who had transported me south to Domignon. About the king's and prince's insistence that I was a Blood-Gifted, all because of our mother's mysterious ancestry.

Finally, I told her about the prince's desire to make me his wife.

She sat down on the bed and listened to it all with rapt attention, but when I'd arrived at the end of my tale, she shook her head and said, "That's all well and good. Now I want to hear the part you're keeping from me."

"Keeping from you?"

"The Fae," she said. "The Fae you met the night you disappeared after we were all in the Raven together." Lowering her chin, she added, "Yes. I know all about it, and I want to know about those who live on the clifftop—*particularly* the one who followed you all the way here. I've seen him, Lyrinn. He's... extraordinary." She leaned a little closer when she said, "He makes the prince look like a toad, honestly—and Corym is as handsome as mortals come."

I clenched my jaw and for the first time, pulled my gaze away from my sister's eyes. How could I possibly explain to her what Mithraan was to me—how my heart and mind fluctuated wildly between despising him and desiring him with an intensity that threatened to split me apart?

How did I express that he was the most confusing creature I'd ever met, and that it would not surprise me in the least if I died by his hand within days?

"He used me," I said dismissively. "As an excuse to come to Domignon, to insert himself into the Trials. Mithraan plans to compete against the prince and me. He has powers—Gifts greater than any mortal I've ever met."

"I see," Leta said. "But that doesn't explain why he looks at you the way he does."

My heart leapt in my chest, and my eyes shot to hers once again. "What are you talking about?"

"I was at the Opening Ceremonies," she said. "I was concealed among the townspeople. The prince wanted my arrival to be a surprise for you—though to be honest, it was all I could do not to run across the arena in the middle of the jousting tournament and throw my arms around your neck."

I wanted to laugh, but my mind was still stuck on what she'd said about Mithraan, so I waited for her to continue.

"I watched you when you were seated next to the prince.

Watched your exchanges, the way you smiled at him. But it didn't take long for me to notice how you were looking at the Fae lord. I've never seen that expression on your face, Lyr—not even when you've looked at the finest chocolate."

"You're mad," I insisted, my cheeks burning. "If I looked at him, it was purely accidental."

Leta smiled again—that knowing grin of hers—then said, "And I suppose it was accidental when he turned to stare up at you like he wanted to eat you whole?"

"He did no such thing," I said with a shake of my head. "He wants me dead. He intends to reclaim his lands, and the only way to do that is by winning the Trials."

"I'd say there's something he wants more than to reclaim Tíria." Leta stretched her arms over her head casually, as if what she'd just said wasn't momentous in scope.

"You still haven't told me where you've been all this time," I finally scolded, recalling suddenly that her arrival here was an absolute mystery.

Leta shimmied up the bed and lay down, her head on one of the pillows. I lay down next to her and waited.

"That night," she said softly, "before Father died, I went into the sitting room to check on him. He told me something was coming, and not to be frightened. He asked me to open a drawer in the cabinet by the fireplace. You know the one."

I nodded. I knew the cabinet where our father kept his paperwork, his correspondences.

"Inside, I found nothing but a sort of double-necklace," she said, pulling at a chain around her neck to reveal two small, round silver pendants. She held one up to reveal a faint, worn shape that looked like some sort of animal—a galloping horse, perhaps, though it was impossible to tell, given how old and tarnished it was. "Father said they once belonged to our mother. He told me to put them on, and when the time was right, to give one to you." She snickered. "I thought it was the strangest thing, honestly. Useless bits of metal. They're not even pretty. But I did it, because he seemed so sincere, and I haven't taken them off since." She unclasped the chain, pulled one of the pendants from it, and handed it to me.

Without thinking twice, I removed the silver chain from around my neck and took off the metal tube I had worn for far too long, leaving it on the nightstand. I put the pendant around my neck and asked her to tell me more.

"Shortly after that," she said, "two men came to the door. Men dressed in black tunics with a single silver wolf embroidered on their chests. They told Father they were there for me. It was the strangest moment of my life. You know how protective Father was—I expected him to pull out a fire iron and beat them with it while shouting at them that they were not entitled to his daughter. But instead, he just looked at them—just *studied* them for a moment, then nodded, like he was resigned to my fate. It was almost..."

"Almost?" I asked when she failed to continue.

"Almost like he had been waiting for that moment for some time."

"I think he did know," I replied. "He told me you would be safe. It's been the only thing keeping me sane this whole time, honestly. My faith that Father was right—that somehow, he knew that all this would happen in spite of his best efforts to hide us away."

Leta nodded. "He was right. The men brought me to a small chateau in Marqueyssal. The owners—a nobleman and his wife —took good care of me and treated me respectfully. They were gracious hosts, though they never did explain why I'd been taken—at least, not exactly."

"What did they say when you asked?"

"Only that my bloodline had to be protected—that it was

safer to keep you and me apart than to have us close together, at least for the near future. That we may not know it, but we have enemies everywhere...and..."

"And?"

Leta pulled her eyes to mine. She looked almost frightened when she said, "They told me all would be revealed at the Blood Trials."

"Did they explain what they meant?"

She shook her head, barely lifting it off the pillow. "Only that I would discover truths that had been hidden for many years. That the mortal realms would seal their fate with these Trials, and that if all went well, we would rule for eternity...and the Fae would be forgotten."

Something stuck in my throat then—something bitter and sharp that made it difficult to swallow.

"That sounds like a promise that would be impossible to keep," I said, reaching for Leta's hand and taking it. "The Fae are powerful, Leta. And believe it or not, they're not so evil as we were always told. Even Mithraan—whom I want to punch much of the time—is noble, in his way. He only wants to help his kind and to bring back the Tíria of the past. But...whatever the case, however weird and mysterious the circumstances that brought us together, I am glad you're here."

"Me, too. Now, Sister, you should get some rest. I hear you have an important task ahead of you tomorrow."

"Don't remind me," I said with a laugh.

We fell asleep with our heads together, and for the first time in what seemed like days, I felt at peace, my head emptying of the tormented thoughts that had been raging through it for far too long.

Tomorrow would bring new challenges.

But for tonight at least, I had my family back.

CHAPTER THIRTY-SEVEN

Though I had seen the other Champions from a distance during my voyeuristic spying sessions and the Opening Ceremonies, it was on the following morning that we were to formally meet them face to face.

There were ten of us now in total: Corym and me representing Domignon. Mithraan and Nihara for Tíria. Two from each of Belleau, Marqueyssal, and Castelle.

As Leta brushed my hair then helped me to dress in my Trial garb, I stayed grimly silent, contemplating the fact that eight of those ten would be dead within a week. And however much I may have wished for fate to take my side, chances were extremely high that I would be among those dead.

"Do you know about the others?" Leta asked, reading my mind as she braided my hair and twisted it behind my head.

"Very little," I replied. "Only that those from Marqueyssal are well-trained and experienced. As is the prince, of course. The Fae are...well, *Fae*. And I don't hold out much hope for Castelle's two Champions, I'm afraid."

"They say the female Champion from Belleau is a last-minute replacement," Leta said with a smile. "So the good news is that she's probably even more lost than you are."

I spun around to face her. It was the first I'd heard of this—though it explained why Elana, the new Champion, wasn't the stunning beauty everyone had said she would be.

"Last minute?" I asked. "Do you know why?"

Leta shook her head. "Not a clue. She must be a Gifted, if she has been chosen. She is the lord and lady's daughter, and just recently came of age." Leta sighed when she said, "She'll probably die first."

"Leta!" I snarked, horrified at how casually she uttered the words.

"It's true, though," she protested, resting her hands on my shoulders. "Look, Lyr, you're going to have to come to terms with all of this sometime. You're about to fight for your life. You've honed your knife-throwing skills, right?"

I set my jaw and narrowed my eyes, but I nodded. "I've been training for weeks," I assured her. "And...some of my Blood-Gifts have developed since I turned nineteen."

"Show me, then," Leta said, moving away and crossing her arms.

"What?" I replied.

"I want to see what you can do. Show me."

I rose to my feet and turned to confront her, irritated that she would make light of my predicament. "Leta—they're not party tricks. I'm not about to summon magic that I can barely control for your amusement."

She smirked and made a sound a little too close to that of a strutting chicken.

"Are you serious?" I asked.

"I want to see my sister in action," she said with a shrug. "I want to assess your chances so I know if I have to prepare myself for the worst."

"Fine," I snapped, reaching for a pair of silver and gold scissors that sat on the dresser next to me. Opening them up, I slid a blade along the back of my forearm, pleased when Leta let out a gasp of horror as the blood dripped down my flesh.

"You quite literally asked for it," I chided.

"That's not a Gift," she said with a hand over her mouth. "That's madness."

"*Magic* is madness."

I lay the scissors back on the dresser, then held my other hand over my arm, closing my eyes, willing the wound to disappear. I could feel my blood run cold then, magic coursing through my veins. I opened my eyes to see the cut vanish, sealing up as though it had never existed.

"What?" Leta leapt forward and grabbed hold of my arm, pulling it close to examine it. "That's amazing! I had no idea you could..."

"Why thank you," I replied with a shallow bow.

She dropped my arm, looking concerned. "Healing won't help you kill people. And I know you think I take it all too casually, but you're going to *have* to kill them, Lyr, whether you like it or not. I insist on it, in fact. I already lost Mother and Father. I'm not losing you, too."

It was a rare moment of raw sincerity from a sister who rarely showed her deepest emotions, and I reached for her, pulled her close, and hugged her tight. "You won't lose me," I said. "But if you do, remember that the same blood runs through us both. Part of me will always be inside you."

"I'm not so sure we share the same blood," she laughed. "I've never managed to heal myself by waving my hands around like a psychopath."

"I didn't wave my hand. I merely hovered it."

"Either way..."

"Come on, you fool," I laughed. "Let's get to the Trial

Grounds and see what I'm up against. I've been told I'm not likely to die today, so *there's* some good news, at least."

"Glad to hear it, you madwoman."

I had dressed in an outfit made up of linen trousers, a purple tunic, a thick leather belt with a sheath attached, and leather boots. It was standard fare for Champions, who could then coat themselves in armor of their choosing. But given that today would not involve combat, I chose not to wear mail. For all I knew, the Champions might have to engage in a foot race through the woods, and extra weight would only hinder me.

When I was finally ready, Leta and I headed down to the castle's large inner courtyard where the prince awaited us in a small, ornate carriage with Domignon's mountain sigil emblazoned on its door.

"My Lady," he said as I approached.

"Your Highness," I replied with a brief curtsy, and Leta did the same.

"It's time for you to see what you—and I—are up against. Though truthfully, I don't think we have anything to worry about."

"You speak as though you've seen all the Champions' Gifts already," I said as he guided me into the carriage.

When he had helped Leta inside and climbed in to sit opposite my sister and me, the prince grinned and said, "Like you, I have been spying on our competition while they train." He slammed a hand against the carriage's roof, and the driver urged the horses forward. Corym leaned toward us, speaking low when he said, "I assure you, we will emerge from these Trials victorious. As I said, we have little to worry about."

"Little," Leta repeated skeptically. "There's a chasm the size of all Kalemnar between 'little' and 'nothing,' you realize."

"Very well, then. We have *nothing* to worry about. The other Champions from the mortal realms are limited in their Gifts. A motley crew of muscular oafs and tricksters, at best. More a traveling carnival than a small army of warriors."

"Though I agree with you about the mortal Champions, you seem to be forgetting the two Fae," I replied, trying to hide the fact that my breath snagged in my lungs as I said it. Today, we would be going up against Mithraan and Nihara for the first time, and I was not looking forward to it.

"The two Fae are hobbled by centuries of confinement to their lands," Corym replied haughtily. "Their magic is weak. Mithraan is a young, arrogant fool. Nihara is impressive, I'll admit. But she has nothing on you."

I snuck a look in Leta's direction before replying, "I am adept with a blade, Highness, but I have not developed any Blood-Gifts that will give me any particular advantage in combat. I've seen Nihara fight Grimpers. She has flame at her disposal, and she is clever."

Much as I hated to admit it.

"Ah. But does she have anything this beautiful at her disposal?" Corym asked, twisting to his right and reaching for a velvet-wrapped package on the seat next to him. He unrolled it slowly, carefully, and extracted a blade unlike any I had ever seen.

Its hilt was silver, carved with an exquisitely detailed face of a dragon. Its blade gleamed in the sunlight, and looked as sharp as any I'd ever seen.

The prince turned the tip toward himself and handed it to me, hilt-first.

"A gift for you, my Lady," he said. "From King Kazimir."

"The High King of Aetherion?" I repeated, taking the blade. "But why would he give me such a thing? I thought..."

Corym laughed. "The High King can occasionally come off as a little cold, I'll grant you," he said. "He has been through wars—and far more. But he told me he was fond of your mother. That his fondness for her made him wish for your victory, that her blood might run for generations through the veins of the victors' descendants."

As much as I should have been pleased, it was a morbid thought, and when I looked at the blade, all I could think of were the lives I might take with it.

But I had to admit that it was an exquisite weapon—one that would have made my blacksmith father gasp with admiration.

"It is crafted from Elven-steel," Corym said. "Strongest in the kingdoms, and extremely difficult to forge. To say that it is worth a small fortune is an understatement." With that, he handed me an ornate leather sheath.

I unfastened my belt and removed my original blade, replacing it with the High King's gift.

"Thank you, Highness," I said with a nod of my head, a surge of strength coursing through my body and mind.

The High King of Aetherion was on my side. He was hoping for my victory.

For the first time, I felt a faint dash of hope that I could possibly survive to see the Trials' end.

CHAPTER THIRTY-EIGHT

An hour or so later, the carriage pulled to a stop.

"Where are we, Highness?" I asked Corym, who was looking smugly amused.

"At the Trial Grounds, of course."

My heart pounding, I said, "We can't be—the grounds are near the Lake of Blood, are they not? I thought it would take several hours to get there."

He let out a quiet laugh. "I told you some time ago—the Lightblood Fae have a hand in all the goings-on at the Blood Trials. As it turns out, rapid travel is among the spells the High King has up his sleeve. It would be tedious, would it not, to have to travel so long just before such a competition?"

"Too true," Leta said with a yawn. "I'm already bored. I can't wait to get this thing started."

"Then let's go," the prince replied, opening the door and helping us out. "Lady Leta, I'm afraid you won't be able to stay for the Trials themselves. But do come and see the grounds. The first event won't begin for a little while yet."

Before long, we were standing at the edge of a long field of swaying golden grass. To our left was the edge of a thick wood leading to the distant mountains that ran up the west coast of Kalemnar.

To our right was the body of water known as the Lake of Blood, so called for its eerie redness. I recalled learning early in life that its water ran crimson because of some mineral or other—but from our vantage point, it looked like a gruesome foreshadowing of the days to come.

Leta and I wandered the grounds, and it didn't take either of us long to realize something felt amiss.

"I don't see any arena," Leta said. "No fighting ring, nothing. Where, exactly, are these Trials to take place?"

"I couldn't say," I told her. "But if the Lightblood are behind the events, then I suppose anything could happen. They're rumored to be the greatest spell casters in all the kingdoms of the world."

"They'd better be," Leta replied with a derisive snort. "Otherwise this will be a dull affair."

As we strolled, a figure in the distance drew my gaze, and the second my eyes landed on him, my heart began to gallop against my ribcage.

Mithraan.

His face was turned toward us, his stunning amber eyes fixed not on me, but on Leta. A deep sadness settled on his features as he studied her, and I wondered what he could possibly be thinking to bring on such an expression.

Probably, I thought, *what every man thinks when he looks at her. "She's the beautiful one. Why was I so unfortunate as to meet the other sister?"*

After a few moments, the Fae's eyes moved to mine. The sadness disappeared in favor of an intense glare, meant, no doubt, to intimidate me before the day's mayhem began.

I narrowed my eyes back at him, refusing to be daunted.

"Lyrinn."

It was the prince who had called my name from somewhere close behind me, and I turned to look at him with a manufactured smile. "Yes?"

"It's time to make our way over," he said, and I took his arm and allowed him to pull me toward the Competitors' Tent in the distance. Leta accompanied us as far as a velvet roped barricade, where a guard stopped her.

"I'm sorry, my Lady," he said. "No family beyond this point. It's too dangerous."

"I understand," Leta said, reaching a hand out to take my arm. In her grip, I felt a quiet desperation.

"I'll travel back to the palace and watch your progress via Birdsight," she promised, pulling her eyes to Corym. "Both of you. I'll send every bit of strength I have your way. I—I wish you all the very best, truly." She looked almost as if she was going to cry when she looked into my eyes and added, "Win this thing, Lyr. For Father. For Mother. For all that's good in this world. Okay?"

I nodded and embraced her before watching her head back to the carriage, where one of the king's men helped her inside.

A minute later, she was on her way back to the capital, and I wondered with a deep sigh if I would ever see my sister again.

Corym and I headed into the tent, where food and drink awaited. Guards lingered around the periphery, keeping watchful eyes on every entrance.

"Keeping people out, or keeping us in?" I asked Corym, who laughed.

"Probably keeping the nobles away," he said. "At this point, we're on our own, and all the important folk are in their own tent, readying themselves to watch the event via their spell-cast birds."

As the prince headed to a nearby table to grab some bread

and cheese, Mithraan stepped over to me, setting my heart throbbing irritatingly fast in my chest.

Don't take another step, I thought when he was a few feet away.

But he did. And then another, and another, until he was close enough to touch.

"You found her, then," he said softly, chin down, his face too close to mine, his dark hair tumbling about his sculptural cheekbones. "You found your sister."

"The prince brought her to me," I replied, throwing a look I hoped would seem affectionate in Corym's direction. "It was a great kindness. He knew it would renew my strength and resolve."

Mithraan snickered. "Does it occur to you to wonder why the prince did such a thing on the eve of the Trials?"

I tightened. "I don't know what you're implying. I told him some time ago that I was concerned about her. Besides, the king's men have been hunting for her ever since I left Dúnbar. It's no great mystery."

"Isn't it?" Mithraan said, issuing me one of his cryptic looks. "Haven't you asked yourself how he just happened to get hold of her yesterday, of all days?"

I glared at him, my eyebrows meeting. "I have no doubt you are trying to turn me against the prince, but it won't work. He is my ally. I trust him."

"Very well," Mithraan replied with a bow of his head and a faint smile. "We will each stick with our own, then, shall we?"

"I think that would be wise," I replied, wishing him away from myself, if only because his proximity was weakening me by the second. I could taste his scent on the air, and it was chipping away, piece by piece, at my resolve.

And perhaps worst of all, he was making me doubt the one person who was meant to be keeping me alive.

Just as the Fae was about to step away from me, a horn sounded and a voice began to shout instructions.

"The first of the Blood Trials will begin in one hour! Suit up, Champions, and prepare to begin!"

"Do not let your guard down," Mithraan warned in a whisper, his eyes locked on Corym. "Though the first Trial is never a battle, it may still prove dangerous for some. Do not try to *win,* Lyrinn. Simply try to make it to the end—that is the only goal that matters in the Blood Trials. Do you understand me? Whatever tricks they pull, do not surrender your mind to them."

"They?" I asked. "Who are you talking about?" I told myself this was more of his trickery. He was playing with my mind. Trying to cast doubt and convince me that I would fail.

"Every single Champion is your enemy, regardless of what you may think," he said. "Every one of them, except for one. Remember it, my Lady."

"Don't speak to me as though I were an idiot, my Lord," I retorted. "I know perfectly well that I have only one ally."

I took a step back, scowling.

The Fae's eyes darkened, then moved from my face down to my chest. He froze, staring.

At first, I felt compelled to cover myself with my hands, though I was fully clothed. But when I looked down, I saw that he was staring at my mother's pendant—the one Leta had given me.

"I have seen that pendant before." The Fae's voice was barely a breath.

"Where?"

"I...I can't recall." He sounded frustrated, as though the memory were sitting at the edge of his consciousness, waiting to be uncovered.

"Mithraan," Nihara's voice purred as she stepped up next to him. I hadn't even noticed her creeping up like a cat, and her ability to move so quietly filled me with dread for what was to come. "We must ready ourselves."

"Yes, of course," he replied. "I will be with you in a moment."

Nihara bowed her head and left us, throwing me a quick, indecipherable look as she moved away.

Mithraan pressed himself close to me. "The other Champions are each strong, in their way. But don't be intimidated. Use your wits—they are, in all likelihood, your greatest Gift."

"I see. And what, pray tell, is *your* particular Gift that I should watch for?" I asked. I had seen much of Mithraan's magic—his ability to change the world around us. The tricks he'd pulled in the inn on the way to Domignon. I knew of his silver talons, sharp as blades.

Now, I wondered what manner he would choose to end me.

"Gift?" His eyes flared with flame, his voice low when he said, "I have no Gift. Instead, I'm cursed with an unrelenting desire to keep an eye on a beautiful woman from Dúnbar who has found herself in an impossible situation. I would not wish to see her fall for anything in this or any other world."

He slipped a hand to my cheek, stroking my skin as he had done before. Offering the touch I craved so often without ever confessing it out loud.

"Should harm come to her," he whispered, "I would suffer a loss like none I have ever felt. I vowed long ago that I would protect her—and I aim to keep my word. Not because of some pact between men and Fae, but because of something far more important. So you needn't watch for me, Lyrinn. I will be watching over you every second of every day, until these damned Trials have come to an end."

With that, his irises faded, and he turned and walked away.

I stood frozen.

Breathless.

My mind reeled with his words, my knees weakening under me.

I had a competition to win, and the charm of a Fae lord was a distraction I did not need.

CHAPTER THIRTY-NINE

AFTER A FEW MINUTES, the ten Champions were summoned outside. The prince, dressed mostly in light leather armor, guided me with him toward a golden rope that separated us from the Trial Grounds.

Behind us and beyond the large tent we had all been standing in was an encampment of various smaller tents arranged in a circle—presumably the ones where we would be sleeping tonight.

Above us, soaring in broad circles in the sky, was a series of birds. A hawk. A dove, an eagle, a falcon, and others, as well. I looked up, intrigued by their magical ability to convey all that they were seeing to the leaders of Kalemnar.

I wonder if those who witness the Trials will be amused or horrified when we die.

A vast, open area unfolded before us, filled with wildflowers and swaying grass. In the distance, the Lake of Blood reflected the sky, its surface an eerie combination of red and blue as it ebbed in the breeze.

Nallach, King Caedmon's trusted servant, strode out to stand before the group of Champions. He wore a long golden tunic emblazoned with Domignon's mountain sigil and carried with him a rolled-up piece of parchment, which he unfurled.

"Champions of Kalemnar," he called out. "It is with great pleasure that I welcome you to the Blood Trials!"

Cheers rose up around me, some of the other Champions thrusting their fists excitedly into the air.

"I will tell you about your first event in a moment. But before I do..."

Nallach stopped, cleared his throat, then pulled his eyes to the sky where the birds were still circling.

I looked over at Mithraan, whose jaw was set tight as he stood next to Nihara.

Nallach pulled his eyes back to us. "The people of Kalemnar would like to wish each and every one of you the best of luck."

Something in his tone felt like a dire warning.

"The first event is the Labyrinth," Nallach exclaimed, gesturing to the open field behind him.

A few of the Champions snickered, then a couple broke into outright laughter.

"Nah, really," Paneth, the young man from Marqueyssal said, "what is it?"

Nallach glared at him. "Do you doubt me, sir?" he asked. "Do you doubt the magic of the Lightblood Fae?"

Paneth immediately clammed up and shook his head, seeming to remember his place.

"The Labyrinth will appear as you approach," Nallach explained his voice softening. "To complete this event, you must each find your way through."

"Sounds simple enough," Gwyr from Castelle chittered, but his co-Champion, Sharilh, glared at him.

"Nothing in this place will be simple," she warned under her breath.

A deep fear was already setting its way into my bones. I had no doubt in my mind that she was right. Something in Nallach's eyes frightened me. I looked over at Mithraan and Nihara to see that their bodies were tight, as though preparing themselves for an onslaught.

"Are you ready, Champions?" Nallach called.

"Ready!" came a half-hearted chorus. A second later, the golden rope before us faded to nothing, and Nallach stepped away from the clearing.

"Stay near me," the prince said softly. "We will find our way to the end together."

I nodded, keeping close as we took our first steps into the clearing.

But almost instantly, our plan failed.

Walls—tall, gray stone, crawling with creeping vines—shot up from the earth, rising instantly on either side of me, separating me from Corym and the rest of the Champions.

Shouts of surprise and disbelief met my ears from every direction. I could hear the others calling out their partners' names: "Sharilh!" "Arvan!"

Cries of "I'm here! To your right!" came back at me.

The only voices I didn't hear were Corym's and the two Fae Champions'.

"Your Highness?" I called out. "Prince Corym!"

But no response met my ears.

I drew my eyes up to the sky, to the birds who were watching us intently. I wondered what their vantage point was like—how clearly they could see our fates mapped out, and how easy it might be to navigate my way through this mysterious Labyrinth if only I, too, were in possession of Birdsight.

As the prince suggested, I began to walk, holding my breath as I stared straight ahead. The narrow pathway created by the two high walls seemed endless at first, as though the so-called Labyrinth were simply a long, drawn-out highway to nowhere.

But very quickly, another wall leapt up before me, forming a junction and forcing me to turn right or left.

I remembered that the Lake of Blood lay off to the right of the Trial grounds, so I chose to go left, aiming north in hopes that I'd gradually find my way to the Labyrinth's exit.

But every time I began to feel that I was gaining ground, another wall sprang up, forcing me to turn sharply in another direction until I was entirely disoriented.

In the sky high above, the birds still circled. I hunted for the sun, hoping to determine my direction. But it was nowhere to be seen, despite the fact that the sky was solid blue and bright.

So, this is the magic of the Lightblood, I thought. *The High King is toying with us.*

After a few turns too many, it struck me that I might well be headed back toward the Champions' encampment without even knowing it.

What happens if I find my way back to the entrance?

What happens if I never make it out?

"Damn it," I muttered under my breath, trudging along and trying to remind myself that every Champion was facing the same problems. *No one has the advantage here. We must each find our way to the end—and none of us knows the path.*

So I walked on, inhaling the crisp autumn air and trying my best to assure myself I was on a pretty hike, rather than facing a terrifying ordeal. *There's no point in exhausting myself or worrying. This may be the least deadly of all the Trials. I should enjoy it while I can.*

And I *did* enjoy it.

For a while, at least.

I walked for an hour or more, careful not to move too fast and risk exhaustion—after all, I had no food or water at my disposal.

I wondered against my will how Mithraan was faring, and

whether his Gifts might allow him to navigate his way directly to the end. I half-expected to look up and see him in his silver eagle form, soaring over the Labyrinth until he reached the end.

But my mind was yanked out of such thoughts when the walls changed all of a sudden. They turned from gray to charred black. The vines that crept along their surface began to move, snakelike, creeping down to slither along the ground.

The green entities moved threateningly close to my feet and ankles, and I leapt forward, trying desperately to outrun them before they claimed me. The Labyrinth that had seemed so unthreatening a few minutes earlier now felt like a monster rising up to destroy me.

I surged forward, my heart racing wildly, until I came to another fork in the maze. I veered right, tearing along a narrow passageway where the vines were growing more aggressive by the second. They no longer looked like plants, but vicious creatures. Small jaws filled with pointed fangs snapped at my heels as I threw myself forward, crying out in panic.

If indeed it was King Kazimir who crafted this spell, he was a sadist.

I pulled the blade he had given me from the sheath at my waist, clutching it in my fist as I ran. I slashed it this way and that, slicing off the heads of the grotesque green creatures so intent on devouring me. The blade made quick work of the vines, clearing a path for me with ease.

But it didn't matter how sharp the dagger was. I would soon tire and fade—and when that happened, I would have no strength left to fight the slithering monsters off.

In the distance, a harrowing scream echoed against the Labyrinth's walls. The cry lasted several seconds before it was cut off suddenly, and a deathly silence followed.

Mithraan's words came to me then. *The first Trial could prove dangerous.*

But I would not allow myself to die, not here. Not like this.

This was meant to be a puzzle, not a death trap.

I ran for some time before I finally came to a small grass clearing with a large sundial embedded in the earth at its center.

Aware that the vines had ceased to threaten me, I finally stopped running, sheathed my blade, and doubled over, hands pressed to my knees. When I had caught my breath, I pulled up to examine the space around me.

The clearing was surrounded by tall shrubberies, and along the perimeter sat a series of stone benches. I strode over to seat myself on one of them, still breathing hard. I stared at the sundial, noting the time: six o'clock.

What did it mean? It couldn't possibly be the real time, could it? It wasn't yet evening, surely. And it certainly wasn't early morning.

I watched for a few minutes as the shadow shifted. The time began to alter with unnatural speed, changing every few seconds despite the lack of sun in the sky.

9:00

6:00.

3:00.

12:00.

A sudden movement to my right drew my eyes to the clearing's edge, where a figure had just appeared, her face coated in sweat, her breath coming in hard gasps.

I immediately recognized Elana, one of Belleau's two Champions.

She froze when she saw me, a hand going to the dagger at her waist. My hand mirrored hers, and I drew King Kazimir's gift, holding it up so that it glinted in the daylight.

Please, I muttered under my breath, *don't make me kill you.*

CHAPTER FORTY

Elana pulled her hand away from her dagger's hilt and said, "I'm not here to fight. I was just trying to get away from those damned vines."

I nodded once before re-sheathing my own blade. "Me too," I said. "I won't hurt you. I could use another set of eyes, actually. I want to figure out how to get out of this place. That is, after I've rested a little more."

She approached with some trepidation, taking a seat at the next bench over. Her hands gripping its edge tightly as though she were readying herself to flee if I made a sudden move. She relaxed after a few seconds, letting the tension in her body go.

"You're the last-minute replacement, aren't you?" I asked.

She nodded, smirking. "The Reluctant Champion. That's what they call me back in Belleau."

"If I may ask—what's the story there?"

Elana pulled her eyes into the distance and took in a long breath before pushing it out again. Grimacing, she spoke. "My sister was meant to compete. For years, my parents knew she would be a Champion—as did everyone else. My family's bloodline on both sides is filled with Gifted. She was talented, too. A mind-reader who could figure out a person's thoughts before they knew themselves what they were thinking. But..."

She stopped speaking and bit her lip.

"She died," she finally said.

"I'm so sorry," I replied, genuinely saddened. "May I ask..."

"What happened?" Elana replied. "It's no secret, so I'll tell you. A few days before she was to come to Domignon, she collapsed. They think it was her heart, though I refuse to believe it. Asa had a strong heart. She had trained long and hard for these Trials. There was no reason someone so young and healthy should have succumbed like that."

I glanced over at Elana, and for the first time I realized why I liked her face so much—why I had felt drawn to her when I'd seen her training.

Like me, she looked like she had no desire to be here. No ambition to compete in the Trials. Unlike the other Champions, she didn't walk around with false bravado or arrogance.

In fact, she wore a perpetual look of quiet fear. But there was something else in her expression, too; a sort of tacit heartbreak.

I was beginning to understand why.

"That's so sad. I really am sorry."

"For Asa's sake, I'm glad I'm here," Elana replied. "To represent her. To fight for her memory. But I never wanted any part of the Trials. I wholeheartedly despise everything about them."

"The killing of so many Champions," I replied with a nod of understanding.

"That's not the worst of it," she said, "though of course I don't approve of the killing."

"What is it, then?" I asked, curious and grateful to be engaging in normal conversation. Anything to distract us from this wretched Labyrinth and the victim it had seemingly claimed only a short while ago.

Elana glanced sideways at me. "I do not wish to be forced into marriage," she said. "Not to any man. I do not want to be a brood mare for a prince or anyone else. I'm afraid there is no outcome to these Trials that will result in happiness for me. Even my Gift has told me so."

"Your Gift," I said. "What is it?"

Elana sighed. "I can see into the future. In bits and pieces only, and sometimes just enough to keep me on my toes. It makes it difficult for enemies to best me, given that I can anticipate their moves before they make them. But my prescience has also told me I was never meant to be here. The Blood Trials weren't designed for one such as myself."

"Are you concerned that you haven't trained long enough?" I asked. "Because I promise you're as prepared as I am. The Trials came as a surprise to me, too—I thought I was too young, that my bloodline was—"

She shook her head. "It isn't anything like that. I am strong, and my mind works quickly. It would take a talented magic-user to best me."

"So what is it that's worrying you?" With a quick smirk, I added, "I mean, apart from the obvious fact that most of us will die very soon."

At that, Elana let out a little laugh. "Some things really are worse than death," she said. "A life without love, for one."

"Ah. I see."

"No," she said, turning to look at me, her eyes sparkling in the dim light. "I don't think you do, Lyrinn. I watched your face, you see, when we were first arrived in the arena. I saw your eyes...when you looked at Lord Mithraan."

I tightened, my spine going suddenly rigid. All of a sudden, I wished the walls that had risen up around us would disintegrate so I could flee this conversation.

"I didn't—" I began, but Elana let out a sad snicker.

"Deny your feelings if you like," she said. "The point is, I can tell you're capable of loving a man—or a male Fae. I, however, am not."

My heart wrenched itself into a tight knot then. "I'm sorry," I said. "I didn't know."

"Little girls in Kalemnar are taught all our young lives that we will grow up to marry men—that our greatest goal in life is to fulfill that promise. These Trials, meant to be such an honor, are based entirely on the concept that men and women must come to maturity and fall into bed together. But the very idea of it is torture to me. There is no chance whatsoever that any of these men—however pleasing to the eye they may be to so many—will ever be the object of my desire." She sighed. "So you see, there is no happy outcome for me. Then again, there is no happy outcome for any of us. The very best-case is that two Champions manage to do away with the other eight and then, by some miracle, manage to forget what they've done to rise to power."

This time, it was I who let out a laugh. It was truly absurd, this system Kalemnar had put into place so long ago —a system meant to create a superior bloodline so extraordinary, so powerful, that no one can hope to challenge it.

Here we were trying to take one another down, all for the amusement of a few wealthy lords and ladies. There was no superiority involved—only a vicious sort of cruelty.

And at the end of it all, two of us were expected not only to forget the trauma we had suffered, but to fall in love and to procreate with someone we might well despise.

"You seem to be the prince's favorite," Elana observed. "Which means you're the most likely of us to survive until the end. So all my concerns are trivial, really. Our fates are likely sealed—whether I see them clearly or not."

"Is *that* the future you've witnessed in your mind?" I asked with trepidation. "Me alongside the prince?"

She went silent for a moment, then said, "Yes. I have seen you seated on the throne next to him. I have seen you with a child in your womb. I have seen..."

But she stopped there, and a realization came to me.

"It's not the *only* future you've seen," I said quietly. "Is it?"

Somewhere above us, a falcon cried out—King Kazimir's bird. I wondered with a frown if it could eavesdrop on our conversation as well as watch us. Did it know what intimate details we were discussing? Were they being broadcast to all of Aetherion via Birdsight?

"I have seen you happy," Elana said, "and I have seen you devastated, Lyrinn. But I cannot—I *will* not—tell you which fate will lead to your pleasure or pain. I will not create a self-fulfilling prophesy for you. All I can say is that you, of all of us, need to fight the hardest."

CHAPTER FORTY-ONE

A CHILLY SILENCE rose in the air between us, but instinct told me Elana was being kind rather than cruel. By keeping my potential fate from me, she was saving me from panic, from torment.

She could not bear to curse me with a grim future any more than she cared to consider her own.

"One thing," she said, "I can tell you is that you and I will survive this day, if we work together." She thrust her chin toward the sundial. "That's our key to getting out of this place. Just don't ask me how."

As I watched, the shadows shifted quickly once again, revealing the same series of hours.

9:00.

6:00.

3:00.

12:00.

"What do you suppose it means?" she asked.

"There's a repeating pattern," I said, rising to my feet and striding over to position myself at the number six. "Nine, six, three, twelve, then a pause. Over and over again, despite the fact that there is no sun visible in the sky."

I glanced around the clearing. There were four exits, each of them leading down a different corridor. One at twelve o'clock, one at three, one at six, one at nine.

Elana rose and joined me, staring as the shadows moved more and more rapidly between the four numbers, always pausing after reaching twelve.

"It's a map," I said, the revelation hitting me like an arrow.

"A map? How? Is the Labyrinth round?"

"No." I stared to my left, at the corridor that led so far into the distance that I couldn't see its end. It was clear of vines, its walls smooth stone. "I think it's something else entirely."

I cast a quick glance toward the sky only to see that the white falcon was circling in the near-distance, its dark eyes still locked on Elana and me. *Why is King Kazimir's bird so intent on watching the two of us?*

"My father taught me to use clock numerals for directions when I was a child," I explained, pulling my eyes to Elana. "Nine is to our left. Six is back, twelve straight ahead. I think the numbers are telling us to go left, then left again, then..."

Elana still looked confused. So instead of trying to explain it further, I reached down and drew a chart in the earth at my feet, showing her.

"But that's only a few turns," she said. "We've been in the Labyrinth for hours. It can't be enough to get us all the way to the end."

"Still, I think we should try," I told her. "You said yourself that the sundial is the key to our escape. Some part of you knows it to be the truth."

The white falcon let out a sharp cry above us, and I laughed. "See? *He* thinks we're right."

"Or he's trying to misdirect us to our deaths," Elana scoffed. "You *did* hear that scream earlier, right?"

"Don't remind me," I said. "I've been trying to convince myself it didn't happen."

I mulled over our options for a moment, then asked, "Do you trust me, Elana?"

"You haven't tried to kill me yet, so...yes?"

I chuckled. "Come on, then," I said, and led her down the corridor to our left. We jogged along warily, relieved when no slithering entity rose up to snatch at our ankles. When we reached the end, we went left again, then right, until we came to another fork.

"One more left," I murmured.

"If you're sure," she replied.

"I'm not sure at all. But it's the best I've got."

I took her by the arm, and we turned and marched down the last corridor. At its end I could already see another wall covered in vine, rising up like a giant hand signaling us to stop.

"There may be another fork at the end," Elana said. "We should keep going, in case we have to repeat the pattern."

I nodded, skeptical and unwilling to allow hope to gestate inside me.

The white falcon was still watching us, and I had just pulled my eyes up to watch him when another shape flew through the air, this time far closer to us.

"Damn it!" Elana said when she saw who and what it was. "Arvan!" she cried, but he was already gone. "My so-called partner," she sneered. "Air-walking. Some help he is."

I could see the soles of his feet as he raced toward the Labyrinth's exit—confirming, at least, that we were headed in the right direction.

Without a word, we both broke into a run, hoping to catch him. But he was too fast, too far ahead of us by now.

"Why didn't he just do that from the start?" Elana asked

with a laugh. "He could have been done with this Trial in minutes!"

"True," I told her. "Still, I'm glad it took him this long, if only for our sake."

When we came to the high wall at the corridor's end, we both stopped in our tracks. It was solid, with no path leading off in either direction.

"Can your Gift tell us anything?" I asked. "What should we do?"

"Wait," she replied, reaching a hand out to take hold of my arm. "Give it a moment."

Sure enough, the wall split apart just enough to form a doorway, allowing us an escape. Arvan was standing in the tall grass on the other side, his arms crossed smugly over his chest.

He grinned at Elana as we stepped through.

"Belleau reigns supreme!" he shouted, thrusting a fist in the air, and Elana glared at him.

"You could have helped us out, you know," she scolded.

"I know," he replied, contrite. "I'm sorry about that. I tried to air-walk early on, but the vines took hold of my ankles and held me in place. By the time I'd fought them off, I was convinced I had to sprint my way out or some other monster would rise up and kill me."

"Wait—was it you who screamed?" I asked, hopeful that Elana and I had been wrong in our assumption that someone had succumbed.

But Arvan shook his head, his expression turning solemn. "No. I'm afraid I saw who it was, though."

My stomach surged, a swell of nausea weakening me to think who might have met their end. I hadn't recognized the voice—but then, I'd never heard the prince scream.

Or Mithraan.

"Who was it?" I asked, my voice trembling.

"Paneth, the huge Champion from Marqueyssal," Arvan said. "He took a wrong turn, and...he..." He looked as though he might heave. "The vines that took him were immense—like enormous snakes, able to swallow a grown man. They..."

I nodded, reaching for Elana's arm. She, too, looked like she was going to be ill. But something told me she had already known the truth of the matter.

"Is he dead?" I asked, swallowing my fear.

"Very," Arvan replied.

Without thinking, I blurted out, "What about the two Fae? Are they..."

"The Fae were out hours ago," Elana said, and when I eyed her curiously, she shrugged and added, "I saw them in my mind's eye. They've been out nearly as long as the prince."

"The *prince?*" I asked sharply.

"He was the first one out. I suppose I should have told you —but I didn't want you to lose your motivation. I needed you to help me get out of there." With that, Elana offered up an apologetic laugh.

I shook my head and said, "It's not your fault my co-Champion chose to abandon me."

Corym had promised to look out for me. *We'll get to the end together,* he'd said.

Then again, it wasn't as though I'd spent my time in the Labyrinth seeking him out.

Just as I pondered my own complacency, Corym came barreling over from inside a tent in the distance.

"Lyrinn!" the prince exclaimed. "I'm so happy to see you made it through—I was growing worried."

"Your Highness," I replied, my tone frosty. "You were quick to escape, by all accounts."

"Oh yes, it took me no time at all to reach the end. It was only a matter of figuring out the Labyrinth's tricks. You should have called out for me—perhaps I could have guided you."

"I did call out," I replied with a rage-concealing smile. "But strangely, you didn't answer."

"Well. Next time."

"Next time," I said, glancing toward the tent to see Mithraan emerging, his eyes locking on my own. I was sure, for a moment, that I saw relief in his features as I attempted to conceal the joy I felt at seeing him whole.

Nihara stepped out to join him, taking his arm to guide him back inside.

"As you can see," the prince said, "unfortunately, the Fae did well. But there was only one victor." He moved toward me and said, "You and I are one step closer to a future together, my Lady."

At that, I looked over at Elana, who was glaring at Corym. In her eyes I saw an accusation, a quiet acknowledgment of a sin that may or may not have been committed.

I wanted more than anything to ask her what it was that she knew.

"If only the rest of us could hope for so much future happiness," Elana said. "The Trials are designed to grant most of us hope, then tear it away. But for some of us, there was never any hope at a joyful end."

With that, she grabbed Arvan and stormed off toward the tent.

CHAPTER FORTY-TWO

Upon our arrival, each of the Champions was assigned one of ten large, private tents arranged in a circle at the encampment's center. Once we had settled into our own quarters, servants brought us food and drink and offered us the opportunity to bathe and change into clean clothing.

I took advantage of all the offerings in the solitude of my tent, still irritated by the prince's disregard for my safety or feelings during the Labyrinth challenge—but admittedly grateful to be alive. I lay on the comfortable bed for a time, contemplating what tomorrow might bring.

After an hour or more had passed, I began to crave fresh air. The sun had set by then, the moon rising in the sky, and I stepped out of my tent to wander toward a large bonfire at the center of the encampment.

I stared at the dancing flame, basking in its heat and enjoying the sound of crackling logs as they succumbed to the fire.

A deep voice pulled me out of my mesmerized state.

"The Trials have always been a cruelty."

I turned to see Mithraan standing next to me, his fiery eyes mirroring the flame before us. I turned back to the fire, telling myself I didn't wish to speak to him—but knowing my own thoughts to be a lie.

"Among the many memories I inherited," he said, "tucked away in the Ancestral Sight my father's blood granted me—I have seen some of the events that took place during the last Blood Trials. I have seen my kind—the two Fae Champions—unhappy in their duty when the end came. Did you know that the last event is always a battle to the death?"

"I've heard something about it," I replied with a poorly-concealed shiver of fear.

"Strong as they were, neither of our Champions had ever wished to kill mortals. Perhaps that is why they fell in the end. Maybe it was their grief that finished them." He turned to look at me, reaching a hand out and touching my own only briefly before pulling back again. It was enough to send a shock of heat pulsing through my veins. "But you must not succumb, Lyrinn," he said. "Do you hear me?"

I turned, seeking the strength to look into his shining eyes.

"I don't understand you, Lord Mithraan," I said coldly. "You are competing against me. So why do you offer me advice like this? And why—"

"Because the Hunt is coming tomorrow," he interrupted. "They will assign us our quarry, and we must pursue it. But with the Hunt come risks. Armed Champions roaming the woods are dangerous. Do not allow your enemies near you. Hide yourself, if you must. Stay alive at all costs."

"I would think you'd wish for my swift death. Isn't that what you've wanted all along?"

I was pushing him now, trying to force an explanation from his lips. If he was so intent on my survival, I wanted him to tell me why he cared so much. Why, when my death would be advantageous for him, did it matter if I lived to see another sunrise? Why had he spoken to me with such intensity before the Labyrinth?

I would not wish to see her fall for anything in this or any other world.

Mithraan reached a hand out, slipping his fingers onto my neck and pulling himself close. His eyes flicked their way from one feature to the next, then back to my eyes. "Do you really not understand?" he asked, his voice tight in his chest. "Do you not know what you are to—"

"Lyrinn!"

It was Prince Corym's voice. I pivoted to see him standing outside his tent, staring out into the darkness.

Mithraan stepped back, dropping his hand to his side and turning to face the fire once again.

"Go back to your prince," he said softly, "but be guarded, Lyrinn. I may not wish you dead, but others certainly do."

He moved away, disappearing into the shadows beyond the bonfire even as a deep sense of loss ravaged my insides.

He had been on the verge of saying something—words that I had wanted badly to hear. Words that might even have begun to mend the hole that had grown inside me ever since my father's death.

But it was folly to allow myself to revel in such feelings. My only goal was survival.

Stay alive for three more days. Live to see the end, for Leta's sake.

Leta, who would be back at the palace by now.

I wondered if she had been able to see today's event—if she had watched me letting out panicked cries as I ran for my life.

I wondered, too, whether she'd seen Paneth being brutally killed.

When Corym stepped up next to me, I forced a smile onto my lips.

"There you are!" he said. "I've been looking for you all evening."

"I have been here all along, your Highness. Preparing myself mentally for whatever is to come tomorrow."

Corym grinned, easing toward me. "The Hunt!" he said gleefully. "You and I should excel at it, given our skill with weapons. I'll stay close to you—we'll work together."

My smile tightened. *Close to me, just as you remained in the Labyrinth,* I thought. *You abandoned me, Highness. Will you do the same tomorrow?*

"Come," the prince said. "You need your rest. The Hunt is a taxing affair. There will be miles of wilderness to navigate tomorrow, so you must get your sleep."

"You're right. I do need some rest after today's ordeal."

Corym escorted me to my tent, parting the door open for me. "I won't go inside, of course," he said softly, "but I must tell you, I am very much looking forward to a time when we can sleep in the same bed."

I glanced over at Elana's tent, wondering if she could see far enough into the future to know if such intimacy between us would ever come to be.

Because at the moment, it was a scenario I couldn't envision for even a second.

Sometime in the middle of the night, I shot awake, startled by a sound at the tent's entrance.

I looked over to see the flap slipping open then closed again. At first, I told myself it was the wind, but I froze when the eerie sound of tight, shallow breaths drew close.

It was too dark inside the tent to see clearly even with my

enhanced eyesight—and as I peered out, the blackness around me only seemed to intensify.

"Is someone there?" I asked, pushing myself up.

No answer came but the hiss of steel slipping out of a sheath—a sound I knew all too well.

I reached over for my blade, which was lying on the night-stand, and grasped its hilt in my hand.

"Who is there?" I asked.

It was then that I made out a faint silhouette a few feet away.

The intruder stood still, seemingly trying to decide how best to attack me. I pushed myself back against my pillows, dagger in hand...

...telling myself to be ready for anything.

"Leave my tent, or I will slice out your intestines," I threatened with more courage than I felt. "This blade is sharper than yours, I imagine."

Still, no voice came in response. The infiltrator's breathing quickened, and the silhouette eased closer.

A sudden noise drew my eyes to the tent's entrance.

A second figure darted inside, and crossing the space in the blink of an eye, hurled itself at the intruder. In the darkness I could see little but a brief, shadowy struggle. I heard what sounded like the swish of a blade, then a thud as something—or *someone*—hit the ground hard.

I recoiled, leaping out of the bed, my blade tight in my fist. Adrenaline coursed through my veins and I let out a sound like a beast's snarl, readying myself to fight.

"Lyrinn—are you all right?" a voice said in a whisper.

Mithraan.

"I...I'm fine," I lied, my hands shaking. *Was he the infiltrator, or the one who had taken them down?* "What happened?"

"Do you have a candle?"

I nodded, remembering that he probably couldn't see me any better than I him.

I reached over and lit the small stub of candle on the nightstand, holding it up as I edged around the bed.

Mithraan was standing over something on the ground, his right hand covered in blood. As I neared, I spotted the body of a young man—Gwyr, one of the Champions from Castelle. His throat was torn out, his eyes open, lifeless, a pool of blood surrounding his head in a gruesome halo.

I didn't have to ask to know the Fae had used his silver talons to take the young man's life.

"He was going to kill me," I said softly, staring at the body. "But why?"

Mithraan crouched down and examined Gwyr's face, and for the first time, I saw the look of terror etched on the young man's features. "I don't think he wished to," the Fae said.

"He walked into my tent with a blade in hand!" I replied in a whispered hiss. "What do you mean, *didn't wish to*?"

Mithraan pulled his eyes to mine. "We sometimes do things against our will," he said. "Neither you nor I would choose to compete in the Blood Trials. Yet here we are, as though some external force has pushed us into this fate."

I shook my head. "Ultimately, we both chose to be here. And that young man chose to come kill me."

"Maybe. Maybe not."

Mithraan reached down, pulled the knife from the Champion's hand, and handed it to me. He then lifted Gwyr's body over his shoulder as easily as if it were a small sack of rice. "I will tell the judges what happened. Will you be all right for a few minutes?"

I nodded as I realized I still held Gwyr's blade in my hand. I set it down on the nightstand, my fingers trembling so fiercely that the blade rattled against the wood until I could bring myself to release it.

It was ten minutes or so before Mithraan slipped back into the tent, stepping toward me with a steaming cup in hand.

"Cornflower tea," he said, handing it to me. "It will help you to get back to sleep."

I hesitated, then, remembering that he had saved my life, accepted it.

"Thank you," I said as he took a seat on the edge of the bed. He looked deep in thought as though trying to solve an unsolvable riddle.

After a few seconds, I finally spoke again. "May I ask you something?"

He pulled his chin up to meet my eyes. "Of course."

"How did you know I was in danger?"

He ran a hand through his dark hair and said, "I felt your fear as acutely as I've ever felt anything in my life." Rising to his feet, he added, "Good night, Lyrinn."

Without another word, he left me alone.

CHAPTER FORTY-THREE

I STARTED AWAKE ON THE TRIALS' second day to the sound of a horn call somewhere in the distance.

For the briefest moment, I stretched my arms and inhaled the fresh morning air, quietly content and oblivious.

And then, I remembered where I was, and why.

A Champion had come for me in the night and because of it, he had died.

Of ten of us, only eight remained—and it was only the second day. Three male Champions were left now: Mithraan, Prince Corym, and Arvan, the air-walker from Belleau.

I wiped at my brow, my heart pounding, only to hear a quiet voice coming at me from outside the tent:

"Lady Lyrinn? I've come to help you dress for today's event."

I exhaled a relieved breath.

It was Anira.

"Come in," I replied, pulling myself out of bed.

The lady's maid stepped into the tent, her chin down as though fearful that I would treat her harshly. I couldn't exactly blame her; I hadn't always been patient with her.

But she didn't deserve my ire; she was innocent of the madness that was the Blood Trials. Like me, she had been raised in a society that revered Champions above all else. To her, Prince Corym was the greatest, most impressive being in the world—and I could hardly fault her for thinking so.

Like me, Anira had been lied to all her life.

"I've brought you some clothing," she said, holding up her arm, which was draped with various leather and linen garments. "I'm sure you've heard by now that you are to compete in a Hunt."

"Thank you," I replied with all the kindness I could muster. "Yes, I have heard."

Realizing I wasn't going to snap at her, she issued me an eager smile and dared to step a little closer. "I have the most incredible leather trousers for you," she said. "They gave me the choice between them and a skirt, but trousers seemed more practical, you know—for running and the like."

"Very wise," I replied with a nod. "I appreciate your thoughtfulness."

She handed me the outfit—a white linen shirt, a long gray vest. Pants of the softest leather, and a pair of black boots.

And finally, a bandolier filled with throwing knives of various shapes and sizes.

"Where did the weapons come from?" I asked with my eyebrows raised, feeling the leather between my fingers.

"The prince," Anira replied. "He said you were good with blades."

"Thoughtful of him," I said absently.

"Is he not the kindest man you've ever met?" she asked, her voice quivering with enthusiasm. "He wanted to give you the best chance at winning today, after his victory yesterday."

"Did you watch?" I asked. "Were you able to see?"

She nodded. "He got through the Labyrinth in astounding time. It's too bad you couldn't hear him calling to you."

"Calling to me?"

"Yes," Anira said. "He shouted your name several times. He was frantic, trying so hard to find you and help you. We all saw it."

"I didn't know," I said, guilt flooding me for doubting Corym's word. I wondered how I could have failed to hear the prince's voice—how other sounds had made it so easily to my ears, and yet...

But I told myself he must have been far away, at the Labyrinth's far end.

"Tell me," I said, "how do Domignon's citizens watch? I mean, I know it's through Birdsight, but I don't entirely understand how it works."

"We hear a call," Anira replied. "A sort of distant voice in our minds, telling us the event is about to begin. Then we stop what we're doing and take a seat—it's safer to sit than stand, in case of disorientation. It's best to close your eyes and let the vision come to you. And it does, very quickly. I watched the entire event unfold from the eyes of King Caedmon's hawk. I imagine it was terrifying to be down there when—" She stopped herself before mentioning Paneth's death, probably out of fear that I would grow agitated.

"It was," I replied, shuddering as the memory came to me. "But I should get ready, if I'm to get to the Hunt on time."

"Of course, my Lady. Will you use a bow and quiver?" Anira asked as I dressed.

"No bow for me," I replied. "I never did acquire the skill. I will have nothing but my blades."

"You'd best hope you're hunting a magical squirrel, then," Anira joked, and I did my best to hide the wince in my smile.

She did raise a good point; I could only hope I wasn't to be in pursuit of a giant bear or a wolf.

When I'd finished dressing, Anira braided my hair and wound it around my head tightly enough that it wouldn't risk falling into my eyes during the course of the day.

"I'll fetch your breakfast now," she offered. "Shall I bring it to you? Or did you wish to dine with the prince?"

I issued her another smile. "I'll eat alone."

I *should* have wanted to dine with the prince, to venture into his tent and exchange strategies.

But after last night's terror, all I desired was solitude.

As I was finishing my meal, the tent's entrance swept open, and a Lightblood Fae strode in, his eyes moving around the space. I recognized him from the previous day; he was one of High King Kazimir's guards.

Without a word, he left the tent again, then the High King strode in, his eyes locking instantly on mine.

I stared at him, my mouth half full of food. After a moment, I remembered my place and rose to my feet, swallowed hard, and issued him a quick curtsy.

"Your Grace," I said.

Kazimir waved a hand dismissively and stepped toward me, his brows knitting together.

"Yesterday's Trial was too easy," he said, the words coming at me like an accusation.

"Was it?" I asked. "I suspect the Champion who died might have disagreed with you. It didn't seem so easy for *him.*"

Kazimir let out a low chuckle. "The mortal realms do not understand the point of the Blood Trials. They believe only in brawn and strength, so they send barrel-chested behemoths to compete against those with far more sophisticated skills." The Fae narrowed his eyes appraisingly. "Tell me—have you only trained with your blades, or have you worked on other talents, as well?"

Confusion tore at my mind.

Why was he here? Why did he care how I had trained?

Then I remembered the dagger he had gifted me—a gift he'd bestowed on me for reasons I could not begin to understand.

"I have primarily trained with my blades. And your Grace, I must tell you—I am very grateful for the weapon."

"It is a fine blade. The finest, in fact. It is sharp enough to slice through air itself. But it will not help your mind. You must focus, Lyrinn, if you wish to prevail."

"Yes, your Grace," I replied, still baffled as to why he had ventured into my tent. "Tell me, why have you been observing me so closely?"

Instead of replying, Kazimir stepped toward me, his eyes moving to my chest. He reached a hand out, and I recoiled involuntarily until I saw what he was doing.

Ignoring me, he took hold of the worn pendant Leta had given me. He examined it, a strange smile taking up residence on his lips. "This is an interesting piece."

"It was my mother's."

"Yes. I know. A pity that it's so worn down. It was once beautiful, I'm sure."

"It doesn't matter to me if it's tarnished or polished to a fine shine. It's of no value other than sentimental."

King Kazimir pulled his eyes to mine, dropping the pendant and stepping back. "You may yet find its value greater than you imagine," he said. "In the meantime, protect yourself. Watch for threats in the woods today."

"Of course, your Grace."

I wanted desperately to ask if he knew who, exactly, wanted me dead now that one potential assassin had already been taken down.

But something in the Lightblood's voice, in his eyes, was daunting enough that I hardly dared question him.

A horn sounded outside, and the High King bowed slightly before leaving the tent.

I grabbed my weapons then followed him out to head for the starting area, where the other Champions had already gathered.

Nallach was standing before the group, his face stern.

"Two of our revered Champions are gone," he said solemnly. "As occasionally happens in the Blood Trials, death came prematurely to Paneth and Gwyr. May their spirits live on in the victors' blood."

A few mutters of vague approval sounded around me as Corym strode over to stand next to me, leaning in close. "Why didn't you come to me and tell me what happened last night? I could have helped you. I could at least have slept in the tent with you, Lyrinn, in case anyone else came along to hurt you."

Mithraan glanced over his shoulder, glaring at the prince as if telling him to be silent.

"I'm sorry, Highness," I whispered out of the side of my mouth. "I didn't want to disturb you and rob you of sleep."

"Very kind of you—but far too selfless. I have offered you my protection. You should accept it, my Lady."

"Today's event," Nallach bellowed, "is a Hunt, as many of you know by now. The quarry has been bestowed upon us by High King Kazimir's magic. You will be looking to take down a silver stag."

The Champions fell utterly silent, a few of them glancing around as if trying to figure out if it was good news or bad.

In Mithraan's eyes, I saw no confusion, but rather a look of quiet rage.

"Yes, it's true," Nallach added, reading the Fae's expression. "A silver stag has not been seen in Kalemnar since the days of old. It is a creature of grace and beauty—and a fine target."

"The silver stag is sacred," Mithraan spat angrily. "Whether conjured through magic or not. To take one's life is a grave sin. In Tíria, the punishment for doing so is death."

"Then don't hunt," Nallach retorted with a smug grin and a narrowing of his eyes. "It's your choice. He—or she—who takes down the stag wins today's Trial. It's as simple as that."

"Of course it is," Mithraan said under his breath. I could feel the heat of his rage from where I stood, and I glanced up at the prince to gauge his reaction. He looked pleased, as though the stag were his idea—a means to thwart the Fae and prevent them from winning.

He knows they won't kill it, I thought. *It's an automatic loss for Nihara and Mithraan.*

"Good luck to all," Nallach said. "The Hunt will continue as long as the stag lives. Bring its body to me, and I will declare you the day's winner." With a sweep of his hand, he added, "And now, the path to my left will lead you to the woods."

As he spoke, trees rose up a mere few feet from where he stood, a dirt path forming spontaneously along the ground.

Once again, I looked over at Mithraan, who was whispering something to Nihara. Her eyes were locked on my face, and a look of intense focus resided in her features. She nodded a response, then the two of them proceeded toward the path that was to take us on today's misadventure.

The prince, smiling from ear to ear, took me by the hand and said, "Are you ready, my partner?"

"I am," I said, examining him. The only weapon at his

disposal was a silver short sword, which seemed odd, to say the least. "I'm surprised to see you without a bow, Highness."

"Archery isn't my favorite skill," he said. "I will hunt the stag silently, and slice its throat when the time comes."

I almost laughed at the absurdity of his plan, but I forced my amusement away and nodded. "I have no doubt you'll excel."

"*We* will win," he corrected as we began to tread down the path. As we advanced, a large, dense forest of flowering trees continued to rise up before us, welcoming us into its clutches.

The other Champions had already run ahead, disappearing quickly into the shadows of the forest. But Corym seemed entirely unperturbed by their head start.

"I'll head right," he told me when we came to the first fork in the trail. "You should go left. Whistle if you see the stag, and I will come to you."

Once again, we were to be separated. But this time I nodded, grateful to be rid of him. After last night, all I wanted was silence and solitude. If I spent the entire day sitting at the base of a tree, I would be more happy than I could ever be running along at the prince's side in the search for a beautiful animal to kill.

"I will whistle for you, Highness," I promised. He took my hand, pulled it to his lips, then sprinted off to the right while I strolled along a path branching out to the left.

I was well aware that losing today's Trial could cost me my life in a few days' time. I was aware, too, of the birds overhead, already sending scenes from the Hunt to the many thousands of people in Kalemnar...including Leta.

But it was the falcon that caught my eye as he came in to land on a branch high above my head. The creature wasn't even pretending anymore to take an interest in the other Champions.

For whatever reason, the High King had his sights set on me. But if he expected a show, he was bound to be disappointed.

"I'm sorry to let you down," I said under my breath as I made my way deep into the woods.

CHAPTER FORTY-FOUR

I WANDERED QUIETLY through the forest, wary of any sound that met my ears.

But I didn't spot a single other Champion—neither the prince, nor anyone else. It was almost as though I had the woods entirely to myself.

After two or more hours of relatively pleasant hiking, I finally heard a sound that made me stop in my tracks.

The crisp snap of a nearby twig.

I crouched down, concealing myself behind the decaying trunk of a fallen tree as I peered out expectantly into the woods and reached for my dagger.

When a flicker of movement caught my eye, it wasn't another Champion that I saw.

It was an exquisite silver beast, as tall as a horse, and more graceful as it stepped through the woods. Its head was held high, its broad antlers elegant signs of age and power. They shone as bright as priceless gems, almost blinding in their sleek beauty.

They were no ordinary antlers. But this was no ordinary stag.

I had told the prince I would whistle, and I did—long and low, letting the sound die away on the wind. Perhaps he would hear it and come. Perhaps not.

In the meantime, I had to make a decision.

I pulled my blade up to position it next to my face, my arm itching to hurl it. The animal had stopped moving now, and was standing a mere twenty or so feet away. Its forehead beckoned to me, a perfect, simple target—and I had no doubt I could hit it with little effort.

Yet when I told myself to fling the dagger, my arm did not obey. Something in me froze, resisting, despite the knowledge that a win in the Hunt would give me a much-needed advantage in the Trials—and put an end to this day for us all.

I let my arm drop slowly and watched as the stag, picking up on my movement, leapt away into the woods.

Just then, a sound sped by my left ear—a sort of *whoosh,* like that of a swift bird.

Or an arrow.

I threw myself to the ground even as I heard the projectile land in the trunk of a nearby tree with a horrifying *thwack.*

Another Champion had spotted the stag. One of those who chose a bow and quiver as their weapon—but not one who was particularly adept, apparently.

I pushed myself up and looked around, hunting for the hunter. But I saw nothing, aside from the trees.

Another arrow flew by my head then, and once again, I threw myself down.

"The stag is gone!" I called out. "You can stop shooting!"

For a minute I lay there, waiting to hear a response, but none came. I pushed myself up again, satisfied that the archer had given up.

But when I rose, another arrow came at me, then another, which landed mere inches from my feet.

I began to run.

I'd been naive to think the archer was interested only in the stag. Naive to hope the attempts to take my life would end with Gwyr's death.

It seemed I had become the day's quarry—and I had no idea who was hunting me.

I raced through the woods, leaping over branches, felled trees, and stones, gasping for breath each time I turned to look over my shoulder to see if I could spot my pursuer. I clutched my dagger in my right hand, prepared to hurl it at the first sign of my enemy.

Arrow after arrow swept by my head. One grazed my right shoulder just enough to cut through my shirt, slicing into my flesh. Suppressing a cry, I kept running until I heard a voice calling my name.

"Lyrinn!"

Still I ran, not daring to halt until I came to the shelter of a hollowed-out tree trunk, where I crouched, breathing hard, and pressed myself into its confines.

A few seconds later, a shadow appeared at the small shelter's entrance, a set of eyes staring intently down at me.

Corym.

I breathed a hefty sigh of relief when his lips curved into a friendly smile.

"You looked like you were fleeing the Devil himself," he said. "What happened?"

I studied him for a moment, assessing. Did he have a bow slung over one shoulder? No, of course not. Corym had told me he wanted to slice the stag's throat. He had nothing with him but a blade.

"I saw it," I said, breathing heavily. "The silver stag. I whistled for you...and then, someone began firing arrows at me."

"At the *stag*, you mean."

I shook my head irritably. "No. At *me.* The stag was long gone before the first arrow came."

Corym sat back on his haunches and sucked in his lower lip before saying, "The sight of the silver stag has been known to play tricks on the human mind. Perhaps you only imagined the arrows?"

A swell of anger was beginning to bubble and roil inside me now. I pushed myself out of the tree trunk, and rose to my full height, pointing at my right arm, at the blood dotting my sleeve.

"Did I imagine *this*?" I asked.

Corym, too, rose to his feet, examining my shirt, my wound. "I'm so sorry," he said. "No, of course you didn't imagine it. Gods, my Lady—did you see who was pursuing you?"

"No. Whoever it was kept themselves well hidden. But I suppose it could have been anyone. Everyone seems to want me dead, after all, and there are no rules about killing each other during the Hunt, are there?"

"I'm afraid not." Corym looked pensive for a few seconds, then asked, "When you saw the stag, did you attempt to take its life?"

I tightened, ashamed.

By refusing to kill, I had failed us both.

I shook my head. "I couldn't," I confessed. "It was..."

"Too beautiful. Yes, I know," he replied with a sigh. "I saw it, too. To kill such a creature does seem like a crime against nature."

I smiled slightly, relieved to know he, too, had qualms about taking the life of an innocent beast.

"Listen," he said. "Stay here. I'm going to do a bit of hunting of my own and figure out who has been after you. But I want you to keep an eye out for trouble, all right?"

I shook my head. Something about the idea of hiding myself away while the Hunt continued seemed pathetic and childish.

"I'll come with you," I said. "I'll help you find them."

The prince lowered his chin. "Lyrinn—we're a team, you and I. Which means I need to protect you sometimes—whether you like it or not. In return, you will help *me* at times. It's an even partnership. But right now, it's safest for you—my future wife—to stay put."

I ground my jaw for a moment, then nodded. "Fine. I'll wait here."

"Good," he replied, taking my hand and kissing it gently. "I will be back soon. Don't move."

He left me, and I climbed into the tree trunk once again, telling myself I was appalling for my cowardice. I seated myself, knees pulled up protectively.

I wasn't certain how many minutes had passed when I finally heard the crack of a nearby branch, then another. Someone was making their way through the woods close by, and from the sounds of it, they were headed in my direction.

It could have been the stag again. But somehow, I doubted it.

I froze, tucking myself into the hollow as deeply as I could go. In the distance, I saw a shape creeping through the forest—a person in a cloak, a hood drawn up over their head so I could not see their face. In their hands, a bow was at the ready, an arrow nocked and prepared to shoot.

And it was pointed directly at the tree where I now sat, as though they knew without a shadow of a doubt that I was there.

The figure moved closer and closer until it stood only a few feet away. In my hand, I still grasped my dagger. I had a bandolier full of blades.

But pinned as I was inside the crumbling trunk, I didn't have enough room to hurl a single weapon.

I sat paralyzed, awaiting my fate as my would-be killer moved still closer.

As they approached, I began to discern facial features in the shadows of the figure's cloak. A pair of large eyes. Dark hair, pale skin.

"Elana?" I said, my voice trapped in my throat as the shock of it hit me. "What are you—"

Without responding, she drew the bow string back, her hands shaking, and prepared to fire.

"Elana," I said again, pushing myself up to a standing position, my dagger still in hand. "It's me. We're friends, remember?"

She shook her head. I could see the whites of her eyes vividly now. A quiet struggle seemed to be raging in her mind... just as my own mind had fought my body when I had aimed at the stag.

She was torn inside. But deep down, she knew what she needed to do.

Of all the female Champions, I had the largest target on my back.

The prince had chosen to take me to the end, and everyone knew it.

If Elana wanted to live, *I* had to die.

"I...I didn't see this coming," she murmured, struggling against some unseen force. "I'm so sorry."

"Please," I said, lowering my blade. "You don't have to be the one to do this. Trust me. Someone else will get to me soon enough."

She shook her head again, tears streaming down her cheeks.

I stared into her eyes, waiting for the arrow to pierce my

flesh. My legs weakened, my heart palpitating, and I slipped down, crashing to the ground in surrender to this vile fate.

Elana drew the bow still tighter, prepared to fire the arrow that I could see in far too much detail.

I closed my eyes as though my eyelids would somehow offer protection from the cruel barb at the end of a such a weapon.

But instead of the sound of the arrow piercing my flesh, I heard a thud and a cry. I opened my eyes to see that Elana was on the ground with another cloaked figure on top of her.

I leapt to my feet, struggling to see who had attacked my would-be assassin.

"Stop!" I shouted when I saw the cloaked figure holding a dagger in hand, reaching down to press it against Elana's throat. "Please, don't hurt her!"

The attacker froze, pulled the knife away, and stared down at Elana, letting out a breath. He turned slowly to look at me, and something in my chest surged as our eyes met.

"Mithraan," I breathed.

"She has been *bent*," he said, pulling himself up to stand over Elana.

"Bent?" I replied.

"Someone has taken control of her mind and ordered her to kill you." He looked around and added, "I did not know we had a mind-bender among us. None of the Champions divulged it as a Gift. It explains what occurred last night, as well—in your tent."

"How do we help her? How do we make her better?"

"Time alone can do that," he said. "But you and I need to leave this place. The mind-bender will no doubt use others for the same purpose, and they may be more successful."

"But who would do this?" My cheeks burned with rage—or something even more potent. I turned to Elana and asked, "Who did this to you?"

She peered at me but shook her head, trembling like a leaf in a stiff breeze.

"If the bender is skilled," Mithraan said, "she won't be able to answer the question. Nor will she recall this incident when she snaps out of it. Whoever did this to her managed to circumvent her ability to see the future. They are obviously more Gifted than most."

"I just don't understand—why wouldn't they just kill me themselves?"

"There are many reasons. Perhaps they're not a skilled fighter. Perhaps they fear you. Or perhaps they know something about you that means you pose a greater threat than they care to admit." With that, he narrowed his eyes in what almost looked like an accusation.

"I'm the least threatening person in this competition," I protested, nearly laughing. "I failed at the Labyrinth. And I failed at the Hunt...I saw the stag. I let him go."

"As you should have," Mithraan said quietly. "But it doesn't matter—you *are* the Hunt now. You are the quarry." He looked down at Elana again, and said, "You need to hide yourself, Champion."

Elana nodded understanding, fear still palpable in her face, and she raced into the woods, leaving her bow and arrows behind.

"As for you, Lyrinn..." Mithraan said, turning to me. He was about to say something more when he noticed the blood stain on my sleeve. "Your arm. May I look?"

"It's nothing," I told him. "Just a scratch, really."

He said nothing as he moved closer, pulling the fabric apart to look at the wound.

"Was this from an arrow?"

I nodded, my throat tight. Suddenly, I was finding it difficult to breathe. I wasn't sure if it was the Fae's presence or some other force that was doing this to me. "Yes. Why?"

He pressed his hands to my cheeks and looked into my eyes. "How are you feeling?"

The question seemed odd. *I'm feeling scared. Anxious. Confused.*

"I'm fine," I lied. "Why?"

But even as I asked the question, looking into his eyes, I saw that they seemed to swim with strange colors—gray, swampy green, pale yellow...and then, his entire, normally beautiful face was swimming.

"Mithraan," I said hoarsely. "What is happening to me?"

"It's a poison," he said. "A rare one, from the jarith flower. It is potent and deadly once it's worked its way into your bloodstream. Lyrinn—listen to me. You need to heal yourself as you healed me that day. Do you remember?"

I nodded. But already, my body was slumping to the ground. I could hear his voice, but it was as though we were both under water. Words and their meaning were suddenly unclear.

My mind, too, was a blur.

"Lyrinn," I heard, and then some other sounds. Whether words or something else, I couldn't say. Mithraan looked so strange now—nebulous and mercurial, as though his skin had turned to liquid.

He bent over me, his lips brushing against mine.

We have little time, a voice spoke into my mind. *Beautiful Lyrinn...stay with me.*

Or maybe I only imagined it.

And then, I saw the sky above me. Above us both.

And we were...

Flying.

CHAPTER FORTY-FIVE

I TRIED TO SPEAK, but no words came.

Twisting my head, I peered down toward the earth, my dizziness amplified a thousand times. I was disoriented, sapped of strength, and lost, all at once.

But I knew one thing for certain: the talons of a giant silver eagle were holding me tight as we soared through the air above the Trial grounds. I could see the Lake of Blood far below, reflecting its strange, eerie redness up at the blue sky. After a time, an enormous tree appeared in the distance, larger than some cities and taller than any building I had ever seen. It could only be the Eternity Tree, its limbs reaching in every direction like outstretched arms embracing the entire world.

It was near the tree that the eagle landed gently, laying me down in the grass next to an enormous, knotted root. As I looked up toward the twisting limbs above me, the world went foggy.

I felt hands lifting me. Arms cradling me. I was being carried again.

We stopped when we reached the massive trunk, so broad that I couldn't see around its girth.

"I have come to ask for payment," Mithraan bellowed. "And you may not refuse."

I couldn't tell how much time passed before another sound met my ears. A sort of grim creaking, and then the odd, huffing snorts of what sounded like a wild beast. A shadow loomed over us both, something large and dark, but when I looked, I couldn't make out its shape.

"Who dares awaken the Taker before the Trials are done?" a grim, rasping voice asked.

"The Lord of Fairholme," Mithraan said. "Protector of Tíria."

"You owe my kind a debt," the Fae said when the Taker didn't reply. "You are obligated to help me now."

After a few seconds, the rasping voice replied, "Very well. Come, then."

Mithraan carried me again, and then we were inside a long tunnel of swirling wood, walking down, then down again, under the tree itself. An enormous, hollow root formed our passageway, and the air smelled of moss and mushrooms.

It was strangely beautiful, this place.

If I die here, I told myself, *it will not be the worst grave in the world.*

Very little of what happened in the next few minutes stuck with me. I knew only that I was lying on a broad table of some sort, crudely cut from another enormous tree.

Mithraan was near at hand, and the creature known as the Taker was arguing with him.

Fragments of conversation came to me, slicing through my addled mind. Some of them stuck like arrows in a target, and I tried my best to focus, to understand.

"You should not be here," the Taker hissed. "This is my sacred place. My roots. My branches. Mine. They *gave* it to me."

"They had no right," Mithraan said. "They never had a right. This is not their land. You betrayed our kind in exchange for your treasure."

"Not a betrayal!" The Taker's voice was high-pitched now, almost hysterical. "I do as I am told! I always obey!"

"The two Fae Champions did not die by another Champion's hand—did they? Yet you took their Gifts from them and granted them to mortals."

The Taker went silent for a moment, its hard breaths cutting through the air.

A memory flashed through my mind of my evening in Fairholme. We had spoken of the Taker then, speculating as to whether it could have been responsible for the deaths of the two Fae.

But this creature—this strangely childish, innocent thing that lived underground—was not malevolent. I could *feel* its mind. I sensed its fear, its profound desire to be left alone.

It was no killer.

"I take only from the vanquished," the Taker said. "If they fall, I must siphon their Gifts. That is the rule. That is the command. I do not hurt them. I will not."

"You *saw* it, though. You saw what happened to them," Mithraan growled. "You know."

I felt the Taker recoil next to me. I turned toward it, my eyes focusing for only a moment to see a gray being, its skin like bark. It was large and lurching, its head attached to its body without a neck. Its limbs were long and jagged like a tree's branches. "I cannot say," it moaned. "I cannot reveal. It is not my place. I will be punished. They will take the tree from me. The roots. The leaves. Please..."

"I will not allow them to take anything from you. Not if you do as I ask. Tell me what happened."

"They were dead," the Taker wailed. "They were dead already. I did not kill them, High Fae."

"I know," Mithraan said, his tone gentler. "Will you tell me who did?"

The Taker let out a screech like that of a hawk. "I cannot! I cannot!" it cried. "I swore! I swore!"

Mithraan reached into the air, holding a hand up in front of him, and said, "It's all right. I will not ask you to go back on your word. But I do ask that you make up for the wrong you committed. Will you do that?"

"Yes, yes," the Taker said. "I can help you."

As I twisted and writhed on the slab of wood, Mithraan pressed a hand to my forehead. "She has a very specific Gift," he said. "She is a Healer. But she cannot save herself, not now. She is too weak from the poison. I need you to grant me her Gift."

The Taker recoiled, then let out another cry. "I take only at the Ceremony!" it screeched. "This is forbidden!"

"As was stealing the Blood-Gifts from Fae who were murdered by an outsider."

The Taker whined like a small, distressed dog, despite its enormous size. It loomed like a shadow, moving toward me, then leaping back as though terrified.

"Please," Mithraan said. "I need to save her. For Tíria. For...me."

"For you?" the Taker said. It sounded intrigued, calm.

"For me, yes," Mithraan said. "She is everything. Please."

I closed my eyes, cherishing the words. Savoring them as though they were the last thing I would ever hear.

And then, it came.

A pressure on my chest, my belly, my legs, my forehead. A hundred palms pressing down on me at once.

I felt suddenly fearful that my blood and bones were about to be pressed from my body.

"No. No," I muttered, trying in vain to shake my head. *I would sooner die than suffer through what's about to come.*

"Lyrinn," Mithraan's soft voice said, a hand stroking my cheek as the pressure continued to mount. "It's the only way. I cannot lose you."

Lose me. Lose me.

Was I his to lose? A precious part of him?

I had told myself so many times that he despised me. That he wanted me dead.

I had to be hallucinating. I was deluded.

He only wanted my Gift so that he could then kill me and take the Trials' victory alongside Nihara.

"No!" I screamed, but this time, I felt my body convulse, my back arching violently as something tore itself apart inside me.

Mithraan's hand left my cheek and he cried out, stumbling backwards as though whatever had just happened to me had hurt him, too. But he rushed back to my side and pressed his hands to my chest, my stomach.

Words wove their way through the air—words I had uttered myself.

Raith min dir.

And then, the pain stopped and his hands were on me again, my eyes locked on the arching ceiling of roots and dirt. I saw little but darkness, but my hands went to Mithraan's and I held them there, against my chest. I felt the heat of them, the power in them.

A strength I had never known surged through my body, my veins ignited, muscle and bone renewed.

The poison had left me, disappearing in sparkling tingles of green and yellow, like toxic fireflies disappearing into the night.

And then, I could see clearly once again.

I looked up at Mithraan, whose hair fell in dark tendrils around his face. His eyes were locked on mine, and for a moment, his irises were so pale as to be almost white.

I turned my head to see the strange shadow that was the Taker—a concoction of wood, bone, earth, twisting vine, so tall that it hunched as it stared at me with bright, surprisingly kind eyes.

"Are you all right?" Mithraan asked, and I pulled my eyes back to his.

I nodded. "I am," I said. "How—"

Then I remembered. He had taken my power. My healing ability. My Blood-Gift.

The one defense I had against my enemies.

"It's gone," I breathed.

Mithraan shook his head. "I'm sorry. But you are healed—you are alive. And you are so much more than one Gift now, Lyrinn. Your mind has been freed at last—as well as your body."

"What do you mean, my mind?" I asked. I should have been angry. Infuriated, even. But as I looked up at him, all I felt was affection and gratitude.

He looked so relieved, so happy to see me alive, that all thoughts of his malevolence and his cruelty left me.

And I couldn't imagine them ever returning.

"It is more than mere poison that has been extracted from you," the Taker's croaking voice said. "A Fae's magic is powerful. All is now as it should always have been. The truth will come to you now—you will see."

I looked over at the creature, but it had turned and was leaving us via a broad tunnel cut into the earth below the tree's roots.

And then, Mithraan and I were alone in the strange subterranean room.

He pushed my hair back, stroking a finger down my neck.

"All of my suspicions have been confirmed," he said. "But there is even more to you than I knew."

"You're speaking in riddles," I replied nervously, pushing myself up onto my elbows. "I don't understand—"

Mithraan took my hands and helped me to my feet, guiding me over to a glass-doored cabinet that sat at the far end of the chamber—one that must once have belonged to the humans who lived above ground.

At first, I thought Mithraan wanted me to look at the cabinet itself.

But as my eyes landed on my reflection, I began to understand what he was trying to show me.

"I knew when I first saw your scars that they weren't caused by any fire," he said. "There is a plant that is toxic—it eats away at flesh, burns it away like acid. But it isn't just flesh that burns away—it is far more. Someone was trying to conceal your true nature. Whether to help you or hurt you, I can't say."

"My true nature...?"

"The wounds you suffered so long ago have been healed by your own Gift, Lyrinn. Your true self has at last been released."

I stared at my reflection, unbelieving, as Mithraan pulled my hair back from my neck.

The scars were...not exactly gone. But in their place trailed swirling, glorious black patterns, like ink had been etched into my skin. They were exquisite and deliberate, beautiful echoes of the pain that had once been inflicted on me.

Mithraan pushed my hair back again to reveal that my ears, too, were intact, the angry red tissue disappeared in favor of black designs created by the same unseen entity.

But that strange metamorphosis wasn't the most remarkable thing.

At each of my ears' peaks was a delicate, unmistakable point...

I was staring at the ears of a Fae.

CHAPTER FORTY-SIX

"How..." I said, my legs giving out. Mithraan caught me, his arms wrapping around my waist.

I was trembling now. With fear, with hope, with a wild excitement unlike anything I had ever felt before. I saw Mithraan's eyes differently now—the amber swirling in his irises like liquid gold, rather than menacing flame. I saw kindness in him where I had only seen coldness before.

He still exuded power and strength, but now, his features seemed to open themselves to me. For the first time, I could read the look deep in his eyes. I could feel the centuries of torment suffered by his father, passed down through the cruel memories that Mithraan carried with him daily.

He spoke gently into my ear, and I could *feel* his words as well as hear them. I felt his heart beating against my back, the blood rushing through his body.

Or was it my own blood—my own heart?

"You were never one of them," he whispered against my skin. "You were always one of us. The reason the Change was so hard on you—that it nearly killed you—was because of the magic suppressing who you are and always have been."

"How long have you known?" I asked.

"Until recently, I only suspected," he replied. "I felt an unmistakable power in you, quiet and contained. I saw the scars on your ears—I had seen Fae disfigured before, in visions from the days long before I was born. But I still wasn't certain that I understood how it was possible, or why anyone would have chosen to conceal your true nature. It wasn't until I saw your sister that I began to piece it all together."

"Leta? Why?"

Mithraan's jaw twitched with tension and he exhaled, readying himself to reveal the truth. "A thousand years ago, my father was acquainted with the High King of the Dragon Court, who had a daughter. I told you about her—a beautiful young Fae with flaming red hair and large blue eyes, who disappeared under mysterious circumstances. In those days, her name was Kaela. He met her at the last Blood Trials—and his memories, as you know, are my own, thanks to my Ancestral Sight. Your sister bears such a shocking resemblance to the young woman my father knew that all my doubt faded when I laid eyes on her."

Mithraan took me gently by the shoulders and turned me toward him, slipping his fingers down to pull the tarnished pendant out from under my tunic.

"I told you once that I've seen this pendant before, but I could not recall where, or when. I understand now that it was in one of my father's memories."

Mithraan stroked a thumb over the pendant, rubbing at its tarnished surface.

I watched as the silver piece began to gleam in the meager light, seemingly renewed by the Fae's touch.

"It seems that a thousand years ago, the Princess Kaela began to go by another name—though I'm not sure why." He gestured to the pendant and said, "Would you mind?"

I removed the chain from my neck and handed it to him, and he held it up, letting it twist in the air until it came to a stop.

Embedded in its silver surface, I could now see the distinct outline of a dragon.

"The sigil of the Dragon Court," Mithraan said. "The sigil of your mother's House."

My heart throbbed in my chest. "That...can't be."

"I'm afraid it is," the Fae said, his eyes landing on my own. "Your mother is our High King's daughter, the princess who went missing so long ago. And your sister is her spitting image."

I took a deep breath and held it in my chest as I assembled the puzzle pieces Mithraan had just given me.

My mother was High King Rynfael's daughter. The woman I had known in my memory as Alessia...had long ago been called Kaela.

"*My mother was a Tírian Fae,*" I breathed, barely able to absorb the words.

It wasn't a question. It was as though I'd known it all my life, every time I'd looked up toward the Onyx Rise, pining for a land I'd never seen and Fae I'd never encountered.

Some part of me had always been drawn to that land, lured by the enticing voices that lived on the wind.

But I had never understood why until now.

"When the princess disappeared at the end of the last Blood Trials," Mithraan replied, "some said she had run away. That her father was too strict, too oppressive. Others thought she had been swept up in the deluge when so many of our kind were changed into Grimpers on that horrible day."

"But she *wasn't* swept up," I said. "She..."

Mithraan pressed the pendant into my hand and closed my fingers around it. "Only you know what happened to her,

Lyrinn. Your mother's memories are inside your mind—you have the ability to access them, if you choose to."

I held the pendant tight, filled with self-doubt. "I'm not like you. I can't simply tap into ancestral memories and extract them."

"You're quite right," Mithraan said. "You're not like me. There is something in you that is stronger than any Fae I've ever encountered—and your strength is only now beginning to build. So I ask of you now—close your eyes. Open your mind to the past, to your mother's mind."

I was about to protest, to tell him it was impossible. But the look in his eye warned me against self-doubt.

With a sigh, I closed my eyes, anticipating failure.

An instant, profound darkness filled my mind. A clean slate, waiting for the writing to come.

A moment later, I found myself inside an empty cavern, hollow and cold. Lost and confused, I walked into its depths. And as I advanced, the darkness only deepened.

A chill ran its way straight to my bones, a fear of what I might discover in this forsaken place.

I found myself reaching out, searching for someone to help me, to offer support.

"Father?" I called out.

But no answer came.

"Mother."

A word I had never used to address the Fae who had given birth to me. I had not been capable of speech the last time my eyes had landed on her.

I could not even remember her.

But the second I called out, a face came to me in vivid detail. I saw the young woman from the portrait my father had kept for so long. Red hair, high cheekbones, bright eyes.

It took a moment to realize I was looking at a reflection.

That of my mother—the daughter of a Fae High King with her long, beautiful red hair twisted in an intricate pattern of interwoven braids. She was dressed for an important event—one that she was anticipating with great excitement.

She wore a dress of light blue silk, a ring of glowing white flowers crowning her head. She smiled as she eyed herself, giddy for the day ahead.

A voice called out from somewhere behind her. "Are you ready, my dear?"

She spun around to see a tall male Fae with a sculpted, dark red beard. He wore an outfit of violet and black, and a crown of silver and gold filigree.

"Ready, Father," she replied.

High King Rynfael, I thought. *My grandfather.*

He offered her his arm and she took it, excited as he led her out to Domignon's main city square. Set up at its center was a makeshift jousting ring, decorated with the colors of all five of Kalemnar's realms.

The Blood Trials, I thought. *I'm watching an event that took place one thousand years ago.*

Time seemed to leap ahead by a few minutes. All of a sudden, my mother was seated with my father to one side, and another Fae to her left—one who seemed to catch her eye. She issued him a shy glance and smiled as her cheeks flushed dark pink.

I concentrated, trying in vain to make out his features.

The image faded, and I opened my eyes.

"What did you see?" Mithraan asked in a half-whisper.

"My mother," I replied. "She was at the last Trials. I saw her sitting with someone—a Fae. But I couldn't make him out clearly. It was almost like—like he'd been erased from the memory itself. But..."

"Yes?"

“I feel like he must be important, though I can’t say why.”

“I’m sure you’re right,” Mithraan said, cupping my face in his hands. “Try to find him. He must be in there somewhere. Lyrinn...”

“Yes?”

“I feel that this Fae could be the answer to the questions that have plagued us both all our lives.”

I nodded and, without a word, closed my eyes once again.

My mother was still seated next to the Fae, who leaned toward her and said something—I couldn’t quite hear it, but could feel her laugh in response.

He was charming. Powerful. He was everything she had ever dreamed of in a mate.

But as much as I tried, I still couldn’t see his face. And when I tried to rifle through my mind for other memories, time jumped forward again.

I could see my mother wandering into a tent on the Trial grounds. It was deep crimson, with elegant velvet furnishings. The tent of a wealthy lord or lady.

As my mother stepped inside, she saw someone—the same faceless Fae who had been seated next to her—pouring a clear liquid from a vial into two small glasses.

He handed them to a servant, who brought them outside on an elegant silver tray.

“What was that, my Lord?” my mother asked him, her tone playful.

“Nothing you need to bother with, pretty thing,” he replied, turning her way. His voice, like his face, was distorted, as though he spoke underwater. This memory, too, was corrupted. “Tell me,” he said, taking a few steps toward her, “have you given any consideration to my proposition?”

Flood gates opened inside me then, and a sea of memories

ran through my mind in a deluge. Torment, trauma, horror, all struck me simultaneously, and my heart began to race.

My eyes opened again and I reached for Mithraan's arm, desperate to steady myself.

"What did you see?" he asked.

"I...I think I know what happened to the Fae Champions at the last Trials." I choked on the last few words, but swallowed and forced myself to finish. "I know what happened to her. To my mother."

"Tell me," Mithraan said. "All of it."

Tears welled in my eyes. I wanted to say no—that I couldn't bring myself to speak the words. But I forced back my fear and spoke.

"The Fae—the one I saw with my mother—sent poisoned drinks to the Champions just before they were to be awarded the victory."

"Do you know why?"

I shook my head. "No. I'm sorry. I can't seem to access a clear memory of him. But..."

Mithraan took me by the arm and guided me over to a broad wooden bench, where he sat me down gently.

"But what?"

"I think he forced her to be with him," I said. "He took her away after the Trials, and imprisoned her. I...I could *feel* it. Her fear, her anguish, her torment. I felt them as though they were my own emotions. And yet, I couldn't see him, however hard I tried."

"Someone has veiled your mother's memories," Mithraan said, scowling. "Perhaps it was she who did it—so that you would never have to suffer through the truth. Or it could have been her Fae captor, if he's as powerful as I suspect."

"Who would do something like that?" I asked, my breath

burning in my throat. "Who would take someone from her family, and force her to stay with him?"

But I wasn't looking for a reply. I knew perfectly well that the world was filled with cruel beings selfish enough to rob a young woman of her life, her family, her future.

"Lyrinn," Mithraan said. "We will learn the truth of it. And when we do, I will destroy the Fae who did this."

I bit my lip and looked him in the eye. "It was a thousand years ago," I said. "My mother found happiness in the end with my father. She escaped her abductor—maybe she even killed him." I almost hoped it was true. I would rather discover my mother was a killer, somehow, than a millennium-long victim of a cruel captor.

"Maybe," Mithraan repeated. "But somehow, I doubt it."

He sat down next to me, and I found myself leaning my head against his shoulder. It wasn't that I was exhausted—if anything, I felt invigorated by all that had occurred since we'd entered the Taker's Lair.

It was comfort that I sought. Comfort granted me by the Fae lord who had saved me from death—who had taught me to see my young mother in the days before her life was destroyed.

The Fae lord I had misjudged so harshly for so long.

CHAPTER FORTY-SEVEN

"PROMISE ME SOMETHING," I said as we sat together in that strange, subterranean place.

"Anything."

"Promise we'll find our way out of this madness. I don't mean the Taker's lair. I mean the Trials—all of it."

Mithraan let out a quiet, bitter chuckle. "If I could promise that, Lyrinn, I would be the most powerful Fae ever to live."

I laughed then, and it felt wonderful. I had been worried for so long—worried about Leta, about myself. About the future of the Fae, of mortals. But for all that time, I had forgotten to live and breathe. To appreciate life's quiet, sweet moments.

Mithraan seemed to read my thoughts, because he pulled away and turned to face me. "We will find our way through," he said. "I don't know how, exactly. I only know that you and I will find our way to the end. You have my word."

"I believe you." I looked up at him, a smile on my lips, reveling in my newfound trust. "You gave me a new life today, one I never knew was inside me. You pulled a veil away from my mind—one that was poisoning my thoughts, and turning me against those I should have trusted. For that alone, I owe you everything."

He slipped a hand onto my neck—a sensation I had come to crave with every fiber of my being—and said, "I would give you a thousand lives every day, my Lady, if you desired them."

I took in a long breath while I hunted my soul for the courage to speak.

"I would desire them if they could be spent with you, High Lord."

Mirroring my smile, he stroked his fingers over my flesh, lifted my chin, and pressed his lips to my neck.

Every bit of my former fear and apprehension disappeared, replaced by a violent swell of desire. I pressed my hands to Mithraan's chest, my eyes sealing shut, my breath shallow. I would not resist him anymore. I wouldn't question his motives.

All I felt now was his desire for me. *But...*

"The Taker," I whispered, remembering the strange, lumbering creature who dwelt in this place.

Mithraan pulled back to look me in the eye when he said, "He will not return until I ask him to. But for now, if it makes you happier, let's go somewhere else."

I was prepared to make any journey with him, however long, but reading my mind, he took my hand and shook his head. "That's not what I mean." Kissing my hand, he asked, "Where do you wish to go?"

I gazed into his amber eyes, understanding the question. "Anywhere?"

"Anywhere."

"The woods depicted in the murals and tapestries of Fairholme," I replied without hesitation. "I want to see those woods."

Mithraan's lips turned up at the corners, and he let out a low, beautiful laugh.

"What is it? Do they not exist?"

"Those woods," he said, kissing me gently on the lips, "are in the far North, in the lands of the Dragon Court. Your mother's home. Your very blood runs through those woods."

My eyes went wide. "I didn't know," I said. "It's only that... something about them called to me when I was in Fairholme. They felt..."

They felt like home.

"Let's go, then," Mithraan said with a wave of his hand. And just like that, we were surrounded by a forest of swaying, white-barked trees, birds singing, sunlight hitting the ground in dappled waves that sent a shudder of joy through me.

We were standing in a small clearing, surrounded by trees that looked as old as time itself, their trunks almost as large as that of the Eternity Tree.

At the clearing's center sat a large, luxurious bed draped in white silk. I laughed to see it.

"Is it presumptuous of me?" Mithraan asked, pulling my tunic down from my shoulder and brushing his lips along my flesh.

"If I were a proper lady, I would say yes and act shocked," I told him. "But it would be a lie. I am no lady."

"You are far more than any lady," the Fae said, his eyes burning. "And I have desired you, Lyrinn, since the first moment I saw you. I have hungered for you, cried out for you in the night. I have doubled over with a brutal ache, because I did not understand my cravings. I railed against them, tried to vanquish them with every bit of strength in me. But I know now that I will wither and perish if I do not have you."

He offered me his hand. When I took it, he scooped me up and I hooked my legs around his waist. He kissed me deeply, and I opened my mouth to his tongue, tasting it with my own as he let out a moan of fierce pleasure.

He laid me on the bed, lifting my tunic and trailing his lips, his tongue, his teeth along my stomach. I laced my fingers in his hair, urging him to move slowly but terrified that this moment would end too soon—that we would be forced back to the encampment, forced into separate tents.

No—we are alone here—we are powerful. No one can take this from us.

Mithraan moved upward inch by inch, his lips caressing my torso, hands pushing my tunic up still more. I gasped when he cupped my breast in his hand, pulling back to watch my face as he slipped his thumb over my nipple. I writhed in frustrated, delicious ecstasy, pleading silently with my eyes to torment me further.

He smiled as my nipple hardened under his touch, delighted to be driving me to madness.

"Devilish Fae," I said softly, pulling him close to kiss him hard. "You're destroying me, piece by piece."

"That's the whole point," he said, slipping down and taking the sensitive tip between his lips. I tangled my fingers once again into his long hair, desperately withholding a cry of ecstatic torment.

"I want you," I whispered. A confession of what I had known all along and been too afraid to admit. "I've wanted you from the first moment I laid my eyes on you."

He pulled away, his chin down, eyes locked on mine as he grabbed hold of one of my leather boots, then the other. He pulled them off and dropped them to the ground before taking the waistband of my trousers and yanking them down, down, until my legs were bare, wrapped around his waist again, beckoning him toward me.

He pushed forward so that I felt his substantial length hardening against me through his clothing. He slipped onto his knees between my legs, which instantly wrapped themselves around his neck.

He kissed one thigh, then the other, then said, "Do you know why I chose to compete in the Trials, against my own judgment, even my own wishes? Do you know why I was so desperate to heal you?"

"Because you knew I was a Fae," I said. "You—"

He pulled his chin up and looked me in the eye. "No. That is not why, Lyrinn Martel." He slid his tongue over me, drawing a loud, long moan from my lips. "I did it to protect you. To be near you. I did it because I cannot fathom existing in this or any world without you."

Another swipe of his tongue had my hips rolling, pleading for more.

"Because," he said, drawing back just enough to drive me mad, "you have stirred feelings inside me that I never thought possible. I have desired you since the first moment I inhaled your scent. Every breath I have taken in since that moment has been in the hopes that one day, I would..."

He stopped speaking then, lowered his chin, and claimed me with his mouth until my body succumbed.

When the climax rolled through me in a delicious wave of the purest pleasure, I cried out, the birds in the trees fleeing in fear for their lives.

"To think all this time, I thought you despised me," I said softly as his tongue lapped gently, calming my body into renewed submission.

He let out a low chuckle, raised his eyes to mine again, and said, "If you and I were the only beings left alive on this earth—if I could make love to you every moment of every day for eternity, it would be more than enough to bring me all the joy in the universe. That is all I have ever wanted from you, my Lady."

A surge of pleasure and pain swirled inside me, an ache like none I had ever known. I knew I should pull back. Walk away.

I was all but promised to the prince. I was to be his wife.

But instead, I lay back and parted my legs, silently begging the Fae lord to give me all of himself.

When I felt his fingers slipping over the slickness between my legs, my back arched, my hips thrusting upwards.

More.

I cried out as he pressed two fingers inside me, his tongue tormenting me again in expert strokes that told me he understood my body more thoroughly than I ever had. I writhed against his hand, against his mouth, begging silently for every inch of him.

I reached down and grabbed at his tunic, pleading silently with him to let me pull it from his exquisite body.

"I want you, Fae," I said again, and this time, he obliged, slipping over me and pulling the tunic over his head.

My fingers scrambled to unfasten the ties at his waist, to free him from the confines of his trousers. I gasped as his generous length sprang free and he pushed himself deep inside me, claiming me as his own. Slowly, he pulled away, my body instantly starved for him, and he thrust his way back in, his lips on my neck, my jaw, my mouth.

"I would walk through fire to keep you by my side," he whispered as my hips rose to meet him, to beg him for more. "I would die a thousand deaths and break a thousand laws, if it meant one more day when I could be close to you. I would gladly take down entire armies, if it meant a future with you."

He kissed me deeply, parting my lips with his tongue. I savored the sweet agony of him as we became one entity, our bodies tangled together, my arms holding him so tightly that I was certain he would never leave, never be separated from me again.

“I claim you,” I said softly, my face damp with sweat as he moved harder, faster, pulling back to lock his eyes on my own. I saw the flames then in his irises, but they were warm rather than threatening. An invitation to dwell inside his soul.

“I claim you,” he repeated to me as he thrust again, a quiet growl passing through his lips. “You are mine, whatever happens...Lyrinn Martel.”

“And you are mine,” I replied, taking his face in my hands, watching as he neared his climax.

When the wave crashed over him, I pulled him close, holding his chest to mine, my legs tight around him as he let out a feral cry.

Tears streamed down my face as we panted against one another.

We were one now.

But there was a quiet war raging out there, back in the world we’d left briefly behind.

And I wasn’t sure that our love for one another would be enough to keep it at bay.

We lay together in our conjured bed for what felt like hours, my head pressed to Mithraan’s chest as I listened to the beautiful rhythm of his heart.

“Who is it that wants me dead so badly?” I asked as he stroked his fingers along my neck. “And why?”

“I don’t know,” Mithraan said. “The mind-bender has concealed their tricks well, even from me.”

“We know it’s not Elana,” I replied. “The question I keep asking myself is, why kill me before the final battle, when they can just wait and take me out then?”

“The most likely motive is to remove you from the prince’s

sights," Mithraan said. "Which would imply that it's a woman. If only I were a mind-reader, I might be able to pinpoint your enemy."

"Mind-reader," I repeated, searching my memory for the last time I'd heard the word. I tensed as it came to me. "Elana's sister. She's the key to all of this."

"Explain."

"Elana told me in the Labyrinth that her sister, Asa, was meant to be Belleau's Champion. She was a talented mind-reader, but she died under mysterious circumstances shortly before she was to come here. You don't think..."

Mithraan tensed under me. "Whoever it is that's trying to hurt you knew of her Gift and killed her for it," he said. "Yes. It makes perfect sense. A mind-reader would make a mind-*bender*'s talent worthless. She would have known exactly what he—or she—was doing, and been able to put an end to it. A mind-bender's Gifts only work if their victims are unsuspecting."

I sighed. "It still doesn't answer our question, though—who is doing this, and why?"

"I know one thing for certain," Mithraan half-whispered. "We will find out soon enough."

CHAPTER FORTY-EIGHT

After a few precious hours spent in a blissful tangle of limbs, Mithraan and I agreed that we needed to return to the Trial grounds. "The leaders' birds will be searching for us," he said. "And if they discover where I took you, it will not go well for either of us. Access to the Taker is forbidden. I have broken a sacred law by bringing you to this place—though it was worth any punishment they might throw my way."

"How will we get back?" I asked. "And how will I explain my physical changes?"

"You won't," Mithraan said, rising from the bed and slipping his clothing on. "Don't forget what you are—what you have always been. You will use glamour, Lyrinn."

"Glamour," I repeated. He was right—I'd already forgotten who and what I had discovered over the last few hours. I was not just a Fae, but the grand-daughter of a High King.

"How do I use glamour on someone?" I asked, feeling suddenly like a toddler learning to walk for the first time.

"In your mind's eye, envision what you want others to see. Whether it be a change in you or in your surroundings, you will coerce their mind into picturing that same vision. It is a Gift that comes naturally for our kind, and you will perform it with ease. Try it now."

"But it won't work on you—will it?"

"It will, if you want it badly enough," Mithraan said with a sly grin.

I slipped out of the bed, pulled my clothes on, then closed my eyes, picturing the version of me I'd seen in the mirror so many times over the years. I wore a long cloak of linen, its hood pulled over my head and most of my face. My dark hair covered my ears and neck, and I kept my chin low, fearful of any eyes that might land on me.

Mithraan's face lit up as I drew the image in my mind.

"Perfect," he said with a laugh. "You're a natural deceiver, my Lady. Just one more thing—remember that you need to look as though you're still wounded."

He was right—I *had* been shot, after all. Whoever was trying so badly to hurt me needed to see I hadn't gotten away without at least some minor injury.

"I'll add it when the time comes," I said. "I promise to make myself appear suitably pathetic."

"Good. Then come—we'll leave this place via one of its longer tunnels, which will bring us to the shores of the Lake of Blood. From there, we'll hike across the field to the Trial grounds."

As he spoke, our idyllic, conjured clearing disappeared from around us, and once again, we stood inside the Taker's lair.

Mithraan kissed me one last time before taking my hand and guiding me toward the long, dark tunnel that would lead us back to the lives we had come to know and dread.

When we staggered into the Trial grounds, Corym came rushing out to greet us both. I focused my mind on convincing him I was still the Lyrinn he'd known—the one with scars and self-consciousness. The one who didn't yet fully understand the depth of Mithraan's feelings for me.

The bloodstain remained on my tunic, the color sapped from my cheeks. One arm was draped around Mithraan as he supported me, and one of my legs dragged slightly along the ground.

"What happened to you?" the prince asked, his voice panicked. "I left you in the woods to go looking for your assailant...But..."

"I found her," Mithraan said. "Lying unconscious in a small clearing. She didn't look well, so I helped her back here."

"My Lady," the prince said, "you need a doctor to tend to your wound."

"I'm fine, really," I replied, deliberately rendering my voice hoarse. "I just need to rest a little. But before I go lie down, tell me—the stag. Did anyone...?"

Corym went silent for a moment, then said, "I managed to hunt it down."

Horror crossed my features, and I was too slow to conceal it. Corym had spoken about the stag's beauty, about how one would have to be a monster to take such a creature down.

And yet, he had done it.

"It wasn't something I enjoyed, Lyrinn," he insisted, seeing my reaction. "But remember, I couldn't find you—and I knew one of us needed to win the event. We must make it to the end, you and I. I did it for you."

"Of course, your Highness," I replied, my voice tightening in my chest. *I never asked you to kill a beautiful creature for me.* "Well...Good night, then."

With that, I glanced at Mithraan only briefly before heading to my tent.

I would bring you with me to my bed if I could, my Lord, I thought, willing the words to find his mind.

~I know, my Lady, a deep voice replied inside my own mind. *But for tonight, we must remain apart. The next Trial will take place soon, and we must sleep at all costs.*

I slipped into my tent and lay down.

Within moments, I drifted into a deep sleep, Mithraan's words spinning around in my mind.

We must sleep...at all costs.

CHAPTER FORTY-NINE

A STRANGE, vivid dream began to unfold in my mind as I slept.

I was standing in one of the palace's corridors when a woman dressed in white appeared. I was certain I'd never met her—not even in my mother's memories. She wore a leather belt at her waist, with an ornate sheath that held an elegant silver-handled blade.

As I watched her, she beckoned me to follow.

The woman's sole purpose, apparently, was to lure me deep into a dark, round tunnel.

I followed mindlessly, trusting her completely as we moved from an elegant marble hallway into a dark tunnel. Immediately, I recognized its shape, its scent.

It was one of the subterranean corridors that led into the Taker's Lair.

I smiled, thinking I had conjured this scenario subconsciously so that I could spend time with Mithraan once again in our secret place. Here, we could explore one another's bodies and renew our bond over and over, far from prying eyes.

Only, Mithraan was nowhere to be seen.

I followed, still hopeful as the woman led me to a small,

round room. Along the walls were slabs crudely arranged into wooden shelves, and covered in objects of every conceivable shape and size. Books. Old shoes. Sculptures. Weapons. Jewelry. Dishes, even, and toys.

I wandered around the room, eyeing the objects, wondering if the Taker had collected them over the millennia for its own amusement.

"Why did you bring me here?" I asked, pulling my eyes to my guide.

The woman smiled. She was pretty, with olive skin and dark hair, her eyes large and friendly.

"This is your penultimate Trial," she said.

"No," I replied, shaking my head and laughing. "This is a dream. I know it is."

"It is a dream induced by the magic of the Lightblood Fae. You have a task to perform in this room, as does each Champion. If you succeed, you advance. If you fail..."

There was no need to conclude the sentence; my flesh crawled at the tone of the last three words. *If I fail...*

I suspect I will not live to see morning.

"What is the task?" I asked, trying not to think how high the stakes might be.

"The Taker has one possession it values over all others," she said. "That possession is in this room. You must find it and show it to me. But choose well. You have only one chance, and you have only a few hours until the sun rises, so you'd best begin your search."

I wanted to ask questions, to clarify the rules.

But the rules were so simple a child could understand them.

The trouble was, the room was full from floor to ceiling with hundreds, if not thousands of items. How could I possibly sort through them before morning dawned?

I took one step, then another, moving along the chamber's perimeter, my eyes perusing the shelves with care.

I noted a doll made of corn husk. A small carriage of delicately carved marble. A book about the ancient castles of Kalemnar. Dozens and dozens of items sat before me, each of them a puzzle.

I steered my mind to thoughts of the creature known as the Taker. But when I had encountered it, I had been ill, confused, dizzy, disoriented.

Think, Lyrinn. What did it say when Mithraan was speaking to it?

I remembered that it claimed to follow the rules of the Blood Trials. It was obedient and loyal, and did as it was asked.

But none of those facts helped me in my search. No item that I came upon seemed fitting for the lurching creature who lived beneath the Eternity Tree.

"An hour has passed," the woman said when I'd made my way around the room only once.

Shocked, I said, "Please—I need more time."

"We all do, don't we?" she asked with a kindly smile.

I kept moving, my mind twisting this way and that, searching my mother's memories for images of the Taker. But none came to me. It seemed she had never encountered the creature, or else she had blocked all memory of it from her mind.

I thought of Mithraan, of what he might think or do in this situation. Of all the items I'd seen, which would he choose?

Every time I passed by the shelves, I noticed objects I hadn't registered before, but still, none stood out to me. I turned fearful after a time, worried that I really would fail.

Another hour passed. Then another, and still, I was wandering aimlessly through the small chamber.

Finally, I stopped in my tracks, my eyes locked on an item I hadn't noticed before.

A small branch, jutting out from the back of one of the wooden shelves. Springing from its tiny limbs was a series of tidy green leaves. *It has to be part of the Eternity Tree,* I thought, *attached to the trunk somehow.*

But when I reached for it and pulled gently, the branch came away easily in my hand, a living branch, surviving independently of the tree itself. Puzzled, I looked closer to see that a series of tiny roots were sprouting from the branch's thickest end.

It wants to be planted. It would one day grow into another massive, beautiful tree.

That was why the Taker cherished it.

Without another thought, I turned to the woman in white and held it up.

"This," I said. "*This* is what the Taker cherishes most."

The woman paused for a moment, then a slow smile spread across her lips.

"You are correct," she said. "Of course."

I placed the branch carefully back in its spot, wondering if somewhere in another dream, Mithraan had just offered up the same answer.

"What happens now?" I asked.

"Now, you go back to sleep. In the morning, you will awaken, and all will be well."

"And the others? Will they be well?"

"Only those who succeed."

I had met the Taker. I had heard its voice. I knew the desperation it felt when threatened. I had felt its love for the Eternity Tree, for roots, leaves, earth.

Most of the others had not. They would have no way to solve the puzzle.

But before I could bring myself to weep for them, I found myself falling into a well of darkness, my mind emptying. The dream had ended, and I was in a deep sleep devoid of thought.

When I finally awoke, the warmth of the morning sun was streaking through my tent. For a moment, I forgot what had happened the previous night, and even when I recalled the dream, I told myself it was just that—a dream, and nothing more.

But I rose from the bed and threw on a thick robe, hurrying out of the tent to see if anyone was around.

In the sky above me, I could see the white falcon circling, but none of the other birds. It swooped down as I moved toward Mithraan's tent, watching me intently. But I didn't care. I had to know the Fae lord was alive and well.

"Mithraan," I called when I'd arrived.

A moment later, he appeared, a smile on his beautiful lips when he saw me.

"You solved it, too," he said. "Of course you did."

"It took me far too long," I told him. "But..." I looked around at the circle of Champions' tents. "The others?"

"Nihara made it," he said. "But I'm a little concerned about the rest, to be honest."

"I'm going to find out."

I darted to Elana's tent, where I found her eating breakfast.

"How did you know?" I asked. "How did you guess the answer?"

"I can see elements of the future, remember?" she said, her mouth half full. "It does come in handy on occasion."

I let out a laugh swollen with relief.

"The others?" I asked. "Do you know—"

"I...haven't had the courage to think about it," she said.

Someone behind me cleared his throat, and I turned around to see Prince Corym standing in the doorway.

"Sharilh—the remaining Castelle Champion—as well as Krita, from Marqueyssal. And..." Looking at Elana, he added, "Arvan, from Belleau."

"All of them gone," I said. "Who..."

"Killed them?" the prince asked. "I'm not sure. Dream Trials are strange, mysterious affairs. But their bodies must be here somewhere, so the Taker can extract their Gifts in the end."

He spoke with such casualness that I wanted to slap him. It was as though he were talking about a pair of shoes and not three humans who had just lost their lives for the sin of choosing the wrong answer in a riddle.

"That leaves five of us for the final Trial," I said, my eyes locking on Elana's. I wondered if she knew anything of what was to come—if she could see the results with any clarity.

She shook her head. "There will only be four," she said, glancing at the prince. "I have seen it already."

"Four?" I spat. "But five of us survived last night. Isn't the final Trial taking place tomorrow morning?"

"It is," Corym said. "Elana, you must be wrong. We will all be staying at the encampment today and tonight—there are guards everywhere. There's no reason to think any harm would come to one of us."

"True," she replied coldly. "But when I went to bed last night, I didn't expect to find three of our Champions dead by morning, either. Now, if you'll excuse me, I'd like to be alone." As she turned toward her tent, she threw me a strange look and added, "Good luck, Lyrinn. Stay wary—and when the time comes, be sure to follow your heart."

CHAPTER FIFTY

The prince brought me back to my tent, whispering that he thought Elana had finally lost her mind.

"She's nervous, I suppose," he said. "It's natural—the last Trial is always a battle to the death, and though she's impressive at dodging weapons, I can't say she's much of a fighter."

"She can see things," I retorted. "She's prescient. I don't think this is mere panic. And she looked at *you* when she predicted one of us would die, Highness. You might want to consider asking your father for extra guards tonight."

He issued me a smile as we arrived at the entrance to my tent. "I'll definitely do that," he said. "I will ask for all the guards my father can spare. I'll have some sent your way, too."

"Thank you," I replied, glancing toward Mithraan's tent, where the Fae was standing, watching us. "I...think I'll lie down for a little, if that's all right. I'm exhausted after last night. I don't feel like I slept at all."

"I'll do the same," the prince said, making a show of taking my hand and kissing it. "My Lady, I will see you soon. And when we fight for our lives—trust that you can count on me."

I'll believe it when I see it.

"Thank you, Highness."

I slipped into my tent, still wearing my robe over my nightgown, and seated myself at the small table where my breakfast was waiting. I poured myself a cup of tea and sipped it, wondering what Elana had seen in her mind's eye. Did she really think the prince would die tonight?

Worry should have invaded my mind at the thought, or sadness.

But all I felt was ambivalent to the notion that Corym could cease to exist.

I was contemplating it when, out of the corner of my eye, I saw a shadow slip its way into the tent. I turned to see High King Kazimir, his white hair gleaming, his eyes flaring bright.

"Your Grace," I said, rising to my feet and curtseying slightly.

"Hello, Lyrinn," he said, stepping deeper into the tent. "How are you feeling this morning?"

As I stared into his eyes, I felt as though I were looking into the face of the falcon that had been watching me for days now. Unreadable. Piercing. Cold.

"I am well, though..."

"Yes?"

"I heard three of our Champions died in the night."

"Ah. The perils of the Trials," he said, slipping a hand onto the back of a chair a few feet from where I stood. "Were you close to them?"

"No, your Grace. I didn't know them well at all. But still, they were so young..."

"May their spirits live on in the victors' blood," he said quietly, repeating the words Nallach had uttered. "But I find it curious that you're still standing before me."

"Curious, your Grace?"

"*You* should have died last night, as well."

I recoiled at the statement, which sounded more like a threat than anything.

"What I mean," the High King said, "is that the Taker is a creature of great mystery, and it takes one with great power to learn its secrets."

I went silent for a moment. Was he prying? Trying to get me to confess what I'd learned the previous day? Or could he see past my glamour, past the thick hair covering my ears and neck?

"I watched you in the woods yesterday," the High King added, bringing his gaze down to the table. He reached over and took hold of a green grape, popping it into his mouth. "I saw that you were injured."

"Yes, your Grace."

"Lord Mithraan saw it, too."

"Yes," I said. "He helped me back to the encampment."

"Hours later."

Every muscle in my body tensed and I found myself staring at the ground beneath my feet. "I was...unwell...for some time," I said.

"Ah. Well, I lost sight of you. I suppose he was...tending your wounds, was he?"

I glanced sharply upward and my eyes met his, wondering what business it was of his. He may be High King of Aetherion, but that land was far from ours. He was not my leader. I owed him nothing.

"He healed me," I said, my voice clipped. "I am grateful to him for it."

"I'm sure you are. So tell me truthfully—how did you solve the puzzle in the Taker's Lair?"

The question came at me like a slap, and in it, I felt a hard accusation from somewhere behind his eyes. Somehow, he knew what had transpired between Mithraan and me, and he disapproved.

"I felt it," I replied. "I felt...the Taker."

"I see. You *felt* a creature you've never met—one made of root and bone. You simply reached your mind out and...what? Melded with its nonexistent brain?"

"I suppose I did."

The High King let out a scalding laugh and said, "You are so much like your mother, you know. A liar. A cheat."

The words shocked me, and I pulled back inadvertently, even as the High King took a step toward me.

He took hold of my long hair, pushing it back, and said, "You think I cannot see, that your thick hair is enough to conceal your true nature from me. But I see her in you—*I can smell her blood through your pores.*"

The threat in his voice was growing, and he now felt as dangerous as anyone I'd ever encountered.

"I think you should leave," I said, struggling to steady my voice.

But he ignored me. "You know what your mother was. You know she was no mere human. But do you know the truth of it? Do you know what she did—where she went, and with whom?"

"I know she loved my father," I said, my voice breaking with fear and anger. "I know she..."

"Your *father,*" King Kazimir scoffed as if he felt nothing for the word but disdain. "A man devoid of honor."

My throat tightened against the scream I wanted to release. I sealed my lips, forcing back the words I could so easily have unleashed in defense of the man who had died protecting me.

"He was the best of men," I replied with all the control I could muster.

"As mortal men went, I'm sure he was...*adequate,*" Kazimir

said. "But he was weak, like all humans. He died a weak man, just as he lived a weak man."

My heart was hammering in my chest now, and I fought to subdue it, tears running down my cheeks. "With respect, your Grace, you do not know how my father died. You were not there."

He issued me a terrible grin then, one that almost made him look giddy, but it left his lips as quickly as it had come.

"No," he said. "I wasn't. You're quite right. My apologies."

He turned to leave, but stopped, spun around, and said, "I will be stationing guards of my own outside your tent until tomorrow's battle. I do not want anything happening to dear Alessia's daughter—whether painful or pleasurable. Tomorrow when you fight for your life, I want you to remember where you came from, *Lyrinn Martel.*"

I stared daggers at his back as he turned and left me alone. Two white-haired guards positioned themselves at the tent's entrance, facing not outward, but in, their eyes locked on me.

"I don't want you here," I said with a scowl. "Leave."

"The High King has commanded that we stay. No one comes or goes. That is his order."

"The High King has no business—" I began, but I stopped myself. Kazimir was powerful beyond words. He could tell the guards to slice my head off and they would do it in a second.

But what upset me far more—what was tearing me apart inside—was the fact that I would not see Mithraan again before the final Trial.

CHAPTER FIFTY-ONE

THE DAY PASSED with all the speed of a hobbled snail.

I paced my tent, rage mounting inside me as I pondered whether my newfound strength might be enough to pit me against a couple of Lightblood guards.

After multiple requests to allow me to leave, I finally surrendered and forced myself to perform a few sparring drills with the blade the High King had given me.

Ironic, I thought, *to be practicing with his weapon when it's him I would most like to use it on.*

He had forced me to my room like a small, disobedient child. I still had no understanding of why he insisted on watching my every move. So he had met my mother decades ago—that didn't give him any right to order her daughter around, did it?

I worked to push my rage into my training. Closed my eyes and envisioned the final battle at the last Trials a thousand years ago—Fae against mortal, spells being cast like arrows flying through the air.

I had no offensive spells. I had managed to heal—though

Mithraan was now in possession of that Gift. I could turn myself into a dark shadow when need overcame me.

As for the rest, I still felt like a foal trying out its new legs. Mithraan had insisted that I would be more powerful than even he was, but I had seen no evidence of this power. I wasn't a soothsayer or an air-walker. I didn't have skin of stone or awesome strength.

I would have to rely on my wits, reflexes, and my skills with blades in the morning.

One thing I had discovered was that the final battle tended to be split up between male and female Champions, which I supposed made sense. There was no good reason to have us all kill each other at once and risk having no remaining Champions in the end.

I had not interacted much with Nihara since our arrival at the Trial grounds, and could only imagine that she despised me more now than ever, particularly if she had picked up my scent on Mithraan. And I couldn't imagine how I could possibly defend myself against her weapons of flame...

Which meant that tomorrow would likely be my last day on earth.

All the more reason to be enraged at the damned High King for ensnaring me inside my own tent.

After dinner, when the sun began to set, the Lightblood guards finally turned to face away and grant me a little privacy—but they remained in their positions, flanking the entrance.

I threw myself onto the bed after a time, still tight with rage that on my last full day of life, I was not allowed to see Mithraan—to touch him, to speak to him, or more.

It was an hour or so later when someone slipped into the tent and over to stand next to my bed. I started, thinking it was one of the guards checking to see if I'd fallen asleep.

But when I looked up, it was Mithraan who stood nearby.

I pushed myself to a sitting position and threw a look toward the door, only to see the guards were gone.

"How..." I whispered, but the Fae lord put a finger to his lips, pulled the covers back, and slipped into the bed next to me.

"I can only stay for a minute," he said. "I drew the guards' attention elsewhere, but the spell won't last long on Lightblood. Still, it was worth the risk—I had to see you tonight."

I lay back, smiling, and he climbed over me, pushing my nightgown up with one hand until he found the place between my legs. His fingers explored me, tantalizing me so that I had to bite my lip to keep from crying out, and then he drew them to his lips and tasted them, letting out a low moan.

"The nectar of every god who ever lived," he breathed.

I reached for him, wanting to pull his clothes away, to feel his naked body against mine, but he shook his head. "It will have to wait," he said.

"Wait for when, exactly? We both know I'll die tomorrow, Mithraan. There's no sense in holding back now."

He leaned down and kissed me, his tongue stroking mine, before pulling back and shaking his head.

"You won't die," he said. "Do you not remember when I made a vow to protect you until after the Trials had finished?"

"I remember," I told him. "But that was a long time ago."

"Not so long. And I am a Fae of my word."

"What if that word means hurting Nihara?" I asked. Guilt was digging away at my soul. "I can't ask you to—"

"You haven't asked for anything," he said. "In fact, you have stubbornly refused my protection more than once. But tomorrow, you will be your own protector, Lyrinn. You will find yourself then—when the truth comes, it will empower you."

"Truth," I repeated. "Everyone keeps talking about it. Leta. The Taker. You. But I already know it—my mother was a Fae. I inherited her blood, but not her Gifts."

"There is more to you than what your mother gave you," the Fae lord said quietly. "Remember that when all else fails. Remember, too, that I love you."

I love you.

Words I had never anticipated from anyone in the world outside my family.

Words that healed my broken soul and made me wish Mithraan and I could flee this place for a land far away and start a new life together.

"And I love you," I replied. "I don't want to lose you."

"That will never happen. Not in this or any lifetime." A rustling came to us from the tent's entrance, and I looked over to see the guards back at their posts. But fortunately, they had not felt compelled to look inside the tent.

"What exactly did you do to them?" I whispered.

"A little mind-bending of my own," he replied with a mischievous grin. "Good night, Lady Lyrinn," he said, kissing me one last time. "Until morning comes."

A piercing blast from a horn startled me awake in the morning. I leapt out of bed and dressed quickly in leather armor, my blade at my waist, bandolier strapped to my chest.

There was no need for a lady's maid this morning—no need for fancy hairstyles or makeup. I was on my own, with the High King's guards still positioned outside the tent.

When a servant I didn't recognize brought me breakfast, I asked how much time I had before the battle began.

"An hour, my Lady," she said.

"And..." The next question wouldn't come so easily. "Do you know how many of us will be fighting today?"

"Four, my Lady," she said.

Four.

I hadn't heard a cry in the night. There had been no evidence of violence. Presumably, guards had been stationed outside of every tent.

What if...

"What happened?" I asked, my voice quivering with fear. *It can't have been Mithraan. He can't be dead.*

"All I know is one of the female Champions was killed," the servant told me. "Stabbed."

"Stabbed," I repeated. "Which one?"

"The one from Belleau. I'm sorry, my Lady, but I can't recall her name."

"It was Elana."

The Reluctant Champion.

She had seen it coming—her own death. Yet she hadn't found a way to stop it. Why not? How was this even possible?

My heart sank as I slouched down in my chair. The servant issued me a shallow bow, then left.

Elana was kind and good. She had told me from the first that there was no end to the Trials that would bring her joy—but I had hoped so badly she would find a way to defy fate.

She did not deserve to die. She deserved a life of happiness with the one she loved.

My heart broke for the woman called Sadia, left behind in Belleau—the lover would learn all too soon of Elana's death. My throat went dry, tears welling in my eyes to imagine how she would weep, how she would shatter inside.

I could only hope Elana had foreseen her own death long ago, and warned Sadia of it. That they had a chance at brief happiness before this day had come.

The thought of it only brought me a small dose of comfort.

An hour passed before another horn blared in the distance, and, after calling on my glamour to conceal my ears and the markings along my skin, I strode to the tent's door, expecting to have to argue my way out. But the guards parted, allowing me through.

"Head to the Fighting Ring," one of them said. "The others will be awaiting you."

Overhead, I heard a bird's cry and I pulled my eyes up to see the white falcon watching me as always.

"Looking forward to my death, are you?" I asked under my breath as I advanced toward a large, dirt-floored arena that had taken up residence overnight in the large clearing next to the encampment.

The prince rushed over to me as I approached. He was dressed in expensive-looking silver armor with large shoulder and wrist-pieces. A long, elegant sword was sheathed at his waist.

I glanced down at my own meager armor and wondered how I thought I could possibly survive the ordeal to come.

"Have you heard?" Corym asked. "Elana was right."

"Yes, it seems she was," I said, peering over to where Mithraan and Nihara were standing, several feet away. Neither Fae was wearing armor, other than leather waistcoats and tall boots. It seemed the prince was the only one sensible enough to shield himself.

"Who could have done this?" I asked. "And why?"

"There's only one reason I can think of," Corym said, shooting a sidelong glance at Nihara. "Competition."

"There's no way a Fae felt threatened by Elana," I scoffed. "She was tiny—and her only real Gift involved avoidance. She was no fighter."

"Then what?" Corym asked. "Why would someone bother to kill her in the night? It seems so cowardly."

"People have been trying to murder me since these Trials began," I replied. "I suppose Elana was thrust in front of the target. It's just so wrong." I had to work to keep my voice level as I spoke. I didn't want the prince or anyone else to see how vulnerable I felt just now.

"Are you ready?" he asked. "We must focus. This will be a difficult battle. I've seen Nihara use her flame in training. She's skilled."

"I know," I sighed. "I don't stand a chance against her."

"I'll help you," the prince promised for the hundredth time, and it was all I could do not to roll my eyes.

"I think I'll need to help myself today, Highness," I replied sharply.

Nallach stepped into the fighting ring and turned to face the four remaining Champions. Before speaking, he glanced briefly upward at the small flock of birds soaring overhead.

When he'd satisfied himself that he was on display to every one of Kalemnar's kingdoms, he spoke.

"Today is a battle," he said. "At the end of which only two of you will remain. One male, one female. Those two will be joined until death."

I looked toward Mithraan, my heart fluttering in my chest. Such a romantic, yet morbid moment. I wanted nothing more than to find myself thrust toward him, told that he would be mine forever.

But the day did not feel destined to end on such a lovely, pleasant note. Something told me it would be one of sorrow, loss, and brutal violence.

"Though the two female Champions will be fighting first," Nallach said, "the other two—Prince Corym and Lord Mithraan—you should know that you can jump in at any time and intervene. If you have already chosen your preferred mate, you are allowed to help her to win."

"Good to know," the prince said too loudly from beside me.

"And now, to all who are watching, I say: Enjoy the Final Battle!"

With that, Nallach looked directly up at the birds with far too much glee in his eyes.

Enjoy the death, I muttered.

CHAPTER FIFTY-TWO

I pulled my hair back, tying it into a knot at my nape, focusing my mind for a moment on reinforcing my glamour. I was confident by now that those watching would see the old version of me, scars and all, rather than the empowered Fae I had become.

It was fitting, given that I didn't feel powerful in light of the opponent I was about to face.

Nihara strode toward the fighting ring and I did the same, turning once to look into Mithraan's eyes.

He looked calm yet sad, as though he had already foreseen the end.

I understand, I said in my mind. *You have to do what's best for Tíria. If that means defending Nihara...it's all right.*

I will not defend her, he told me. *I am here for you.*

Nallach offered up a brief set of rules:

"You may use any weapon, magical or otherwise, at your disposal. You may not offer your opponent mercy, unless you aim to let her take your life. Understood?"

Nihara and I both nodded, and to my surprise, when Nallach backed off, she stepped forward and embraced me.

I put my hands awkwardly on her shoulders, confused. Was this some trick? Was she about to squeeze the life out of me?

Mithraan and Corym stood just outside the arena, both looking as though they were prepared to charge in, should the moment demand it.

But Nihara simply whispered, "I will not hurt you. For him. For Tíria. I know who you are—even if you haven't realized it yet."

I pulled away, looking at her with a furrowed brow.

"You need to figure it out, Fae," she said quietly. "Or he will take you down." With that, she nodded toward the two male Champions.

"Who will?" I asked.

She backed away, shaking her head as though trying to free herself of a nagging insect. Her eyes, normally piercing, went dull as she fixed them on me. And for a moment, she stood still, fighting against something inside her.

"Nihara?" I asked. She looked like a statue, frozen. Immovable. Powerless.

I took a step backward, my hand on my blade's hilt. Above me, the white falcon screeched a cry that was now as familiar as my own voice.

"I won't attack her," I called out. "Not like this."

"Do it!" Corym called. "Now is your best chance, Lyrinn!"

I looked at Mithraan, who was staring, confounded, at Nihara. He didn't appear to understand what was happening any more than I did.

But then, Nihara leapt toward me, throwing herself across the arena, her powerful hands on my throat.

I fell to the ground, gasping for air as I struggled against her clenching fingers. I managed to free myself just long enough to roll to the side and leap to my feet.

Nihara let out a feral cry, lunging once again, and this time, I managed to evade her attack.

"What are you doing?" I asked, locking my eyes on hers. They were still dull, still cloudy, as if...

As if someone had bent her mind, as they did to Elana during the Hunt.

I looked around to see if anyone was close by, but all I could see were Nallach, Mithraan, and Corym.

I glanced up toward the white falcon, wondering if there was any chance that the Lightblood could cast such spells through birds. The High King hated me, after all. Why not take control of others and prompt them to take my life?

Horror flowed through my bloodstream as I backed away slowly, pulling my blade. "I don't want to do this," I said softly. "Please...don't make me do this."

Nihara held her hands before her chest, twisting them in the air until flames spun between them. I had seen her fire the night the Grimpers had attacked Fairholme.

I knew what she could do.

I pulled my blade back to hurl it just as Nihara readied herself to shoot flame at me.

But before either of us could attack, something flew through the air, knocking her off her feet.

A great silver eagle, its wings spread wide.

He pinned her to the ground, his talons digging into her flesh.

"Mithraan!" I cried as Nihara shrieked in pain. But still, she locked her grim eyes on mine and pushed her hands toward me.

A bolt of flame shot through the air, but because she was so twisted, it missed by a few inches.

Nihara let out a frustrated cry, then hurled another fire bolt, then another. I dodged my way around them, my skin searing with their heat as they flew by my head.

When one grazed my arm, tearing through my clothing, the eagle let out a tormented, protective cry, and clenched its talons harder.

The sound of crunching bones met my ears.

I cried out in horror as Nihara went limp and Mithraan, returning to his Fae form, sank to the ground next to her.

His shoulders shook with sobs and I ran to his side, my arms around him, falling to my knees to hold him.

“I’m sorry,” I said. “You should never have had to do that.”

“She knew,” he whispered. “She knew what was coming.” He turned to look at me, his cheeks damp. “She knew the mind-bender was coming for her—and for you.”

He turned to Corym, his expression turning to one of pure hatred, and rose to his feet.

“Prince,” he snarled. “It’s time for you and yours to answer for your crimes.”

CHAPTER FIFTY-THREE

"Corym?" I whimpered. "But it can't have been him. He—"

I pulled my eyes to the prince, realizing I had no defense to offer.

Perhaps, after all, his greatest Gift lay in subterfuge.

It explained the death of Asa, Elana's sister, killed for her ability to read minds. It explained why Elana had come to kill me in the woods during the Hunt, mere seconds after I had whistled for Corym. He had sent her to take my life, just as he'd no doubt sent Gwyr in the night.

I wondered suddenly if he had bent the minds of all of Domignon, including Anira, who was certain she'd seen him calling for me in the Labyrinth—despite the fact that I had never once heard his voice.

"All of this—it was your doing?" I asked the prince, rising to my feet and striding toward him.

I was all too aware that all of Kalemnar was watching this strange, horrible altercation as it unfolded. But I didn't care. *Let them call me treasonous for hurling accusations at their beloved prince.*

Nallach leapt toward the arena then, his hands in the air.

"This is highly irregular!" he shouted. "The battle between female Champions is over. The fight between the males must now commence."

I shot him a glare. "You told these two they were allowed to help us fight," I said. "Does the same apply in reverse?"

"I'm afraid I don't follow, my Lady..."

"Am I allowed to fight the prince?" I asked, my voice seething with rage.

"I..." Nallach glanced up at the king's bird, the hawk, and swallowed hard. "Yes, I suppose so..."

"Good," I growled.

"Lyrinn," Mithraan said. "You don't know what he's capable of. You should stay out of the arena."

In his eyes, I saw desperation and resolve combined. It came as no surprise that he wanted to kill the prince as badly as I did.

I turned to Corym. "What do you have to say for yourself?" I asked. "Will you be honest with me, just this once?"

At first, the prince stared back at me innocently, his eyes wide with confusion.

But they quickly narrowed, his lips curving up at the corners.

"Honest?" he asked with a disturbing laugh. "Certainly. I've had no end of amusement these last few days, brainwashing these poor saps."

"You cannot brainwash a Fae," Mithraan spat. "Nihara was powerful. She was a skilled fighter."

"As am I, my Lord," Corym said with disgust. "Oh—right. You don't know all of it."

"All of what?"

Corym glanced up at the white falcon, then at me. "You don't know how helpful your kind has been to me...*Princess.*"

I glanced at Mithraan, speaking silent words.

He knows what I am.

~*Yes. He's probably known his whole life.*

I let my glamour go, exhaling as the spell faded. Corym smiled again when he saw my ears, the marks on my skin. "Ah, there she is," he said. "So much more beautiful than before, no?"

"She was always beautiful, you filth," Mithraan snarled.

"To you, perhaps. My taste runs more along the lines of, say, redheads. Like her younger sister, for instance. Leta is quite something, don't you think? She looks just like her mother."

As he spoke, nausea attacked my insides. I fought against the urge to double over, to release my breakfast onto the ground.

I saw his mind now with all the clarity of a mountain creek. How had I not seen it sooner? How had I been so patient with the jackass who had been so close to becoming my husband?

"You have never cared about me for a second," I said. "You've only ever wanted my bloodline."

The prince clapped once, twice, then laughed. "Very good, Lyrinn," he said. "But that's the beauty of this so-called 'final battle.' Don't you see? Whatever happens today, your blood is mine. If you die, I receive your Gifts. If you live, we marry—and I still receive your Gifts. At least, my offspring do."

"Only if you win," I snarled.

"Oh—I'll win." He flashed another quick glance at the falcon, but flicked his eyes quickly back to my own.

Nallach, who had been watching the conversation unfold, stepped up next to him and said, "Highness—we must continue with—"

"Shut it, you tedious oaf," Corym snapped. "We will fight when we're ready." With that, he turned back to me. "By the way, Lyrinn, I'm so sorry about your friend Elana." He began to examine his fingernails, as though the emotion he was expressing was as banal as the weather. "Such a shame, what happened to her. I didn't want to do it, but you know—now she's with her sister, so in a sense, it's a happy ending. Ironic, isn't it? She's the only one I killed with my own two hands."

My hand went to my blade and I pulled it from its sheath, desperate to use it. But the prince hadn't yet stepped into the arena. *Not yet. I want his death to be the spectacle he deserves, for all of Kalemnar to witness.*

"It would have been a terrible idea to allow someone like Elana into an arena such as this one," Corym said. "She might have foreseen everything. But what stuns me is what *you* fail to see, Lady Lyrinn."

He was right. I had failed to see what a monster he was. I had failed to understand the extent of his malevolence.

But something told me he was talking about another thing entirely.

"Enlighten me," I said.

"You have not yet seen what you are," he replied. "Not fully. Let me tell you something of your ancestors." He began to pace just beyond the arena's borders, smiling as he spoke. "You know when the Fae were turned at the last Blood Trials—when many of your kind were made into Grimpers, and the mist began to flow down the Onyx Rise?"

I sealed my lips tight and said nothing.

"It was your father who did it," Corym added. "After he murdered the two Fae Champions, that is."

"Don't be ridiculous," I snarled. "My father was not alive during the last Trials. He was a mortal."

"No," Corym laughed. "He wasn't. The man who *raised* you was a mortal."

"Raised me?" I asked, barely aware that Mithraan had just reached out to wrap his fingers around my arm. I could feel him telling me something silently—something I didn't want to hear.

"You really have no idea?" Corym scoffed. "Well then, I'll give your liar of a so-called 'father' credit—he managed to keep you in the dark all those years, despite what blood runs through your veins."

"My father kept my identity from me to protect me from people like you," I hissed.

"No. He did it out of selfishness while your *true* father sought you out. Your *true* father, you see, is far more powerful than a duplicitous blacksmith who hides stolen children away in hell-holes like Dúnbar."

With that, the prince pulled his eyes up again to the white falcon.

And just like that, my mind exploded with a whirlwind of memories. They came to me hard and fast, clear as day, vision after vision that I wished I could push away.

I saw my mother, a beautiful young Fae, pressed to a wall by a handsome Lightblood with hazel eyes. Even as she tried to squirm free of his painful grip, pleading with him to release her, he caressed her cheek, kissed her. He told her he would give her the life she'd always dreamed of.

My breath halted when I saw his face clearly for the first time.

Kazimir.

Another scene slipped into my mind, this time of Kazimir throwing her onto a bed, tearing her dress from her body and...

No. I will not be witness to this.

I forced the vision away, repulsed by the violence of it.

I saw my mother poisoning herself to keep from bearing his children. Sick, pale, suffering in pain and torment as he confined her in a palace of black and white stone.

I watched as she escaped, making her way across the sea to Domignon. After centuries of cruel imprisonment, she looked so happy, so relieved, when young King Caedmon welcomed her with open arms. Fearing discovery and hoping to begin a new life, she renamed herself Alessia.

But Caedmon sent word to High King Kazimir about his prisoner, and the Fae traveled across the sea once again.

A secret visit, he had once said.

And now, I understood at last.

Kazimir had found her once again. And this time, she had no access to poison. No escape.

Choosing to remain in Domignon as he schemed with the king, Kazimir impregnated Alessia, and she bore him a black-haired daughter—a hair color common to young Lightblood Fae.

Alessia named her daughter Lyrinn.

When she fell pregnant the second time, her cruel spouse allowed her a little freedom, telling her she could roam the palace grounds for the sake of her health.

One day while wandering, the red-haired Fae met a young apprentice smith.

When her second baby was born, she and the smith hatched a plan to escape the palace. She burned away the pointed tips of her two daughters' ears, weeping when the acid ran down their flesh and scarred each of them permanently.

Alessia had done it out of love, to hide the girls away from their brutal father—but it still broke her heart.

Casting a sleeping spell on those in the palace—including her cruel husband—she ran off with the smith to the town of Dúnbar in the North. She remained there only briefly before disappearing forever.

The man who came to be known as Martel raised the two girls himself, telling them little about their mother over the years—other than that he loved her, and she loved them.

All of this came to me in the span of less than a second,

winding me as though I had been the recipient of a vicious blow.

For the first time, I knew the truth. I understood Kazimir's fascination with me.

But there was one thing that made no sense.

"Why does he want me dead?" I asked of my birth father. "Why has he been helping you?"

"I'm not sure he does want you dead," Corym said, looking up at the falcon once again. "But I suppose there's only one way to find out. What say you, Kazimir?"

The bird cried out, and Corym laughed. "Still, I *do* want you dead. So let's get on with it." With that, the prince moved into the fighting ring.

"Stay outside the ring, Lyrinn," Mithraan commanded, his voice low and threatening. But the threat wasn't being leveled at me.

Reluctantly, I stepped out to the same area where Nallach was standing, arms crossed as he chewed on his nails fretfully. I wanted to slap him for pretending to care so deeply about the Trials' rules.

If rules mattered to you, you wouldn't have allowed the Champions to be murdered in their sleep.

I watched, my dagger clutched firmly in my hand, as Mithraan and Corym circled the ring, their eyes locked like two wild cats about to tear one another's throats out.

Corym had revealed so little of his power that I wasn't sure how frightened to feel.

"Come, Fae," the prince sneered. "Do your worst. Or are you simply going to wander the ring for the rest of your days?"

"I'm biding my time," Mithraan said. "Contemplating how best to take your life. Slowly and painfully, or quickly...and painfully."

The prince let out a derisive laugh. "You will do no such

thing," he said, flicking a hand toward Mithraan. A projectile shot through the air—something white and sharp, and it took me only a moment to realize it was a dagger of ice.

As suddenly as a lightning bolt crashing from cloud to land, Mithraan flung a hand up, and instantly, a wall of flame rose up to stop the weapon, which sizzled against the heat and disintegrated harmlessly.

"Fire," Corym snickered. "How dull. Such a cliché for you magic users."

"As is ice."

"Fair enough. What say we stop with the spell-casting and fight like men?" Corym called out, drawing his sword and raising it into the air. "Oh—but I see you have no weapon."

"I have no need of a sword," Mithraan retorted. "But please—come at me—unless you're too fearful."

The prince lunged, and Mithraan raised a hand, flicking it rapidly in the air.

I'd seen him use this gesture once before. In the Feathery—the inn on the way to Domignon.

Corym was frozen in place, one foot off the ground. He looked as though he might topple over, except the very ground beneath him, too, went rigid, hanging onto his other foot with all the grip of a steel vice.

A faint sound met my ears—a sort of whimpering, and it took a moment to realize it was coming from the prince.

The birds in the sky above lowered their circle, straining to move closer out of a desire to hear him.

A moment later, a sound like fracturing glass invaded the air and Corym, pulling himself out of the spell, took a step toward Mithraan.

"You won't beat me, my Lord," the prince scowled. "You may as well fall to your knees and beg for mercy. I won't *give* it to you, of course—but it'll make for a nice spectacle."

"I would sooner choke on a blade," Mithraan growled.

"Suit yourself," Corym shrugged, advancing on the Fae, who flicked a hand in the air once more. Corym briefly froze in place again, clearly agitated, but he fought off the paralysis spell and took another step.

Once again, Mithraan gestured and Corym stopped, and the pattern repeated itself several times before the prince lost all patience.

"When you've finished choking on my sword," the prince hissed, "I'll give Lady Lyrinn something to choke on."

Mithraan's eyes went feral then, his lips pulling back in an animalistic snarl. I watched as his fingers turned into the vicious talons I'd seen him use before—the claws of an enormous bird of prey. He leapt at Corym, throwing him hard to the ground.

Raising his arm, Mithraan brought it down to tear at the prince's thick armor, shredding it open so that his flesh was exposed underneath, torn and bleeding.

The Fae clawed at the prince's face once, twice, leaving deep red slashes in his cheeks, then lifted Corym by the tunic and pulled the prince's bloodied face to his.

"You are a coward," Mithraan snarled, "a traitor to mortals and Fae alike. You are not fit to be a prince, let alone a king. And I will die if I must, to keep you away from Lyrinn. You will never have her. You will never have her Gifts. You do not deserve them. Do you hear me?"

At that, Corym let out a snicker, then a full-on laugh, and nodded toward the sky.

"I'm not working alone, Fae. I have powerful allies—or are you forgetting? Kill me, and I promise you—Tíria will suffer for far longer than the next thousand years. In the meantime, however, I'd like to call on my good friend and future father-in-law for aid."

Letting out a high-pitched whistle, he pulled his gaze skyward again.

Instantly, the white falcon shot downward, clawing cruelly at Mithraan's back, his face. The Fae leapt to his feet, readying himself to shift into his silver eagle form.

But before he could do it, the prince shot up, blood trickling down his face, and thrust a hand out toward the Fae. Ten brutal-looking, barbed arrows materialized in mid-air, then flew with blinding speed at Mithraan's chest.

The projectiles pierced the Fae's chest, his shoulders, his neck. He tumbled to his knees, suppressing a cry of agony.

I leapt into the arena and, snarling in rage, hurled my dagger at Corym. It landed deep in the prince's side—a serious wound, but to my devastation, not serious enough.

Kazimir had told me the weapon was sharp enough to slice through the air itself. Another lie.

"Heal yourself!" I called, pulling my eyes to Mithraan's.

"Your pleas won't work, Princess," the prince hissed, extracting the blade from his side and raising it as though he intended to hurl it back at me.

But instead, he ran at Mithraan and grabbed him, pressing the dagger to his neck.

"I *will* slit his throat," he threatened. "It's a little hard to come back from a wound such as that."

"Take him down, Lyrinn," Mithraan said, his voice hoarse with the pressure of the blade. Blood trickled down from the side of his mouth, and I winced with the pain he was suffering. "I will gladly die for you, and for Tíria. But do not let this bastard live. Seek the power inside you—the power given to you by your mother's bloodline—and kill him."

Somewhere above us, King Caedmon's hawk let out an anguished cry, then went silent.

I heaved a hard sob, trying to understand Mithraan's

meaning.

The power given to me by my mother's bloodline? What is it?

And then, I remembered.

My mother was skilled, they said, at summoning conjured beasts.

I closed my eyes and, through some memory I'd never known I possessed, pictured a small army of enormous wildcats and wolves. Made of pure light, they were beautiful, their claws razor-sharp as those of the Grimpers.

I knew without a shadow of a doubt that they would obey my silent command and tear the prince to pieces.

Raising my arms wide, I pulled my eyes open.

"I will not let you take him from me, Corym," I said, my voice hoarse with emotion. "You have no right—and you will never be king."

With that, I flung my arms forward, conjured the beasts.

They came then, materializing from nothing but light itself and, springing forth in fast-moving waves of iridescent blue, they leapt through the air to take down their prey.

Mithraan, the blade at his throat, closed his eyes and smiled as the creatures came, and I watched in horror as Corym's grip tightened on the blade in his hand.

A cry split the air in two.

And then, in a flash of pure, blinding white, the world disappeared.

I could no longer see anything—not Mithraan, not Corym.

I stared out into space, waiting for the brightness to fade, for my mind to grasp what was happening. *I need to know the prince is dead, and that Mithraan lives.*

But the light did not break.

A final, shrill cry of a falcon broke out somewhere in the sky above, then I collapsed to the ground...

And the world went black.

CHAPTER FIFTY-FOUR

I awoke on a bed—a strange, narrow thing that rocked back and forth like an oversized cradle.

I pushed myself up, my head darting around to assess my surroundings...and then I remembered the cry of the white falcon, and the flash of blinding light.

No...no. Mithraan needs me. He's hurt...he...

"Ah," a deep voice said from the shadows around me. "You're awake, Daughter."

High King Kazimir glided toward me from a far corner. When he got to the bed, he pressed a hand to my forehead and smiled even as I recoiled in disgust.

"Where are we?" I said, my voice a fraught rasp in my throat.

"On my ship," the king said, pulling up a nearby chair and seating himself. "Heading for Aetherion—your new home."

Panic ravaged my insides, my hands grabbing the edge of the mattress. There was nowhere to run. No way to escape, if indeed we were sailing across the sea.

"What have you done?" I asked, fighting back tears. "How could you—"

But I had not forgotten how he had taken my mother so many years ago. Against her will, he had cruelly stolen her from her father and broken his heart in two. He had violated her, taken her very life from her.

"It was a close call back there, you know," the king replied with a dismissive snicker. "Employing spells you're not familiar with is a risky business."

With a jolt, I remembered the wild beasts that had manifested around me, blue and glowing, crafted out of light itself. How they had leapt at Corym...

Then I remembered the prince's hand on the silver dagger —and I wondered if my spell had been quick enough to save the life of the Fae I loved more than anything in this world.

"What do you mean, risky?" I asked, bile rising in my throat.

"You tried to weaponize the Light, just as many of our kind do. You failed, Lyrinn. But don't worry—I saw to it that you will not be punished for your transgression."

"What...what do you mean? Why would I be punished?"

"You don't know? Really?" Kazimir's expression was smug, heartless as he let out another laugh. "It's against the rules to slaughter the only two remaining Champions in the final Battle. Doing so defeats the whole purpose of the Blood Trials—you would have killed your future spouse, Lyrinn, and that's a no-no in the Trials."

"You said slaughter..." The words fell from my mouth like a lead weight.

"You are new to your Gifts," Kazimir said with a judgmental click of his tongue. "It's understandable that they aren't yet... shall we say... refined. So I simply cast the necessary spell to protect you. I extracted you from an unfortunate situation— which is why we're now fleeing Kalemnar."

"The white light—that was your doing?" My heart threatened an explosion in my chest. "Mithraan—is...is he..."

The Lightblood's face twisted into a look of sympathy. "There was no hope for the Tírian. The prince would have killed him within seconds. You know that as well as I do."

"The prince," I breathed as a vision came to me of the blade pressed to Mithraan's throat.

But I didn't see it. I didn't see Mithraan fall...

"There will likely be consequences for my actions—but we'll cross that bridge when we come to it, shall we?" Kazimir leaned forward, looking horrifyingly like he intended to embrace me.

I pulled away from him, my eyes moist with tears, my throat tight.

"The good news," he added almost gleefully, "is that Prince Corym still lives. I made his father a promise years ago, you see —to keep him alive at all costs. It was a sort of thank-you for alerting me when your mother showed up in Domignon. I owed him a debt."

"I don't care about the prince, or the king, or your dealings with those monsters," I snarled. "What about Mithraan?"

But Kazimir simply shrugged and offered up an exaggerated frown. "We lose the ones we love sometimes. It's a part of life's natural cycle. But then, you already know that, having lost both your parents—don't you?"

"He can't be dead," I murmured, pulling my eyes to the far wall. Better to look at nothing than the cruel bastard's cold eyes. "I would feel it. I would *know* it..."

Kazimir shrugged. "It's best to push him from your mind, Daughter. Forget him. He was never worthy of you. Don't you see? You and your sister—you are unique to this world. You two are the product of a melding of Lightblood and Tírian Fae. Mithraan is...well, he's nothing special." He sat back and chuckled, adding, "Do you know, I asked King Rynfael of the Dragon Court for your mother's hand during the last Blood Trials, and he rejected me? The arrogant bastard thought his daughter too high and mighty for the likes of me. It's why I took her when I did."

I glared at the Fae who was my alleged father. I despised him. *I wanted him dead.* "You're cruel," I said. "Heartless. You're a monster."

Kazimir laughed. "I beg to differ. If I were heartless, I hardly think I would bring you across the sea with me, risking a prolonged and violent conflict with the mortal realms. I wish simply to bestow upon you riches beyond your wildest imagination. I want you to live the life you have always deserved—the one your mother stole from you."

Shaking my head, I said, "The life I want is in Kalemnar. My sister is there. My..."

My mate.

The words hit me like a bittersweet blow.

Though I had fought against it and railed against my desire, I had always known Mithraan was meant to be mine, and I his.

And now...

I reached my mind out, searching in vain for him. For his voice in my mind, for any small sign that he might be alive. Was it even possible that he'd survived, after so many arrows had pierced his flesh? Could he have fought the prince off after the blast of white light?

He can heal, I reminded myself. *Thanks to the Gift that was once mine.*

"Do you know why I did it?" Kazimir asked.

"Did what?" I muttered, wishing him a million miles from me.

"Joined forces with the mortals in the last Blood Trials, a millennium ago. Why I killed the Fae Champions, granting their Gifts to mortal-kind."

"I don't care."

The High King ignored my sour expression. "Because," he said, "the Blood Trials were nothing more than a vanity project for the Fae of Tíria. The competition should never have existed. It was pure arrogance to think the Fae would always win—would always prove their dominance and continue to steal away any meager Gifts humans had developed over the centuries. If there was any cruelty, it was on the part of those Fae."

"You *destroyed* Tíria, so I don't see that it matters."

"On the contrary," he said, his voice rising with irritation. "Tíria was saved. It now has a chance to be reborn, to flourish in isolation. The Fae are finally learning humility. That land, like Aetherion, will be far better off without the contamination of the mortal realm, and the Fae are learning that truth."

"You're wrong," I retorted. "The Blood Trials may be horrible, but the Tírian Fae are good, and kind. They never deserved the fate you forced upon them. They did not deserve to lose their beautiful lands."

Kazimir's expression softened again, and he reached for my hand, but I drew it back and shot him a look of pure hatred.

"Daughter..." he said.

"Do *not* call me that," I snarled from between gritted teeth. "I despise you. And I will *never* call you Father."

"So be it," he said, rising and turning to walk away. When he reached a set of stairs at the room's far end, he said, "By the way, you're free to roam the ship. I have little fear you'll leap off and try to swim away."

I glared after him as he went, and only after he had left the room did I pull myself out of bed.

My head pounded as I slipped up the stairs to the ship's deck only to take in the enormity of the vessel, the sigil of a flaming sword proudly displayed on its massive sails.

My heart split in two when I saw that Kalemnar was only faintly visible in the far distance.

Even if Mithraan is alive, he's too far from me now.

Unless some miracle occurs, I'll never see him again.

I stared out at the land until it disappeared on the horizon. Hot tears streamed down my cheeks, falling mercilessly to the deck.

A small army of white-haired Fae roamed the ship, bowing their heads to me as they wandered by. "Princess," one or two said as they passed.

It was a title that I already despised.

I descended to my room and lay down on the bed, letting the tears come in torrents. Tears for my sister. For my lover. For a land I would never see again.

After a time, Kazimir's servants brought me dinner, but I did not eat it. I slept fitfully that night, tossing and turning as my mind twisted with attempts to recall what had occurred just before the flash of light in the arena.

Had I seen Mithraan's life end?

However hard I focused, I failed to see his fate, and my heart, already broken, seemed to splinter with each passing minute.

I awoke in the morning to the sound of a loud, clanging bell somewhere on deck.

A wild commotion erupted above me, agitated shouts coming from every direction. I leapt out of bed and ran up the stairs, eager to learn what was happening. I almost hoped to find the ship was sinking—that my misery would end quickly and my fate would seal itself at the bottom of the sea.

But I had no such luck.

Instead, a few of the Lightbloods had gathered at the ship's stern to stare into the distance.

Kazimir came leaping out of his quarters, pulling on a tunic as he strode across the deck.

"What the hell is going on out here?" he growled, ignoring me as he stormed past.

"Your Grace!" a golden-eyed Fae in the crow's nest shouted from above.

"What the hell is it, Tvor?" the High King called.

"Someone is in pursuit," the lookout shouted, a telescope in hand. He was pointing back toward Kalemnar. "A fast-moving ship, far from us, but gaining rapidly."

Kazimir ran to the stern, pressing his hands to the railing, and stared into the distance. "Did you see a sigil?" he asked, his jaw clenching tight.

"I...I...yes. There was a sigil." The Fae looked terrified as he spoke the words.

"Well? What is it?" Kazimir asked.

"Your Grace..."

"Spit it out, you jackass! What did you see?"

My heart threatened to leap from my chest as I awaited the reply. And when at last it came, I fell to my knees, a torrent of tears blurring my vision.

"It's a silver eagle, your Grace," the lookout said, his voice trembling. "The sigil of Fairholme."

End of A Kingdom Scarred, Fae of Tíria, Book One

COMING SOON: A CROWN BROKEN

Book Two in the War of the Five Realms series is coming soon!

Pre-order here until release day: A Crown Broken

AVAILABLE NOW: A DARKLY FUNNY APOCALYPTIC YOUNG ADULT NOVEL

What happens when the first day of school is the last day of the world?

For sixteen-year-old Virtue, navigating 11th grade is hard enough. Throw in the mass carnage of the Purple War, the brain-mangling Lemming Plague, and the overnight, post-apocalyptic breakdown of civilization, and suddenly, arguing with her parents, being picked on by bullies, and tyrannized by her teachers doesn't seem quite so devastating.

Instead, her new priorities are saving her best friend (and potential boyfriend?), fending off Clique Baiters and Serial Daters, and rescuing Beynac—her golden retriever service dog. Oh, and surviving.

It took sixteen years of torment and insecurity to make Virtue a wallflower. It took a single day of classes (and an academy full of brainwashed killers) to turn her into the school's most feared and deadly badass.

Available now on Amazon: *Apocalypchix*

ALSO BY K. A. RILEY

If you're enjoying K. A. Riley's books, please consider leaving a review on Amazon or Goodreads to let your fellow book-lovers know about it.

Dystopian Books:

The Cure Chronicles:

The Cure

Awaken

Ascend

Fallen

Reign

Resistance Trilogy:

Recruitment

Render

Rebellion

Emergents Trilogy:

Survival

Sacrifice

Synthesis

Transcendent Trilogy:

Travelers

Transfigured

Terminus

Academy of the Apocalypse Series:

Emergents Academy

Cult of the Devoted

Army of the Unsettled

The Ravenmaster Chronicles:

Arise

Banished (Coming in January 2022)

Crusade (Coming in April 2022)

Fantasy Books

Seeker's Series:

Seeker's World

Seeker's Quest

Seeker's Fate

Seeker's Promise

Seeker's Hunt

Seeker's Prophecy (Coming Soon!)

To be informed of future releases, and for occasional chances to win free swag, books, and other goodies, please sign up here:

https://karileywrites.org/#subscribe

Follow K. A. Riley on TikTok: @karileywrites

K.A. Riley's Bookbub Author Page

K.A. Riley on Amazon.com

K.A. Riley on Goodreads.com

Printed in Great Britain
by Amazon

16018329R00242